BLOOD-BONDED BY FORCE

BY

TRACY TAPPAN

Cover by Steven Novak
Edited by Faith Freewoman and Jessica Slade

Also by Tracy Tappan

The Choose A Hero Romance™ reading experience
JUSTICE
Keith Knight's Story
Brayden Street's Story
Pete Robbins's Story

The Community Series
Paranormal Romance
PREY (free novella)
THE BLOODLINE WAR
THE PUREST OF THE BREED
BLOOD-BONDED BY FORCE
MOON-RIDERS

Wings of Gold Series
Military Romantic Suspense
BEYOND THE CALL OF DUTY
ALLIED OPERATIONS
MAN DOWN

For more information, go to www.tracytappan.com.
Sign up for Tracy's author updates and find out about FREE books today!

ACKNOWLEDGMENTS

Special thanks go to Robyn Segel Shifren for her invaluable help with ballet questions. Also to my editor, Faith Freewoman, for her expertise in the world of dance, as well as Tarot card reading. How lucky am I that one of my editors is such a Jack of all trades?

Jessa Slade, also my editor extraordinaire, once again applied her genius to peeling back deeper layers of my characters. I am indebted to all of these fine woman.

All mistakes are my own.

To my readers.
Every day I sit at my keyboard is pure joy
because so many of you have reached out to
share your enthusiasm for my writing.
It feels really danged good.
Thank you.

Celtic Quaternary Knot

Celtic Meanings of the Five Fold Symbol

Inner circle = fifth element binds the other four

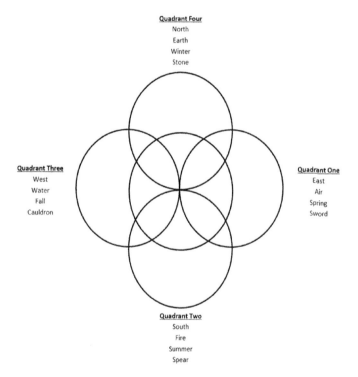

Quadrant Four
North
Earth
Winter
Stone

Quadrant Three
West
Water
Fall
Cauldron

Quadrant One
East
Air
Spring
Sword

Quadrant Two
South
Fire
Summer
Spear

BOOK ONE

CHAPTER ONE

PANDRA PARTHEN CRUMPLED TO HER knees with a hiss, clutching at the bloody slash in her stomach, pain burning through every vein in her body. Her hands shook as she grappled to shove her intestines back into her belly, but the slippery ropes were uncoiling faster than she could push them back in. A scream slammed up her throat and battered at the backs of her teeth. Blood fountained through her fingers and splashed to the floor. *Not my blood. Can't be. There's too sodding much.* She panted roughly, her cheeks working like bellows. *Do. Not. Scream.*

Her father despised weakness.

So did she, in truth.

Raymond came to stand dispassionately over her, his Gucci loafers stopping just short of the spreading stain of her blood. She didn't look up—couldn't, really. Just as well. Raymond's eyes were such a startlingly clear blue, they appeared almost colorless when he was enraged. Like now.

Not the jolliest of sights.

The room fractured into a prism around her as the electrical charge of her father's power seared through her once more, tearing the hole in her belly wider. A gritted, "No," made it past her lips. She toppled over, landing with a hard splat in the pool of her own blood. Her viscera boiled up and out of her, piling onto the floor around her body.

Silence.

No. The thunder of her heart and the harsh cadence of

her breathing were deafening.

Wetness soaked through her jeans and into her knickers. The books on the shelves she'd been scanning mere moments before Raymond's arrival slanted sideways and grew moss: Charles Dickens, Charlotte Brontë, James Joyce... Through pain-slitted eyes, she stared up at Raymond. Tall and refined, his features sculpted and handsome, his hair a rich mane of silver-blond falling to his collar, he was a man who could be as warm-hearted as ruthlessly cold. Let a soul act according to Raymond's rigid specifications of behavior and all would be dandy. Break a rule and the poor sap earned herself one beastly punishment.

Until recently she and her father had an unspoken agreement about those rules. If she chose to break a minor one, she would do so outside of his general knowledge and make sure her actions wouldn't damage his reputation in any way. The one exception was her penchant for dressing like a tart. She did that with full awareness it cheesed him off. But then...he'd never overtly told her not to do so.

On his end, Raymond wasn't supposed to act behind her back. He would tell her what to do and she would do it, but it was understood that there was always this communication.

He'd broken this rule.

Without asking, Raymond had used information Pandra had acquired regarding the Vârcolac, the bloodsuckers who held the dubious honor of being Raymond's mortal enemies. They'd earned this unenviable status by kidnapping Toni Parthen, Raymond's daughter from his first wife. Toni and her brother, Alex, possessed an extremely rare and powerful gene called Royal Fey Dragon; a gene Raymond wanted bred into his grandchildren. With this scheme in mind, Raymond had always planned on reuniting with the daughter he'd abandoned. But the Vârcolac had ruined that by abducting her instead.

For nearly a year now, Raymond had been trying to

snatch Toni back. To no avail. He needed to find an easy way into the Vârcolac's secret, underground town to wage a proper war. His brilliant plan? To kidnap a Vârcolac delivery woman—Pandra had unearthed her schedule, and this was the information Raymond had swiped—and *persuade* her to reveal the entrances to the Vârcolac's lair. But Videon, Pandra's mental half-brother, had tortured the poor girl to death, which had inadvertently led to another woman getting captured: Marissa Nichita. She was the pregnant wife to one of the Vârcolac, making her a perfect bargaining chip to trade for Toni. Except…

Pandra had released Marissa a little over an hour ago.

Two could break the rules in this sick game she and Raymond played, eh?

But, of course, Pandra's actions had violated her father's most stringent and unforgivable rule: never openly defy him.

And so here she was… sweat running in rivulets down her neck, her vision tunneling.

Raymond clasped his hands behind his back and gazed down at her coolly. "What a perishing disappointment you turned out to be, Pandra."

She gritted her teeth against a stab of pain piercing through her sternum…her heart. Not from her father's power, but his words. What a pile of wet lettuce she was. Here her guts were spewed around her like tangled macramé, and what made her want to cry was one, wee sentence of Raymond's. And he was only confirming what she already knew. She'd thrown away her status as her father's favorite—or his *second* favorite—with both hands.

Raymond turned and walked crisply for the door, the tap of his Gucci loafers across the marble floor managing to sound both elegant and lethal, the same as on his trip into the library to mete out her punishment. Her father's power shot out of her like someone yanking a cord from an outlet. Her bowels jerked once against her fingers, then came to a quivering rest.

"You may put your ring back on now." Raymond's voice floated back to her as he disappeared down the hall of this Fairbanks Ranch mansion that served as both her home and prison.

My immortality ring. She squinted up to the top of the desk where she'd left it. Enchanted specifically for her, that red crystal ring would take away the worst of this horrendous pain and heal her with miraculous speed. But up there on that desk it might as well have been in Siberia.

Other options? Lie here and let herself waste? *What a perishing disappointment you turned out to be, Pandra.* She blinked slowly. Tempting.

"You sure as hell dropped a clanger by lettin' that girl go, Pandra, you dimmock."

She carefully angled her vision toward the doorway.

Her older brother, Murk, was standing just inside the library.

She stared at him dully. He could be here to insult her as much to help her. It was anybody's guess. "I hadn't realized that," she rasped past the dry lump of her tongue. "Thank you ever so much for enlightening me."

Murk crossed the library and knelt at her side, heedlessly planting a knee into the shimmering pool of her blood. "Sufferin' fuck, he really brasted you, didn't he?"

At twenty-six, Murk was two years her senior and the eldest of the seventeen-sibling blended family who'd been brought into this world—same as Toni and Alex—to be Raymond's breeding machines for the ultimate Fey race he planned to propagate for regular human takeover.

Murk was a right frightening-looking blighter, tall, broad, muscular, and black-eyed like her. He kept his hair shaved off, exposing a ghastly array of black flame tattoos that began above his ears and trailed over the top of his skull.

All seventeen of them wore black flames, the tribal markings denoting them as born of Yavell, the last Om Răn female in the world with pure demonic bloodlines.

Pandra's flames had been on her stomach, now utterly buggered.

Murk inspected the snarled mess of her intestines. "Hurts a shitload, doesn't it?"

Her focus automatically shifted down to Murk's belly, where she knew a gnarled scar was. So he'd been privileged to endure this same punishment, had he? For what transgression, though, she didn't have a Scooby.

She swallowed tightly as nausea speared up her throat. A spate of vertigo tilted her senses upside down, and her eyelids dragged down.

"You're going into shock," Murk informed her.

"My ring," she croaked, her lips trembling.

Murk used a small crystal dish to scoop her ring off the top of the desk. He couldn't touch it directly because of the painful shock it would give him. "You'll close up soon after you stick it on, so first we'd best put you back together a bit."

She sucked in a sharp breath as her brother painstakingly started cramming her intestines back into the gaping hole in her belly. A halo appeared around her pupils and her pulse beat frayed.

CHAPTER TWO

PANDRA LEANED TOWARD HER DRESSER mirror and applied her fire engine red lipstick, smoothing on the finishing touches for her upcoming night out.

One of her *extra-special* nights out.

She was dressed in one of her few slutty outfits that didn't expose her midriff; something she wouldn't be doing for a while now that the tattoo on her belly was shanked through with an ugly red scar. Feck knew where her jewel belly-button ring had chipped off to.

A leather romper was tonight's outfit of choice, the garment hugging her like skin to a grape. Plenty of cleavage was exposed from the plunging metal zipper in front, and the half-moons of her arse were put on display by the short-shorts—although her cheeks were covered by fishnet stockings that rode down to her knees. Below that, she was wearing tall black "pirate" boots, the leather hugging her tight over the ankles and calves then flaring into a wide cuff at mid-thigh.

In the reflection of her mirror she saw Jorgé, the Parthen butler, come to attention in her bedroom doorway. "Your gentlemen friends are here, Miss Pandra." The butler stepped aside to allow two men access to her bedroom: Bo Bo and Duane.

Hardly her friends.

The two were a couple of deviant masochist grotbags who mucked about with her because they got their rocks off on the shocking and aberrant life she led outside of this prissy mansion...and for the skill she had at terrifying them. Their relationship was symbiotic in its way. Whenever she needed an extra-special night out to blow off a head of steam, these two found her something vile to do. As a reward for their efforts, she lavished plenty of abuse on them.

Bo Bo, real name Beauregard, was short, stocky, and suffering from early pattern baldness. He vaguely resembled George Costanza from *Seinfeld*, but without the glasses. Base humiliation got him off, and he generally didn't give her much trouble.

Duane was a different article altogether. He was a long streak of piss, tall to Bo Bo's short, and lanky of build with greasy hair. He had a complexion riddled with acne and beady eyes like a shithouse rat's. He was into full-on physical domination and pushed Pandra to make things worse for him. He was the dodgy tosser she had to watch.

True to form, as soon as Duane saw the mean look in her eyes, his expression brightened maliciously.

She squinted at the two in the reflection of her mirror. "It's going to be blood sport tonight, lads." She needed to clobber someone more than she needed oxygen. "What's the crack on that?"

"Fight at the pits," Duane answered.

"Blades?"

"Just fists."

She turned around and settled her bum on the edge of her vanity, putting the lid back on her lipstick tube with a sharp *click*. "Dull as dishwater, Duane."

"Well, there's a—"

"Goin' out?" Murk propped one shoulder against the jamb of her bedroom door.

She showed Murk her teeth in a smile. "Private party, love. No big brothers allowed. Terribly sorry and all."

Murk surveyed the length of her body. "It's too soon afterward, Pandra," he said quietly.

She caught back a flush of heat. Did the gobbin really

think she needed to be reminded that five hours ago she'd been wallowing in a mound of her own guts? She hooded her lids at her brother. "No worries, mate. I'm hale." She lifted her right hand and wiggled her immortality ring at him.

Murk shook his head. "You still lost a lot of blood, Pandra."

She could practically hear Duane snicker.

She flashed her brother a murderous look. Fecking asshole, Murk, giving away a weakness in front of her minions. Anger moved like heavy mire into her chest. "I'm touched, truly, at your show of brotherly love." She picked up a pack of Camels from her dresser and pinched out a ciggy with the tips of her sharp, red-painted fingernails. "But if you're worried I'm too dicky, I could pan your head in to prove otherwise." She tucked the cigarette between her lips.

Murk watched her in silence. The threat was real, and he knew it. By some genetic anomaly, she'd ended up with the strength of three of her half-Rău brothers put together. Considering the power of even one half-Rău, that was no piddly thing.

She picked up a lighter and, with a stroke of her thumb, ignited it. A one-inch flame shot up and she leaned the tip of her Camel into it. "You want to see me lamp my brother, lads?"

"Yeah," Duane answered.

Such a good little laddie.

"Uh, oh, Murk, that's hard cheese for you." She picked a piece of nicotine off her tongue. "I like to please my lads, don't I, boys?"

"Yeah."

"I'm taggin' along tonight," Murk announced.

She laughed, then cut off the sound with an abrupt closure of her mouth. "Don't think you want to be privy to what's going to happen with me tonight, old mucker."

Duane made a *mrm* sound and Bo Bo ran his tongue over

his lips, back-and-forth, back-and-forth. That's what Bo Bo did when he got excited. Lick, lick, lick… *sick arse.*

She flicked a gesture at Murk. "Push off now."

Murk grinned at her. He had a surprisingly handsome smile for such a nasty piece of work. Fact was, all of Raymond's progeny were exceptionally good-looking, herself included. But for some reason Murk felt the need to ball it up. It'd probably been a thrill getting his nose broken twice by the Vârcolac, both times when he'd been on a mission to kidnap Toni.

Murk folded his arms in front of him. "You don't think you owe me a little fun tonight, ducky?"

She dragged on her cigarette. She owed Murk her life. If he hadn't come along when he did and helped her replace her immortality ring, she'd be pushing up daisies. Had Raymond just assumed that someone would happen by and save his daughter? Or had he given it a moment's thought? A burning coal lodged in her chest. Jaw squared, she rounded on Duane. "What other blood sport is going on tonight?" she demanded.

"No punch-ups, Pandra," Murk intervened. "Not tonight."

Anger seeped into her head and made Răus红 red spark at the corners of her vision. Aye, her beastie had been riding dangerously close to breaking free ever since her punishment today. But "going Răus" was like a nuclear temper tantrum; she might grow invincibly strong when she slipped into the demon side of herself, but at the expense of complete loss of control. *No, thank you ever so much.* She didn't care for that. "You should shut your cake-hole, Murk. Protective Big Brother doesn't suit you."

Murk merely stared at her again.

She turned aside, sucking in a huge lungful of smoke and exhaling it sharply. Murk *had* been through this before, though. He must know how weak she was feeling. How painful it was to have this burning coal of helplessness residing inside her. How filled with self-loathing she was. Mashing out her cigarette, she twisted it hard into the ashtray, then shrugged. "All right, I'll indulge." She looked at Duane. "What else do you have on the agenda?"

"I know where the Iron Cock is tonight."

"Ah! Now there's a brill idea." The Iron Cock was a sex club where anything could go on and usually did. The illegal part of people shelling out brass for "favors" kept the location constantly changing. That, and the drugs that were generally being passed about. She arched a brow at her brother. "You like taking it up the arse, don't you, Murk?"

Murk's expression didn't change. "Not the last I checked, ducky."

"Bo Bo does." She lavished a nasty grin on her minion. "Don't you, Bo Bo?"

"No," Bo Bo squeaked even as his tongue darted out and slithered across his lips. Lick, lick, lick…

THEY ALL PILED INTO PANDRA'S car: a Porsche 996 Carrera 4-seater coupe, jet black on the outside, pristine beige leather upholstery on the inside, and an in-dash 6-CD changer, plus plug in for an MP3, with speakers that could blow a girl's head clean off. Blimey, but she loved this car. She ragged it onto the I-5 freeway with hardly a sound from the purring engine. She had the Foo Fighters playing, and the rock band was belting out "Free Me." Pandra tightened her grip on the steering wheel. How apropos was *that* sentiment? She drove faster.

Careening off the I-5, she came to a red light at the end of the ramp and braked to a stop. Reaching into her small black purse, she pulled out two Camels. She lit them both and handed one to Murk.

"Hey, we're back here, too, you know," Duane whined. "How the fuck 'bout one for us?"

She unbuckled her seatbelt, handed Murk her ciggy, then

leaned into the back seat and slammed her fist into the side of Duane's jaw. His head bounced off the passenger side window and cracked it.

Duane cried out.

"Shut your fecking trap." She sat back down. "And if you get blood on my car, I'll make you eat your own conkers." She reclaimed her cigarette from Murk, catching Bo Bo's reflection in the rearview mirror. His eyes were wide with terror. "Neither of you get to ask for anything tonight. You hear, you lousy piece of shites?"

Bo Bo licked his lips. *Bleeding spacko.*

The traffic light switched to green. She put the Porsche in gear and continued toward Barrio Logan, the scrotty part of town where the Iron Cock was operating tonight. Dragging steadily on her cigarette, she struggled to ignore the sharp pain in her belly. Her immortality ring didn't take away all sensation, and considering her intestines had been playing *Twister* on the floor earlier today, she was feeling right cattled. She should be home soaking in a hot bathtub at this very moment, and if there was anyone in her life with an ounce of sense or an ickle of real affection for her, that's exactly where she'd be.

In a sudden aching rush, she missed Inga, one of the nannies who'd cared for the brood when they'd been growing up. Raymond certainly hadn't let them be raised by their mean-as-piss demon mum, Yavell. When Pandra was a little girl and had an ouchy, Inga always made her feel better with songs and biscuits and kisses. Those days were long away now, though. She couldn't remember the last time there'd been a nurturing female influence in Raymond's household.

She switched lanes, gunning the Porsche past a Corvette. "Do you remember Inga?" she asked Murk.

Murk glanced at her. "Our hot Swedish nanny?" He made a rough sound in his throat. "Who could forget a set of milkers like those?"

She snuffed out her cigarette in the ashtray. "Don't be a shit-face, Murk. She was a good sort."

Murk paused. "She was." He turned his head to stare out of the window. "I liked her cookies."

"Raymond got rid of her because of you lads, you know. You wankers got too interested in shagging her."

"Hey, not me."

"Aye, I forgot," she drawled. "You're as innocent as a bairn."

Murk tapped his fingers on his knee. "Maybe we should give Inga a bell."

She snorted. "Can you imagine what Inga would say about us now? She'd be right proud of what we've become, for dead certain."

Murk went back to staring out the window.

Twelve-thirty in the morning on a Saturday night and the streets were empty in this part of town, with only the occasional cluster of dicey-looking gangbangers milling about. The roads were slick from a recent sprinkle of November rain, the shiny black asphalt reflecting the lights of the traffic signals and the street lamps in a way that seemed surreal.

It *wasn't* real. This world. Her. How could any place where a father all but killed a cherished daughter be real?

With a hard punch of her finger, Pandra forwarded CDs to the Red Hot Chili Peppers and the solid drumbeat of "Dani California" pounded through the Porsche.

She drove the rest of the way in silence.

CHAPTER THREE

THE BOUNCER STANDING GUARD AT the Iron Cock tonight was Curtis, a huge black man with gold-rimmed teeth and a crisscrossed starburst of scar beneath his right eye that he'd earned from Pandra one night at the Pits.

He let Pandra and her group walk past the front of the line and directly through the door. *Please, have one of the other waiting partiers bemoan that.* She'd thrape him in the mouth. But, no, this crowd was too street-smart for that kind of chuff.

Inside the old warehouse serving as playground tonight, the place was typically dim, illuminated only by unnatural blue lighting that left faces in shadow. The occasional strobe flashed, the white lasers streaking across a throbbing mass of people on the dance floor, bodies undulating and dry-humping to a pulsing beat of music that was sex itself. Most of the attendees were decked out in their sleaziest duds, others barely clad, some were outright nude.

Dolf, the man in charge of this travesty, stood just inside the main entryway. He was a thick, knotty fellow with a square head like a bolt rammed into the wide block of his neck. He straightened abruptly when he saw her. "I don't want any trouble tonight, Pandra," he said, his focus zeroing in on Murk.

"Piffle, Dolf. You love trouble." She reached up and pinched Dolf's cheek, a good hard squeeze of flesh between thumb and forefinger. "It's why you keep letting me come here." Not to mention how much money she threw down the pan in this pisshole. She shoved five hundred dollars into his

TRACY TAPPAN

hand. "We're going to need one of your special rooms tonight. Boys and girls. Toys. The usual fecked up bag o' shite." Without waiting for a reply, she headed to the bar. A stool was quickly vacated for her, and she slid onto it. "Four Wild Turkeys with beer backs," she told the bartender.

"Only beer," Murk corrected. Turning to the fellow on the barstool next to hers, Murk hard-stared the man out of it, then sat. "You don't want to be gettin' foxed and goin' Rău," he said just loud enough for her to hear over the music. "Not in this place."

Murk had a point. Hard alcohol and drugs had the inconvenient effect of making those of them with demon bloodlines go Rău. But this Monsieur Expert routine was getting bloody tiresome. She sniffed. "An hour into this night, and I'm already regretting bringing you along. Naffing killjoy."

The bartender plunked down four beers, and she passed them out to Duane, Bo Bo, and Murk. She lit a cig and took a sip of her drink. Over the rim of her mug she spotted one of Videon's mates across the bar. Edgar. The bloke was hot for her junk, and a prize sleaze about clueing her into that factoid. He emailed her nearly every day, although to suggest what, she didn't know anymore. She always pushed "delete" without reading what he had to say. Although tonight, *hmm*, maybe she'd use him for a bit of rough. Making a man weep in bed could be just the thing to take the edge off.

Dolf came up to her and aimed his square head toward a hallway. "Third door on the right."

"Top! That was fast."

"Slow night," Dolf answered. "I'll send your drinks in."

"Brilliant." She paid the bartender, adding a generous tip, then hopped off her stool. "Right-o, lads, it's fun time. Do make me proud." She took two steps, then stopped and turned back around.

Her brother hadn't moved off his stool.

"Don't sit around cabbaging, Murk," she snapped. "Shake

a leg."

"Think I'll pass on the room, Pandra."

Edging one of her eyebrows up, Pandra strode back over to Murk. She took a slow drag on her cigarette, exhaling twin streams of smoke from her nostrils. "My party," she drawled. "My rules." Almost hysterically, the thought came, *It's my party and I'll cry if I want to…* Sod that.

Murk drank his beer.

She narrowed her eyes. "You wanted to come out with me tonight, Murk, so you'll get your knob waxed if I say so."

"I'm not going into that room with you."

"It didn't sound to me like I was asking."

Murk regarded her blandly. "Any other night you could force me to go in there, we both ken that, but…" He went back to his beer. "Not this night."

Heat shot in searing waves to her face. *Think I'm that much of a sad arse, do you?* Clenching her lit cigarette between tight lips, she lashed her hands out and fisted up Murk's leather jacket by the collar. "You dead cert about that, old boy?" Răzu red bled into the edges of her vision, that fiery coal inside her chest burning hotter and hotter. A *crackle* snapped apart inside her ears. If she let herself go Rău, she'd do Murk over till there was naught left of the wank rag, enough to kill him if not for his ring.

Murk's lips pressed in on each other as he waited for whatever she would dole out.

She gave her brother a hard shove as she let go.

His stool skidded backward, knocking into the one behind.

The man on it scampered off.

"I'm just here to make sure you don't do anything too bollock-brained," Murk said in a low tone.

She pushed her face into her brother's. "What's your angle, Murk?" No one in the brood ever did anything "nice" without an ulterior motive. True, she had helped Murk get his bum out of hot water with Raymond when Murk and the lads had botched a mission to turn over three Dragon women to the Underground Om Răscu to pay a debt. The Vârcolac had ended up stealing those women: Hadley Wickstrum, Kendra Mawbry, and Marissa Nichita née Bonaventure. Still, that didn't mean she trusted Murk any further than she could lob him.

"Nothing," he said.

She caught sight of the hard kick of Murk's pulse along the skin of his throat. That was somewhat mollifying. "You're a fool," she growled, stepping back. "We'll be revisiting this later, you and I."

"I have no doubt."

She rounded on her minions. "Offer up your gratitude to Murk here, m'lads. He just made your night a whole lot worse."

Inside their room, Dolf had provided them with a smorgasbord of choices as ordered: two women, one black-haired and goth-like, the other blondish and sweet-looking...as close to sweet as one could get in a place like this. Plus there were two men, one Caucasian, one African American, both dressed only in spandex shorts. They were athletically built, their bodies slicked down with oil to emphasize that fact.

She strode over to a high bench positioned in the center of the room. It looked like the type of gym equipment one might use for bicep curls, but it was for something else entirely. "Alrighty, Bo Bo." She patted the bench. "Get over here. It's time to grab your ankles."

"No." Bo Bo shook his head violently. "I don't want to."

Oh, yawn. Always the same with him. She'd say, "Come," then Bo Bo would say, "No"—even though he was really gagging for it—and she'd have to make him. *'Round 'n 'round we go.* She stalked over to Bo Bo, blood hot inside her eardrums.

He backed away from her, sweat dampening his upper lip,

and…

There went his tongue. Lick, lick. *Effing twat.*

She fisted her hand into Bo Bo's shirt and yanked him to the center of the room. Grabbing him by the back of the neck, she forced him to bend over the bench. "You move from this spot, Bo Bo, and I break your snotter." Holding her glowing Camel between the vee of her long, pointed fingernails, she jabbed her cigarette at the black guy. "Listen, mate, you lube your todger up nice and good before you go poking around, right? You hurt him, and I hurt you."

She spun hard on her heels and made for Duane, shoving him down into a chair. "You know what you get tonight, Duane?" She leaned into him. "Nothing," she hissed. "You have to sit there and watch Bo Bo and only give it a tug."

Duane's eyes blazed into hers, fury and defiance. "That's not fair."

"No?" She waited for it. *C'mon, laddie…*

"Y-you bitch."

There it is! "It's going to be like that, is it?" Securing her ciggy into the corner of her mouth, she grabbed Duane's hair with one hand and shoved his head back against the wall. Using her other hand, she slapped his face, again and again…three times, four. She released him and stepped back.

He was breathing with effort, blood trickling down his chin. His langer stood erect as Big Ben in his trousers.

Jesus wept, I'm surrounded. "Poor babby." She sneered. "Got a lob on and no one to do."

Duane dragged his tongue across his lip, licking up his own blood. "Maybe I should do *you.*"

She belted out a laugh. "Bold words, love. Either you're in the mood for a right hard stomping or just plain thick as a brick." She snapped her fingers at the "sweet" one. "Come, Petunia. Time to put that kisser of yours to good use."

There was a scuffling noise over by the sex bench, Bo Bo whimpering. Pandra didn't look.

The blonde scurried over and planted herself in front of Duane.

"Make bloody well certain you dig your fingernails into his bollockbag while you're about it." Pandra dropped her cigarette to the floor and ground it out beneath the toe of her boot. "Or I'll be stomping you." She strode over to a chair set against the wall and dropped herself down into it, the leather of her pirate boots *squiching* as she crossed her legs. She pulled out another Camel and a lighter from her purse, and blazed up.

She heard the wet slap of flesh on flesh and Bo Bo squealing. Her airway tried to close off, but she ruthlessly stopped it. Out of her periphery, she saw the blonde's head bobbing rhythmically against Duane's crotch.

She stared straight ahead, shutting her vision off to as much as possible, and smoked. Her lungs congested. Her lower intestines writhed and ached. *Dirty tossbags.* This was supposed to have been one of her extra-special outings, a night of violence and bullying and depravity to make her feel better. But nothing at all had changed. She still felt small and mean and insignificant, no better than she had five hours ago.

Sod you, Raymond.

She tilted her head back and puffed smoke rings, letting her Rău fire scorch her insides until she was nothing but a burnt ruin wrapped in a cold, impenetrable shell.

CHAPTER FOUR

Țărână: two and a half weeks later, November 28th, Thanksgiving Day

NYKO BRUN LEAPT BACK AS the gym locker next to his exploded, shooting out a cloud of snowy powder that engulfed the top half of his younger brother, Jacken.

Stunned, Jacken just stood and blinked, two black eyes peering out of a mime's mask.

Nyko snorted and quickly ducked his head to cover further laughter. Heck, that was funny as all get-out.

The other warriors in the locker room weren't as discreet, every one of them breaking into hoots and guffaws. The Costache brothers, Arc and Thomal, threw back their heads at the same time and roared with laughter, and Gábor Pavenic sagged down onto one of the benches, his left arm—the one with the bull skull tattoo on it—clutched around his middle. Even Breen Dalakis, who usually blank-faced most things in life, bowed his head in quiet laughter, his black hair hanging into his eyes.

"Man, Jacken," Dev Nichita gasped between laughs, his teeth bright white against his black goatee. "I've never seen you look so...so..."

Like a baby seal? Nyko gulped down another laugh. Jacken Brun, leader of the Warrior Class, was hands-down the toughest of their group. So this was just too much.

"I don't know..." Dev opened his own locker. "Like a—"
Sh-wham. A burst of red powder shot out of Dev's locker and splatted against his bare chest and face.

With a ha-whoop, Gábor fell off his bench.

Breen clunked his forehead against the locker, his shoulders full-on shaking now.

"What the *hell*?!" Dev snapped.

"Whoa," Thomal said. "You look like an Om Ră*u got the squirts on you, man." Thomal, Dev's best friend, had tried to dead-pan that, but his lips were twitching pretty badly.

"Okay, guys, we need to watch our asses here." Sedge Stănescu, a better-looking version of the WWF wrestler Hulk Hogan, cracked open his own locker and peeked inside.

"Nah, the rest of us don't need to worry." Arc, the older and slightly taller of the Costache brothers, threw open his locker without incident. "This is just Alex using his special effects skills to mess with Jacken and Dev. His two brothers-in-law."

Nyko made a *ah* noise of understanding. Alex Parthen had bonded with black-haired, sweetheart Vârcolac, Luvera—sister to Dev, who was now vaguely Clifford the Dog looking—a week ago, and Alex's sister Toni Parthen, illustrious co-leader of this refuge underground community called Țărână, was wife to Frosty the Snowman over there. Guess this was how Alex said "howdy" to his relations.

"I'm going to rip Alex's head off," Dev snarled.

Arc looked taken aback. "You can't do that. This was a prank, Nichita. You have to prank him back."

Dev's eyebrows bunched together.

Arc frowned. "Didn't you ever joke around with Luvera when you two were growing up?"

"She's a *girl*."

And all but ignored in the Nichita household her whole life. Nyko pulled on his workout shirt. Kind of wished he'd known that about Luvera. He would've made an effort to talk to her more, even though his vow of celibacy generally had him keeping his interactions with the fairer sex on a *hi, how're you doing today?* level and not much more.

Arc turned toward Jacken and Nyko. "Didn't you guys prank each other?"

Nyko shrugged. "Not really." Nyko, Jacken, and their younger brother, Shon, had been born and raised in Oṭărât, the neighboring underground town of the demon Om Răŭ race. Life had been cruddy enough there without them messing with each other.

"Unbelievable." Arc rolled his eyes. "Well, we"—he gestured back and forth between himself and Thomal—"used to pull shit on each other all of the time." A light of amusement brightened in Arc's eyes as he kept his focus on Thomal. "Remember when I put pink hair dye in your shampoo?"

Thomal chuckled. "I looked like a punk rocker for a week. Till I got sick of it and shaved my head."

Arc and Thomal laughed together, their gazes holding for a moment of brotherly camaraderie.

Hmm. Maybe Nyko should have pranked his brothers.

A knock interrupted them. "Hey there," Toni Parthen called out. "May I come in?" The locker room door cracked open. "Everyone decent?"

When no one protested, Toni stepped all the way inside. She was dressed professionally in brown pants and a silky-looking blue blouse that matched her eyes. The top half of her strawberry blonde hair was tied back, the rest left to drape her shoulders. "Jacken, I need you to—my God." Her brows rose into a high arc. "Why do you look like you barely survived a Johnson's Baby Powder factory mishap?"

The warriors chortled.

Jacken's voice was brittle with annoyance. "This is your brother's idea of a damned joke."

"Alex did this? Uh, oh, you'd better not get it wet, then."

"Aw, hell!" Thomal shouted toward the showers. "Nichita!"

Dev reappeared into the main part of the locker room, the sound of water running behind him. He was naked as the day he was born, except for the twinkle of his trademark gold hoop earring in his left lobe. He spread his arms to show off a soaking wet body now stained with dripping red lava-marks. "What *is* this stuff, anyway?"

Another raucous burst of laughter erupted out of the men. God knew how any of them were ever going to get work done today.

"And there," Toni sighed, "is Dev's penis again."

Jacken's head whipped around so fast, white powder jet-sprayed off the top of his black hair.

Nyko snort-gulped another laugh.

Jacken pointed a rigid finger at his wife, the long black teeth tattoos along his forearm bulging. "Out!" he ordered her.

Toni's lips twisted. "You can't really expect me to take you seriously when you look like a French pastry, can you?"

With a low, rumbling growl, Jacken started for his wife.

Toni scuttled backward, her eyes sparkling. "All right, all right."

Once upon a time, back before Jacken and Toni were together, Dev had tried to seduce Toni in his bedroom—naked, so the story went—and Jacken was a little sensitive about it. Kind of understandable. Nyko wouldn't want his wife, doctor or not, glimpsing Dev's, er, the size of Dev's...you know, his, um.... Never mind. And not that *he* made a habit of noticing. But, heck, it was sort of like a car wreck, impossible not to at least take a glance at something like that.

Jacken body-blocked Toni out into the hallway.

"I'm going," she insisted, her voice still warm with amusement. "As soon as Your Snow Whiteness can get himself cleaned up, I need you and the men to come to my office." Toni's voice faded down the hall. "There's something you need to see."

CHAPTER FIVE

THE OTHER WARRIORS TRAMPED INTO the locker room to full-on change for the meeting with Toni, while Thomal just yanked on a pair of sweatpants over his workout shorts and headed out of the mansion—the warriors' training gym was in the basement—and headed down Main Street. Now he could duck into Aunt Ælsi's, just down the way, and grab a to-go cup of coffee.

The TradeMark Clothing Store, his sister-in-law's place, was right next door, and Beth Costache was also inside Ælsi's, ordering a drink that would probably throw her into sugar-shock. Thomal secretly rolled his eyes. *Women.*

As far as sweet went, though, Beth had the lock on that, with the type of ultra-nice personality that was somehow reflected all over her skin. If Thomal didn't know better, he'd say Beth was one of those sparkly vampires from Twilight. He snorted. Sparkly? Regular humans got nearly everything wrong about the breed, but *sparkly* had to take the cake.

Thomal chatted with Beth, then paid Ælsi and grabbed his cup, full of straight black coffee as man was meant to drink it. Meandering down Main, he came to Garwald's Pub, located just before the road forked, and spotted Dănuţ, exiting the bar with a bag of ketchup bottles. Dănuţ was manager of the community diner, and by the looks of it, he'd run out of some supplies.

Thomal lengthened his strides, passing the pub to head down the right fork. Dănuţ wasn't dressed in a way that was especially bleak, but Thomal still only saw a depressing blend of charcoal, black, and grey whenever he looked at the dude, and that wasn't how he wanted to start his morning.

"Hey, Thomal!" Hadley was just coming out of the grocery store. "What are you doing out and about?" His girlfriend drew close and smiled up at him. Her teeth were so white they seemed to catch the pretend sunshine from stadium lights overhead and reflect it back tenfold. "I thought you were training this morning."

"I was. We got interrupted to have a meeting with Toni." He gestured down the street toward the hospital. "I'm heading to her office now."

"Oh. Well, I'm glad I ran into you. I wanted to tell you something last night, but couldn't find you."

He sipped his coffee, pretending great interest in it to avoid Hadley's eyes. He'd been avoiding his girlfriend, lately, afraid he might somehow give away how frustrated he was feeling toward her these days. Which made him a total dick—both the avoidance and the frustration. Because he should do nothing but count his lucky stars that Hadley was in his life.

This community ran extremely short on mate-able females: specifically, women like Hadley who were in possession of an ancient, rare gene called Dragon. These females were the last frontier of breeding options for Vârcolac since their dying species had reached the limits of their DNA and now couldn't procreate with their own kind. To go back to the lucky for him part, Hadley was awesome; she had a million-dollar smile, a righteously hot bod, honey-blonde hair, a very pleasant personality, and—after an initial freak-out when she found out he was a fang-bearing sub-species of human—now wanted to be with him as much as he wanted to be with her: marriage, kids, lots of sex, the whole nine yards.

The catch?

She suffered from a needle phobia.

And, yeah, to take a pit stop in Obvious Land for a moment, his fangs were much sharper than needles, more like blades, which equaled a bunch of *hurry up and wait, already* on his end.

Hadley was working on overcoming her fear of his fangs with the community therapist, using some technique called "systematic desensitization." But after five months of treatment—*five long months*, during which time he'd been privileged to watch warrior buddies Dev and Gábor nab wives—Hadley didn't seem much further along than when she'd started. He was growing sick of plastering a smile on his face and pretending that dating her with no end in sight was just super-okay, and that's where the avoidance had come from. He was also pretty damned sure that if Hadley found out how horny he actually was, it wouldn't help his campaign to ultimately convince this woman that he and his fangs could be oh-so-sweet to her.

"I had a B12 shot, Thomal."

He whipped his eyes up. "What?"

"Yep." Her expression glowed with pride. "I focused on happy thoughts and kept my heartbeat even, and I did it!"

"Holy crap."

"I know, isn't it great!? I need to manage a few more shots, but otherwise, I think we can be together soon." She moved closer and widened her smile.

Her scent—that of an unmated female—drowned him in the smell of *mount-me-now-and-hard-baby*, and he jolted. Grinding his teeth, he tried to pinch his nostrils off from it. And, yeah, he'd go ahead and solve world hunger and create peace for all, too, while he was about the easy shit.

She reached up and palmed his cheek. "That is, if you still want me."

"Of course." As the words left his mouth, he felt something twinge in his conscience. He had a knack for seeing the true side of people—a throwback from his artist days—but with Hadley, he felt like he was overlooking something. There was some kind of...essence about Hadley that pulled him

27

toward her, but as if he didn't have a choice in the matter and the hell if other shit got ignored.

She threw her arms around his neck and hugged him. "I'm so sorry, honey. I know this wait has been difficult for you. It's been hard on me, too, unable to be with you when I love you so much. But..." She turned her head to whisper directly into his ear, "I promise to make the wait worth it."

Lights, camera, action. A porno movie instantly lit up his brain, a string of endless variations of what her promise implied parading through his mind. Hadley in a bikini shot instantly to the screen. Every time the two of them went to the Water Cliffs he just about blew his load in his swim trunks...metaphorically speaking, of course, because he couldn't get the ol' bone daddy going until he was a mated male. Hadley had a cute little birthmark sitting high on her left hip—in addition to the one on her back that marked her a Dragon—which for some reason he always wanted to lick. It was shaped like a lopsided "3," and sucking on it while he peeled off her bathing suit was the movie going off in his head that—

Prickles of pain needled his cock, his blocked-off sexual plumbing saying *hey, watch it, bub* in full contradiction to his mind shouting *yahoo, let's rock!* Such fun to have schizophrenic sex organs. He stepped out of Hadley's arms. "Hey, now, don't start in on that. I'll end up on the floor." He was smiling, though, really happy for the first time in a long time. "I gotta go, Hadley, but let's have dinner tonight to celebrate."

She laughed. "It's Thanksgiving, silly. We're going to the Bruns' house, remember?"

"Oh, yeah. We'll celebrate there, then." What better place to raise a toast to his future than with his family and friends? "I'm really proud of you." He gave her a quick kiss and took off down Main Street again.

ŢĂRÂNĂ'S HOSPITAL STOOD BETWEEN THE community grocery

store and the beginnings of the residential neighborhood where couples with children lived. Every house there was painted a different bright color, but each one had a white picket fence out front surrounding a lawn of artificial turf. Various other fake plants and potted flowers littered the yards, depending on individual preferences, creating the illusion of any upper-middle-class neighborhood from topside rather than the inside of a cave. At the end of the street, there was a schoolhouse on the right, and on the left a path leading toward the Water Cliffs park, where sand, waterfalls, and pools provided for fun family outings. It was very happy-go-lucky stuff, and Thomal grinned so widely it was a wonder the sides of his mouth didn't knock his ears in. He'd be living here soon. He knew just how he'd arrange the plants in the front yard, too…although he should probably leave that to Hadley.

Toni Parthen's office took up a huge corner of the ground floor of the four-story hospital building. A desk of pale wood sat to the left of the door and a cluster of couch, chairs, and coffee table were situated opposite. Straight across from the entrance was a frosted sliding glass door which led out to a garden courtyard where convalescing patients could sit or hobble about. Above the couch hung a rectangular picture of one-hundred-percent girlie crap: flowers on a hillside. On the wall by the door was mounted a state-of-the-art flat screen TV.

Raln Dodrescu, Țărână's media tech guy, was currently kneeling beneath it, fiddling with the TEVO. Raln was in charge of television programming for the community, which mostly consisted of him flip-flopping shows to meet Țărână's backward day/night cycle. Nighttime topside was daytime here, and vice versa, and it wouldn't go down well to have primetime TV playing, like the risqué *Three and a Half Men*, during kids' breakfast while *SpongeBob Squarepants* was the only thing available for adults in the evening.

Raln was a decade older than Thomal, part of the "lost generation" of Vârcolac. He was married to a woman of his own breed and had suffered through the birth of two stillborn babies before he and his wife gave up on the idea of a family. Devastated by years of death and loss, most couples of this lost generation had stopped trying for children even long before Roth Mihnea, Toni's co-leader of Ţărână, had forbidden all future Vârcolac-to-Vârcolac reproduction. Real tragic stuff.

"Forward to the spot when the police officer leaves the house," Toni directed Raln. "Then freeze-frame as soon as the door swings open."

Nodding, Raln super-slow-forwarded the picture. On the TV, a female newscaster was reporting in front of a single family home, the tag of "El Cerrito" on the lower right hand corner of the screen, indicating where she was in San Diego.

"Who did the reporter say was kidnapped?" Dev asked, focused on the TV.

Devid Nichita was leader of the Special Ops Topside Team, an expert military unit created to deal with problems occurring up on planet earth. All of the team were at this meeting—Gábor, Sedge, and Thomal—as was, Jacken, their ultimate boss.

"A young woman named Elsa Mendoza," Toni answered. "Sister to Ria Mendoza."

Sedge pulled his long blond hair into a ponytail. "The name Ria Mendoza sounds familiar."

Toni nodded. "Ria's a San Diego prosecutor. Kimberly probably knows her." Kimberly was Sedge's wife, a champion-class attorney who lived down here, but also practiced law topside, working cases for her own firm as well as attending to issues for the community. "In the middle of the abduction, Elsa's live-in boyfriend came home and was killed by the intruders."

They all watched in silence as the TV picture moved forward frame by frame. The door to the house swung open in slow motion and a uniformed policeman moved into the entry.

"Okay, stop there," Toni said to Raln. "Now move back to when the door first opens." The frame click-clicked back. "There." Toni pointed at the television screen, indicating a bloody mark on the wall just inside the house: a piece of crime scene evidence TV viewers weren't supposed to see...and nobody probably had, because the door opened and closed so quickly at normal speed.

Jacken gave his wife an incredulous look. "How the hell did you spot that?"

"I don't know. I just...did." Toni swept her gaze over the warriors. "That blood mark is what I think it is, isn't it?"

Thomal cursed below his breath. The red stain on the wall was in an unique, symmetrical starburst pattern, one that could've only been created by the enchanted exploding knives both the underground and topside demonic Om Rău used to devastating effect. So, yeah, it was what Toni thought. The boyfriend had been killed by a Bătaie Blade.

"Shit," Dev confirmed.

Thomal frowned at the TV screen. This didn't make shit for sense, though. "What would an Om Rău want with a Mendoza?" he asked. Dark-eyed and dark-haired, a Latin girl was the farthest thing away from the fair, blonde Dragon females that both the Vârcolac and Om Rău races need-ed...and fought each other to possess.

Jacken crossed his arms. "Good question, Costache. Let's find out." He glanced at his watch. "It's a little after eight at night topside now." He looked directly at Dev. "If you hurry, your team can probably arrive at this Ria woman's house around nine or so, get some questions answered. I want full optics on this as soon as possible."

"Got it." Dev bought off on the mission without hesita-tion, but Thomal caught a flicker of disappointment pass through his friend's gaze.

Dev and Marissa's baby crib was being delivered today, and Thomal knew Dev was excited about putting it together. Why deprive a man of his pleasure for something as benign as a fishing expedition?

"Why don't I take point on this?" Thomal said, tossing his empty coffee cup into Toni's trash can. "Charm is needed for this mission, right?" He flashed the men a cocky smile. "And who better to finesse answers out of a woman than a Costache?"

A laugh rumbled out of Dev. "True enough. Take Arc with you as backup, then. He's been on half duty for a while with Beth's pregnancy and wants to get back in the game." Dev smirked. "He's the one with the real charm, anyway."

Thomal didn't actually flip his team leader the bird, but put plenty of that sentiment into his gaze.

Toni sat down behind her desk. "Just make sure you and Arc are back by two o'clock for Thanksgiving dinner. I've got a twenty-two-pound turkey cooking."

CHAPTER SIX

Topside: Manhattan, New York, same day, EST 2:00 pm

FAITH TEAGUE EDGED HER COMPUTER mouse sideways until the arrow on the screen hovered over the email entitled *new ballet company*. She double-clicked it. How many times had she read this email today? A dozen? More? She read it again as the subtle aroma of cucumbers and tomatoes wafted around her.

"So what're you going to tell him?" Her sister, Kacie, glanced at the computer screen from behind the kitchen counter, where she stood chopping salad fixings.

This Soho apartment Faith shared with her sister was quaint, but small, and space needed to be maximized. Hence the kitchen table where Faith sat doubled as an office desk. "What do you think I'm going to tell him?" Faith replied. "A huge and enthusiastic *yes*."

Kacie grabbed a handful of mushrooms, but paused before slicing into them. Two small lines appeared between her brows.

It was an expression Faith knew well—on her *own* face. In family photos, it was always Faith who looked out at the world with the practicality those two small forehead creases represented, while Kacie usually wore a big, vivacious grin. But since her identical twin sister possessed the same face as Faith's, the expression was hauntingly familiar.

"He's asking me to serve as Artistic Director of his new ballet company." Faith shoved the hair pins deeper into her bun, a task she probably performed a hundred times a day.

Her copper hair was unusually thick and rebelled against all attempts to contain it. Something her theatre hairdressers had lamented fervently over the years.

Kacie fingered a mushroom, still not chopping. Not speaking.

"And he wants you to join his troupe as well. Insists on it, in fact." Faith swept out her hand in a gesture that encompassed her sister. "Why wouldn't we both want to say yes to this opportunity?"

Kacie's amber-gold eyes—that arresting color which had earned them both so many comments over the years, second only to the extraordinary happenstance of their identicalness—filled with skepticism. "It doesn't make sense, for one. I'm a nobody. A dancer in the corps de ballet."

"Oh, twaddle. Don't say that." Faith smiled supportively. "You're a beautiful dancer."

Her sister exhaled. "And what about you? You *can't do it*, Faith. Your knee hasn't fully recovered. This man"—she gestured at the open email with her kitchen knife—"does he even know that?"

"My knee is all but sound," Faith responded firmly, her back going stiff.

Kacie hacked a plump mushroom in half with a single stroke of her knife. "Don't try to pull the wool over my eyes, Faith. You know I can tell it isn't."

Faith and Kacie enjoyed—or suffered—the identical twin oddity of sometimes being able to feel each other's pain. Many days her twin's healthy knee ligament probably twinged as much as Faith's unstable one.

Faith's eyelashes twitched as she was suddenly reliving the sequence that had devastated her life. *Chassé, coupe jeté en tourné*—and *clunk*. She'd torn an inner knee ligament coming out of that turn.

Air leaked past Faith's lips as her stomach iced, same as it did when the doctor had told her that her Medial Collateral

Ligament, or MCL, had been severely damaged. Besides being told both of her parents had died from E. coli poisoning when she was ten years old, she'd never received worse news. Maybe that made her small-minded. How many people in the world were worse off than she was? But dancing and performing on stage were the only dreams she'd ever had, and now they were...put on hold.

How long and hard had she fought to become a success? At the prestigious Joffrey Ballet, she'd studied dance 24/7 while Kacie had bounded off to NYU to enjoy a normal university experience. After four years of grueling work at Joffrey, Faith had thankfully been discovered by a choreographer from New York City Ballet during a summer intensive program. That next spring, at the age of twenty-two, she'd joined their company. Which naturally had led to more punishing work, first as an apprentice, then in the corps de ballet, then as a demi-soloist, a soloist, and finally she'd reached the pinnacle so many ballet dancers aspired to but few achieved, that of prima ballerina. She'd enjoyed the spotlight as a star for one year before she hurt her knee—*one*. Not nearly enough. Not at only twenty-six years old.

She stiffened her spine another notch. "I *can* dance, Kacie."

"Only with a brace on," Kacie reminded her with a level-headedness Faith should've celebrated in her flighty sister.

Except she didn't particularly care to hear anything logical right now.

"You can't wear a brace onstage," Kacie added unnecessarily.

"Well, I'm not ready to quit."

Kacie dropped her gaze to the mushrooms.

Why wasn't Kacie agreeing with her? Their opinions matched as inevitably as their appearance. "So here's what we'll do," Faith said in the matter-of-fact tone that always got Kacie hustling along in the right direction. "We'll fly out to

---

San Diego next week and meet with this man. I'll tell him about my knee and we'll hear what he has to say. After that, we can travel to Los Angeles for Christmas with Aunt Idyll. We haven't seen her in a long time, and we owe her a visit."

Kacie chewed on her bottom lip.

Faith pushed to her feet, impatient now. If Kacie wouldn't go, Faith certainly couldn't. Her sister needed to stop hemming-and-hawing. Because Faith *needed* to go. "What harm could it do just to talk to this"—Faith glanced at the name at the end of the email—"this Raymond Parthen?"

"I guess it couldn't hurt," Kacie finally conceded. Looking up, she smiled tentatively. "Okay, let's go."

CHAPTER SEVEN

Topside: somewhere in San Diego, same night, close to midnight, Pacific time

THOMAL BREATHED HEAVILY THROUGH ROUNDED nostrils, his teeth gnashed around the gag in his mouth. He probably should've been scared shitless, considering he was chained to a chair in a seedy downtown hotel room, and the Topside Om Răoo ass-can who was in the room with him looked like he planned to do some serious tap dancing on his balls. But he could only muster pissed-out-of-his-skull. A slanting glance at Arc, similarly bound to a chair next to his, confirmed his brother was in an identical foul state. It didn't help either of their moods that they'd landed in this goatfuck by seriously screwing up.

We're only talking a few questions, right? had been the absolute wrong attitude to take. Thomal had been way too chill about this mission, which had left him unprepared to find that lip-scarred Om Rău lunatic, Videon, already at Ria Mendoza's house. *Yeah, go figure.* A Bătaie Blade had been used during the crime against Ria's sister, so, surprise-surprise, an Om Rău had been at her house. *Fuck me...*

Videon had opened the door with a Taser gun already pointed and ready to deploy.

Thomal and Arc had proceeded to stand in place like a couple of dickless wonders and let the Om Rău take them out with about as much effort as shooting fish in a barrel. After that, they'd been tied up and transported to this shithole of a hotel room, then for some reason, handed over to Murk.

Maybe Videon's schedule was too full of ripping the wings of butterflies and skinning live cats for him to waste time River Dancing on the balls of a couple of dickless wonder Vârcolac. Maybe Videon knew how much Murk hated Arc, and so he'd done Murk a solid—Arc had viciously broken Murk's hand seven month ago.

It probably hadn't been necessary to break the guy's hand to get his immortality ring off, but Arc had been fresh from getting knocked out a four-story window—along with Thomal—in a fight with the Om RăU, so he hadn't been feeling especially generous toward their kind.

As far as hate went, Thomal and Murk had their own baggage. On the night of Toni's kidnapping at Scripps Hospital, Thomal had stabbed Murk in the neck with a pair of medical scissors. So Thomal would probably have his own turn at the table for whatever Murk was dishing.

Blah, blah, blah. Bottom line was: tonight was going to be filled with some major hurt. Kind of might've been better if the community hadn't released Murk back when they'd had the Om RăU in their custody. But Murk was Toni and Alex's half-brother, and that had clearly colored the decision.

Murk moved to loom over Arc. "Time to duff you up now, vamp. Figure bouncin' you off every wall in this room will be a good place to begin." He ripped Arc's gag out of his mouth. "You think?"

"Yeah, sounds good." Arc smiled. His fangs weren't fully elongated, but still nice and pointy. "Unshackle me, little man, and we'll get our game on."

Murk chuckled, a dark noise deep in his chest that—

The hotel door swung open and a woman strode inside with a couple of Laurel and Hardy lowlifes: one tall and skinny, the other short and fat.

Thomal's attention snapped into extra-sharp focus. Something was...very wrong about her.

She was dressed raunchy as a two-dollar crack whore, her

body squeezed into a short leather skirt so tight it molded the mound of her mons, and her tits were hiked nearly to her chin by a bright red satin snap-up lingerie-thing resembling an old-time corset. And, of course, no sleazy outfit would be complete without a pair of red stiletto fuck-me pumps. But more than the sleaze-factor, the weird thing was that she didn't look entirely real.

Thomal had spent his whole life around stunning women, but this chick went so far beyond striking that there wasn't even a word for her. Thick golden hair fell in a gleaming cascade down her back, her face was artful perfection with its thin nose, flawlessly molded cheekbones, and erotically lush mouth, and she had the most killer body he'd ever seen on a female, athletic and muscular along her set shoulders, tight abs, and long legs, yet also soft and rounded in womanly places, her hips slightly flared and her breasts full. The most wrong part about her, though, were her eyes. They were exceptionally black, even for an Om Răuu, and very flat, as if the woman was dead inside.

Thomal fought back an involuntary tightening in his throat. *Can you say "bad to worse," anyone?*

"Bloody buggers," Murk ground out. "How did you find me, Pandra?"

"Having a bit of a razzle here, are you, Murk?" The slut called Pandra slicked a cigarette out of her purse. "Very unsporting of you, love, not to invite me along." She set the cigarette between her lips and gave Murk a hard stare.

"I've got shite I'm wantin' to work out with this bloke." Murk cut a gesture at Arc. "So bog off."

Pandra lit her cigarette, squinting at Murk through the coil of rising smoke. "I can help you with your endeavors, brother dear."

"I don't want your soddin' help."

Pandra *tutted*. "How cheeky. I let you come out to play with me when you wanted to, and this is the bleeding thanks I get? But no bother. I'm in the mood to fight you for him, so we're brill."

Murk's black eyes held Pandra's for a long moment.

The taller of Pandra's two lowlifes sniggered.

Pandra sniffed. "I owe you a good pasting, after all."

Thomal exchanged a quick glance with Arc. *What the hell is going on?*

With a low, hissed curse, Murk shook his head. "You're a prize hatstand these days, you know that? Would you just talk to Raymond, for fucksake, and save us all the rest of your spleen. It's been two weeks."

Pandra jetted out a lungful of smoke. "Raymond doesn't fancy talking to me, and I can't say I care for the same." She gestured at Arc, her cigarette trailing a ghostly tail of smoke. "So are you going to let me help with this bloke or will you and I be having arms?"

Murk sneered. "Well, I don't know, ducky. I suppose that depends on what plan on doing to the chap."

"Why, I plan on fucking him, Murk."

Murk froze.

Thomal froze, too.

In fact, every man in the room had gone extremely motionless.

"That's shite," Murk accused, his tone suspicious. "You're havin' a laugh."

"Am I?" Pandra stabbed out her cigarette in the nightstand ashtray, then began to unsnap her corset-thing, *snick, snick, snick.*

Murk's eyebrows lifted as she flung her top aside.

Pandra unzipped her skirt and stepped out of it, exposing a warped mess of black flame tattoos on her belly cut through with a bumpy red scar.

Her lowlifes' jaws came unhinged nearly in unison.

She was wearing a naughty black-and-turquoise bra and panty set, and was even hotter than Thomal had originally thought, supple and nubile as a she-cat. Obviously, she was also dead serious about her plans to bang Arc. Thomal's pulse kicked into a higher gear. From the side of his vision, he saw Arc's cheekbones grow hard and prominent against his skin.

Pandra started for Arc, and Thomal's upper lip lifted around his gag.

"'Allo there, my good man." Pandra placed a hand on the back of Arc's chair and leaned toward him.

Arc's nostrils flinched at the same moment Thomal's did.

She reeked of that disgusting corrosive smell, like battery acid or brake fluid, which was particular to Topside Om Răx, whose immortality rings made their blood acid.

Without warning, Pandra punched Arc in the gut.

Exhaling a blast of oxygen, Arc toppled out of his chair and crashed to the floor, his chain bindings clanking together.

Thomal gnashed a string of curses around his gag. What the hell was up with this half-Răx bitch? His brother had never been taken to the mat with only one hit before.

Pandra grabbed a fistful of Arc's shirt and ripped it off his body.

"Shit the bed!" Murk exclaimed. "Look at that dragon on his back."

"Shift your arse, Murk," Pandra commanded. "Hold the bloke good for me. I need to get his trousers off."

Blood roared into Thomal's ears as Murk stomped over and hauled Arc to his feet, bear-hugging him tightly against his body.

Pandra reached for the zipper on Arc's jeans.

Snarling and snapping, Arc kicked out and arched his body, shoving Murk backward a couple of paces.

"Jesus wept," Pandra hissed.

"Well, he's bastarding strong, Pandra," Murk gritted, struggling to push Arc back toward her.

Sweat ran down Thomal's cheeks as he strained at his chains.

Pandra grabbed her purse off the nightstand and took out a length of telephone cord. "Use this." She handed it to Murk. "Be careful not to top him, though, you hear?" She gave Arc a thin smile. "Ready for a second go?" She slammed another punch into Arc's stomach.

Arc folded in half, retching and coughing. In the moment that he was weakened, Murk slipped the cord around Arc's neck and pulled it taut, tugging Arc upright.

Thomal's heart ricocheted into his ribs as his brother's face stained an alarming shade of purple.

"Each of you sit on a leg," Pandra ordered her lowlifes.

The two men scurried over to Arc and grabbed hold.

Pandra reached for Arc's fly again, and before Thomal knew what was happening, his brother's pants were down.

"Now that's a good'un," Pandra murmured, wrapping her hand around Arc's dick.

Acid rushed up Thomal's throat along with a shout, the muscles in his neck spasming as he tried to push the yell past a mouthful of gag and bile. The bones in his wrists throbbed from the fight he was waging with his chains.

A threatening sound erupted from Arc. He managed to drag-step sideways a couple of paces before Murk tightened his hold on the garrote, and the lowlifes put all of their body weight into restraining his legs.

"There, there, be a good laddie." Pandra stroked Arc's shaft, her blood-red fingernails evil-looking against such sensitive flesh.

Murk and the two lowlifes followed the motion of Pandra's hand, mesmerized.

Another sound boiled out of Arc, nastier than the last.

Pandra quickened her strokes.

Nothing happened.

Murk cracked off a laugh. "The git's got a lazy lob."

Pandra glanced up sharply. "Ease back, Murk. The chap can hardly get a stalk when he can't fecking breathe." She slid her hand over Arc again, up and down, tip to root and back again.

Bile burned Thomal's throat and nose. Sweat soaked his shirt. He flexed and released his fingers. If he concentrated hard enough, maybe he could make his hands small enough to slip through.

Air rushed in and out of Arc's closed teeth, his chest expanding and contracting, his face sopping with sweat, worse than Thomal's. Still no lift-off.

"Well, fuck me backward," Murk said in a snarky tone. "It appears the almighty Pandra has lost her touch."

"Not effing likely." Pandra stepped back and studied Arc. After a moment, she made a noise of understanding and crossed to her purse, this time pulling out a comb. No…*schnick*. A knife punched out of the top of the handle. It was a switchblade. She waved off her lowlifes. "Chivvy along, lads. What I have to do now isn't for your ruddy perving."

"That's not fair," the tall lowlife whined.

Pandra's fist flashed out so fast, Thomal barely saw it. A solid thwack announced knuckles meeting flesh, and then the complainer was lying flat on his back, lids closed and mouth flabby. Not doing a whole lot of moving.

"Get him out of here," she told the short one.

The guy's lips quavered. "I can't carry Duane."

Pandra's chin edged down. "Move him or join him, Bo Bo."

Somehow the short lowlife managed to grunt-drag the taller one outside. The door shut, and Arc's rapid breathing filled the hotel room. The whites of his eyes showed as he craned to keep his gaze on Pandra and her knife.

"So what're you about, Pandra?" Murk asked, his attention also on the switchblade. "I thought you didn't want to snuff the wanker."

"I'm going to make the vamp pop his fangs." She flipped the blade into her other hand. "I couldn't do that in front of my lads, could I?"

Murk frowned. "Why the hell are you goin' to do that?"

"He's Vârcolac, durbrain," she said in the impatient tone of someone dealing with an especially stupid stupid person. "He likely needs the scent of blood to get a knob on, you ken?" She pulled off her immortality ring and set it on the nightstand, then slashed the switchblade across her finger. A line of red blood pebbled to the surface of her skin.

Thomal's nostrils twitched.

Pandra moved toward Arc, her strides lithe and feline, her black eyes glittering with feral intensity.

Arc thrashed against Murk again, but with that cord around Arc's neck and his hands and feet bound in chains, he couldn't do much of anything to free himself.

Murk tightened his grip, and Arc jerked and wheezed.

Pandra swiped a finger across Arc's upper lip, smearing the area under his nose with her blood.

Arc let out a short howl.

Thomal's bones rattled from it and he pressed his eyes closed briefly, feeling his brother's pain. The blood of anyone but Beth, Arc's bonded mate, would smell utterly wrong.

Pandra made a noise of satisfaction. "Ah, there're your wicked ivories. Let's see how your plonker does now, shall we?" Pandra dropped to her knees at Arc's feet.

Thomal exhaled through his nostrils in abject shock when Pandra grabbed Arc's cock in her hand and swallowed the head of it between her red lips. Sweat streamed through Thomal's lashes. *No. This isn't happening.* A loud buzz droned through his brain, trying to shut down functions. He could do no more than stare, his teeth rhythmically chewing his cloth gag as Pandra rode down Arc's shaft, taking him deep into her throat, then pulled slowly back off his length, her mouth wrapping him in a tight grip. She paused at the satiny cap to work it with several quick, hard sucks.

Arc's dick went rock-hard.

Murk grunted.

"There's ol' Percy," Pandra said, a note of triumph in her tone.

The muscles in Thomal's crotch tautened. He started to tremble, from boots to scalp; he couldn't stop the body-quakes.

Pandra licked a circle around the rim of Arc's cock with her tongue, and a sound echoed through the room, horrible and raw, the kind of noise an animal might make when it was being slaughtered.

His brother.

Panic sent Thomal staggering to his feet. He yelled, bit the ragged gag in two, and yelled again. "Stop it! For shit's sake, *stop*, you're killing him!"

Pandra turned her head towards Thomal, her eyes dark and blank. "Nobody ever died from getting gobbled, love."

"You don't understand." He huffed the words out, never so close to losing it as he was right then. "You don't know how it is with Vârcolac. He's married, *bonded* to his wife, which means that every instinct inside him will fight against being with another woman. Look, he's bleeding from his ears—just *look*!"

Pandra rose to her feet and peered at the side of Arc's head, where, *see that, you little whore*, blood had pooled in the cup of Arc's ear. His eyes were also narrow and glazed, his breathing erratic.

"You don't want to kill him," Thomal went on hoarsely. "I heard you say that."

Pandra jerked her head around, her brow darkening.

"But if you keep messing with him, he'll fucking implode, I swear it."

She crossed her arms beneath her black-and-turquoise hooker bra. "We're in a bit of a spot, then, chum, because I'm not ready for this bash to come to an end."

Thomal lurched forward a step. "Then take me."

CHAPTER EIGHT

THOMAL WAS A SOLDIER. ANY given day on the job, he faced pain and death from a state of mental calm. Dancing Le Freak while in hot water never helped a man save his ass. But, right now he was skirting embarrassingly close to a full-on panic attack, his heart lodged like a gooey lump in his throat and his head trying to do a James Bond *shaken not stirred* number off his neck into outer space. Because it was an absolute certainty that if he didn't convince this skeezy 'ho to leave Arc alone, his brother was going to die, and living even one day of life without his big brother in it was impossible.

Pandra tilted her head to one side as she considered him. "Are you promising to be a good little egg, is that it, all agreeable to my...appetites?"

Thomal drew in a deep, steadying breath. "Yes," he forced between parched lips. "If that's what you want."

Murk voiced his dissent with a, "My arse."

Pandra glanced at her brother.

"He's talkin' tommy rot," Murk said to her. "Tryin' to trick you into something."

"Well, he's right about him." She nodded at Arc. "The bloke looks manky."

Murk's face grew tight. "Are you forgettin' this is my show, Pandra?"

Thomal blazed a look at Murk. "If you want Arc to suffer, Om RăU, you'll get your wish. I'm his brother, and he'll hate it if she takes me instead."

"It's an interesting proposal, Murk." Pandra crossed to

Thomal and unlocked him. His chains clattered to the floor. "All righty. Let's see what you're offering, vamp."

Thomal stood in place, rubbing the ache from his wrists. What he was offering?

"Your body," Pandra prompted. "I want a gander at you, eh?"

Heat flushed over him. He flared his nostrils as he kicked off his shoes and socks, then peeled his jeans down his hips and stepped out of them. Finally, he jerked his T-shirt off and his underwear.

Pandra's gaze roamed over his naked body, raking him boldly from head to foot.

The muscles in Thomal's stomach flexed and released, echoing the back-and-forth chaos that had just lit off inside his brain. Being treated like a slab of meat wasn't exactly his idea of a day at the park, but also…the feminine appreciation in Pandra's expression was very genuine, and undeniably arousing.

"Now your bum." Pandra twirled her index finger in the air. "Turn around."

He turned, anger and tension throbbing in his head.

"Bloody 'ell," Murk uttered. "Another one of those dragons on his back."

Thomal completed his circuit and faced Pandra again. Arc's strained and shallow breathing created a bizarre counterpoint to his own harsh breaths.

"You're a right fine piece, vamp." Pandra's eyes were bright black, like rain over tar. "I believe we have ourselves an accord. Get on the mattress and lie on your back, spread eagle." She grabbed her purse and pulled out another length of telephone cord.

Thomal's gut seized. "You don't need to tie me down. I told you I won't fight."

She gave him a droll, almost bland, look. "For effect, love, for effect."

He stared at her.

She threaded the cord through her fingers. "My party, my rules."

"I get that," he snapped. "It's just..." He pushed his fingers through the short hair of his flat top. More chaos in his head. What he had to do next was disgusting, but also...it ignited a primitive fire in his belly, a bloodlust that pounded through him with such feral intensity, thoughts of betraying Hadley were pushed to a barely visible, pinpoint spot at the back of his mind. "I have to bite you first."

"Come again?"

"I can't get a boner without your blood in my body, so I have to—"

Arc groaned.

His brother couldn't see what was going on—Murk had Arc's head wrenched back in what had to be a painful angle—but Arc obviously could hear what was happening, and he fully understood the devastating, life-altering consequences of what Thomal was about to do. Well, hey, if there was time to gather a war council and come up with a better way for saving Arc's life, he'd do it. As it was, he was hanging onto this situation by a thin thread.

"Your brother didn't need to bite me," Pandra pointed out.

"That's because Arc's married, as I told you. He's already taken the blood of a woman into his body, so the scent of your blood was enough to get him...him..."

"Proud?"

"Yes," Thomal ground out. "That's not the case for me." *Put two and two together and you'll figure out I'm a virgin.* Luckily, she wasn't concentrating on Vârcolac math at the moment, otherwise fuck knew what this cruel skank would've done with that intel.

"That's the biggest load of cack I've ever heard," Murk declared. "The maggot's tryin' to dupe you into lettin' him bite you so he can drain you dry, Pandra."

"That's impossible," Thomal shot back. "Even if I wanted to do that, I couldn't. Mother Nature installed a safety valve in Vârcolac, so my fangs will automatically retract once I've taken enough blood." And how fun was it that he was having this entire conversation bare-assed naked? "There are many ways I could kill you, half-Răul, but feeding on you isn't one." That much was true. 'Course while is fangs were elongated, he could rip out Pandra's throat, then get back to the task of dishing pain with Murk.

A smile flitted across Pandra's mouth, a genuine one this time, and if it'd remained in place, Thomal had the sense his insides would've done weird things. "You know, I like you, vamp. You're a bit of a brass-neck." She set down the cord. "All righty, let's take a whack at it."

She strode up to him, stopping an inch away.

He swallowed hard. And again. Night and day, black and white, apples and oranges…the difference between how she smelled now, without her ring on, and before went beyond his ability to describe. The closest he could come was to say she smelled somewhat like Toni, who, with her Fey blood, had smelled better than any other Dragon out there, mind-and-crotch-blowingly fantastic—that was, before she'd hooked up with Jacken and killed her scent for any male but her husband. And Pandra had Fey blood, as did all Topside Om Răul. Still…somehow Pandra smelled even better to him than Toni. Better than Hadley, too, which was a mind-fuck on levels he never thought possible. How could an ice queen like this smell so damned good?

"Was there something else?" Pandra inquired blandly.

"My bite's going to hurt."

Her lips curled into an ironic line. "What a perfect gallant you are to warn me."

He knotted his jaw. "I just don't want you to think that I'm trying to kill you, half-Răul, and retaliate."

A Vârcolac's first bite always hurt. Not only that, but the feel of blood being siphoned from the body often set off a new host's survival instinct, and when that happened, struggling and screaming came next. Bonded males spoke in soft, guilt-ridden voices about their wives' first time, and Thomal had never particularly looked forward to that part of his own wedding night. Not in a millennium of years would he have thought he might *relish* the thought of inflicting pain on a host. But with this floozy, he damn well would've corked up his fangs and stopped the pleasure elixir of Fiinţă from coming out, if it'd been within his power to do that.

"The very thought of my pain must have you sick as a parrot," Pandra said in a droll tone. "But no worries, mate, I can hack it." With a sweep of her hand, she brushed aside her long hair, baring her neck to him. "Feed away."

Air blasted from his nostrils as his eyes ignited on the smooth flesh of her throat, his Vârcolac vision zeroing in on a particularly juicy artery: the carotid. He watched the steady, throbbing pulsebeat there and his own pulse jerked forward a pace. Bloodlust consumed him, instantly and savagely. His mouth watered and, before he could stop it, a primitive sound broke from him.

Pandra angled a questioning glance at him.

Hands shaking, he set a palm on her bare hip and drew her closer, bringing her breasts to within a bare inch of touching his naked chest. Oxygen seared a path through his lungs. He felt the prick of his fangs against his tongue. He hadn't even had to think about elongating his fangs, like the concentration it required with a donor. They were just out, ready to puncture a vein and bring him some serious culinary ecstasy.

Sliding his other hand around the back of her nape to hold her in place, he bent his head to her throat and pressed his open mouth to her downy skin, sampling the salty-sweet flavor of her flesh. Something twisted in his gut. She tasted kind of…fresh and outdoorsy, as if she'd gone for a dunk in the ocean earlier today, then washed off with lavender soap. Was this the real Pandra? Thoughts of neck-ripping vanished. His next breath tripped out of him as he found the intoxicating throb of her pulse with his tongue. It was the beat of a necessary life-source. His fangs pulsated to the same rhythm, an exquisite ache running into his upper jaw. He flexed his fingers into Pandra's supple flesh and groaned.

"Thomal," Arc wrenched out. "*Don't.*"

To hell with *don't*. There wasn't any such thing as *don't* anymore.

The hum in his canines told him exactly were to punch in. He inhaled a thick breath, then, with a hard clamping motion of his jaws, he drove his fangs into the velvet softness of Pandra's throat, sinking in, Jesus, so deep. She barely even reacted to his bite. A small, swift exhale was the only acknowledgement she gave of being virtually stabbed in the neck with a couple of blades. He came half out of his skin as her warm blood filled his mouth, saturating his tongue with viscous pleasure and forging a path of eternal ecstasy down into his stomach. A growl thundered in his chest. The taste of her was sensation itself: power, heat, potency, energy, elation, life. The earth swayed beneath his feet and bright colors raced across the screen of his closed lids. A tingling warmth started at his toes and spread upward, engulfing him in a sensation he'd never felt before: a feeling of absolute *rightness*. Like his life was clicking exactly into place and he was finally finding the true fit of his skin.

Strength poured through him, Pandra's Fey blood nourishing him like some violently fantastic drug. Every cell in his body stood up and did a posedown, and his crotch… Something was happening down there. Like the Panama Canal, valves were opening, liquid rising, locks swinging wide. The blockage that kept him from getting erect was *gone*. Blood surged into his cock and swelled him up against

Pandra's belly. Another groan rumbled out of him. Against his tongue, he felt her pulse quicken. Fear? No, it tasted like excitement. A strange thrill coursed through him. He sucked harder, pumping his jaw against her throat to push blood out of her artery even faster. Alarms resonated in his head when he felt his fangs retracting. *No.* He dug deeper into her artery, a misplaced thought racing through his mind that Hadley would've hated him for such rough treatment. Then it was over.

As his fangs tucked back into his upper jaw, he staggered a step away from Pandra, the bones in his knees feeling like nuts and bolts clanking around in a tin box. His lungs pumped, and his whole body felt like one big throb: the veins in his head, the aftershocks in his fangs, and his dick—*definitely* that part of his body. His organ wanted to go spelunking right now.

He observed Pandra, and his stomach caught. Her gaze was soft and hazy, the pleasure on her face changing the look of her completely. It was as if that fresh outdoorsy scent of hers *was* her true self, and in a startling flash, he realized this woman wasn't dead inside, just so ruthlessly contained that her emotions probably rarely saw the light of day.

"Hey," Murk butted in. "You okay, Pandra?" More sharply. "Pandra?"

"Yes. Yes, Murk. That was…" She laughed breathlessly. "Bejesus, you have to get yourself a Vârcolac, brother dear. That was the absolute berries."

Murk expelled a *tch* noise. "Well, it worked, whatever it was."

Her attention drifted down to Thomal's erection. "So it did," she murmured.

He followed her gaze down to himself, and…*thank God.* Shallow of him to do an internal happy dance at this particular moment, maybe, but this was the first time he'd ever seen his organ at full readiness and…he was imposing.

"Time to play sex slave now, vamp." Pandra flicked her hand. "On the bed you go."

Thomal's head came up, his hands jerking into fists, his neck stiffening. The thought of playing "sex slave" was an abomination now. Didn't this woman know what had just happened between them? What they'd shared by him feeing on her? Couldn't she feel it? *No.* Whatever tiny softness had been on Pandra's face before was gone now, so utterly obliterated it was like it'd never happened.

She lifted her chin. "If you've decided against being a good egg, no worries." She indicated Arc with a tilt of her head. "I've still got him to play with."

Thomal clamped his jaw so hard his molars creaked under the pressure. "No," he said. "I'm still all goody gumdrops for this trip to the dark side." Fighting the shakes, he crossed to the bed and lay down. Calling on every ounce of willpower he owned, he spread himself out, stretching his hands and feet toward the corners of the bed.

CHAPTER NINE

EYES PINNED ON THE CEILING, Thomal locked the bones of his face in place while Pandra tied his wrists and ankles to the low bedposts.

She pulled the telephone cord taut, then stood at the side of the mattress for a long moment, gazing down on him. "My, such martyrdom." She clucked her tongue. "You might actually enjoy it, vamp. I've been told I have a tight vadge."

He dropped his lids closed as his engorged cock leapt against his belly. *Don't tell me shit like that.*

"Bring the other vamp over there, Murk," he heard her say. "Make him kneel down on that spot to watch."

Feet shuffled. "*Thomal,*" Arc rasped out. "Oh, God, please, don't do this to him. I'm the one you really want, right? I'll go along with you this time—"

"Shut up, Arc." Thomal squeezed his lids tighter. "You can't do this and you know it, so just *shut up.*"

There was more shuffling movement.

Murk laughed coarsely.

Thomal sprang his eyes open as Pandra climbed on top of him. He understood Murk's laugh. She was spectacularly naked now, a vista of bare, fair flesh…except that she'd left on those fuck-me pumps, which on a totally naked chick was, admittedly, sexy as hell.

She gave him a sultry smile, as if she'd plucked that "sexy" thought out of his brain, then arched her spine slightly forward in an alluring pose.

After over twenty years of suppressed sexuality, the last

few months of which were spent with babelicious Hadley dangling before him as the proverbial sexual "carrot," and with a raging boner currently standing up between his thighs, it was impossible not to devour the sight of Pandra. Her breasts were the premiere event, round, ripe, and buoyant, flawless cream lined faintly and sumptuously with blue veins, their crests topped with flirty pink nipples. The flat plane of her marred belly flared into slim hips, at the juncture of which was...*oh, man*. No hair. She was all smooth skin and a little slit down there, the dusky petals of her sex peeking out. He ran his tongue over his upper lip as his cock lengthened and thickened. He'd never thought he'd like a hairless koochie, but it appeared his dick had its own opinion.

Pandra glanced down at the growing proof that his cock had no standards. "Hmm, Pandra approves." She folded her warm fingers around his sex and gave him a firm squeeze.

He threw back his head and gritted back a moan against a lightning rush of feelings through his groin.

"The head of your dobber is nice and fat." She circled her palm over the top of his cock. "I like that."

A muffled sound escaped him. He'd had no idea his organ could feel so damned much. It was like he'd grown a mass of new nerve endings in the last few minutes. Which meant he was in serious trouble. He *had* to keep himself from coming. Feeding and sex combined to create a permanent blood-bond for a Vârcolac, so the only way to stop himself from becoming inextricably bound to this hose beast was not to ejaculate inside her. A vein beat at his temple. *Sure, easy as—*

Pandra slapped him across the face, the blow whipping his head to the side with a sharp snap. Jesus, no wonder Arc had been taken down by this cum chugger. She was strong as fuck. Snarling, he brought his head back around and glared at her.

But Pandra wasn't looking at him. Her attention was off to the side on Arc. "Listen, bloke," she warned. "You stop watching us at our business and I hit your brother here. Each time harder than the last. Savvy?"

"Yeah," Arc said in a rigid voice. "I got it."

"Brilliant." She turned back toward Thomal, and smirked when she saw his expression. "Ready to spit tacks, are you, love? Get as jarred off as you want." She winked. "It gives me more of the hots." She rose off Thomal's thighs, lifting up high onto her knees, and wet her fingers in her mouth.

Something pulled tight in his chest as he watched her transfer that wetness to her sex. *This is really happening…*

Her hand froze at her crotch, a look of surprise darting across her features. "Already wet," she murmured.

Fucking Fiinţă.

She grabbed his erection and set it against the soft *squish* of her opening.

No… No…"Wait," he gasped.

"Nope." She sat down on him.

A guttural roar ripped helplessly out of his mouth as her sheath slid the length of his rampant shaft, her firm butt cheeks coming to rest on his balls. His wrists and ankles strained convulsively at his bonds. *Oh, Jesus.* He panted. *Jesus.* How long had he wondered what it would feel like? How long…but he'd had no way of knowing…not even the remotest idea in his head that…that it'd be like….*Oh, Jesus Christ.* Tight vadge was the biggest understatement ever uttered. He felt like his dick had just been shoved into a wet, warm blood pressure cuff.

"It's a corker, isn't it?" Pandra planted her hands on the mattress above his shoulders and started to move up and down on top of him, the powerful muscles in her legs flexing against his sides, her long, soft hair brushing his face and chest.

Oxygen scrambled in Thomal's lungs. He twisted his wrists so that he could grab his bindings and hold on for all he was worth. Pandra moved faster and faster. Each time she sat down, she rammed him deep inside her, the walls of her sex clamping around his dick in a relentless grip. Sweat flooded his eyes, blinding him. He blinked hard, forcing himself to focus. *Come on, Costache, you can get through this.*

Murk laughed, that low, coarse, sick sound.

Arc was silent as death itself.

Thomal sucked ragged breaths between the grate of his teeth. His cells felt like tennis shoes in a clothes dryer, *tumble, tumble, clunk, clunk* as they moved into The Change. He was already half-bonded to Pandra from that bite, and every natural Vârcolac instinct in him was pushing him toward completing the bond. The scent of Pandra's sex swamping his senses didn't help with the whole don't-climax restriction. The strong urge to do exactly that tingled through his balls and into the root of his shaft. Somehow he managed to grit it back, but he sure as hell wasn't going to last much longer. He needed to pull a fake orgasm on her, groan and buck up his hips, but… As close as he actually was, pretending would probably push him into the real deal.

Murk made an interruptive noise. "This vamp isn't mindin' anymore, Pandra."

Pandra stopped pumping her hips and drove her fist into the side of Thomal's head.

Pain splintered through his cheek, the corner of his eye splitting open and releasing a torrent of blood down his cheek. Cursing savagely, he shook the stars out of his vision, then jerked his head over to his brother. "Would you get your act together?" he seethed.

Arc's expression was ravaged.

Don't like that you're being forced to watch? Well, screw you! Arc wasn't the one staked out like a sacrifice to the Demon Goddess of Sex Torture. "I'm trying to concentrate here," Thomal hissed.

"Is that so?" Pandra stuck a finger under Thomal's chin and forced his head back toward her. "Concentrate on what? You aiming to keep yourself from chucking your muck?"

Tension pulsed in his head. His lungs suddenly felt

blocked; he struggled for air.

"Uh, oh. Pandra doesn't like to be defied." She *tsked*, as if he should've known better. Snatching up a pillow, she jammed it under his head to prop him up, preventing him from anymore ceiling stare-downs. "It's your turn to watch." She spun around and straddled him on her hands and knees, facing the opposite direction, her slick sex and her perfect ass now pointed at his face.

A tightness pulled at Thomal's spine.

Pandra twisted her head to look at him. "You keep an eye on your donger going in and out of my vadge, you hear? If you stop, Murk'll rat on you, and then I'll sock your brother's head into the next room. Right-o?"

He swallowed, or tried to; his mouth was suddenly as dry as if he hadn't fed in a week instead of only a few minutes ago. No way he could make it through that.

Pandra gave a mild lift of her eyebrows. "Or maybe I should lace into your brother now."

"No. I'll do what you say. I'll watch." *Watch, watch, watch*…just the word tugged his balls into his body.

"Brilliant." She faced forward and reached between her legs for his cock, propping it upright, her red fingernails groping toward the head as she positioned his length at the entrance to her body.

Panic crawled up his spine as those tight pink lips of hers gulped up the head of his dick, then suctioned around the circumference of his shaft as she rode down him. A small explosion of ecstasy went off in his pelvis and blasted down his legs. He shook all over, nearly crying out in pleasure as she started to pump up and down again, her pearlescent labia flexing tightly around his cock on each plunge.

It's only a porno movie. It's not my own dick. But it didn't work. It just felt too fucking good. She was all silky heat and snug inner muscles, and—as she'd obviously planned—seeing that hot kooch of hers work his member was too much. His orgasm shot up from his nuts and through his cock like a geyser, as unstoppable as water from a broken dam. Every muscle in his body went rigid, his hips straining upward on their own. His seed erupted into her, and he gave a hoarse shout, the feelings of pleasure so powerful and intense, he actually grayed out a little. Panting and groaning, he slumped back onto the lumpy mattress, his wrists sagging at the cord.

Pandra slid herself off his cock. "Well, that was a rum go." She swung her leg over, as if dismounting a horse, and hopped off the bed. From the corner of his half-mast lids, Thomal saw her scoop up her clothes. "All righty, brother dear." She stepped into her skirt and jammed herself into her top. "Let's leave the vamps. I have a craving for tequila."

The two Topside Om Rău left, and the door swung shut gently, like they were trying not to wake a baby. There was a muffled conversation in the hall, probably Pandra with her lowlifes. A moment later, two car engines roared to life, then faded away.

Thomal stared at nothing, trying to locate his reason and some energy. Time spun out, filled by the steady *plink-plink* of a leaky faucet in the bathroom and an annoying electrical whine coming from the TV. A sleazeball in another room down the hall asked a working girl, "Hey, tootsie, how much for a hum job?"

Thomal heard Arc swallow. "This is bad."

He didn't look at his brother. Arc had just seen Thomal get ridden like the Pony Express, and on a scale of one to ten that ranked about an eleven on embarrassing and a twenty-five on mondo bizarro. "I'm sorry," he said. He'd tried his best not to come.

"Don't you *dare* apologize for what that whore did to you," Arc blared back, his voice oddly both ferocious and quavery.

Thomal traced a water mark on the ceiling. The side of his face ached relentlessly.

"Do you think you can get loose?" Arc asked after another long pause. "The key to my shackles is over there on the table."

"I should be able to." Thomal hauled in a breath, and in a burst of focused power, he pulled inward simultaneously with all four limbs, snapping the bedposts. One *smacked* his shin as it flew across the mattress, and he growled. Sitting up, he chewed the bindings off one wrist, untied the other, then untangled the cords from his ankles. He rose to his feet, feeling both a little unsteady and like he was thrumming with more power than he'd ever known. Another psychiatric mind-fuck, knowing that his newfound strength came from Pandra's Fey blood. He finally glanced at his brother.

There were deep gouge-marks around Arc's neck from the telephone cord, blood and swelling and bruising. But nothing was as bad as his brother's expression. Arc knew exactly where this little incident left Thomal, although he wouldn't say it. No way. Saying it out loud would make it too real for either of them to handle.

Thomal grabbed his jeans and staggered as he dragged them on. His legs felt like slush, and his depth perception was shot to hell by his injured eye, already crusted over with blood. He moved over to the table and braced his palms flat on top of it, the key blurring before his vision. His arms shook violently. "Shit," he hissed. "Sh-shit. What...?"

"It's bonding withdrawal," Arc explained. "Your cells are making the biological change into being a bonded male, but your mate's not here to scent."

Emotion pushed into Thomal's throat and his fangs thrust down. He nearly choked on the howl tearing up from his chest. The primal urge to rip the door off its hinges and hunt down that woman, sink his teeth into her again, rose rampant in his blood. *Shoulda ripped your throat out.* Another wave of near-seizures steamrolled over him. "It's really messing me up, man."

"I know." Arc scooted forward on his knees. "Get me out of this crap and I'll help you." Somewhere along the way Arc's jeans had been hiked back up to his waist. When had that happened?

Thomal shook his head, but not about the key. "We don't know where Raymond Parthen's new operation is," he said hollowly. "And we're not going to find out where he keeps his Topside Om Răn holed up any time soon, Arc, not with a man as smart as Parthen."

"Don't say that."

"I'm never going to see her again." Ten days without Pandra's blood and Thomal would go into a blood-coma. Ten days... Sweat dripped from his face and fell onto the table, droplets attracting, clinging, congregating into small puddles. "I'm going to die, Arc."

There. He'd said it out loud, and, yeah, it was too damned real.

CHAPTER TEN

Topside: Clairemont Mesa, San Diego, same night

DETECTIVE JOHN WATERSON CUFFED UP the sleeves of his denim shirt as he scanned the crime scene photographs spread over the Formica table in his kitchen. They were scattered together with sheets of notes he'd taken over the last year about the serial abductions of young, beautiful blonde women, plus the spare notes he'd made about the crime handed off to his occult crimes unit earlier today: the kidnapping of Elsa Mendoza. Even though the Spanish girl didn't fit the serial abduction case in most ways, there had been a starburst pattern of blood on the wall of her home.

Same as in Toni Parthen's room at Scripps Memorial Hospital when she'd gone missing back in January, the first women to get kidnapped in this bizarre case.

John drew in a slow breath. Had it really been almost a year ago since Toni had first disappeared? The last time he'd seen her—a little less than a year ago—she'd been in the company of a man with black eyes and hair and large black teeth tattoos along his forearms: a description that fit the perpetrators of the serial abductions. When John had tried to question Toni about her miraculous reappearance in San Diego, this asshole had punched John into Sandman's Land, then absconded with Toni for good, denying John the chance to get some answers…and to date Toni.

Yes, after months of chasing the gorgeous doctor of hematology—ever since they'd started working crime scenes together—he'd finally convinced her to go on a date with him. A date that was supposed to have put them on the path toward marriage, kids, a house in the 'burbs, vacations spent camping or skiing: the whole blissful enchilada. John flexed his jaw. Teeth-Tattooed Asshole had cheated John out of that, and now it was John's main purpose in life to crush the man. And find Toni.

John stared down at the photos again as, behind him, his apartment-issue refrigerator *whirred* into a higher gear and his coffee maker *grum-grum-wheezed* in the process of brewing some freshly ground Columbian. Sane people wouldn't be drinking coffee at this hour, but the only things his finicky system seemed able to tolerate these days were nicotine and caffeine. Not exactly the diet of champions. It was amazing he hadn't keeled over, yet.

He was betting on any day now, though.

It was probably time to go on medical leave, but the hell if he was dropping this case before he'd solved it. *Eight* women total had now been taken now; Toni, the first, then two in April, four in June, and now Elsa Mendoza.

John wrote down the names of the women who'd been taken in June: Marissa Bonaventure, Hadley Wickstrum, Kendra Mawbry, and Ashling Lafferty. This group was important because two of these women had returned.

After tracking down Kendra Mawbry at her home, John had found out some interesting information. A four-man special security team had saved her from her kidnappers and then taken her to the refuge of a research institute. *Very* interesting. Because the last day John had seen Toni at Scripps, Teeth-Tattooed Asshole's friend had shoveled some dung about Toni disappearing to interview at—*drumroll, please*—a top-secret research institute. Without a single word of goodbye to John before she'd left? No way. He wasn't buying it.

But just as John was about to question Miss Mawbry further about the institute, her abductors had returned for her.

In the ensuing attack, John was shot.

John returned the favor and shot his shooter, then in the middle of their gun battle, another man had showed up: black hair, black goatee, gold earring, wielding an M4 carbine assault rifle.

John shot him, too.

The wound had landed the buttinski in the hospital, bringing to light more interesting information. The blood of the M4-wielding guy, name of Devid Nichita, had tested as *not quite human*. Same as some blood found in Toni's hospital room at Scripps when she'd originally disappeared.

All the threads were starting to intertwine, weren't they?

Although, oddly, in the process of being treated for his own gunshot wound, John's blood had tested with a "not entirely human" element in it, as well. Not exactly the same inhuman as Nichita's and the blood at Scripps, but still with an unidentifiable marker. A tight sensation pinched the back of John's neck. Had to be a mistake.

Nevertheless, there was something about this case and blood.

To tangle the strands further, five months after her disappearance, Miss Bonaventure had returned to San Diego bearing the last name of *Nichita*.

It was getting more and more difficult to tell where one string of the web ended and the others began.

John heard the coffee maker burp to a stop, and took a cup off his mug tree. He grabbed the pot and started to pour, but midway through, one of his shaking fits overtook his hands. The pot clanked against the lip of the mug, sloshing hot coffee onto his fingers. "Ouch!" The mug slipped out of his hand and shattered on the kitchen floor. "Dammit!" That had been his Police Academy mug.

Holding his hand under cold running water, he waited for the shaking to stop, then slammed off the faucet. Snatching up the small broom and dustpan from under the sink, he swept up the shards of the mug with hard jerks. He was having these fits four or five times a day now. Soon he was going to do something in front of his partner that would give away his condition…whatever his condition was, exactly.

According the bomb his mother had dropped on him when he was sixteen years old, John suffered from an inherited disorder called Blestem Tatălui. But when he'd looked that up on Google and in medical books, he hadn't been able to find it.

Don't worry, honey, his mom had assured him when symptoms had appeared in his twenties. *You can take these pills to manage your condition.*

The pills still arrived monthly by mail, no prescription needed. Detective though he was, he chose to ignore that oddity. Whatever kept him out of a doctor's office was worth a little feigned ignorance. He'd been gulping the little green babies, called another foreign-sounding name, Suprimarea Patrimoniu, for twelve years now with only minimal problems. It was only in the last couple of years he'd started feeling like absolute crap. More and more each month.

Something was obviously wrong. But since doctors had killed his dad, he was steering clear of letting *that* be another inherited condition. At some point he should probably talk to his mom, but he got the sense she didn't know anything more than she'd already told him. The day she'd filled him in on his condition, it was as if she'd been reading off a script, using someone else's words. John didn't see any point in worrying her.

Dumping the broken remnants of his mug into the trash, he put away the dustpan and broom just as someone knocked. He crossed his living room, frowning at his watch. It was midnight. Squinting through the peephole, he saw—*Ria?* He opened the door. "Hey."

It'd been a couple of years since Ria Mendoza had darkened his doorstep, so to speak. These days he saw her only through work. She was a prosecutor and he was a detective, so their paths crossed at the courthouse with the shared mission of trying to put away bad guys. Although even those encounters had become few and far between now that John worked exclusively night shifts.

"Hi, John," Ria said, her voice that kind of hoarse women got after they'd been crying. "I hope it's not too late to come by."

"Don't worry about it." He stepped back. "Come on in."

Petite with dainty features and soulful brown eyes, Ria didn't look at all like the Amazon warrior she actually was in the courtroom. Walking inside, she hesitated beside his couch, blinking for a moment, probably letting her vision adjust.

He kept his apartment dim these days. Maybe a sign of oncoming depression?

"I'm sorry, I…" Ria faltered. "I don't mean to bother you, John, but I'm really worried about my sister and I heard your unit was given her case." She glanced over his shoulder at the photos on his kitchen table. "Have you…made any progress, yet?"

"No, not much, sorry. But it's only the first day." He headed into his kitchen. "You want some coffee?"

"Oh." Ria followed. "No, thanks."

Maybe not him, either. "No news from your end? No ransom demand?" He'd planned to question her tomorrow, but…she was here now about her sister, and the first twenty-four hours of a missing person case were the most crucial, so why not?

"No." Ria's eyes shifted down and to the left.

He nodded noncommittally and blanked his expression in reaction to her tell. Now why would Ria lie to him?

"Do you have any wine?" she asked.

"I think so." He went to his refrigerator and pulled out the bottle he found there. "White okay?" He didn't drink it himself, but his partner, Pablo, liked it.

"That's fine."

"Can you think of anyone who might want to hold leverage over you?" he asked her as he found a goblet in his cupboard. "Are you working on a case like that?"

"No." Her tone was firm and straightforward: the truth.

He poured. "So you have *no* idea why anyone would want to take your sister?"

"No. None." Her eyes shifted again. *Back to lying.*

Weird and weirder. It made absolutely no sense for her to hide facts from him. Without all the information, his ability to solve this case would be impaired. Unless... "Ria, are you being threatened? Because it feels like...no offense...but I get the sense you're not telling me the entire truth."

Her cheeks flushed. "No, I... John, the truth is I'm also here because I don't want to be alone right now, and... There's no other man in my life, but...I don't want to make things awkward between us, you know?"

He nodded again, once more putting a bunch of meaninglessness into the gesture. The history between him and Ria could account for her strange behavior. But also, maybe not. He smiled reassuringly, anyway. He knew enough about interrogating witnesses to back off; badgering a scared woman wouldn't get him anywhere. "Well, hey, you and I are still friends, aren't—?"

She was against his body in an instant, her arms tightly wrapped around his waist, her face buried in his chest.

He hesitated with a mental *um* for about half a second, then did the natural thing and put his arms around her. He'd meant only to give her a comforting hug, but the act of embracing her pressed her feminine body close to his, and he flooded with heat. She felt so warm and supple, and if memory served, they'd been fantastic in the sack together way back when. He also hadn't been laid in over a year...since before Toni had said "yes" to a date with him, her answer putting a spark of hope in his mind that soon she'd be the one gracing his sheets.

"Do you ever think about us?" Ria asked quietly.

Hmm, the situation was getting sticky. Ria had come here tonight for reassurance, not a bootie call. "Sometimes," he lied. "It was a good six months we had together."

Why it hadn't been great was still somewhat of an enigma. Ria had everything he could ever want in a woman; she was smart, beautiful, owned a passion for catching criminals equal to his, and was a dynamo in bed. He supposed it came down to some women being able to just *look* at a guy and make him feel like she'd reached inside his chest and grabbed his heart. Or between his legs and squeezed his cock. Ria hadn't done either of those.

No, the only woman who'd ever had that effect on him was a certain hot hematologist.

As Toni Parthen's beautiful face flashed through his mind, he stepped back from Ria. "Uh...I think...I know you're feeling vulnerable right now, Ria."

She smiled a little. "I know how I'm feeling, John, and it's exactly why I want to be with you. I just...with everything that's going on with my sister, I need intimacy right now, warmth and affectionate human contact. I know I can get that with you. If...you don't mind."

Mind? He almost snorted. Pulling her back into an embrace, he kissed her, their lips finding an instant, comfortable union. Her mouth opened eagerly, her tongue sliding inside to tangle with his. *Daaaamn*. She was game for sex big time. Securing her more tightly against his body with one arm, he tunneled his fingers into her hair with his other hand, holding her as he twisted his lips against hers. He explored deeply with his tongue, tasting her softness. The moist warmth of her mouth bounded his heartbeat forward and heated his blood. Nothing much was happening down below, though.

Please, no. Not tonight.

He hadn't seen hide nor hair of a boner on himself in a

good long while, hadn't even tried to beat off in ages he'd been so disgusted with himself. But this was a real, live woman in his arms, pliant and sweet-smelling and raring to go. His cock should absolutely rev up with that kind of provocation. Shouldn't it?

He pushed his hips forward, trying to get his engine going.

Ria groaned.

The hot little noise went through his ears, traveled into the super-sexual command center of his brain, and lit off a "wanna get busy" lust in flashing neon…then careened down to the southern regions of his body and fell into an abyss. *Shit.* His breathing speeded and his nerves bunched up.

Ria dipped her hand to the front of his jeans and palmed him through his zipper. She rubbed him…

Nothing happened.

Twin spigots turned on inside his armpits, sending sweat streaming down his ribcage and pooling at his belt. What the hell was wrong with him? Face flaming, he stepped back from her. "Uh…" The monosyllabic utterance hovered awkwardly in the air between them. His cheeks grew hotter. "I…had the stomach flu last week," he lied again. "I guess I'm not completely over it."

Ria's lashes moved rapidly, her breathing uneven. "Really?" she said, her disappointment obvious.

His face now officially needed a fire extinguisher. *Hey, this is cool. I'm in the middle of every man's dream: a nasty case of impotence getting in the way of sex with a gorgeous woman.*

"Maybe," he half-mumbled, "you should go."

She stood there and stared at him—stared and stared like maybe if she looked at him long enough with disappointment in her eyes his dick would feel guilty and magically take itself to task and get erect. Golly, why wasn't that working?

He cut a quick path to his front door. "I'll call you as soon as I know anything about Elsa's case." He opened the door.

Ria moved reluctantly across his living room, then hovered in his doorjamb.

He caught back the urge to shove her into the hallway. *Go already!* "Well, bye." He eased the door closed, leaving her no choice but to step past the jamb and into the hall. The door *clicked* shut, and he cursed softly to himself. *John's third most embarrassing sexual experience*, topped only by farting loudly while in the process of losing his virginity, and ejaculating in his pants during piano lessons when Miss Sonum had leaned forward to do nothing more racy than place his hands properly on the keys.

He crossed through his kitchen, switching off lights as he went, then trudged into the master bathroom. He stripped out of his sweaty clothes, opened the door to the floor-to-ceiling cabinet, and examined his reflection in the full-length mirror mounted there.

Kansas born, he'd worked horse and cattle ranches throughout his teen years and into his young adulthood, and had always had a muscular build because of it. Now he was a shadow of his former self: sunken belly, bony cheeks, circles under the eyes, thinning muscles. His ashen skin glistened with so much perspiration, he might've just gone swimming. Yes, sirree, a new symptom was exactly what he needed: uncontrollable flop sweat. He shifted his gaze down to the useless member between his thighs and felt despair slide into the hollows of his gut. Maybe he *should* go to a damned doctor. There weren't many things worse than—

Movement flashed behind him.

He spun around, fists coming up. Then froze. "Ria?" He blinked stupidly. How had she gotten in here?

She had the white wine bottle in her hand.

He frowned at it. "What are you doing?"

He got his answer in the form of her slamming the bottle against his head.

He keeled sideways, a snowstorm of white lights blasting apart in front of his vision, pain shredding through his skull. Gasping raggedly, he crashed into the cabinet door and slumped against it, his feet slowly skidding forward until his ass met the floor. He tried to maintain a sitting position, but couldn't. He wilted onto his side.

Ria moved quickly toward him, regret on her face. "Don't struggle," she said, kneeling at his side. "I have to draw some of your blood, and I don't really know how." She grabbed his arm and tied a rubber tourniquet around it. She had a syringe in her hand.

"What…?" he tried to ask as he felt a sharp prick at his arm. Then another prick and finally one that went deep.

Stars and meteors collided before his eyes, mottling his vision. He almost didn't see Ria leave, gliding like a wraith out of his bathroom.

The front door to his apartment open and closed distantly with an efficient snap.

CHAPTER ELEVEN

Ţărână: eight days later

NYKO'S LEG MUSCLES TIGHTENED AS he strode into Ţărână's conference room, meeting place of the community's twelve-person Council. The last time he'd been here the wall partition had been pushed back, transforming the conference room into a courtroom, and he'd been watching his little brother, Shọn, defend himself in a criminal trial. Not that much defending had been going on.

"The reasons I did what I did are nobody's business" was all Shọn had been willing to say when challenged to explain why he'd attacked Luvera Nichita, now Luvera Parthen.

So this room wasn't exactly Nyko's favorite.

He came to a stop in front of the U-shaped conference table, standing at parade rest on the far right side of the rest of the Special Ops Topside Team members: Dev, Sedge, Gábor, minus Thomal, but Arc was here to take his place, and since Arc was half-crazed with worry these days, Jacken had secretly asked Nyko to tag along as a potential team member. As strange as Arc was acting these days, he probably shouldn't have been a part of any operation right now, but with Thomal's life on the line, Arc wasn't letting anyone put him on the sidelines.

Roth Mihnea, black-haired, nicely dressed, and seated in the top dog spot at the head of the conference table—even though Toni was the real head honcho around here—glanced expectantly at the team.

Nyko felt tension roll off of Dev.

During this Thomal crisis, the Council had insisted on a daily check-in from the team. Which meant every day Dev, as team leader, was forced to admit they weren't any closer to finding Pandra Parthen than they'd been when they started. And failure didn't sit well with Dev, especially when his best friend's life hung in the balance.

"Any progress?" Roth asked, even though the four of them probably would've run in here, whooping and hollering, if there had been.

"No, sir," Dev answered.

Same-old, same-old. Or maybe not…

Roth rounded on Jacken, who was seated on the right arm of the U, across from Toni on the left. "It's been eight days."

"I'm aware of that." The grooves around Jacken's eyes and mouth made it look like his face had been wrung out. He wasn't feeling too fond of the warriors' lack of success, either.

"Were you also aware," Roth continued with a harder edge in his voice, "that Thomal fell unconscious this morning?"

Now Arc's tension boiled into the room.

A muscle pulsed in Jacken's cheek.

That was news to everyone.

"The situation has become dire," Roth pronounced.

An expression crossed Jacken's features that Nyko couldn't entirely interpret—he'd go with disgusted impatience, though. "The warriors have always treated this situation as dire, Roth. Alex has been working around the clock to find evidence we can use to track down Parthen, but whoever's running things on Parthen's end has security locked down extremely tight."

Nyko shifted his attention over to the empty Council seat next to Toni. Where was Alex, anyway?

Alex Parthen wore two important hats in the community, that of computer expert and Soothsayer. The latter meant Alex was the only person who could read the Strǎvechi Caiet, the ancient text of the Vârcolac...although *read* wasn't the most accurate description. Alex *saw* certain future possibilities, or answers to questions, or law interpretations through visions. Unfortunately, Alex didn't have any control over visions of the future. They came when they merry well pleased. Otherwise Alex would surely have told them where Pandra Parthen was by now.

Funny enough, Nyko and Alex had recently become friends. Funny, because Big Bad Nyko and a computer nerd were as opposite as two men could get. But he and Alex were trying to map out the Hell Tunnels—a network of torturously hot passageways that led from Ţărână to the demon town of Oţărât—and they needed each other for that. Alex would go into a meditative state to try and *see* the pathways using his Soothsayer skills, while Nyko followed his directions via a headset...and tried not to melt. As soon as the tunnels were completely mapped, the Vârcolac could turn the tables on the Om Răuc, who'd always been able to get at them and not the other way around. Once the Om Răuc knew that they could be pursed into the Hell Tunnels after an attack on the Vârcolac, said attacks would undoubtedly lessen, or stop altogether. And, more importantly, the Vârcolac could finally get into Oţărât to save the human women there.

Roth sat forward in his chair. "The unbreachable security we're facing is exactly why we need to discuss the option of negotiating directly with Mr. Parthen himself."

Jacken barked out a laugh. "Parthen isn't going to negotiate with us."

"Mr. Parthen won't negotiate with *you*," Roth came back concisely. "He most certainly will with her." He nodded toward Toni.

Jacken sat back in his chair in a posture of false calm. "So let me see if I've got this right? You want me to bring my *pregnant* wife topside to meet with a man whose main goal is to steal her and pair her with one of his sociopathic half-Rău.

A man who's already shown that he doesn't have a qualm about using abortifacients, seeing as he nearly jacked up Marissa Nichita with one. And the baby Toni carries—*my genes*—sit about as high up on the evolutionary scale to Parthen as gum on the bottom of his shoe. Is that what you're saying?"

Oh, boy. Nyko dropped his gaze. He really wished he was off fixing a toaster right now instead of here.

Syrian Popovici, Jacken's former blood donor, turned to look at Jacken from where she sat on his right. "We trust the Special Ops Team to keep Dr. Parthen safe during the meeting, Jacken."

Jacken turned his cold gaze to Syrian. "That from someone who's never faced down Parthen's power, thank you." He addressed the entire Council again as he added, "We don't know Parthen's full potential, yet, but you can be damned sure that he'll blast my men with everything he's got in order to get Toni. So, I'd be sending my men into what could easily be a suicide mission, only to end up losing Toni and our chance at this Pandra woman, too. Combating Parthen head-on isn't the way to do this."

Balc Oargă, one of Țarână's electricians, who was wearing jeans and a T-shirt even though this was an official meeting, spoke up. "Doesn't Dr. Parthen have the power to handle herself now?"

"That doesn't play into this," Jacken shot back.

For some reason, Toni didn't like to use the enchantment power she'd acquired when she'd bonded to Jacken.

Ælsi Korzha, gray-blonde owner and operator of *Aunt Ælsi's* coffee shop, pinched her lips together. "Then come up with another plan, Jacken. The only thing I hear you doing is shooting down everyone else's ideas, but not recommending any of your own. Thomal will be dead soon."

"All right, please," Toni finally inserted. "Nobody is in any doubt about how grave this situation is. But this isn't a

Council decision. Jacken is my bonded mate and it's his right to protect me as he sees fit." She looked at Roth. "I'm actually shocked you're not respecting that. Would you allow the Council to make decisions about your wife?"

Roth's expression chilled. "My wife isn't one of the leaders of this community. You don't have the luxury of being only a mate in this, Toni."

"Any decision that affects my marriage," Toni returned, "is a mate issue, and will be made exclusively by Jacken and me."

Nyko shifted his feet. That sounded pretty danged final.

Some of the rigidity eased from Jacken's mouth, and he captured Toni's gaze across the U.

Toni stood. "We'll let the Council know our decision shortly." She exited.

Jacken followed, then the team.

In the hall, Toni turned to face Jacken. "Roth does have a point about my position, Jacken. We have to fix this." She rubbed her eyebrows. "Contact my father, anyway, and say that you want to meet with him. He might agree out of curiosity. I don't have any idea how to get Pandra out of him. We'll have to be creative."

Jacken nodded. "The last few days, I've been brewing some—"

"Hey!" Alex hurried down the hallway toward them, dressed, as usual, in khaki pants and a button-down shirt; most days Nyko thought of the professor from *Gilligan's Island* whenever he saw Alex. He also wore gold-rimmed glasses, and—because he was Royal Fey like his sister—had a bit of red streaking his hair. "Sorry I'm late," Alex went on. "But I had a vision, and wanted to gather more information on the Internet before I brought it to the Council."

"The Council has somewhat adjourned," Toni said drolly. "What have you got?"

Alex held out a piece of paper. "This is the air manifest for

Delta Airlines. A flight arranged by Raymond Parthen is arriving in San Diego tomorrow evening with two very interesting women on it."

Jacken's brows edged together. "Interesting how?"

"According to my vision, they're Royal Dragons." Alex glanced at Nyko, probably figuring Nyko, as a man of half-Răй bloodlines who could only ever hope to have a future with a Royal woman, would be the most invested in that information.

And, definitely, Nyko's heartbeat had lurched into a couple of strange beats.

Alex pushed his glasses higher on his nose. "I know it's probably pushing things to save them with everything that's going on with Thomal, but—"

"No," Jacken cut in. "Actually, this is perfect. We'll try to grab one or more Topside Om Răй dickheads while we're saving the women on this mission, give ourselves some bargaining power." He looked at Dev. "Get your team ready to deploy."

CHAPTER TWELVE

Topside: Lindberg Field, San Diego Airport, the next evening

"OH. MY. GOD," FAITH WHISPERED, hearing an echo of the exact same three words from her twin, standing next to her near the baggage claim area.

They'd both just caught sight of the man holding up a sign with *Teague Sisters* hand written on it, and clearly they were in agreement that he was the most breathtakingly handsome man ever created for visual consumption.

The sign-holder saw them gawking and walked forward…with a smile.

The flash of his pearly whites turned the man into pure Adonis…and Faith's belly into warm honey. She glanced at her sister. *Dream?*

No.

Okay. Faith looked back at the man. He had a Bluetooth stuck in his ear and was dressed in the kind of dark, conservative suit worthy of a businessman. But no one observing this fellow could ever mistake him for a mere bean-counter. Faith had been around the well-honed physiques of male dancers for long enough to recognize the musculature and bearing of a very active man, probably an athlete.

He stopped in front of them. "Faith and Kacie Teague?"

They executed a perfectly choreographed double-nod.

His smile broadened.

Faith tilted, bumping shoulders with her sister. She didn't date much. Her fast-paced career—at least, pre-knee injury—hadn't left her with time for more than the occasional tryst with a dance partner. This man was making the area between her thighs feel that lack acutely.

"I'm Arc Costache," he introduced himself. "Raymond Parthen's assistant." He reached out and shook each of their hands. "I hope the change in your flight didn't cause you any problems?"

"Not at all," Kacie said, sounding as breathless as Faith felt. "It was only an hour difference."

The man glanced back and forth between the two of them, marveling. "You two really look the same, don't you? So, who's who?"

"I'm Kacie," Kacie answered. "This is my older sister, Faith."

Faith patted her bun to check for disobedient hair pins.

"Older?" Adonis asked.

"By four-and-a-half minutes." Kacie tinkled a laugh.

Faith eyed her sister sideways. What kind of laugh was that?

"But despite our age difference," Kacie went on, her chin tilted at a coquettish angle, "most people can only tell us apart onstage. Faith here dances like a swan, whereas I tend to resemble something close to an ostrich in a tutu."

"I bet that's not true." Adonis chuckled. "Besides, I can tell you two apart, no problem."

Kacie tinkled again. "Maybe now. We're dressed differently and my hair's in a ponytail. But trust me, if we wanted to fool you, we could."

Faith silently agreed. The Teague girls had been tricking people ever since they'd left the womb.

But Adonis merely tossed them one of his charm-loaded smiles, this one seeming to say *not me*.

With a *plonk* and a *whir*, the carousel belt started moving. A suitcase pushed through the flaps and one of the other passengers grabbed it.

"After we get your bags," Adonis said. "We'll go someplace to talk. There are a few things about Raymond Parthen I need to clarify with you."

Faith frowned. "About the ballet company?"

Adonis watched as more bags were belched through the flaps. "Not at all."

Faith nodded. *Okay. Good.*

More bags came through and were claimed until they were the last people waiting there.

Kacie crossed her arms. "Shoot, I hope they didn't lose our luggage."

"No." Faith pointed. "There's yours."

"I'll get it." Adonis stepped forward and reached for—

A large hand shot through the baggage flaps and grabbed Adonis's wrist, yanking him downward.

Adonis hit the conveyor belt chin-first and let out a bark of pain.

Faith jumped.

A man rocketed through the flaps and landed on top of Adonis. He was dressed in a TSA airport security T-shirt. Although she'd bet her good knee he was a fake—his bare skull was tattooed with an array of ominous-looking black flames, and that just didn't look…official.

Faith clutched Kacie to her as the two men turned into a whirling knot of wrestling and cursing, fists swinging, hands tearing at clothing, boots gouging licorice strips of rubber off the belt. Sweat and spit streaked the air.

Faith scurried sideways with her sister. *My goodness!*

Kacie's eyes rounded. *What's happening?* Faith heard her sister's voice in her head…not in any way that was overtly telepathic. She just knew exactly what her twin was thinking.

I don't know. We need to get help. Faith whirled around, one hand still on Kacie, and—bounced off a man's concrete chest. Gasping, she staggered back. Then her jaw dropped.

The muscular man standing in front of her had black hair, a black goatee, and bright wolf's eyes, like the hulking predator Wolverine. He was wearing a headset and was also dressed in a TSA T-shirt, although just as unbelievably as Bald Guy. She darted a glance over Wolverine's shoulder. The closest people were at the farthest baggage claim area.

"Not a word," Wolverine warned her.

The expression in his silver gaze sent Faith's belly into a deep dive for her knees.

"You two are in danger," Wolverine added.

The conveyer belt chugged the two snarling combatants past them. Adonis had his hands manacled around Bald Guy's neck and was squeezing. *Hard*. So hard that a dozen wormy veins pushed up along Adonis's forearms and his arms began to shake.

Bald Guy's face went blue, then violet. He wrenched at Adonis's hold, but Adonis's eyes were ablaze with some kind of violent insanity, and his grip never wavered. A grinding metallic sound spilled out of Bald Guy, like the noise a car engine makes when it's already running and the driver turns the key again. And then…there was…another noise.

Crunching spinal bones?

"Faith," Kacie squeaked.

Faith hugged her sister closer, gaping in speechless horror as Adonis dumped Bald Guy to the floor and staggered off the belt. She'd never seen a dead person before, and Bald Guy had clearly given up the ghost. His neck looked like a pillar of wet clay an enraged sculptor had clutched between his fists, deforming it into uneven ridges.

Adonis moved over to them, breathing heavily. One sleeve of his blazer was torn and dangling. "Crap, that dirtbag was strong."

"Yes," Wolverine said shortly. "We don't want to still be in the airport when he wakes up."

Faith blinked. *Wakes up*?

"I'll carry him on our way out the back." Wolverine smirked. "Murk is just going to *love* that we've captured him to use as leverage again. You see to the women."

See to...? Us? Faith glanced over Wolverine's shoulder again. There had to be *real* airport security somewhere.

Wolverine pivoted to address Faith again. "I need you two to listen to me, quickly. My name's Dev Nichita. I'm head of a special military unit that's been tasked to save you. We need to—"

"Save us from *what?*" This was beyond ridiculous. "We're a couple of ballet dancers."

"The simplest version I can give you right now is that you and your sister have been duped by Raymond Parthen. He's not the head of a dance company, but the leader of a faction of individuals who want you and your sister for a very special gene you carry. My people found out you were being flown into San Diego to be kidnapped, so we changed your flight to protect you. But Parthen's men have shown up and are trying to grab you back. Your situation is extremely perilous, Miss Teague. I need you and your sister to come with—"

"Wait a moment," Faith interrupted, her throat jerking around her words. "I'm sorry, but..." *He's not the head of a ballet company.* "Are you sure? The website for Mr. Parthen's company was impressive and his credentials, impeccable."

"That was faked."

Kacie blew out a sigh. "I thought that email sounded too good to be true."

Faith pressed a hand over her mouth. *You've been duped by Raymond Parthen.* Breathing became an effort.

"Miss Teague," Wolverine tried again.

Faith shook her head. "This still doesn't make sense. My sister and I don't have any kind of special gene." She stepped back on a surge of impatience. She needed to get away from this man and make some phone calls, figure out if this was really true. "We're normal, everyday identical twins."

Wolverine grabbed Adonis by the shoulder and spun him around. "You two have brown birthmarks which indicate the existence of this gene: they're pieces of a dragon, actually. Most probably you have a strip of wing here." Wolverine arced his finger high up on Adonis's right shoulder. "Or a blotchy spot here for the nose." Now he pointed low on the left scapula. "Or here"—the lower back to the left of the spine—"for the foot. Correct?"

The conveyor belt *shissshed* to a stop.

Kacie's lips parted. "We have all three of those marks."

Another cause for lament by their theatre makeup artists over the years.

Adonis craned his neck around to look at Wolverine, eyebrows high.

"Royals," Wolverine said cryptically. "They've got a shit-load of the Dragon in them."

Faith placed her hands on her hips. "How could you have known about our—?"

"You *are* the women I'm claiming you to be," Wolverine insisted, turning tetchy. "So unless you want Raymond Parthen to get his hands on you and subsequently pair you with a man like *that*." He cut a gesture at Bald Guy. "Then you'll come with me and my men. *Right now.*"

Faith met her sister's gaze. *This man is certifiable. Nothing he says makes sense.*

I'm not going anywhere with total strangers. Kacie took a step back next to Faith. *Let's keep moving.*

Wolverine pressed an index finger to the earpiece of his headset. His predator eyes turned to flint as he aimed a look at Adonis. "Gábor just spotted one of the enemy outside."

Adonis's attention sharpened. "Who?"

"*Her,*" Wolverine growled low.

Adonis went rigid and the violent insanity returned to his expression. "Let's go," he snapped. "We don't need Murk if we've got that bitch."

"We have to take care of them first," Wolverine countered.

Take care of...? Faith exchanged an alarmed look with her sister. The two of them had managed to sneak away from the men by a couple of feet, but the exit from baggage claim was still several yards away. *We need to run.*

"We don't have time for this," Adonis argued.

"No, we don't," Wolverine agreed. "Let's deploy Plan B. You carrying?"

"Fucking A."

"Kacie—!" *run!* The second word never made it past Faith's lips.

Wolverine was suddenly *beside her*, his hand clamped around her arm. She opened her mouth again to scream, but her voice box seized up and her vision blurred.

Wolverine had just jammed a syringe into her arm. "We've been authorized to use whatever means necessary to rescue you," he said, then scooped her into his arms.

Terror filled Faith's nose with acid.

"You'll thank me for this someday, I promise." Wolverine laid her gently on the motionless conveyor belt, then climbed up behind her. Grabbing her under the armpits, he ducked back through the flaps and zoomed her through with him to the other side. He set her on a transport carriage. Next, came a couple of suitcases, then Kacie.

Her sister's eyes were glazing over, but Faith could still see the panic in them. *They're going to kill us.*

Faith's tight throat muscles locked out all possibility of sound. She couldn't move at all.

Wolverine leaned over her. "We don't want to hurt you." His features were rendered cartoonish by whatever drug had been injected into her, his nose slipping sideways off his face. "We injected you and your sister with something called ketamine, so you'll be unconscious in a second. When you come to, you'll be safe."

Pretty rainbows soared across Faith's field of vision and sparkly fireflies flitted. She felt the transport lurch into motion beneath her spine. The hairs on the back of her neck rose straight out from her flesh like icicles. Her vision tunneled into a tiny pinprick.

End of act. Curtain down. House lights fade to black.

Chapter Thirteen

Pandra leaned back against her Porsche and crossed her feet at the ankles, lightly slapping the instep of one strapless high-heeled shoe against the sole of her foot. She should've worn boots. Her toes were going numb from the cold weather.

Just another inconvenience to add to this blighter of a night.

Going out into the field with her brothers was supposed to have been a lark, giving her a chance for more shit-stirring. But Murk had turned out to be too much of a bossyboots for her tastes, and finally, fed to the teeth with him ordering her about, she'd bunked off and come here to wait. After those sisters were grabbed, Pandra would drive home Teer and Dace, while Hutch would go with Murk and the women.

It seemed to be taking the lads bloody forever.

She shivered as she leaned in through the driver's side window and fished an emery board out of her purse. Ten more minutes and then she'd wait inside her car, even though she hated the limited visuals it gave her, and would set the Porsche's heaters to blasting.

She filed her nails vigorously, planning how she was going to pan Murk's head in at the end of this, take out her chopsy temper on—

Headlamps sliced onto the service road where she was parked behind Delta's hangar. It was a Sky Chef van. She returned to filing her nails. *No worries, blokes, I belong here.* The vehicle slowed as it drove closer. *See something you like, nosy parkers?*

The van stopped so suddenly, it rocked violently on its shocks. The side door slammed open.

Bother. She was in no mood to make explanations to some half-sharp airport employees about—

There was a blur of motion, and—*ha-shisssh*. A breath rushed past her lips as a muscular arm was suddenly banded around her throat in a choke hold. Who the bleeding hell moved that fast? The scent of Vârcolac hit her at the same moment an animal growl resonated in her ear. *Ah.* A vamp. Looked like she was going to get into a ruck tonight, after all. *Bully.* Dropping her nail file, she missiled an elbow into her attacker's gut, doubling him over, then spun around and drove a fist into the back of his neck.

He fell to his knees, groaning.

She flung off her high heels and kicked out.

He moved with that inhuman speed again, hooking her heel with his palm and flinging it up.

She stumbled backward a few paces.

Her attacker sprang to his feet. His eyes and blond hair blazed in the headlights.

Shit a brick! It was that handsome crumpet of a vamp whose cock she'd sucked off about a week ago. She laughed, a razor-edged thrill coursing through her. After what she'd done to this bloke, he'd surely try to kick seven shades of shit out of her. This was going to be a right awesome fight!

Standing poised on the balls of her feet, her breath leaving her mouth in a vapory cloud, she aimed a nasty smile at the crumpet as—

He was *behind* her again. A ruthless shot to her kidneys had her biting back a shout. He swept out her legs and took her to the ground, planting a solid knee in her lower spine. His palm came down on her head and ground her cheek into the asphalt. She grunted. *Impressive.* She herself was fast, but the crumpet was blinding fast.

He jabbed a hypodermic needle into her arm.

Oops. Hard cheese for him. Drugs didn't knock her out, just made her go Rău. Vicious. Powerful. Unbeatable.

But then...

The landscape teetered and grew heavy, pushing her lids closed. *What the devil...?* Well now...Turned out she might be in a bit of a pickle here, after all.

WHEN NEXT PANDRA OPENED HER eyes, she was surrounded by inky blackness and the smell of oil, petrol, and the distinctive aroma of Vârcolac. She heard the steady *hum* of an engine plus the monotonous *whap-whap-whap* of rubber tires over asphalt.

She was in the boot of a car.

Testing her wrists, she found that her arms were bound behind her back, both with hard plastic spot-ties and metal handcuffs.

She almost laughed. She'd wanted to find herself some trouble, hadn't she? *Wonder what's in store?*

The vehicle slowed, easing forward over a bump, then stopped. The engine shut off, and she tensed, preparing herself for battle. The double whammy of security around her wrists would be a piece of piss for her to break. She just needed more space than this boot provided.

Helpful to know the vamps had no idea who they were dealing with, though.

But battle didn't come.

A cacophony of peculiar noises started up instead: the slithering *whisk* of a bicycle chain derailing and the reverberating *clank-clank* of a wrench hitting a pipe. Then Finn McCool—the giant from her childhood fairy tales—mumbled in his sleep, the steady *mum-mum* signaling movement again, this time downward. Down? Right odd, that. She kept herself at the ready, waiting. Seconds ticked into minutes and minutes ticked into a small eternity. Where the feck were they heading? Into Hell itself?

She had plenty of time to ponder how the crumpet had managed to trank her. Nothing existed that had the super-capabilities of rendering a half-Ră…u unconscious, not that she knew of. So had she been dosed with an enchanted drug? But none of the Vârcolac possessed the power of enchantment. Did they?

Finally, with a jolt, they stopped. The bike chain *whisked* again. The car roared to life and drove slowly forward, maneuvered, then stopped once more. The engine shut off. For good this time, it seemed. Car doors slammed and voices spoke, one sounding urgent. Footsteps pounded off and faded. Keys rattled at the boot.

Pandra pulled in a long breath, bringing her power into focus.

As the lid swung upward, she snapped her elbows wide, flinging her bindings off, and exploded out of her confined space like a dynamite-activated Jack In The Box. She landed light on her feet with her fists up.

The man who'd opened the boot swiftly stepped back and settled into a sure-footed fighting stance, too. He had long, swooping teeth tattoos running the length of his forearms and jet black hair. He was some breed of Om Rău by the look of his black eyes.

She flew at the man like a deranged character spawned out of Mortal Kombat, a lifetime of martial arts training turning her into a blitzing machine of kicks and punches—spinning back kick, hammer fist, back fist, roundhouse kick, knife hand, elbow strike.

Her opponent blocked everything, moving as fast as she did.

Breathing roughly, she large-stepped back out of his striking range and stared at him. Now what? She'd kept him on the defensive the whole time, stopping him from landing any offensive blows, but she hadn't sorted him out, either. No headway was being made here.

"You done?" her Om Răn opponent drawled nastily, his voice sounding like it came directly out of Hell.

Shite, how far down *had* they traveled into the earth?

She sensed movement behind her and whirled, planting a brutal fist right into the chops of some dodgy black-haired Vârcolac.

He stacked it backward onto his arse, then clumped the rest of the way to his spine, completely buggered out. Blood welled up into the chalice of his mouth and gushed over the sides, running down his cheeks to paint the floor in burgundy.

Another Vârcolac standing nearby, also black-haired, but with prominent sideburns, stared down at his chum in frozen shock.

Her Om Răn opponent sneered his upper lip at her, exposing the tip of a fang. So he was one of those part-vamp, part-Om Răn she'd heard tell about. Wonder if this chap was Toni's hubby and thus Raymond's most-hated? Wouldn't want to be that.

She took another large step backward as the Răn-vamp stalked over to the fallen Vârcolac and crouched down at the man's side, examining his mouth.

The Răn-vamp's head snapped up. "You broke his fang," he growled.

The one with sideburns looked even more gobsmacked than he had a moment ago.

What was all the fuss about? People got cabbaged in fights all the time.

The Răn-vamp powered to his feet, his voice lowering into deeper octaves of Hell. "You'd better hope he can still feed, lady. If you issued Breen here a death sentence, there's nothing on this earth that will save you. Vinz," he barked at Sideburns. "Get a couple of Dragon warriors down here now. As damned strong as she is, I doubt we can take her hand-to-hand. We need men with speed."

Like the crumpet at the airport? *No blooming thanks.* She

wasn't dossing about for that. As Sideburns sprinted off, she dove into the driver's seat of the vehicle she'd arrived in—a Lincoln Town Car—and slammed the door shut, locking it.

The Răˇu-vamp gave her a frigid glare as he stalked toward her.

"Sorry, love, my regrets and all." She cranked over the engine. "But I'm otherwise engaged and can't piss around with you." She knew bog all of where she was, but maybe if she started bashing into the walls of this garage she'd eventually get somewhere. She put the car into gear and gassed it forward, aiming to run down her opponent along the way.

The Răˇu-vamp took a single large step up, planting a combat boot on the hood of the car, then continued to the right and down, landing by the driver's side door with amazing agility for a man of his size. He punched her car window. The glass cracked and bowed inward.

Not bloody good. One more blow like that and the man would have access to her. She gave the Town Car some welly and roared toward a wall hung with items of a mechanic's trade, each tool chalk-outlined on a pegboard.

Her Răˇu-vamp opponent materialized in front of her, both hands slamming onto the hood of the car, denting metal. Forward motion ceased. The wheels kept spinning, throwing up gray smoke and the ghastly scent of burning rubber. The high-pitched squeal set her teeth on edge.

"Get her out of the car!" the Răˇu-vamp ordered.

Another man had just entered the garage.

Not a blond Dragon as requested. This vamp was—Her hands tightened on the steering wheel. *Bejesus*…she'd never seen his like on earth. With his massive body, eyes of blackest black, hair that was a shaggy beast's mane, and a face built of steel girders and concrete, augmented by a broad nose crooked from a former break, he was the most fearsome being ever created. He was tattooed with long, swooping teeth on his forearms, like her Răˇu-vamp opponent, but also around his neck.

Heart pounding, she stomped the gas pedal to the floor. Wheels complained *eeeeee*. The Răhu-vamp's arms shook on the hood.

Whopping Vamp stepped forward and peeled the car door off the vehicle like it was no more than tin foil from a frozen ready meal.

Jesus suffering—

Her new adversary plucked her out of the car.

Răhu-vamp let go and jumped aside. The vehicle skidded sideways, ramming into a rack of wood-working tools. Saws, hammers, screwdrivers, *plunkity-plunkity*, all came crashing down onto the hood.

She threw a hard purler at Whopping Vamp.

He swatted the hit aside, and drove a punch into the side of her face.

Holy double fuck.

His fist was Thor's hammer.

The room went black as she thumped down onto the cement of the garage floor with enough force to crack her kneecaps. She garbled a curse, unable to manage anything coherent.

That monstrosity's blow had unbolted her lower jaw bone from its hinges and now her mandible was hanging by the skin of her cheeks. Her immortality ring kept the pain from completely overwhelming her, but she still staggered as she pushed to her feet. The room reappeared into scrambled images of gray. She thrust a hand against her chin to puzzle-piece her bones back into place. Her acid blood laced through her fingers and dripped to the garage floor, *siss-sissing* onto the concrete.

Whopping Vamp arrowed behind her and grabbed both of her arms, cranking them behind her back until her elbows met. Her jaw swung loose again without her palm as a prop, more acid sizzling to the floor.

Concentrating on her power, she gave an experimental tug. *Well, shite.* She'd be buggered if she could break this trog's hold. Clenching her hands into fists, she dipped her chin down, preparing to fling her head up and splatter the Whopper with her acid blood.

"That's enough, Pandra," commanded a female voice.

The familiar timbre of power in the woman's tone dug deep into a place inside Pandra, making it impossible for her to disobey. She froze long enough to draw in two breaths, then lifted her head slowly and met the woman's gaze. Cold dipped her from top to toes.

This woman's eyes were the same startling shade of blue as Raymond's.

It was the infamous Toni.

Chapter Fourteen

Pandra cautiously watched Toni take a step closer.

"You and I have some extremely vital business to conduct," Toni told her. "I need you to stop fighting. No more violence of any kind. Can you promise me that?"

Pandra's heart skipped a beat. How absurd that Toni would be willing to trust her word, but it was obvious she did, and somehow that...made her want to comply. She nodded.

"Please, let her go, Nyko," Toni said to the Whopper.

Pandra's arms were released. The Whopper—Nyko—stepped back from her, though he didn't go far.

The other Rău-vamp also remained nearby, heavy boots planted in a wide stance.

Pandra shoved her chin back up again, keeping her focus on Toni as she waited for her immortality ring to work its magic and re-secure the joints of her mandible bone. Cor, but Toni was beautiful. Raymond would be pleased to know just how stunning she'd turned out.

Toni's gaze moved over to the black-haired bloke laid out on the garage floor. "What happened to Breen, Jacken?"

"She broke his left fang," Rău-vamp retorted.

Toni's blonde eyebrows rose. "I thought fangs were too strong for that."

"Usually that's the case, but..." Jacken sneered. "She's a bit on the strong side."

Two vamp males raced into the garage, one had cowlicked light brown hair, the other had hair so blond it was nearly white.

Jacken gestured them to a stop. "Kasson, Jeddin, stand down for now."

The two men gawked at the bloody-mouthed, unconscious vamp sprawled out on the garage floor. He was quite the spectacle, that one.

Pandra dropped her hand from her jaw and rotated it once to test it. When it didn't fall apart, she spoke to Toni. "You have Raymond's power."

Silence.

Chatter-chatter-chatter went an air vent, like pebbles tumbling through an aluminum pipe.

Toni gave Pandra a flat stare.

Pandra glanced at the vent. "You're his favorite, you know. He has a picture of you in his den, the only of his children who made it into his precious man lair. You're about two years old, holding a red ball—"

"That's not the matter of importance I need to discuss with you." Toni kept her expression neutral, but Pandra sensed emotional currents roiling below the surface. "The man you…attacked, Thomal, is lying in the hospital on the verge of death. Because of you."

Near death? "Well, that's not my doing." Pandra made a blithe sweep of her hand. "God's truth, someone else must've thrashed him after I left the hotel."

"You don't understand." Toni offered her a wintry smile. "When a Vârcolac feeds on and has sex with an unmated female, as Thomal Costache did with you, he goes through a cellular change that biologically connects him to that female. Thomal is now physically dependent on your blood, Pandra, and yours alone. Because of that, for the last nine days, we've watched Thomal wither steadily towards death while we've scrambled to find you."

She went silent for a long moment. Of all the convoluted bilge water, she'd never expected to hear something like this. "That doesn't make a whit of sense. If this Thomal chap is so dependent on my blood, what the bleeding hell did he do before I came along?"

"He fed on donor blood. But that option is no longer available to him now that he's gone through The Change and is bonded to you."

Bonded? That didn't sound like something she wanted to be, not to a vamp. Not to anyone. "Well, how do we undo this effing change?"

"There's no undoing it."

"What? You're codding me."

"Unfortunately, no. The bond is permanent, Pandra."

"But…" The beginnings of dread stirred at the back of her throat. "Truly? Never?"

Toni spread her hands. "As long as you're alive on this planet, a sixth sense radar within Thomal will know it and make it impossible for him to take in any other blood but yours."

The hairs on the back of her nape prickled up. "I see." Her chest burned, the hot coal that lived inside her flaring up. A *crackle* echoed through her ears and red flashed at the corners of her retinas.

"Pandra," Toni interjected quickly. "We're not going to hurt you."

"I'm sure not," she drawled. "I mean you didn't just say this Thomal chap will be released from his bond if I'm dead, did you?"

"No one's going to kill you," Toni insisted. "Thomal's too weak to endure the wrenching process of unbonding right now. Moreover, that's not our way. We don't kill without proper cause."

Pandra blew out a laugh. "What more does a girl need to do?"

"Believe me," Jacken stomped in. "We're keeping the option on the back burner in your case. Meanwhile, you're stuck here because Thomal needs your blood. You don't like it? Go fuck yourself. You sealed your own fate the night you abused two of my men. So that means you put your attitude in check, lady, or your time here will be spent hanging from a meat hook as no more than a vein for Thomal. We clear?"

Pandra hooded her lids, trying to hide a flicker of alarm. Could they really keep her here against her will, if they had a mind to? Of course they could. That long trip down meant she was umpteen meters below the soil. "I should jolly well think so," she returned dryly. "You didn't exactly beat around the bush, chum."

The bicycle chain *whisked* again.

She swiveled her head toward the noise, and saw two large garage doors sliding open, revealing a Pathfinder vehicle sitting on an enormous elevator platform. The idling engine shut off, no doubt because the Pathfinder had nowhere to go. The Lincoln Town Car was all skew-whiff in the way, wispy strings of smoke still eddying from the two back tires.

Three men climbed out of the newly arrived vehicle. One had long blond hair caught back in a ponytail, a bloody cut on his brow, another had a black goatee and a small gold earring, and the third, stubbly black hair and a bull skull tattoo on his arm. Each owned the kind of sculpted, muscular bodies seen on men who fight for a living...or for their lives. Hard-nuts, all, not a jellyfish among them.

Pandra's chest shook with a tremor of claustrophobia. The three didn't come down off the platform, but her situation squeezed in on her all at once; she was enclosed on all sides now by men of supernatural power whose breed had always been hostile enemies to her own. She didn't know where the blinking heck she was, only that she was underground, deep enough to render escape extremely difficult, if not impossible. She was trapped, surrounded, and possibly helpless.

"No one's going to hurt you," Toni repeated. "As long as you cooperate."

Pandra sucked in the garage smells—oil, petrol, WD-40,

Windex—to tamp down another upsurge of Rău. The demon state was flaring up to protect her, but Rău often did her more harm than good.

Somewhere out of sight, a door slammed, followed by the thunder of running feet.

"They're coming." Toni strode forward, palm outstretched. "I'll need your immortality ring now, Pandra."

She made no move to comply.

She rarely took off her ring, certainly never removed it in an overtly threatening situation like this one. And hard-shit to anyone who wanted to force it off. Bribe, threaten, torture…there wasn't anything anyone could do to confiscate her ring if she didn't fancy having it removed.

Except for Toni. Aye, Murk had firsthand knowledge of Toni's extraordinary ability to get around Raymond's enchantment and remove their rings without receiving a shock.

Pandra supposed that meant her ring was coming off, will her, nil her. So, either she could continue to stand here being a stubborn knothead, and then the Vârcolac would hold her down—maybe tank her full of more of that enchanted drug—and take her ring off that way. Or she could make a show of being "cooperative."

"Very well." Pandra held out her right hand to Toni, her brows arched high. *Let's see if you can do what they say you can, Sunshine.*

Toni slipped her ring right off.

Blimey…

Tucking the ring into a small box, Toni trousered it.

Ice washed through Pandra's belly. "I thought you only needed to change me into real blood for this Thomal chap?"

"That's true," Toni responded.

"But you're not giving me my ring back?"

"No, I'm not."

"Right. I almost forgot. You want to leave the snuffing-

Pandra option open to the Răù-vamp over there, don't you?"

"Please don't refer to my people as vamps, Pandra."

The pounding feet grew louder, and then four men exploded into the garage.

A nattily dressed black-haired Vârcolac with a medical bag rushed in first, casting a surprised glance at the zonked-out vamp. Next came Sideburns and her nemesis, Crumpet, the two carrying a fourth limp bloke between them. They had the fellow propped between them, each with a hand under the chap's thighs and the fellow's arms looped around their necks, making it look like he was sitting in an invisible chair. Or *slumped* in a chair, as the chap's head was lolling off his shoulders as if held there by no more than an imaginary length of fishing line.

"Put him against her," Crumpet ordered Sideburns. "Hurry!"

The unconscious fellow was shoved into Pandra's body. He drooped against her, his breath cold as deep water fish against her flesh. She quickly stepped back.

"Don't move, you fucking whore!" Crumpet lashed out a fist, the punch catching Pandra with a vicious crosscut to the jaw.

Her head whipped to the side so hard she felt her cervical vertebrae grate together. Her lungs bottomed out of air. Bejesus, she hadn't been braced for that.

"Arc…" Toni began.

"See what you've done to him!" Crumpet bellowed at Pandra.

Pandra back-paced several more steps, little spasms leaping through her belly like a herd of hunted gazelles. The garage rolled arse over kettle before her eyes, then righted itself. Bile was a rotten lemon in her throat. Now that her ring was gone, all the aches and pains from her recent fighting bouts were coming to life, some nagging, most screaming: kneecaps, cheek, kidneys… Crumpet's punch to her face just now was *really* fecking reminding her that her jaw had been broken by Whopping Vamp a short time ago. She had the sudden, silly urge to lie down.

"Hey, I got this." The Vârcolac with the goatee came down off the elevator platform and walked up to Crumpet's side, speaking quietly. "This has been a tough couple of weeks, Arc. So why don't you let me take care of Thomal on this one?" Without waiting for an reply, Goatee pulled Thomal out of Crumpet's hold, then looked at Pandra. "You ready to give this a shot?"

She didn't budge, didn't answer, too overwhelmed by another ludicrous urge. She wanted to hum the song Inga used to sing to her when Pandra's childhood world would spin into a rage, an all-too-often occurrence in a house full of half-demons and a father who always insisted on his own way, and woe betide the person who didn't give it to him.

Där satt en liten fågel i päronatä. Å sjongde så många vackra viser...

A little bird sat in the pear-tree. And sang so many beautiful songs...

But that was before Pandra had grown into a woman and learned that life was to crush or be crushed.

"Look, Pandra," Goatee said. "Thomal's one of my best friends and I don't like to see him hurt. But you released my wife, Marissa, from Raymond's control, so I don't have a beef with you. I only want you to make my friend better. Can we be cool with that?"

Why was it so ridiculously relieving to learn that there was at least one person here who didn't want to have her guts for garters? The pain of her injuries making her weak-minded? She took a step forward, catching a better gander at Thomal. Shitting hell, *this* was the man she'd sported with eight nights back? *Couldn't be.* Her bloke had been unfathomably attractive, golden skin, sharply carved features, vibrant blond hair, and iridescent blue eyes flecked with gold. He'd had a docking great body, too, a perfect combination of muscle and leanness. His sleek, supple form had suggested the ability to move at lethal speeds while the width of his shoulders and the honed shape of his muscles promised his agility came with substantial strength.

At first she'd been so focused on his brother, the crumpet, she hadn't realized how attractive this one—this Thomal—was. She'd wager that was a common mistake, too. Most women probably thought Crumpet was the better looking of the two brothers. But no.

Either man could've been splashed all over the cover of GQ magazine, without question, but it was Thomal's face which hadn't been Photo-shopped into plastic perfection. A tiny scar nicked through his right brow, his lips were a little off-center, and his eyes were full of a hidden darkness; profound waters moving through his soul, warning that he just might be fighting as many inner demons as she was. All of this gave Thomal character, and made him way more handsome than his brother.

That magnificent fighting animal was gone now, though, reduced to a Raggedy Andy doll in the arms of Goatee—who she now knew was Nichita. Thomal was definitely on the verge of death, with sallow skin stretched like parchment over wasting muscles and his shimmering blond hair faded to a sickly straw color. A strange knot gnarled up Pandra's heart. How long would this man have lasted if boredom hadn't lured her out to the San Diego airport tonight. One day? Two? The thought was oddly disturbing.

She nodded. "All right."

Nichita moved forward.

"Wait a moment, Devid," Natty interceded. "I'll need to shock Thomal. His fangs won't elongate without it. He's too far gone." The doctor opened his medical bag and pulled out two long probes, wires trailing down to a black box.

Nichita changed his hold, securing Thomal against his

chest with one arm, the other hand pressing Thomal's head back to his shoulder. "Okay, Doc. Fire away."

"You'll feel this, too," Natty warned.

"Just light him up."

Dr. Natty set the probes onto each of Thomal's canines and squeezed the trigger. A small bulb on the box blinked on.

A biting snarl whiplashed out of Nichita.

Thomal's body went rigid, his spine bowing, the cords in his neck knotting up. The light went out, and Thomal wilted lifelessly in Nichita's arms again, his thick, dark blond lashes lying against his cheeks like the wings of a dead bird.

Crumpet howled.

Curses erupted from the warriors.

Nichita met Pandra's gaze. "I need your help," he told her quietly. "Thomal has to get your scent into his head, okay?"

Feeling right knackered at this point, she didn't protest when Nichita propelled Thomal toward her again, pressing him right up against her body. With a hand on the back of Thomal's head, Nichita angled his friend's face into her neck.

She stood there, arms limp at her sides. Her body hummed as Thomal's breath hit her flesh in ragged bursts. If memory served, this bloke's bite gave quite a lot of pleasure and, as shagged out as she felt at present, she could stand with a bit of that. "He's warmed a bit," she told Nichita.

Nichita pulled Thomal back. "Hit him again, Doc," he told Natty.

Natty set his probes. The small bulb reignited.

Thomal came awake with a shout, thrashing in Nichita's embrace, his body convulsing and his legs kicking out.

His left foot missed Pandra by mere millimeters.

"Hey, man, it's me, Dev. Everything's fine. Your woman's here and you gotta feed now, okay?" Nichita placed Thomal against Pandra once more.

Thomal's chin came to rest on her shoulder and he shuddered against her, a jumble of quaking, shivering muscles, his body jerking over and over. A low growl reverberated out of him and then his head came up, his eyes locking on hers like blue laser beams.

The two of them stood frozen in place, suspended in a strange tableau for she didn't know how long. She started to speak, but...what was she supposed to say? *So sorry about all that raping bosh, my good man, didn't mean to give offense* seemed...rather gauche. She wasn't sure if she was sorry, anyway.

Thomal broke contact first. With another low growl, he pulled her hard against his chest and drove his fangs into her throat.

She tensed, then air eased out of her lungs. His bite didn't hurt this time. She gripped his shoulders as the sound of his frantic gulping filled the garage. Her eyesight grew fuzzy at the corners, but she still could make out Nichita, forehead bowed to the middle of Thomal's back, and everyone else in the garage, also with lowered heads, as if to give them privacy for some intimate act. But they were only—

Oh, my giddy aunt. Her belly liquefied. She'd bloody well forgotten how intense the pleasure of this was. A quiet moan slid out of her before she could catch it back. She was suddenly sitting on a volcano, hot lava ecstasy boiling up all around her, lifting her up until it felt like she was floating outside of her own body on a cloud of steam. The heated sensations seeped into every cell, swirling through her body in hundreds of mini twisters that funneled directly into her naughty bits. Her knees turned to porridge, joining her belly in the land of mush. She dug her fingers into Thomal's shoulders as her nethers throbbed with a primal, aching need, wetness slicking the area. She arched in his hold, only a thin remnant of willpower keeping her from slamming her hips forward into Thomal's and biting him back: his earlobe, his throat, his nipples...

With a torn breath, Thomal extracted those lovely ivories

from her neck and surged back against Nichita.

She stumbled out of Thomal's hold, her lungs working heavily.

Thomal's eyes glinted like sapphires, his cheeks ruddy with color. His wanger was erect as a Scottish caber in his trousers.

She swallowed carefully. *Intimate, indeed.* Her own knickers were practically stuck to her.

Nichita lifted his head. "How're you doing, man? Can you stand now?"

Thomal didn't answer. His chest moving, he kept his gaze nailed to hers, his face a churning cauldron of savage emotions, too many for her to read. She was savvy enough to ken most weren't good, though.

Toni broke the spell. "Oh, crap," she hissed.

They all turned around.

Visible over the backseat of the Lincoln Town Car were two identical faces, both wearing the same expression of utter, jaw-breaking shock.

Faith and Kacie Teague had woken up and been watching this drama play out for…how long?

To judge by the looks on their faces, they'd seen every-blooming-thing.

Chapter Fifteen

Faith sat with the cup and saucer balanced on her knees, the tea cold, the spoonful of honey she'd added two hours ago congealed at the bottom like a modern art blob. She'd barely been able to swallow, much less drink anything, during Dr. Parthen's lengthy explanation of everything that had…happened…in that garage.

All three of them, Faith, Kacie, and Dr. Toni Parthen, were currently gathered in the sitting area of a well-appointed bedroom located on the third floor of some glorious mansion. The door to the room was decorated with an opulently painted mural of a Flamenco dancer in traditional Spanish dress, her skirts flared out in swirl of color against the backdrop of a soaring cathedral.

Inside, the décor was equally dramatic. The walls were covered with dark red velvet wallpaper inlaid with golden whorls, a huge four-poster bed had swags of gold cloth draping the canopy, and over in the sitting area, where they were now, a three-foot-tall earthenware urn was filled with bright silk flowers of the type a Flamenco dancer might wear in her hair. The three of them were seated in iron-framed, black-cloth-upholstered furniture, Dr. Parthen in an armchair, Faith and Kacie on a couch.

When the doctor had first arrived, a man in a white serving coat had trailed her inside, pushing a tea cart. As if Darjeeling, scones, triangle-cut cucumber sandwiches, and salmon canapés—none of which a ballet dancer would eat, by the way—could soften the blow of what was about to come next. *Not quite.*

"I realize everything I've just told you sounds far-fetched." Dr. Parthen's slim hands were folded in her lap, her legs elegantly crossed.

Far-fetched? Faith smiled wanly. According to the last two hours' worth of explanations, they were currently in a town built inside a subterranean cave, complete with its own plumbing, electricity, Internet, houses, a water park, football field, movie theatre, several restaurants, and myriad shops. It was a refuge for a human species called Vârcolac. This species' blood makeup was different from "regular" humans, requiring them to frequently ingest blood by biting a host using a set of…No, she couldn't even think that word.

Oh, and also demons, referred to as Om Rău, lived in a neighboring town and caused all kinds of trouble. Up in the city of San Diego, which was "topside," there was another group of these nasty characters under the leadership of the now-infamous Raymond Parthen. This Raymond had wanted to capture Faith and her sister for some kind of special DNA they possessed—looked like Wolverine had been telling the truth at the airport—called "Dragon." This was the same gene which most of the other humans living in this town carried…except Faith and Kacie owned a supercalifragilistic-expialidocious version of it, making them *Royal* Dragons. Faith sighed. Like most little girls, she had once dreamed of waking up one day to find out she was actually a princess, but *this* wasn't exactly what she'd had in mind by being dubbed royalty.

Honestly, she didn't know what she'd had in mind after seeing all she had in that garage. She and Kacie had been left alone in this bedroom for only about fifteen minutes before Dr. Parthen had arrived with the tea. In that short time, "ketamine-induced hysteria" and "cruel prank" were about all they'd come up with. Unfortunately, everything they'd seen had looked very real.

Drawing a shallow breath, Faith scrunched her toes together inside her shoes, rubbing her calluses together. Too much excitement with Adonis, Wolverine, and their aberrant gang, plus being drugged, were making her punchy. Not to mention that everything had happened after a cross-continental flight which had landed her in California with three hours of jet lag; her body said it was 1:00 o'clock in the early morning, her watch read 10:00 at night local San Diego time, but down here, it was actually 10:00 in the morning. She was really starting to feel like vomiting should be her next course of action.

Dr. Parthen smiled reassuringly. "Luckily, you two are way ahead of where most people begin when they come to Ţărână. You've already seen for yourselves the truth of everything I've described."

They had, at that. Faith swallowed tautly, the tea cup *clinking* softly beneath her trembling fingers.

"Do you have any more questions?" Dr. Parthen asked.

Faith pushed to her feet and crossed to the tea cart, setting her cup and saucer down on it. "I just think…we need some time to let everything percolate for a bit, doctor."

"Of course. Take all the time you need." Dr. Parthen rose from her chair. "The Lucerne room two doors down has been prepared for your use, as well." Apparently every bedroom door in his mansion was painted with a different European theme to distinguish one from the other. "Rest a bit, and I'll be back at dinnertime to give you two a tour of the town. Hopefully when you see what a great community we have here, it'll help you decide to stay."

Faith offered up another pallid smile, the best she could manage at the moment. She'd lived her entire life in big cities, her days and evenings filled with dancing, rehearsals, fittings, dinners, the theatre, and premieres. She didn't need more than a peek outside her bedroom window at the dinky town of Ţărână to know she absolutely did not want to stay.

Dr. Parthen extracted what looked like a small cosmetic pot from her pocket. "You'll need to wear this special mud before either of you can go into town. A double hit of Royal scent will knock the single men over like bowling pins."

Faith moved her brows together.

Dr. Parthen chuckled. "That'll make sense once you've read the community manual, which I left for you on the desk." She crossed to the nightstand and set the cosmetic pot there. "A dollop behind each ear will do. It's been cleaned and treated to remove allergens. Okay, then. You have my cell number if any questions or problems arise." She paused at the door. "I would like to apologize once again that you two were drugged. I can relate to how disconcerting and frightening it feels. I also want to reiterate that you were brought here for your own safety. You're free to go at any time. I only ask that you carefully consider the danger that Raymond now poses to you before you make such a decision." With a nod, Dr. Parthen opened the door. "See you soon."

As the door closed, a ripple of incredulous laughter escaped Kacie. "Wow."

A little too simple of an exclamation for all this, but Faith supposed there weren't any other words descriptive enough. "Do you believe everything Dr. Parthen said? I mean..." *Vampires, demons, and Dragons.*

"I wouldn't have if I hadn't seen it, but..." Kacie waved airily. *We both saw some very unnatural stuff: that one man stopped a moving vehicle with his bare hands, and the other extremely large...creature just yanked the car door off. We saw that woman bleed white acid and her broken jaw heal in minutes. And we saw that hunky blond guy suck on the woman's neck using a* definite *pair of fangs.* "They didn't know we were watching them in the garage," Kacie added. "So I think we can trust they were being their true selves."

"Yes," Faith uttered the single syllable on an exhaled breath. Was she actually agreeing or just uttering? Her brain was numb from the effort of trying to digest everything she'd heard about this outlandish community while simultaneously processing the news that she'd flown to San Diego for nothing. Certainly not to rejuvenate her career.

Kacie pushed up from the sofa. "Dr. Parthen also came across to me like a perfectly reasonable and rational human being." She moved over to the tea cart, standing across from Faith. "So what do you want to do?"

"What do you want to do?"

Kacie caught her lower lip between her teeth. "Find out more of this place, for sure. I… I'm curious about what it'd be like to live here."

Faith gaped. "You're seriously considering staying?"

"I know it sounds crazy, but…" Kacie shrugged. "They really need us here. You heard that sad story Dr. Parthen told."

Sad? Mostly, bizarre. The Vârcolac were apparently a dying breed, the result of a one-hundred-year-old betrayal leading to the deaths of a majority of them. With so few left, the Vârcolac family tree had become somewhat of a straight line over the years. No surprise that hadn't worked out. Vârcolac had ceased producing live offspring nearly thirty years ago, landing them on the endangered species list. Their future had looked extraordinarily bleak for a while…until it was discovered that Vârcolac could procreate successfully with Dragon humans, women like Faith and Kacie, along with others like them. There were twelve currently living in this community, four singles, the rest already married.

"From the sound of it," Kacie went on, "they treat their women like queens around here. I think it would be nice to be special."

"Are you kidding me?" Faith set her hands on her hips. "We've always been treated as special. Too much so."

"We've been treated as a circus act," Kacie countered. "Not for what we can do. Well, you maybe, but not me."

"They want us to have babies." The pitch of Faith's voice was rising. "That's what they want us to do."

"So?" Kacie threw out a hand. "You've always wanted to have a family, Faith, but you've kept it on hold because of ballet. Now that your career is over, maybe we both can finally—"

"My career isn't over!" Faith shouted.

Kacie lowered her head with a long sigh and pinched the bridge of her nose.

Faith mashed her eyes closed, so tight she felt her lashes fluttering against her cheekbones. "I'm sorry," she pushed out of her mouth. "I didn't mean to yell at you."

"And I don't mean to hurt or upset you. But…." Kacie hesitated, the *but* hovering over them along with a heavy cloud of tension. "Your knee isn't ever going to go back to normal," she said quietly. "I'm sorry, but it's just not. It's been a year now, and… I really think you need to accept that so we can get on with our lives."

Defeat closed in on Faith, like every door in the world had suddenly and simultaneously slammed shut.

Kacie's brow pleated. "Here in this town we could also have some close friends for once. Our whole lives we've sat on the fringes, always assuming we didn't fit in because of the quirk of being identical or because we were raised by Aunt Idyll after Mom and Dad died."

Faith glanced down. She'd always thought the same thing, especially about Idyll. The kooky aunt who'd taken them in when they were orphaned had never lacked in love to give to her two nieces. But the hippie-guru-shaman priestess-Tarot Card reader-sprightly woman hadn't exactly excelled at providing a normal, stable living environment. Faith had always needed to be the responsible one. It made perfect sense that she'd been drawn to the structure and discipline of ballet.

"But now we know we've been outcasts because of this Dragon-thingy we carry." Kacie's gaze was earnest. "There's nothing wrong with us, Faith, and I want to feel that, experience it, *believe* it every day."

"And you think you can accomplish that *here*?" Faith pointed a rigid finger at the sliding glass door which led out to a small wrought iron balcony. "Have you seen that town?"

Kacie's lips pressed together. "Would you not be so closed-minded? Just because there's no dance company here doesn't mean you have to automatically turn up your nose at it. You're going to miss out on a great opportunity to—"

"What opportunity, Kacie?! We're in a cave!"

"Tell me, then," Kacie snapped back. "What you think we'd do if we returned topside? More *not* dancing, same as the last year? Not only that, but we'll also have to spend the rest of our lives looking over our shoulders, trying not to get kidnapped again. You heard what Dr. Parthen said: now that we've been identified as Royal Dragons by this Raymond, he'll never stop hunting us."

"M-maybe," Faith stammered. "Maybe not. We could at least—"

"No, Faith," Kacie flared. "It's my turn, okay? I've followed you everywhere besides Joffrey: into a ballet career, apartments, our lifestyle. I haven't regretted it, because…well, there wasn't anything else I wanted to do. But now I might want to stay in Ţărână. And if I do, you need to support me in that."

Faith's hands trembled as darkness swallowed her up. What could she possibly say? She loved her twin more than words could describe; she couldn't live without her. Yet…she didn't see any way she could survive in this Podunk town, either.

"No response?" Kacie marched over to her suitcase and grabbed the upright handle. "Fine." She rolled it toward the door. "I'll be in Lucerne if you care to offer comment."

As her twin disappeared through the door, Faith stared down at her teacup, little pink roses on white porcelain. So delicate. So breakable. Her legs shook, threatening to bend her into a plié deep enough to dump her onto the floor. Her right knee attacked her with pins and needles. The teacup blurred, and she swayed. There were two things she required to live: her twin sister and ballet. And now for the first time in her life, it looked like she might not be able to have both.

CHAPTER SIXTEEN

THOMAL SQUEEZED THE HIGH BAR stool between tight thighs, hunching over his drink like a prisoner protecting his stash. Muscles all over his body were gnarled into aggressive knots. He'd fed a little over an hour ago, but instead of making him go all Tao-chill like it should've, his mood was downright abominable.

He was back to bonding withdrawal. Oh, joy.

Every artery, vein, blood vessel, and capillary inside him was a wild beast snarling at him for more of Pandra's blood. Besides the stuff tasting like orgasm-in-a-can and being laced with Fey Super Powers, he'd sort of been inches from dead an hour ago, and one dosage of red yummy wasn't nearly enough to get him completely back on his feet. He wanted—*needed*—more. Then there was the insistent roar of his dick. Vârcolac males weren't wired to feed on a new mate and then not get down to the business of bumping fuzzies. The boner he'd sprung in the garage hadn't ever entirely settled down, leaving his body filled with several quarts of adrenaline with nothing better to do than make him want to kill every organism on earth. Big wonder no one else was sitting at the bar.

Picking up his shot glass, he clonked it on the bar. "Another, Luvera."

Luvera Parthen cut him a look from beneath her black lashes while she finished drawing a beer at the tap. Luvera was a long-time waitress at Garwald's Pub, now part owner, seeing as Garwald had recently entered his elder phase.

Since marrying Alex Parthen, Luvera had changed a lot.

First off, she'd given up wearing baggy, formless clothes, astounding everyone with just how pretty she was, and now she radiated all kinds of newfound confidence. Overall, she was doing a better job of de-nerdifying herself than Alex. That dude was holding onto his pocket-protector like it was a childhood blankie. In her time slinging drinks, Luvera had probably seen men and women in every state of crappy disposition, yet the look she tossed Thomal leaned really heavy toward worried.

"Um…hold on a sec," Luvera told him, heading off to deliver the beer. Or maybe she was stalling for time while she figured out how to handle him.

The hell if he needed handling. Hiking himself high on his stool, he leaned over the width of the bar and snagged the bottle of Jack Daniel's from among the other—

A strong hand on his shoulder re-parked his ass on his seat. None too gently. The bottle of Jack was pointedly removed from his grip.

He pivoted on the stool, his upper lip wrinkling toward a preemptive sneer. *Wunderbar.* Jacken and Toni. The Bobbsey Twins of Buzz Kills. He narrowed in on Jacken. "You in the mood to get skull-fucked?"

Toni heaved a sigh.

Yeah, not exactly a career-promoting thing for a guy to say to his boss. But Thomal didn't see any point in being subtle in his current frame of mind.

"Sure, sounds like something right up my alley," Jacken returned in a tone blasé enough to bring Thomal to his feet.

Jacken gripped Thomal's shoulder again and shoved him back down. "Soon as you're not weak as a guppy, Costache, you go ahead and hand me my balls. Meantime, go to your mate."

"My *mate*?" The word dropped a Harry Potter Jelly Slug vomit jellybean onto his tongue. "You mean that bitch with a capital C?" He glared at Jacken. "May I please have my Jack

Daniel's back?" He left off the *you fucking asshole*, but still showed Jacken a set of half-jacked canines. "We can toast my miraculous return from the grave."

"You've re-awakened your bonding withdrawal," Toni told him.

"No shit, Sherlock."

Jacken bit out a snarl. Probably not feeling the love for Thomal's tone.

Why was Toni here, anyway? Probably because a female should be a calming influence on a newly bonded male—which he still sort of was, seeing as his cells had never completely settled—but this particular female happened to be half-sister to the slut-bag. And the only thing that would truly *settle* him was the slut-bag herself, which was a thought that made him want to tear his brain out of his head and bean Jacken with it.

Toni held up a hand. "Exactly, Thomal. You've been through this before, and you know how miserable you're going to be if you don't go and scent Pandra."

"And," Jacken grated, "you're putting other people in danger."

Thomal scanned the bar. True, but he couldn't help that, except maybe to remove himself from the public arena, which was probably Jacken's exact *point*. A Vârcolac male newly out of The Change went into automatic protection mode, treating every male like a rival and a threat to his woman, no matter who the guy was. Even if his brother, Arc, got within spitting distance of Pandra, Thomal would want to kill him. Thomal laughed hollowly. *Arc close to Pandra*? Right. And tomorrow morning angels would fly out of his butthole, too. "I don't want anything to do with that black-eyed human trampoline." Over the bar, Thomal eyed the bottle of Maker's Mark snuggled with its other amber buddies.

"Very well," Toni said. "You should know, however, that I've had Pandra moved from her jail cell. She's now in

Budapest up on the third floor of—"

Thomal let out a mighty roar as he catapulted off his barstool; no thought, no consideration, only the animal instinct of *my mate is no longer contained but accessible to other males* taking over his frontal lobe and sending him lunging off his seat.

He was immediately slammed back on it, his ass hitting the top of the stool and then his boots reaching for the ceiling as he flipped over backward. He landed on his stomach, peanut shells and sawdust billowing around him. He hissed air through set teeth and long fangs. High idiot points awarded to the reptilian part of his brain for making him move in a hostile manner near the pregnant mate of a Vârcolac male.

It'd gotten him punched in the chest by Jacken.

Thomal pushed to his feet, a vague part of his mind aware of the entire bar holding its breath, waiting to see what would happen next.

After all the growling and hitting that'd just gone down, the bar's gawking rubber-neckers probably hadn't expected Thomal to run. But that's what he did. His brain wouldn't allow him to do anything else but race out of the bar, traveling at invisible speeds for the woman he hated down to the deepest part of his soul, the woman whose very existence carved a huge slice of shiny siding off the persona he'd tried to create of himself as a badass warrior. Now everyone probably thought he didn't have what it took to kill a woman. Damn him, he should've ignored that *something* about Pandra and ripped her throat out.

Crashing into the mansion, Thomal took the stairs three at a time to the third floor, careening past Seville, Stockholm, Lucerne…till he saw the door with the red, white and green-striped Hungarian flag painted on it. Did someone think it'd be so ha-ha-ironic to give Pandra the room Thomal had lived in before all males had been moved downstairs to the second floor, all females on the third? *Buncha douches.*

He burst into Budapest without knocking and skidded to a halt.

Pandra was flipping through some paperbacks at an exotic-looking desk, the wooden legs carved into twining vines of flowers.

Not much had changed since he'd lived here. The whole place still mimicked the inside of a hookah bar: dark, earthy colors and gauzy lampshades, large beaded pillows and a beanbag chair mounded in the corner like a lopsided pile of soft serve ice cream. Being in here had always made him feel weirdly out of place, like he should've been shuffling around in a pair of dirty slippers with his head haloed in ganja smoke. He much preferred his new home in Oslo downstairs.

Pandra startled to her feet.

He did his own startling on the inside, his stomach seesawing at the sight of her.

She appeared like she smelled now, so…fresh. Her black eyes were no longer flat and dead, and her facial structure had lost some of its toughness. Was it because she was sans immortality ring now? Or because she was their prisoner and cowed a bit? Or was it all an illusion created by what she was wearing: light gray stretch pants and a tank top in lavender, both of which showed off her nubile hotness to the nth degree and seemed way too plain and nice for her usual sleaziness. A wayward tendril of blonde hair had escaped her braid to curl demurely against her throat, and her bare feet displayed cute little toes squishing into the carpet that simultaneously made him want to crack them off at the stem and paint a cool, retro design on each nail—something that would totally fit her. And how the fuck would he know that?

He hardened his jaw. He was sick and damned tired of feeling batshit crazy around this woman. "Go over to the bed," he ordered her.

No reaction.

Not a single thing registered on the little ol' wifey's face, not surprise or a *go blow yourself*, not the hint of scorn or even a desire to smoke-check his balls. Nothing.

Thomal smiled sharply. *Nicely done.* But he was too good at reading adversaries not to sense the heightened tension in Pandra, despite her robotic outerwear. He prowled forward, circling her, tasting her scent in the back of his throat. "When I come in here to feed," he said in low, distinct syllables, "you are to stand over by the bed, your back against the bedpost, hands at you side. Do. You. Understand?" He stopped in front of her, trying to make himself look threatening, but found himself distracted by the front of her tank top. Was she wearing a bra? The way her nipples pushed out from the cotton like bubblegum balls, he'd say not.

She shrugged. "Very well." She took up position at the bed as he'd described, her hands wrapped around the post behind her. The posture thrust out her breasts, her tank top pulling taut across the two succulent, generous mounds, the sweet peaks, both nipple and aureole now, outlined against the fabric.

His cock stirred. *Ignore it, Costache.* He strode up close to her. A misting of perspiration glistened in her cleavage, and he found ruthless satisfaction with that. This close, her scent wafted into the core of his brain like an opiate, settling the *thumpity-bumpity* his insides had been going through for, hell, days now. His upper lip quivered toward a sneer. He hated that she made him feel okay.

He leaned into her, stacking his hands one on top of the other on the bedpost just above her head, his chest crushing her breasts. He licked his lips, his blood thrumming a wild beat. His strike was purposely aggressive, his fangs plunging deep, the suction of his mouth rough. Blood poured onto his tongue, too fast, too much, drowning his cells. His knees shook from the rush of sensation. He couldn't get over how good this woman tasted. Salty-sweet. Rejuvenating. Right. *His.*

Pandra squirmed a little. Not from discomfort, despite his lack of gentlemanly treatment, but because Fiinţă was working its magic. She released a low moan and pressed closer, her beaded nipples caressing his chest through both of their shirts. His cock swelled up stiff against his Levi's, the answering force of his own desire nearly making him go bug-eyed with the effort it took to hold it back. He needed to get his fangs out of her. But the newly awakened part of him only wanted to fill himself up with her, so full he'd never feel wrong again. How hosed was that? This woman was actually poison.

Forcing himself to wrench out his fangs, he jolted backward, the rapid cadence of his breathing matching hers.

Her gaze was smoky with desire. She tilted her chin up, her lips soft with invitation.

A wave of black rage boiled up from his gut, like magma from the core of Hell. "Do you think I'm going to kiss you now? You've *got* to be kidding." He curled his upper lip. "I've seen where that mouth of yours has been." The image came to him in a blinding white flash: Pandra's lips wrapped around Arc's cock, sucking it into her throat. The bonded male in him yowled *mine! mine! mine!* corroding his anger into cold fury.

He grabbed Pandra by the back of her neck, swung her around toward the bed, and shoved at her. He felt her tense in objection for a moment, but then she let him face-jam her into the mattress, her hips hanging off the side of the bed. "Bet you're the type who likes a good, hard fuck, don't you?" Bracing one knee beside her, his other foot planted on the floor, he ripped her stretch pants down the backs of her thighs. No panties. His cock jerked painfully against his jeans.

"Force me now, you fucking cum dumpster." He grabbed a handful of her butt cheek and squeezed. "Let's see how well you do when you don't have your little helpers with you and I'm not locked in chains." He swept two fingers down the valley between her buttocks and arrived at her labia, soft and slick. Sweetly aromatic. His stomach stumbled into a roll-over. Fiinţă had prepared her for him. He ground his jaw as he tried to make himself ram his fingers inside her, violate and humiliate her like she deserved.

But someone started playing a discordant drum set inside his head, a pounding, painful rhythm against his cranium. The scent of this woman blared MATE to his neurons in high def surround sound, and his brain was telling him that he was trying to do a very bad thing here.

Well, shut up! Shoving a hand into the small of Pandra's back, he held her in place as he moved to stand behind her. One-handed, he wrenched open his blue jeans, his erect cock jutting into readiness between the vee of his zipper. He took hold of his dick in his fist, then shifted his gaze to her face.

She was staring at the headboard blankly, her hands resting on either side of her head. Not doing a thing. Just lying there. *Fight me, bitch!* He grabbed her hips and muscled her back toward his cock. Her body was limp as an empty pillowcase. *Fuck!* Breathing through his teeth, he moved back from the bed. No matter how much he might want to hurt this slag, he couldn't. Now that he was bonded to her, his male Vârcolac instincts were all about protecting his woman from harm. He'd had his chance to fuck her up in that seedy hotel room, and lost it. Because he'd been weak.

Tucking himself away and zipping up his jeans, Thomal jolt-stepped over to the desk and sank down into the chair, propping his elbows on his knees. He buried his head in his hands against the memory that had been jostled loose; Thomal in fifth grade on the playground, straddling Dănuţ and whaling on him for calling Thomal "stupid" one too many times. Thomal had gotten in a good half dozen hits, including a bone-breaking tag to the nose, before he realized that Dănuţ was just lying beneath him, arms over his face, whimpering. Not fighting back. Dănuţ was a complete dick and had deserved to pay, but something about beating on a person who wouldn't defend himself had left Thomal feeling…really wrong. The experience had stayed with him, and as a young adult, Thomal had ended up deciding that protecting people who needed it was a helluva lot more noble than painting pictures of them. He'd switched gears and followed Arc into the Warrior Class, a decision that had earned him his father's approval, locking in the rightness of it.

"Pull your fucking pants up," he growled at Pandra. His eyes watered. It was from bile sitting in his throat, but a part of him also wanted to cry.

He heard her rustling with her clothes.

"For as long as I can remember," he told her in a hoarse tone, "I've dreamed of what it would be like to mate. To gain my other half, to become a man, to spend every hour of every day making love to my wife, *loving* her. That's what other Vârcolac males get to do. It's what I've watched my friends do." He glanced up, his upper lip trembling.

Pandra was sitting on the edge of the bed, her hands on her knees, her feet hooked on the bedrail. Her face displayed its usual utter lack of emotion.

"I was supposed to have had that with Hadley, my girl-friend…*ex*-girlfriend now that you've come along and screwed my life away." Hadn't *that* been a delightful meeting with Hadley when she'd come to see him in the hospital nine days ago. He'd never forget the look of devastation, pain, and—this one had been peachy keen—betrayal on her face. She'd left Țărână the next day, completely removing herself from his life. He wouldn't even be able to secretly keep tabs on her because Hadley had decided to change her identity to avoid getting kidnapped again for being a Dragon. "Hadley was sweet and nice and affectionate. She would've been a great wife, a fantastic mother to my children."

Pandra's face remained an impassive mask.

Thomal closed his hands into hard fists. *So much* he want-ed to be able to hit her, sock that nothingness clear across the fucking room. "You *stole* that from me," he seethed, glaring. "Do you have any idea how much I hate you for that?"

She waited in silence, maybe thinking he didn't expect an answer. Finally, her blonde brows twitched upward, and she cleared her throat. "Yes, I believe I'm beginning to cotton on to that." Something passed through her gaze.

He couldn't tell what it was. How could he? Her eyes were like vats of black sludge.

"I do appreciate your candor on these matters, thank you." She stood and crossed into the bathroom, shutting the door.

With his jaw knotted and twitching, he sat back in the chair and absently reached for a small glass bottle on Pandra's desk. He flexed and released his hand around it for several moments, then glanced at it. Nail polish, in a flashy, fluorescent blue. The perfect color to make Pandra's toenails into something killer.

He bent forward again, squeezing the nail polish in his hand and pressing his fist to his forehead.

What the hell was wrong with him?

Chapter Seventeen

FROM THE TIME PANDRA WAS sixteen, her ring hadn't been off her finger for more than an hour, maybe two—however long it took to shag a lad—and that was it.

Now, it had been about twenty-four hours.

In that time, her surroundings had become a sensation bombardment, her hyper-aware nerve endings processing everything as her body fought to find a place in this new world. The chair she was sitting on outside of Toni's office had a slightly pilled cushion. One of the wooden back slats was shedding a prickly splinter. She could feel where her skin was attached to her muscles, how her blood fizzed through her veins. She could sense her god-blasted hair growing. She could also tell her clothes fit perfectly. Whoever had dropped off four sacks of duds outside of her door had gauged her size bang on, although hadn't judged her style very well. Unless she'd been given "nice" clothes on purpose. Today's ensemble of a light blue skirt that flowed all the way down to her knees—cor, the thought—a soft cottony white blouse, and a pair of slip-on Vans made her resemble a sweet Gidget off for a day of boating. Sideburns Vinz had dropped his mouth nearly to his belt when he showed up at her door to usher her to a morning meeting with Toni.

Vinz was now leaning against the wall outside of Toni's office and fiddling with his cell phone, taking pains to ignore her. He was one of many of that ilk. On her walk down Main Street, she'd been coldly disregarded by the entire town.

Unfortunately, she'd felt that, too.

Aye, discovering a deeper set of emotions was the worst part about being ringless. She'd actually woken this morning with an unfamiliar tightness in her throat and belly, her conscience needling her about ruining Thomal's chance for an idyllic life with that Hadley bit of skirt.

The office door to her right opened and Toni appeared, wearing an emerald blouse and loose black slacks cut on the bias so the silk-like material flowed gracefully around her when she walked. Pandra sat frozen in place, again struck by what a stunning sort Toni was. Pandra herself was attractive, she knew that, but where Pandra was sexy hot, Toni was beautiful in an elegant way. The kind of classy looks Pandra would've preferred, and why the devil was she thinking rot like that?

Vinz pushed off the wall. "Do you need me to wait around till you're done, Toni?"

"Thanks, Vinz, but you can go. I'll call you if I need you." Toni waved Pandra inside. "Come on in."

Pandra stood and entered Toni's office.

Toni moved over to her desk and sat down behind it.

Pandra glanced at the couch and two chairs opposite Toni's desk. *Ah.* So there'd be no dishing the dirt over in the comfy chat area, eh? *Right, then.* Strictly business today. Pandra sat in one of the chairs in front of the desk.

Toni picked up a daisy-painted coffee mug and took a sip out of it. "How'd you sleep?"

Pandra propped her elbows on the armrests and bared her teeth in a smile.

One side of Toni's mouth crooked upward. "That bad, huh?"

"The bedroom's a far sight better than a jail cell, that's for dead cert." Pandra could've gone in for a different flatmate, though. But, unfortunately some strange Vârcolac bonding need had required that Thomal remain close to her scent for a while. He'd stayed in her room all night, spending the first half of the evening planted in front of the TV, staring hard-jawed at a marathon of re-tread *House* episodes. *It's lupus, no, it's sarcoidosis, no, it's syphilis, no, it's lupus…*over and over again.

A serving gal had brought a meal at supper time. Thomal ate his in front of the television. Pandra had sat at the desk reading *The Help* from a stack of books someone had left for her. Thomal's freeze-out would've been complete had she not caught him studying her on more than one occasion when he thought she wasn't minding. She'd sneaked eyefuls of him, too. Blimey, but two boshes of her blood had certainly awakened the bloke back to his perishing good looks.

Beddy-bye time had come, and Thomal had just stripped out of his clothes and climbed under the covers of her bed. That had stumped her. Should she join him or make a place for herself on the floor? She'd ended up sleeping on her own side of the mattress—not starkers like him—figuring if he'd either wanted to kill her or shag her, he would've done so already. It had still taken her a long time to get to sleep.

Toni leaned back in her chair. "The Costache brothers are well-loved around here, Pandra. There's no short road back from what you did to them, not with the people of this community or with Thomal."

Heat washed up the back of Pandra's neck as she relived her walk down Main Street, people pointedly turning their backs on her. "Did I give you the impression I wanted to travel that road?"

"No." Toni settled her mug on her lap. "And how you spend your time in this town is entirely up to you. Nobody can force you to make an effort. I just didn't think Jacken's suggestion to hang you from a meat hook sounded appealing."

"Ah, yes." She crossed her legs and flipped her foot. "Best I not forget that I'm trapped here till I'm a wrinkly gimmer, eh?"

Toni released a soft breath. "I'd prefer you didn't think of it that way. Your stay here doesn't have to be unpleasant. If you work hard, keep your nose clean, and show yourself disposed to be a good person, then the people of this community might give you a chance."

"A good person?" Pandra snorted. She supposed pigs did fly in a frozen-over hell every now and again.

"Sure, and why not?" Leaning forward, Toni set her mug on her desk. "Don't underestimate yourself, Pandra. Wearing a ring enchanted by Raymond has affected you. There's darkness in his power. I know this because I feel it in myself whenever I use my own power, which is why I *don't*, besides learning how to enchant medications and a few other things. But I'm very cautious about it." She sat back again. "Look, take some time without your ring on your finger and heal yourself, figure out who you really are and what you want to do. I imagine some great possibilities lurk within you."

Pandra bore down on her teeth, creating another unpleasant smile. "Lawks, sis, I do appreciate the whole sunshine-up-my-arse-thing, but I already know who I am, and it certainly isn't anyone who can keep her nose clean. Sorry to disappoint. Shall I go now?"

Toni picked up her mug and sipped her coffee as she searched Pandra's face. "I don't believe that's true," Toni said. "You're my half-sister, and in my mind, that makes you—"

"Just one of Fate's little laughs, old mucker, so I wouldn't get yourself in a dither about it." Pandra cocked her head to the side. "Do you know that Raymond wanted to have all of his nippers with your mum. Her Fey goes back to the Irish fairies, see, and that's a right powerful lineage. But there were complications with your birth and your mum couldn't have any more babies after you, so Raymond had to settle for a Pure Om Rău female, *my* rank mum. A kick in the ballocks for you, though, getting abandoned by your father because of the accident of your own birth."

Toni gazed down into her mug and ran the tip of her finger around the rim. "I'm offering you a second chance, Pandra. A genuine offer from my heart, no strings attached, besides the requirement that you adhere to the town laws, same as everyone else. You can continue to try and sabotage that by attempting to hurt me…an endeavor you'll probably succeed in if you keep using my losses against me."

Pandra re-crossed her legs. Slowly. She couldn't believe Toni had openly handed her a weapon like that.

Toni looked up. "But I sincerely hope you won't. If you agree to this offer," she went back to the topic at hand, "we'll find you something useful to do. You'll be assigned to various jobs in the community until you've had a chance to try a little of everything. Hopefully, this will help you figure out what suits you best. The only thing you won't be allowed is access to our computer systems. I know it's where your expertise lies, but there's a security issue involved. Everything else is available." Toni slid a file folder across the desk to her. "The other requirement is that you go to twice-weekly sessions with our therapist. She comes down here from topside three times a—"

"A what? A blooming head shrink?"

"Don't make it sound like that. Karrell's a great person to talk to, someone to help you work out your…for lack of a better term, your Raymond issues."

Pandra smirked. "Maybe you should go, too, then."

Toni smiled, maybe a shade too nicely. "I'm not the one who's trying to self-destruct."

"Is that what I'm doing?" Sod the woman, she was frighteningly close to dead-on with that.

Toni turned the mug in her hands. "As to Raymond, what kind of retribution can we expect from him for taking you?"

A laugh launched up Pandra's throat. Raymond would hardly pass up on another opportunity to send Pandra the message she wasn't of any cop to him. He would do exactly nothing.

"I'm sorry," Toni said after a short pause.

"Don't be," Pandra shot back. "I myself couldn't give a kipper's dick."

Toni paused again. "Okay."

Pandra tapped her fingers on the armrests. She was getting restless to be done with this meeting. "So if I say yes to your offer, promising to be well-behaved and such, you'll trust me at my word?"

"Yes. Until you give me cause not to."

"I'll be allowed to"—she swept her hand through the air—"run amuck?"

"You'll be watched to a certain degree, of course, but not guarded outright. That is, if you agree to abide by our rules. I'd like Ţărână to feel like your home, Pandra, as much as possible."

Pandra lowered her gaze against a rush of unexpected emotion, pretending a sudden interest in her fingernails. Home: the most frightening concept of them all. *Home* had never contained a sister like Toni, who was, from all appearances, caring and just, open and honest. The next oldest sister in the half-Răsu brood was Opal, ten years younger than Pandra at fourteen and born of Boian—Raymond's pure Fey partner in their procreation program—making her a complete bum nugget, as all of Boian's progeny were. Pandra wanted to claw the cowbag's eyes out more than she ever imagined having a chin wag with her over tea and scones.

Pandra coughed lightly. "I suppose I'll give it a bash." She had no illusions that this place would ever truly become a home to her, but she was stuck here for now, by gum, and Toni was right; she didn't fancy hanging from a meat hook while she figured out her next move.

"Great." Toni beamed. "Your first assignment is with Hannah Crişan in our library. You start today. The particulars are in there." She pointed to the file folder. "It also contains a map of the town and the community manual. I recommend you read that without delay. It'll get you up to speed on Vârcolac culture. Any questions?"

Pandra picked up the folder. "Actually, yes. I've developed…there's something that grew on my back overnight. A dragon." The thing had surprised the devil out of her in the bathroom mirror this morning. It was fashioned out of actual scales, brilliant blue on the body and wings, red on the belly, claws, and choppers. The dragon's noggin sat in profile over her left shoulder blade, the wings arched over the right, and the reptilian tail snaked along her lower back with its clawed feet aimed at imaginary prey to the left of her spine. It was the same kind of beast she and Murk had seen on Thomal's and Arc's backs in that rubbishy hotel room, although the Vârcolac's dragon had been green and red.

"The dragon is a tattoo of sorts," Toni explained. "It means you're Fey now."

"It means…?" Pandra's mouth dropped open. She was too shocked to stop it. *I'm Fey?* "But that's impossible."

"I have one, too, as does Alex." Toni pushed her intercom button. "Donree, could you please send in Dr. Jess, if he's not too busy."

"You're pulling my plonker." Raymond had been going mad planning the next generation because it was only his grandchildren who were supposed to be fully Fey, not his children.

Toni laughed. "Nope." She stood, turned around, and lifted the back of her blouse, flashing a dragon—the exact same one Pandra had.

Well, I'll be damned.

A knock sounded at the office door, then Natty entered, dressed in a white lab coat over an impeccable dark suit, the garment rich enough to pass even Raymond's high standards.

"Dr. Jess," Toni introduced, gesturing to Natty. "This is

Pandra Parthen."

Pandra rose.

The doctor offered her his hand. He striking turquoise eyes were warm with welcome.

Pandra took the offered hand, giving it a firm shake.

"Pandra popped her dragon," Toni went on. "I wanted you to look at her enchantment designator. I never know what those symbols mean."

Designator? Ah, the symbol off her dragon's nose.

"Neither do I, usually," Dr. Jess admitted. "The Fey bloodline has been suppressed for so many years. But, indeed, let's have a peek. If Miss Parthen doesn't mind lifting her shirt in back."

Pandra half-smiled. A bit of a silly worry, considering her usual wardrobe choices. "I don't mind a'tall. I'm rather curious myself." She turned around and gathered her shirt up.

"It's the letter V," Dr. Jess mused.

"And you don't know what it means?" Toni guessed.

"I have no idea," Jess confirmed, chuckling. "But Miss Parthen's power will come out soon enough, and then we'll all know."

Bully. More power for Pandra. Just what she needed to inspire everyone to hate her more than they already did. She pulled down her shirt and faced the doctors. "How did it come to be there?"

"Well, the enchantment itself has always been with you," Toni answered. "But Thomal's Ființă activated it."

"Ființă?"

"The elixir that comes out of a Vârcolac's fangs when he or she feeds. Funny, isn't it?" Toni added in a sardonic tone. "Raymond considers Vârcolac to be the scum of the earth. Yet, it's the Vârcolac who can trigger enchantment powers in a person with Fey bloodlines. Here and now, *today*." Toni's eyes twinkled mischievously. "I don't think we should tell him, though, do you?" She winked at Pandra, such the conspiratorial sister.

Pandra experienced the oddest stirring in her chest. How to respond to this attempt at connection? She didn't have a bloody clue.

CHAPTER EIGHTEEN

NYKO STOOD WITH HIS BACK jammed against the wall outside of Toni's office, his hands thrust into the pockets of his black cargo pants. He sullenly eyed one of the waiting room chairs. He could maybe fit one thigh into that thing.

His abnormal size was never cause for celebration, but his recent encounter with the Teague twins had his grumpiness about the whole issue up a few hundred points.

It had happened about an hour ago. He'd been on his way downstairs to the mansion's dining room for breakfast, the sisters had been going in the same direction, and, *Hello*— they'd all ended up standing on the grand staircase together. He'd skidded to a stop, and managed to get his senses unboggled enough—dang, they smelled good—to offer them a smile. Not a grin wide enough to show his fangs. *Gosh, no.* The Teagues knew what he was, of course, but they were still getting all snug as a bug with the whole Vârcolac idea, so why push it? Besides, he didn't need to dial up his own menace by showing off the sharper parts of himself.

Little good his precautions had done him. Not *any* good, in fact, at least where it counted…with Faith.

He liked both of the sisters; they seemed equally nice. Considering they'd been drugged and kidnapped—and, ugh, no one in the community felt happy about doing that again— and also considering their lives had taken a really bizarre turn in the last few days, it was a testament to their good manners that they were trying to be polite. They were both super pretty, too, with swanlike bodies and eye-catching grace, and they smelled like cookies. Not literally, but rather the idea was they smelled like his favorite thing in the world.

He loved every kind of cookie there was: peanut butter, lemon cream, cinnamon applesauce raisin, sugar cookies, chocolate chip. But his all-time favorite were oatmeal butterscotch. One of the best parts about babysitting for Maggie and Luken was that Maggie always made him a batch of her World Famous Oatmeal Butterscotch Cookies whenever he came over. Well, besides the *main* best part of being able to spend time with their two-year-old daughter, Amabel, his little cutie-pie baby with curly blonde hair like her momma.

He adored kids, and had let it be known around town that he was available for babysitting anytime—no cookies required. He didn't get as many gigs as he would've liked, though. Not because of how scary-looking he was. Nah, kids always saw beneath the surface of a person's outer appearance to the real personality beneath, and all kids loved him. It was because there were still so few offspring in Țărână—only ten—so he had to share babysitting duty with half the community. There were lots of single gals with loads of maternal love to give while they waited for more Dragon males to be brought in so they could start their own families.

Anyway, while Kacie Teague could best be compared to chocolate chip cookies—yummy, for sure—Faith drugged up his senses with one-hundred-percent-pure oatmeal butter-scotch. The Best Scent in Creation. She smelled like a mate. Which meant that she was his, but how in heck he'd ever convince her of *that* was a complete mystery.

When the three of them had been grouped on the grand staircase, Kacie had managed to dredge up a return smile for him. It'd been strained and had come after some extended wide-eyed gawping, but she'd done it.

Faith had let out a horrified yelp, stumbled back from him, and stayed far away. She hadn't meant to hurt his feelings; they were both well-brought-up ladies, as he already knew. She'd just been too appalled by him to do anything else. And could he blame her? Besides his looks, she'd seen him punch a woman's face off yesterday.

He'd been at an utter loss about how to smooth over the situation. He knew as much about flirting as he did about ballet. Another mark against him, he supposed, that he didn't know jack diddly squat about his future mate's passion. So he'd ended up mumbling something about forgetting his wallet, then clambered back up the stairs. *My vow of celibacy is good, yes it is.* He'd do himself a favor by keeping that sentence at the forefront of his mind.

Donree, Toni's assistant, rescued him from any more morose thoughts by leading the group of them—team members Dev, Thomal, and Gábor, plus Jacken and Alex— into Toni's office.

Toni was seated behind her desk, a newspaper open in front of her. "Where's Sedge?" she asked, glancing at Nyko.

Yep, once again Nyko was today's insert-substitute-warrior-here.

"In hibernation," Jacken answered.

Toni's face brightened. "Oh, that's great."

A Vârcolac male went into a three-day hibernation state after he'd exhausted himself with the grueling process of Vârcolac baby-making.

"I knew Sedge and Kimberly were planning to start a family soon," Toni continued. "I just didn't think it would happen this fast."

Gábor plopped down on the sofa. "Nature called," he drawled.

Jacken strode up to Toni's desk. "So what's your security issue?"

Toni spun around the newspaper in front of her, showing Jacken the bold headline: THE SYMBOL KILLER STIKES AGAIN. "Have you seen this?"

Jacken nodded. "Yeah, we've all been reading about this maniac."

The Symbol Killer had earned his, or her, moniker by cutting a strange symbol into the right side of all the victims' foreheads. Four people had been murdered in San Diego county in the past ten days.

"How does the Symbol Killer affect Ţărână's security?" Jacken asked.

"He may not," Toni admitted. "But Alex had a vision about who the killer is, and it's somebody way out of the SDPD's league. I thought we might want to help."

Now that Alex was a Soothsayer, he could read the Străvechi Caiet, the ancient text of the Vârcolac...although *read* wasn't the most accurate description. Alex *saw* certain future possibilities, or answers to questions, or law interpretations through visions. Unfortunately, Alex didn't have any control over visions of the future. They came when they pleased.

Jacken crossed his arms. "Which Om Rău is it?"

That hadn't taken a huge leap.

Alex set his briefcase on the desk. "Videon."

Thomal leaned against the back of the couch. "Oh, goodie."

Thomal, Dev, and Gábor had all had confrontations with the malicious Topside Om Rău, whereas Nyko had never encountered this noteworthy bad guy. It would've been fine by him to have kept it that way, too. Insane, strong, and cruel didn't make a man Nyko ever wanted to meet.

"I hacked into the San Diego Police Department's database," Alex said, grabbing a stack of files out of his briefcase. "And I was able to snag some information and photographs about the case." He passed the files around.

Toni opened hers. A dead guy's empty eyes stared at her from an 8x10 glossy photo. "Yuk."

Even though Toni was a medical doctor, she hated gory

stuff. Funny.

Nyko opened his own file, finding the same photo on top. He studied the intricate swirling design carved into the bloody forehead. "Any idea what the symbol is?"

"It's a Celtic knot," Alex answered. "Called a Quaternary. It's based on the number four. See how it sort of has four quadrants? This indicates the four seasons, or the four directions—north, south, east, west—or the four elements—earth, fire, water, air—or something *four*."

"Which?" Toni asked.

"It depends on what Videon is trying to accomplish, I suppose."

"Any visions about that?" Jacken asked Alex.

"Not a one."

Jacken flipped through more pages in his file. Stopping on one, he read off the surnames of the men killed, "O'Connolly, Fleming, Eagan, Dowdall...these names sound Irish."

"They are," Alex confirmed.

Toni stood up. "There's probably a connection between that and the fact that the symbol is Celtic." She headed for her office door. "Let's dig into it."

Alex's eyebrows peaked. "Are we done?"

"No. I just need to go barf."

Jacken leapt forward. "Toni—"

Toni waved him off. "It's not the pictures, only the pregnancy hormones." She made a face. "I guess the pictures didn't help. I'll be back in a second." She shut the door quickly.

There was a pause, then Alex asked Jacken, "Are you okay?"

Jacken scrubbed a hand across his brow. "Sure."

'Course, it was a lie. Most days Jacken didn't know whether to wind the cat or put out the clock, he was so worried about his wife and unborn child.

Dev made a thoughtful noise. "This pregnancy talk has

got me thinking about the last time we were in Toni's office. It was ten days ago, the same day Marissa and I got our crib delivered and Thomal and Arc went topside, where they had a run-in with Videon at Ria Mendoza's house. So we know for sure Videon was involved in that kidnapping. Doesn't it seem coincidental that the first murder occurred"—Dev checked a paper in his file—"only one day after the abduction of Elsa Mendoza? I'd bet my right nut that Elsa's kidnapping and these serial murders are somehow related."

Jacken nodded. "Sounds reasonable with Videon being a part of both." He swept the group of them with a questioning look. "Any suggestions about the connection?"

The question was answered with empty shrugs. Apparently, no one had the foggiest idea.

Gábor stretched out on the couch, ankles crossed in front of him, his hands linked behind his head. "You guys just tell me who I need to shoot."

CHAPTER NINETEEN

Țărână: two weeks later, December 22nd

FAITH'S INSIDES SLIPPED SIDEWAYS AND a lump pushed into her throat. "What did you say?"

"You heard me," Kacie returned. "I said the community has offered to ship our goods here from New York, and I think we should take them up on it. I want all of my clothes and my ballet gear, some of our furniture...or *all* of it. I think it's time to give up the Soho apartment."

"Give it up?" Faith's voice nearly squeaked. She wasn't hearing this. She absolutely couldn't be. Faith had only stayed in Țărână because she'd assumed that after several weeks without New York's culture and fast-paced lifestyle, Kacie would be begging to leave. Her sister was supposed to be coming to her senses, dang it, not growing more attached to this hick town. "You can't do that!"

Kacie's chin came up. "The lease is in my name."

This was a nightmare. "But what if we want to go back?" *When* we go back.

Kacie expelled a long, hard breath. "I'm not leaving here, Faith. I've been trying to tell you that. I wish you'd listen."

Faith clasped a hand to her throat. Her sister had gone utterly insane. "You've only been here two weeks, Kacie. How in the world could you possibly know if—"

"I *know*," Kacie insisted, her jaw set mulishly. "I've never been happier than I am here. I belong. I'm making friends. I firmly believe you'd be happy, too, if you'd get off your butt and give this place a chance instead of holing up here in your

room and"—she flung a hand at Faith's television set—
"watching old videos of yourself dancing while feeling sorry
for yourself. Real productive, Faith."

Faith's chin trembled. How could Kacie, of all people, not
understand what Faith was going through?

Kacie leaned forward, her voice growing earnest. "Do you
know that no one around here has accidentally called me by
your name, not once—at least not the Vârcolac. To them, I
smell like *me* and no one else. It's amazing. For once in my
life"—she threw out her arms and tossed back her head, as if
soaking up accolades on stage—"I'm unique!"

Tears burned Faith's eyes. "I didn't realize being my twin
was such a trial."

Kacie slapped her arms back to her side. "That's exactly
the problem. I've always been *your* twin; the sister of the ballet
superstar. I love you, Faith, but I haven't loved not being my
own person. The second people see you and me, everything is
instantly about *you and me*. Those Teague twins. It's robbed
me of the chance to have my own space in this world. I don't
even get to have my own birthday. When we were kids, we
always shared the same cake, the same party, and even today I
have to remember to buy *you* a gift on *my* day."

Faith bowed her head, tears falling. She couldn't believe
this. She'd always thought Kacie had found comfort in being a
twin, same as Faith did. To her, their sameness grounded her
with the confidence that there was always one person on earth
who knew her down to the kind of impossible depths that
only came from sharing matching DNA.

Kacie's voice softened. "Don't cry, Faith. Listen, I'll make
you a deal. Go out on a date with Nyko, and I won't get rid of
the New York apartment."

Faith whipped her head up. "*Nyko!*"

"Don't say his name like that. He's a great guy, and you're
the only type of woman who a half-Răumm like him can have
children with. Or Shon, but he's—"

"Children!" Good God, Faith couldn't fathom seeing that monstrosity naked, much less having intercourse with him. "He's not my type, Kacie. Not at all."

"How could you possibly know that? You've never even talked to the man."

A quiver stole across Faith's lips. Because her *type* was someone who could live topside, in the sun, in a city, where she could dance. "He hit a woman. Have you forgotten what you saw in the garage the day we arrived?"

Kacie brushed that aside. "If you'd bothered to find out about it, you'd know that woman was a prisoner trying to escape and one of the half-Răú enemy who'd been part of the plot to *kidnap* us. Nyko was doing his job, that's it." She headed for the door, pausing there, her hand on the knob. "If you're so miserable here, then go, Faith. But I'm staying."

Faith held herself very still as loneliness tried to suck her into a black hole, like the time when she was eight and her parents had come up with the bright idea to send their twin girls to different summer camps for "individuation." Faith had cried for twelve hours straight and was finally sent home— where Kacie was already waiting. "I can't leave without you."

"Then *stay*. And make an effort." Kacie turned and left the room.

Faith stared at the closed door, her insides slipping sideways again. A moment later, she heard a male voice downstairs call, "Hey, Kacie," not an ounce of doubt or confusion in his tone.

Faith pressed both hands to her face and fought back more tears. *I'm unique!* Why was Kacie so overjoyed by that? Faith truly couldn't understand it. If they weren't the Teague twins, who in the world were they?

Swallowing and sniffing, Faith dropped her hands and walked over to her DVD machine. She would watch as many videos of herself dancing as she wanted, and this town could go hang. She pressed *play*. The picture flickered once, then the machine made an ill-omened *zuzzz* sound and the TV screen went blank.

She dug her fingernails into her palms. *On top of everything else today!* She disconnected the DVD from the TV set, then jerked the electrical cord out of the wall socket and scooped up the machine. Scowling, she left her bedroom in high dungeon. She didn't know which hillbilly around here did the repairs, but the computer command center was on the first floor. As she turned down the main staircase, she screamed and stumbled back, nearly dropping the DVD player.

Nyko reached out a hand to steady her.

She lurched back another pace, her heart surging into a runaway beat.

Nyko quickly dropped his hand, his face flushing scarlet.

Her own face heated on a rush of embarrassment. Her method of greeting him was really quite awful…and probably getting tiresome. "I'm sorry," she murmured.

The door to Vienna opened and the warrior with the disarming cowlick poked his head out. Seeing it was only Nyko, he went back inside.

"You, uh, startled me, is all," she lied. He scared the unholy pants off her.

His size went beyond anything she felt capable of dealing with. She was a woman of small stature, but being around him made her feel miniscule. He was like Popeye OD'd on spinach, minus the comic charm of the quirky sailor man. No corncob pipe protruded from his mouth, rather fangs, and instead of anchor tattoos on his arms, this giant was marked all over with swooping black teeth, a hideous array of them even surrounding his neck. She couldn't get used to the sight of him, although—if she were going to quote her annoying sister—she hadn't exactly tried, either.

"Do you need help with that?" Nyko pointed to the DVD machine. "Is it broken?"

"Oh." She hugged the machine closer to her chest.

"I can fix it for you." Nyko speared a hand through his black hair, sending a ragged clump of it flopping forward onto his forehead. His hair stylist must be a lawnmower with the DTs.

"Thanks, but… I was about to go down to the—"

"They'll only send you back to me." He ascended one more stair, bringing himself up to her level, a mighty colossus looming over her, blocking out light and life. "I have all my tools right here in my room. It'll just take a sec, no problem." He reached out and eased the DVD player out of her arms.

She immediately let go, not about to let him touch her breasts inadvertently. Or on purpose.

He started down the hall.

She dropped her eyes to the knife strapped to his hip. A waste of weight and space, that. Here was a man whose entire body was a weapon, from the incredible rack of shoulders stretching his T-shirt to near seam-splitting limits, down to his mountainous biceps, and thighs that were each as thick as her waist. *Thicker*, probably.

Nyko disappeared into Amsterdam.

Should she follow him? She bit her bottom lip. He'd absconded with the DVD of her premiere performance as a prima ballerina—she'd brought an entire collection with her to show to Raymond Parthen—and she definitely wanted it back. She glanced around. She was alone, but noises were coming from Oslo and Vienna. She could scream if Nyko tried anything. The cowlicked fellow had come to her rescue once, and he surely would again.

She entered Nyko's room and stopped inside the door. Squinting, she—*goodness*. She'd never seen so many shelves. Every wall was covered with them, top to bottom, and there were even several shorter ones placed around here and there. More amazing, every shelf was weighted down with a staggering array of tools and other doo-dads related to the trade of handyman.

A workman's table, high and long, was stretched out in front of the longest line of shelves, directly across from the door, with three stools placed randomly around it, a couple of metal boxes on top. To the left, a super-sized bed was jammed into the corner. The bedspread was a shade of plain dark brown, as austere-looking as the lone lamp sitting on the single wooden nightstand and the picture-less walls. No frills around here. The room radiated as much unpretentious masculinity as its occupant.

"I guess you are the fix-it guy around here," she said.

A smile touched the corner of Nyko's mouth. "What gave me away?" He picked up a screwdriver and peered at the back of the DVD set in front of him on the work table. "Single guy, no girlfriend. You can imagine how it is. I have to do something to keep from getting bored."

"Your job doesn't do that?"

"Job's a job, hobby's a hobby." He concentrated on his task, twisting the screwdriver to take out one screw, then the next.

Faith watched the ropes of muscles flexing along his forearm as he worked with the tool. She swallowed. "Why are you carrying a knife?"

He carefully removed the plastic back of the DVD player. "The warriors are always armed. It's only a precaution against trouble." He flashed a glance at her. "Don't let that scare you. You're safe in Țărână."

"I don't feel scared here." *Bored and depressed, yes.* She flitted a hand over her bun, found a hair pin sticking halfway out, and pressed it back in.

Another small smile crossed his mouth. "Just scared of me."

"No."

He snorted softly.

Guess he'd seen through that lie. "Well, a bit."

"Try to think of me as a Clydesdale." He slipped a tray full of copper innards out of the back of the DVD player, like a sheet of cookies from an oven. "Those horses are huge, right? But the nicest animals there are. They're even called gentle giants. That's me."

Gentle? The image rose again of Nyko punching Pandra's jaw off. Faith gripped the doorjamb, a cold shudder rippling down her spine.

"What are you thinking?" he asked.

"Excuse me?"

"Your scent just changed."

Faith placed a hand to her breast and frowned. How...vulgar was it that he could tell that?

Nyko went back to his task, poking around the gizmo board. "Looks like you've blown a fuse," he told her, as if she cared or understood.

"I was remembering," Faith said in a rush, "about you punching that woman in the face."

Nyko's hands froze momentarily. "I'm sorry you saw that." Throat moving, he rummaged through a box of tiny thingies. "Even more sorry that I had to do it. I don't hit women, Faith," he added quietly. "I think women should be treated like...women need to be...they just shouldn't ever be hit."

Faith watched Nyko pick up one of the thingies and examine it. She would've expected someone of his size to have sausage-like fingers, but, although his hands were definitely large, his fingers were nimble. It didn't seem to fit who he was, but then—to go back to her sister's rebuke again—she had no idea who he was, did she? *You've never even talked to the man.* "Um, Kacie said you were doing your job, so, uh...I'm sure you were."

Nyko tossed the thingy back in and continued his search. "Kacie's real nice."

And I'm not? No. I'm the twin with bats in her belfry who

can't stop screaming and cowering around you.

Nyko picked up another thingy and snapped it into the gizmo board. He slipped the guts back in and screwed the plastic cover in place. "This ought to work now."

"Thank you."

"I'll hook it up for you." As Nyko picked up the machine, he knocked a file folder off his work bench. "Let's go back to your—" An 8x10 photo shot out of the folder, skidding across the floor and landing at Faith's feet.

It was a picture of a dead man, his bloody forehead scored with some kind of design. "Oh!"

"Crud. Sorry." Nyko set down the DVD player and bent for the photo. "Here, let me—"

She picked it up before he could and frowned at it. Something about the design on the corpse's head was ringing a bell of familiarity. "What is this?"

"A serial killer's handiwork." Nyko grimaced. "I usually don't have gross stuff like this around, but the special operations team I've been assigned to is working on catching this guy." He reached for the photo again.

She angled it away from him, focusing more intently on the mark. "It's a quaternary knot."

"That's right." Nyko gave her a curious look. "How did you know that?"

"My Aunt Idyll, the woman who raised me and Kacie, is an expert in Celtic lore. She's a shaman and Pagan priestess, a Tarot Card reader, and an all-around nut. Esoteric symbols like this were lying around the house all of the time." Faith gestured at the photo. "The quaternary is a symbol of protection."

Nyko's brows lifted. "Really? I think you need to tell Toni about this, maybe get her in touch with your aunt, if you wouldn't mind? We don't know squat about this case and could use any and all help."

"Okay." *Why not?* She had nothing else to do. "I'll make

an appointment with Dr. Parthen for today."

"Great." He picked up her DVD machine again. "I'll hook this up for you back in your bedroom."

Faith blinked. *My bedroom?*

CHAPTER TWENTY

UP ONE FLOOR IN SEVILLE, Faith opened her bedroom door and let Nyko carry the DVD player inside.

He went over to the television and attached its wires to the back of the set. After plugging it in, he pushed *play*. "Ah, here we go. Works." Nyko went down on one knee.

The Faith onscreen was dressed in a white tutu and matching leotard embellished with silver sequins, an elegant cap of white feathers curved around her head. She was in the middle of a turn sequence, spinning one fouetté after another.

She moved up next to Nyko to observe his reaction to the dance, and an incredible warmth awoke inside her. He looked fascinated.

"Why do you keep putting your foot down?" he asked.

"Well, I can't just go off like a top," she answered, her voice warming with amusement. "I use the muscles in my legs to turn, so I have to keep dropping my foot and throwing out my leg to maintain my momentum."

"You must be really strong, then." He chuckled, his attention never leaving her image. "Look at you go!"

The warmth inside her heated and spread. Her dancing had been complimented many times, but the way Nyko had just said that made him sound so…proud of her.

"What's up with your head, too?" he asked.

"That's called spotting. I focus on one point across the room and keep my eyes coming back to it on every turn. It prevents dizziness." On the screen, she came out of her last fouetté and went up *en pointe* in arabesque. "See? If I hadn't been spotting, I wouldn't have been able to do that. I would've toppled over."

He chuckled again. "I can see how that might be bad."

Her dance partner, Harold, moved into the picture, his hands wrapping her slim waist as he swept her into an overhead lift.

Nyko jutted his chin toward the TV, his gaze narrowing as he watched her and Harold flow across the stage. "That guy likes you."

"Oh, no, we're merely acting. Dance is very sensual, but…"

Nyko glanced up at her, although he didn't have to look up by much; even down on one knee he was almost as tall as she was standing.

"Harold had a thing for my sister. So, sometimes I think he let that get the better of him onstage with me." She gave a one-shouldered shrug. "Just one of the many oddities of being an identical twin."

A grunt was Nyko's reply. Returning his attention to the TV, he pointed to the right side of the screen, where the corps de ballet of other "swans" where gliding on stage. "Hey, there's Kacie."

Faith watched the image of her twin, affection stirring in her chest. "Yes. She's great, isn't she?"

Nyko concentrated on Kacie. "You're much better."

"Kacie's good," she defended.

"I'm certainly no expert, but it seems like you put passion into every move you make, and Kacie kind of…doesn't." He switched back to Faith's image as she danced in front of her *Swan Lake* entourage. "Dang," he murmured. "You're amazing."

She actually felt herself blush a little. What was it about the way Nyko complimented her…? As if the words just fell from his lips, not spoken thought or flattery, but absolute truth.

"Kacie told me about your injury." Nyko turned his head to look at her again. "You miss it, don't you?"

She laughed breathlessly. "Only every moment of every day and with every particle of my soul."

He ran his eyes over her, beginning at her collarbone and drifting down. His perusal was simply exploratory, ultimately landing clinically on her right knee, but the journey tugged strangely at her belly. "So your leg still hurts?"

"It doesn't while I'm standing here, but my knee pops and crackles whenever I dance without a brace."

"So wear a brace."

"I can't wear it to perform. Not professionally. It would look funny on stage."

His mouth angled downward. "I guess it would." He paused, his gaze clouding. "Well, that sucks."

Three little words that completely encapsulated her situation. Faith's smile felt soggy. After being so misunderstood by Kacie earlier, Nyko's understanding was…felt really good. "Yes," she agreed. "Very much." Maybe his eyes weren't so disturbing, after all. A woman just needed to learn how to read beyond their blackness. "I didn't know you were so interested in ballet."

Nyko pushed *stop* on the DVD player. "I am now."

She blinked a couple of times. Her heart fluttered. That was…was…

Nyko stood up and stepped back. "I, personally, would love to see you dance someday, Faith, and I don't give a hoot if you wear a brace."

She tried to smile again, but it wobbled away. "That's the nicest…um, a very…"

His expression softened. "You make me want to hug you. But I won't," he added hastily, putting up both hands. "Don't worry."

She glanced down. People often accused dancers of being overly obsessed with appearances, the natural consequence of mirrors surrounding them 24/7. She'd always considered herself above such shallowness, yet she couldn't deny that she'd outright rejected Nyko based on his appearance. "It's all right. I'm kind of getting used to you now." She looked up. "I think you're like…well, to quote Jessica Rabbit: you're not bad. You're just drawn that way."

Nyko laughed. It was a deep, vibrant sound, and very pleasant—another contradiction, like his nimble fingers. "I like that better than Clydesdale, for sure."

She managed a small smile now.

"So…" He sidestepped, suddenly seeming a little nervous. "I'm going to press my current advantage and ask you out to lunch right now. You know…to celebrate the rebirth of your DVD player."

She stilled. She *was* getting used to Nyko, but…maybe too much. Entanglements weren't a good idea when her ultimate goal was to leave this town. On the other side of matters, if she appeared to be giving this place a genuine chance, then she'd have more of a leg to stand on with her sister. *I gave it some effort, like you said, Kacie, and I still hate it here. So can we go now?*

Nyko dipped his hands into his pockets in response to her lengthy silence. "Oops."

"Oh, no, I'm sorry. Yes, I would love to have lunch with you, Nyko. I just…can't believe you want to go out with me, after the way I've treated you."

"I totally do." She got her first glimpse of Nyko's fangs, he smiled so widely. "You smell like someone I'll get along with real well."

She cast a look at him from beneath her lashes. *What?*

"DO YOU WANT TO HEAR A secret?" Faith asked Nyko.

Nyko looked up from the menu and his eyes brightened. "Definitely."

They were seated in a small booth in Marissa's Restaurant,

the perfect choice for a date. It was a romantic place, lit mostly with candles, the tables and booths elegantly set with china and crystal, and discreetly positioned to provide privacy for diners. For either lunch or dinner, there was always a *prix fixe* menu, each day featuring a different cuisine. Today was French food—Marissa's specialty, apparently—with lunch consisting of canapés, quiche, and profiterole pastries. The fare was a bit on the heavy side for Faith, but she'd splurge today and try a little taste of everything.

She'd already gulped down half a wine spritzer and was feeling a bit reckless. Was that why she'd asked Nyko such a question? No, she knew why. Two weeks spent barely out of her room—she'd even had a makeshift barre put in her room so she wouldn't have to leave to practice—and her fight earlier with Kacie had left her feeling especially deprived of human contact. She didn't want to spend this date talking about the weather…which would be even more boring than usual since there was no weather inside a cave.

"I have a tattoo as well," she said, glancing at the wedge of tattooed flesh exposed by Nyko's open shirt collar. Was there anywhere the man wasn't marked?

"Really?" Nyko's eyebrows hiked up. "Let me guess. It's a tarantula."

She laughed. "It's a ballet dancer, smart guy. She's up on her tiptoes, arms down in first position, wearing a wide tutu— same as the ballerina in a little girl's jewelry box."

"You're totally blowing my image of you." Smiling, Nyko set his menu aside. "Where is it?"

"High up on my right hip, where it's easily covered by a leotard."

"Covered? Shucks, I was kind of hoping to see it the next time you went swimming at the Water Cliffs."

Faith chuckled, then glanced down. "Well…" She fiddled with her menu. "I've stopped liking it, anyway."

"Why's that?"

"When I got it, I imagined I'd be a ballet dancer forever, but now my injury has put it in my face that all dancers stop dancing. Eventually."

"Maybe you should get a brace added to the leg of your tattoo. Kind of an *up yours* to the industry."

A breath tumbled out of her. "Maybe."

The waitress dropped off the canapés, pointing to each as she described what was on the little rounds of bread. "Herb cheese, caviar, and fruit puree." She took their menus and left.

Nyko leaned forward and peered down at the appetizer. "How about I leave the fish egg ones for you?" He slid an herb cheese canapé off the plate.

Faith took a fruit one. "Do you regret it?" she asked him.

"Regret what?"

"Getting your tattoos?"

Nyko popped the canapé in his mouth and chewed. "They weren't exactly my choice in the first place."

Faith sniffed her canapé. Smelled like mango. "How is that possible?"

"My father forced them on me. They were supposed to make a man out of me, at least according to the old man, who happens to be a Pure-bred Om Răsu and a full-blooded asshole."

"But…" Faith took a bite. *Oh, delicious.* "How do tattoos make a man out of you?" Maybe because they were scary teeth…?

"My father put them on with tacks, so it hurt. A lot."

Faith blinked, then her stomach dropped. "Oh." She ate the rest of her canapé in silence. "Where was you mother during all of that?"

Nyko considered a fruit canapé. "She was protecting me and my brothers, for sure, but there was only so much she could do." He glanced up from the serving plate. "Have you heard of Oţărât?"

"The neighboring town of bad guys?" It was a town full of

demons, in reality, but that sounded too weird to say. "Underground here, too, right?"

"That's it. My brothers and I spent the first years of our lives there. A very nasty place, lots of violence." Nyko picked the fruit canapé and set it on his appetizer plate. "My mom used to wear these gloves, see, the knuckles sewn and glued with shards of broken glass and bits of metal. Anyone who tried to mess with her boys, she'd sock 'em a good one." One side of his mouth lifted. "And with her Vârcolac strength, that was no small punch. The only person she never challenged was our dad. Maybe she thought it would ultimately make it worse for us. Maybe she knew she couldn't beat him and was trying to stay healthy in order to keep an eye on us in other ways. I don't know. But she shielded us from a lot of hassle, I'll tell you, and in the middle of all that Oţărât crazy, she taught us to be good men. As best she could, at least."

"Well, it shows." She smiled a little. Goodness, and she thought her childhood had been stressful.

Nyko's cheeks flushed slightly. "Mom got us out of Oţărât, too, risked Lorke's wrath stealing maps of the Hell Tunnels in order to save us. Too bad the heat of those tunnels disintegrated the maps, otherwise we could've gotten more people out."

Faith chose a caviar canapé. "Your brothers have the same tattoos. Does that mean…" she hesitated over the question. "They went through the same thing as you?"

"Yes." Nyko exhaled a long-winded breath. "I tried to get them out of as much as I could. I'm the oldest, you know, so I can't help looking out for them. Even today, I still worry about my younger brothers sometimes. Despite our mother's love, Jacken came out a hard man. If Toni hadn't happened into his life, I don't know what would've become of him. And Shon…" Nyko poked the fruit canapé around on his plate. "He…uh…" Nyko trailed off again.

"You don't have to talk about him, if you don't want."

Kacie told Faith that Shọn had been temporarily banished from Ţărână. Kacie hadn't known what the man had done to warrant that, but it must've been pretty terrible if this community had been willing to oust a Vârcolac to topside. They seemed very prickly about their anonymity and secrecy around here. For some reason, Kacie was fascinated by Shọn, or maybe just the idea of him, like she was harboring some fantasy of the Teague twins marrying the half-Rău Brun brothers.

"Oţărât wasn't fun for any of us," Nyko said. "But I think it was especially tough on Shọn. He…got lost, and I feel bad. I should've done a better job protecting him."

Faith felt her heart roll over. "You can't save everyone," she said softly.

"I have to," he said, completely serious. "I mean, look at me, Faith. Who else is going to do it, if not Big Nyko?"

She smiled gently. "I can kind of relate, actually. After my parents died, I shouldered all of the responsibility for parenting Kacie." She coasted a hand over her bun. "And my Aunt Idyll."

A thin line appeared on the bridge of Nyko's nose. "How old were you when they died?"

"Ten."

"Wow, that's…shoot, that's not good."

"No." Pain pressed outward from her chest. "They say bad things happen to good people, though, right?"

Wolverine suddenly appeared at their table. "Hey, guys."

"Hi, Dev," Nyko said. "What's up?"

Dev…yes, that's right, Wolverine's name was Dev.

"Sorry to interrupt," Dev said. "But Alex just had a vision about the Symbol Killer's next victim. Videon is taking out the dude in about an hour, so we need to go wheels up right now. Sorry." He repeated, casting an apologetic look at Faith. "Otherwise I wouldn't have cut in on your date."

"I understand." Faith said. "If you have a chance to catch

a madman, you need to take it."

Nyko scooted out of the booth and stood. "We'll pick up when I get back, okay?"

"Absolutely." She gazed up at him, dressed in dark slacks and a dark blue button-down shirt, looking so large and virile. Invincible. But nobody was invincible, not even the biggest Vârcolac on earth. She swallowed, struck by the sudden urge to kiss the top of his scruffy head. "Be careful, Nyko."

His eyebrows shot up, then he smiled. "I sure will."

CHAPTER TWENTY-ONE

Topside: downtown San Diego, same night

THE PARK PLACE CONDOMINIUM COMPLEX sat at West Harbor Drive and Kettner Boulevard in San Diego's swank Marina district, soaring thirty stories into the night sky. It was a ritzy-looking tower of sparkling lights and balconies stacked one on top of the other, zipping up every side of the structure.

Not many stars were visible, blotted out by the power of the surrounding city lights, but the moon hung like a bulging eyeball off the building's right shoulder. Across the bay, a US carrier hulked in port at the North Island Naval Air Station on Coronado. In the other direction, the city skyline spread out its arms, the view rendered distinctly San Diegean by the neon green lights circling the tops of eight skyscrapers: "Emerald Plaza," as it was officially known.

Nyko lurked in the shadows of a parking lot on the south side of the condominium complex on West Harbor Drive. Dev, Thomal, and Gábor were stationed at the other three points of the compass around the building, their team maintaining full surveillance. Videon's next victim, Samuel Preston, had an apartment on the sixth floor, but Alex hadn't known which side of the sixth floor. It would've been nice if Alex had also been able to tell them why he'd had this vision; his future ones only came when the episode somehow involved the Vârcolac. But Alex had drawn a *nada* on that, so it was anybody's guess what they were going to face.

"Jay-sus," Gábor's voice crackled through Nyko's earpiece. "Who is this rich prick Preston, anyway? An astronaut

156

or something? Knows the secret ingredient for converting dog crap into gold?"

"Plastic surgeon, I think," Dev crackled back.

"Ho, hear that, Costache?" Gábor returned. "After we save this Preston guy from Videon, maybe he'll offer you a freebie for that face of yours, transplant a few whiskers onto that girlie chin and rid you of some of your Barbie."

Nyko heard Dev laugh. Blond, Mixed-blood Vârcolac couldn't grow facial hair, and it was a constant source of ribbing from the black-haired Pure-breds who could.

Oddly, Thomal didn't shoot a comeback. He didn't laugh, either, but that part wasn't odd. Thomal didn't laugh so much these days.

"Heads up," Gábor suddenly clipped out. "I've got six nut-fuckers doing the human fly up my side of the building."

"Damn, right on time," Dev said. "Another gold star for our Soothsayer. Okay, everyone meet at Pavenic. Double-time."

Nyko took off, running in a low crouch and staying close to the shadows. His sheathed knife lightly banged his thigh and his handgun pressed against his lower back as he crossed West Harbor and headed east up Kettner to Gábor's position. He arrived first, a moment later, Thomal, and finally Dev, who'd been clear on the other side of the building.

Dev narrowed his focus on the six black-clad forms swinging lithely from one balcony to the next up the side of Park Place.

The bad guys were already at the third floor.

Dev cursed. "They're moving fast. We need to haul balls. Pavenic, you're with me, Spider-Manning after them. Costache and Brun, main entrance. Meet us on the east side of the sixth floor. Whichever door the bad guys go for is our rendezvous point.

Dev and Gábor disappeared.

Nyko sprinted across the street with Thomal at his side.

Adrenaline pounded in his ears as he slipped up to the main entrance and pressed his back against the outside wall, peering through the glass doors into the interior. More ritzy-looking stuff, with a floor done in shiny white tile, the middle decorated with a black geometric design, and a latticed partition wall that partially concealed a line of three elevators. To the left was a black grand piano, and the right, a...*oh, no.*

A doorman.

Spotting the man behind the desk at the same instant, Thomal glanced at Nyko and made a face.

Might've been smarter if Dev had sent Big Bad Nyko up the wall instead of into possible public confrontations. Even not dressed in his current black-and-gray camo pants and black turtleneck sweater, he couldn't go anywhere without being noticed and remarked upon.

"That Costache charm everyone's always talking about?" Nyko whispered to Thomal. "Now might be a good time to put it to use."

Thomal exhaled an unhappy-sounding breath, but pushed inside the building, buttoning up his overcoat to hide the weaponry strapped to his body.

The doorman came to his feet. "Good evening, sir. May I help you?" The man was clearly curious about the newcomer's all-black attire, but Thomal did his job and plastered a magnetic smile on his face, keeping the guy's curiosity from becoming anything more than mild.

"Yes, thank you." Thomal walked forward and slammed a fist into the doorman's jaw.

The man's eyes rolled into the back of his head and he sank limply to the floor.

Nyko hurried inside. "What the heck was that, Thomal?"

"You have a better way for me to get you in here?" Thomal shot back.

Good point. "All right, let's—"

The elevator *dinged.*

"Shoot," Nyko hissed. More people.

Thomal chopped his hand at a spot behind Nyko, indicating the other side of the piano.

The lobby stairs!

Nyko flew up them, Thomal on his heels. At the top, they ducked through an employee doorway, finding themselves in an emergency stairwell. Racks and racks of metal stairs going up, up, up—six flights for them.

Thomal growled. "This is taking too long."

No sooner had he spoken those words than the muted sounds of gunfire spilled down from high above. Dev and Gábor were already engaging with the enemy!

"Dammit!" Thomal blasted up the stairs, his Dragon speed immediately putting him two flights ahead of Nyko.

Nyko followed at top velocity, running harder than he ever had. Careening onto the fourth level, he caught a glimpse of Thomal.

The warrior had unbuttoned his coat and unholstered his pistol.

Panting, Nyko pulled out his own gun.

Overhead another employee door opened and shut. Pounding feet rattled the stairs, heading down. *Incoming bad guys.* Another surge of adrenaline poured into Nyko's system, speeding his heart and rushing his blood. He caught sight of Thomal, rounding the last turn with his gun held straight out in front of him. Then he froze. Didn't shoot.

What is he—?

The deafening report of a gun being fired roared through the stairwell.

Blood spackled the wall by Thomal's side and he was jolted back on his heels.

Nyko stopped, watching Thomal struggle to regain his balance.

Thomal's boots slipped.

Nyko shouted as Thomal tumbled butt over brainbox

down the flight of stairs, the flaps of his overcoat slapping over the top of his head. His comm headset flew off and clattered down the stairwell, cartwheeling along steps, bouncing off handrails, plummeting into nowhere. At the bottom of the flight directly above Nyko, Thomal hit the wall, his skull doing most of the hitting with a sickening *crack*.

Nyko yelled again, his chest on fire with rage. He thundered up the last stairs and leapt over Thomal's still form, the scent of blood assaulting his senses. Whoever had shot his partner was about to get—

He stopped so suddenly the soles on his biker boots made a rubbery fart sound. Gripping his gun in a hard fist, he blindly reached out his other hand for the support of the handrail. Now he knew why Thomal had hesitated, why he'd been too stupefied to shoot.

A pair of black eyes glared at Nyko over the snout of a smoking pistol.

Nyko knew those eyes. Thomal did, too.

Shọn.

CHAPTER TWENTY-TWO

IN THE SIX WEEKS SINCE Nyko had seen his little brother, Shọn hadn't changed much. His mouth still shaped a permanent pout, his black hair stood up in spikes all over his head, and his black Om Rău eyes looked coated in a bright ceramic glaze. His body type was Nyko's exact opposite; where Nyko was all bulk and bulges, Shọn was lean and mean. The youngest Brun was marked with the required teeth tattoos and, like Jacken and Nyko, wore them on his forearms. Unlike Jacken and Nyko, that was the only place Shọn was marked.

Shọn's upper lip tugged up, displaying one of his unnaturally long canines, as he continued to point his gun directly at Nyko…and didn't seem at all nervous about it.

Nyko let his own gun wilt down to his side.

A police siren skirled its high-pitched *woo-woo* into the night, the noise drawing steadily closer. And another.

The employee door above banged open. "Shọn!" a man shouted. "Take care o' that cockhead, then leg it! It's the fuckin' bobbies!"

Shọn's nostrils quivered as he inhaled and exhaled.

Down the stairs, Nyko heard Thomal groan and stir. "Shọn." Nyko uttered his brother's name in a rush.

Shọn pulled the trigger.

A bullet slammed into Nyko's right bicep, catching his muscle on fire. He bellowed in pain—bellowed in shock and anger. His fingers went lifeless, his gun clanking down the stairwell to join Thomal's headset in the abyss.

Shọn turned around and darted up the stairs.

Teeth bared, Nyko exploded after his brother, then checked himself at the employee door, pausing to do a quick glance into the hallway. No one. *Stupid fast idiots.* Nyko stole down the hall. The door to apartment 6G was hanging woozily on one hinge, and he slowed his strides as he approached. Shọn and his cohorts had to have gone in here. Nyko did another quick check. *Clear.* He entered and cautiously made his way across the living room, one hand gripped around the hilt of his sheathed blade. The blood from his bullet wound was seeping slowly down his arm, oozing past the ribbed cuff of his sleeve to trace his fingers then trail over his knife hilt.

He swept the room with his eyes. The apartment was spookily quiet. There was only the intermittent creak of the front door behind him as it twisted in a breeze brought in from the open terrace. The noise ran up his spine. He skirted the edge of a wide puddle of blood at the far side of the living room, his fangs pulsing. *Whose blood?* Dang it, where were Dev and Gábor?

He pushed the "speak" button on his headset. "This is Nyko," he said in an undertone. "I'm checking in. Where is every—?"

"Freeze!"

Nyko spun toward the open doorway, and his pulse leapt forward a beat.

A police officer was hunkered in the jamb, his black gun leveled at Nyko two-fisted, his legs braced wide. "Drop your weapon!"

Weapon? Oh, the knife. Nyko carefully peeled his bloody hand off the hilt of his blade.

"I said drop it!" the cop blared. "You're under arrest."

Nyko remained still and watched the cop. Jail was a *no way, José* option for their sun-allergic breed. *Where to escape to…?* His mind raced in rhythm with his heartbeat. He heard more people clomping down the hallway. Soon he'd be outnumbered. *Now or never.* He turned and leapt through the open sliding glass door of the terrace, catapulting himself into a handstand on the guard railing, then back-flipping over the other side into open air: a full rainbow arc, a perfect ten from the judges for the harrowing gymnastic maneuver. Now the question was: would he stick the landing?

The Park Place building whooshed by him as he fell through the night, down and down, lights and colors a messy whirl. His hair whipped into his eyes. He circled his arms and cycled his feet, all the while drawing in great lungfuls of air to harness the power of the moon. He hadn't been topside in so long... A bolt of panic shot through him as the pavement rushed up fast to meet him. *Come on...* He blanked his mind, going into a near trance as he reached deep inside himself. His body thrummed. A bubble formed around him, providing buoyancy just as his feet hit the asphalt—hard. His ankles compressed painfully, but...he wasn't dead. He stumbled forward a few steps, caught his footing, then shot a glance over his shoulder and up.

The cop was gaping down on him from the sixth floor balcony, his handgun hiked back next to his ear, his entire face sagging as if pulled there by four G-forces of shock.

Oopsy-daisy. *Here's hoping the guy is a heavy drinker.*

Headlights swiped across Nyko.

He leapt out of the way, but the driver chased after him. Nyko ran, but his sore ankles bobbled sideways, and the car was able to catch up and ram him. He caught air, flew several feet, hit, and rolled across the street for several more feet, tearing the elbows out of his turtleneck. He sprawled to a stop onto his back, dizzied.

Car doors slammed.

A man's face loomed into Nyko's vision. His mind registered: *bad guy.* But in the next breath, he knew he'd be okay. The man's scent spelled R-E-G-U-L-A-R, and there wasn't a human alive who could take him out.

Nyko moved to rise, but the man pushed him back down, the hand on his chest *very* strong. *What's this?* Nyko backstepped his senses and caught it then; the man's scent was sort of off. *Who the heck is—?* A fist rocketed toward his face and his lights blinked out.

NYKO POPPED HIS EYES OPEN. Tied to a chair. Pain in right arm. Om Rău male nearby.

He tabulated sights, smells, and sensations in 3.5 seconds.

"Welcome back to the livin', half-Rău."

The Om Rău male Nyko had scented was standing directly in front of him, making it impossible to ignore the sheer size of him. Shirtless, dressed only in combat boots and tight black leather pants, the man was a towering fortress of muscle with the body of a heavyweight boxer, shoulders, arms, and chest bulging with thick, hard slabs, his abdomen striated. Black flame tribal tattoos whipped up the entire front of his torso, erasing all doubt that this was a Topside Om Rău. A lip scar tugged the man's mouth into a sneer, adding more menace where none was needed. *Lip scar...*

So Nyko was finally meeting Videon.

Three other men were in the room, smelling like regulars, but kind of not, too, like the guy who'd punched Nyko.

Their odd group appeared to be gathered in the living room of a condemned building. The windows were closed off with crisscrossed boards, drywall had crumbled away in sections, exposing the bowed and splintered wood frame beneath, and there was a fire-charred hole in the middle of the floor, revealing part of an empty apartment one floor below. No electricity equaled lanterns set up around the room. Wisps of black smoke curled up from their glass chimneys, adding a distinctive kerosene stink to the stench of Videon's caustic acid blood.

Nyko concentrated for a second on the sort-of-regulars.

To a man, they were big, their bodies covered with a staggering variety of tats, and their eyes were narrow and mean. Probably ex-cons, the kind of men who asked questions, *maybe*, after all the killing had already been done. They didn't seem like the type to wear jewelry, but necklaces glinted at each man's throat. Nyko squinted. Not necklaces, amulets. He nearly shivered from a feeling of evil enchantment.

"Ye havin' a brown-trouser moment, fella?" Videon asked, then smiled cruelly. "If not, ye should be."

Probably so. The advantage-disadvantage ratio was fairly obvious. Nyko was currently chained from ankles to collarbone to a chair that felt bolted to the floor, and even though he was bigger than Videon—because Nyko was bigger than every man—in this case, it wasn't by much. "What do you—" *want*? The last word dropped off the end of Nyko's sentence as Shǫn sauntered into the room.

His little brother crossed to a rusted-out radiator and sprawled against it, crossing his arms, his eyes cold, black ice. Just watching.

Videon indicated Shǫn with a nod of his head. "Yer brother here says he don't know where the entrances to yer lair are. Says he gets transported in and out in a vehicle with blacked-out windows."

Nyko glanced at Shǫn again. That was true. The community doled out information about their secret entrances on a need-to-know basis only. The Travelers knew, of course, since they brought supplies into the community, and the Special Ops Topside Team, as they did their own driving on missions. The Dragon women had found out, too, because once they'd engineered an escape from Țărână. But no, Shǫn didn't know.

"Says *ye* know, though. So ye'll be tellin' me." Videon grabbed a gym bag and dropped it at Nyko's feet. "I couldn't break that fuckin' mare o' yers tryin' to get the information out o' her. What was her name?"

"Candace," Shǫn supplied.

Bile brewed in Nyko's throat. Candace was the Traveler Videon had tortured to death, which had led to Marissa getting captured, which had led to Pandra letting Marissa go—a whole chain of events had been set in motion by Videon's brutality.

Videon rolled his neck, cracking vertebrae. "Goin' to get it out o' ye, though."

"No," Nyko said. *No, you won't break me* and also, *No, I won't let you hurt me.* Covered all over with marks that had come from torture, he was done with that. Plain and simple. There wasn't a man on this earth, regular, demon, large, or larger, who could make him endure it anymore. Death would come first.

Videon's laugh was coarse and grating. "I was hopin' ye'd be full o' piss about it. Funner that way."

Nyko shifted against his restraints. They were tightly secured. "Why do you even care about our entrances?" he asked. "You're not after Toni."

"But Raymond is," Videon answered. "And since I'm gettin' myself into a bit o' a war with that scunt, I'm acquirin' what he wants."

Another ex-con entered the room. It was the guy who'd punched Nyko. He was also wearing an amulet. "Preston's ready," he told Videon.

So these jerks had succeeded in capturing Dr. Preston. An ache speared through Nyko's throat. It was his fault the team had failed to save the plastic surgeon. If Nyko wasn't such a freak of nature, then he and Thomal would've made it up to the sixth floor in time to help Dev and Gábor fight the bad guys, and the outcome would've been different.

"I'll be there in a tick, Kevin," Videon answered, an ugly grin still aimed at Nyko. "I ain't finished with this tonk, yet."

"I don't think Preston has much life left," Kevin said. "He's bleeding out fast."

Videon growled. "All right. Is Jerry ready for the ritual, too?"

"'Course."

"Let's crack on, then." Videon waved his men toward the door. "Shọn, ye guard this bloke."

Kevin frowned. "They know each other, Videon."

"Aye, they do. So it'll be another test o' his commitment to us." Videon shot Shọn a heavy-lidded glance. "He'll pass." Videon left with his men, the gym bag swung over his shoulder.

CHAPTER TWENTY-THREE

NYKO LET HIS GAZE WANDER around the squalid living room, looking anywhere but directly at his brother. Not that there was anything much to see in here besides rat poop and mold. After a thick silence, he finally forced himself to meet his brother's eyes. "What are they doing to Dr. Preston?" he asked, avoiding the real questions. *What the heck are you doing here, Shọn? Why are you betraying your people?*

Shọn hitched a shoulder. "Don't know. I'm not that far into their inner circle, yet."

Yet. "Ah. So…" Nyko coughed. "So how long have you been hanging out with the Topside Om Rău?"

"A while," Shọn answered vaguely.

"And, uh… Well, why are you with them, Shọn?"

Shọn scoffed. "I'd think that'd be obvious. The community banished me, so I headed where I was wanted."

Nyko's mouth fell open. Shọn thought they'd abandoned him? "But… No, Shọn. You were sent topside *temporarily*, to help you get better, to give you a break from the community for—"

"It was a *punishment*." Shọn's words slammed into Nyko. "And if the community thinks it can keep my loyalty after a maneuver like that, then the whole damned town should be nuked for its idiocy."

"It was partly a punishment," Nyko admitted. "But it absolutely wasn't a rejection of you. You were supposed to come back. Jacken and I, the whole community, want you to—"

"I'm not going back." Shọn sounded bored now. "And don't worry about my survival, either, when you stop sending my blood donor up. Videon keeps a stable of whores around. I'll feed off one of them until Videon kills her, then move on to the next."

Horror invaded Nyko's chest. His brother really hadn't just said that. "Don't do that," he pleaded. "You'll hate yourself if you do."

Dark, predatory emotions rolled off Shọn. The bones in his jaw moved into a menacing position. "I already hate myself."

Nyko's ribs squeezed his heart, his own emotions a nearly overwhelming tide—worry, guilt, confusion, fear. "Why?"

"None of your fucking business."

Same as at Shọn's trial. Nyko drew a breath with difficulty, the chains draping his body suddenly feeling like an impossible weight. "Tell me what's bothering you?"

"Bothering me?"

"Something torments you, Shọn. I…I've known it for a long time." Nyko wet his dry lips. "You need to get it off your chest. Purge yourself of it. Then you can move on."

Shọn laughed. The sound wasn't pleasant. "You really want to know?" He sprang off the radiator and stalked over. "Okay, big brother, let's have share time." Shọn planted his hands on the armrests of the chair and shoved his face close to Nyko's. "It was because of you!" he yelled.

Nyko didn't know how he remained still, but he did.

Shọn straightened, but didn't move back. "When was the last time you saw yourself in a mirror, Nyko? You're covered in tattoos from top to bottom, marred with more teeth than Jacken, way more than me. And why is that?" Shọn's nostrils flared. "Because you took Lorke's torture for us, you fuck!"

Nyko blinked hard for a moment, an ache building behind his forehead as too many memories pushed around inside his skull. There was just so much awful stuff he didn't like to remember, and getting those tattoos was the biggest: the pain, the blood, the knowledge that his agony was being doled out by his own father. Then there was the daily question mark of whether or not he'd even live to see another day in Oțărât, and the horrible realization that if he didn't, that actually wouldn't be such a bad thing. He'd survived to look out for his younger brothers. That was the only reason.

"You…" Nyko licked his lips again. "I'm sorry, but…" He grimaced. "You couldn't handle it, Shọn."

Another ugly laugh cracked out of Shọn. "You're right. I couldn't. Rambo Jacken could take it. Big Bad Nyko could. But not Baby Shọn." A darkness as deep as death took over Shọn's eyes. "Lorke *knew* you were taking all those tattoos for me, you ass, so he…" Shọn broke off, his face losing some color.

A quake ran through Nyko's jaw. There was leftover blood in his mouth from Kevin's punch and it leaked past his lips.

Shon turned around and walked back to the radiator, staring down at it. His voice lowered. "Lorke had to make me into a man, didn't he?"

A rat scratched inside the walls.

Shọn swung around, glaring. "Didn't he!?" he snapped.

"Yes," Nyko forced out.

"But you'd taken away the tattoo option with your hero-ics, so Lorke had to come up with another way." Shon's chin dipped down. "Do you know what he did?"

Nyko's throat knotted.

"I'm going to tell you. Not to purge myself, big brother, but because I want you out of my life forever and this will make sure you go." Shọn slouched back on the radiator and ran his thumb along the side of his nose. "Do you remember the whipping boards set up over by that part of the cave we used to call Death Ridge?"

Nyko's throat closed down another notch. How could he

not? He'd had his stint on the boards like everyone else, although by the time he was twelve years old, nobody'd been strong enough to strap him onto them, except for the two Pure-blooded demon leaders of Oţărât, Lorke and Josnic. "Yes," he whispered.

"There was a table over there, too. We used to try and play a version of ping pong on it when the boards weren't in use."

A better memory. "Yes."

"That's where Lorke did it," Shọn told him, his eyes like over-polished eight balls.

Nyko swallowed heavily.

"Lorke gathered a bunch of guys around the table and then had Bollven bring Deborah over. You remember Deborah?"

Nyko briefly closed his eyes. He didn't want to remember. Her loss had messed him up pretty badly. "Krolan's mother," he said.

"Faðe and Havel's, too."

"Oh, yes. I'd forgotten them."

"Deborah killed herself," Shọn said tonelessly. "Threw herself off Death Ridge. You remember that part?"

"I…" Deborah's face flashed through Nyko's memory, her gaze unseeing, her neck cranked at a wrong angle. He willed his thick tongue to form the words. "I remember."

"Do you know *why* she offed herself?"

For a moment, Nyko wanted to cry uncle: enough was enough already in the memory department. Deborah had been one of the better human women in Oţărât. Many others had only been able to look out for their own survival in their violence-riddled world, maybe that of their children, and that was it. The rare few had managed to be motherly and protective toward all the little ones. Deborah had been in that second category, and life in Oţărât had turned a lot crappier after her suicide. "I suppose I figured that life as one of

Bollven's women became too much for her."

"Oh, it was so much more than that, Nyko." Bowing his head, Shǫn dragged his thumb and forefinger down both sides of his nose. "You see, Lorke laid Deborah out on that ping pong table and made that circle of guys start in on fucking her. There must've been ten of us, one guy thrusting into Deborah while the rest jacked on their cocks to get ready. The next guy would mount her and get going, and the next, and…and I'm standing there with my stomach in my knees as it gets closer to my turn, thinking, what the hell is Mom going to say if I screw Deborah?"

Nyko's stomach convulsed. That was…he couldn't imagine it.

"So I come up to bat all nervous-like, Lorke yelling at me to get my cock out of my pants and get on top of Deborah. I'm twelve fucking years old! But I…I yank on my dick like a maniac, right, screaming my lungs out because my loin blockage hurts so damned bad, but terrified of what Lorke will do if I stop."

Nyko sucked in an uneven breath through his mouth and nostrils. Nausea writhed through him as he pictured it.

"I didn't know that a Vârcolac had to be blood-bonded before he could get a hard-on. None of us knew, except Mom, but she hadn't told us *that*." Shǫn dug his fingernails into the thighs of his pants. "The other men were laughing their heads off at me, of course. *They* could get boners. But not me, not impotent little Shǫn. Lorke didn't laugh, though. Ho, no. He was humiliated. *He* was humiliated. Isn't that rich?" Shǫn scraped his nails up and down his thighs. "So back I went to the ping pong table, again and again. Every day for four days in a row, and still no boner. Then on the fifth day Deborah offs herself because she's…well, I think the reason's obvious. She couldn't stand it anymore. The sixth time I'm brought to the Boards, Lorke says to me, 'You little pussy, if you're gonna act like a woman, then I'll treat you like one'. So he…uh, he…"

Nyko tightened the muscles in his neck to keep himself from shaking his head at his brother. *You don't have to tell me anymore, it's okay.*

"He bent me over the ping pong table, bare-assed, and straps me down. I broke three ribs and my wrist fighting not to get tied down like that, but…it didn't work out, so… Lorke chose Bollven to do the honors, knowing that the bastard blamed me for Deborah's death and would make things extra rough for me." Shọn's eyes blanked as he stared straight ahead. "Thousands of times I've relived the scene in my nightmares; Bollven moving up behind me, that big cock of his brushing my ass cheek, his fist gripping my hair, and the throaty sound of his breathing. I hate that the most, like he was actually into what he was about to do. I wake up gasping and sweating, tearing at the bedsheets in a panic. But I always wake up before it happens." Shọn's gaze dropped back to Nyko's. "Because it never did. Mom showed up with her gloves and saved me."

The oxygen Nyko hadn't realized he was hoarding rushed out of him. *It never happened.* Mom had stood up to Lorke, the one man she always kowtowed to. She must've paid dearly for that.

"Later Mom got it out of me what happened, and then explained the whole bonding requirement for Vârcolac being able to throw wood, but by then it was too late. I already felt like a total pansy." Shọn noticed his nails scraping his pants and stopped, pressing his palms flat to his thighs. "What I did with Luvera in Țărână three months ago…that Blood Ride…" He shook his head.

Blood Rides were a new invention of their breed, thought up, not surprisingly, by the rebellious Stânga Town kids as a means to participate in some kind of sexual activity outside of a life-bond. It entailed consuming enough blood, usually by licking it off the skin, to temporarily unblock a Vârcolac's sexual plumbing. According to the community's Non-Vârcolac-Fraternization-Law, it was an illegal act, and both Shọn and Luvera had landed in court, and then jail, because of experimenting with it.

"I just…" Shọn faltered. "I wanted to see what it was like to be with a girl, to finally feel like man. I wanted my *dick*, Nyko." Shọn dragged a hand through his hair. "I never meant to hurt Luvera. But…ingesting her blood during that Ride lit off my deepest bloodlust and made me go apeshit. I ended up trying to force her." Shọn's head came up, his eyes churning with dark turmoil. "Do you understand what I said? I tried to *force* Luvera. I did exactly the same thing to her that was done to me, the thing that gives me nightmares. There's no coming back from that." He pushed off the radiator. "So I'm hanging with the Topside Om Rău now. It's where a guy like me belongs."

"No," Nyko croaked, desperation clearing out a hole in his chest. "Please, don't give up on yourself, Shọn." He tried to scoot closer to his brother, but, dang it, that's right, the chair was bolted to the floor. "You're okay…I mean, you *can* be okay, if you just give yourself a chance and some time working with your therapist. This is my fault, not yours. You said so yourself, right? If I'd let Lorke tattoo you, then he never would've tried to turn you into a man by making you have sex with a woman. Okay? Please."

Heavy footsteps sounded in the outer hallway.

Nyko clung to Shọn's gaze, his panic wound so tight, it hurt. Had he reached his brother, even the smallest bit? If he lost Shọn, he didn't know what he'd do.

Shọn's face lost all expression. "Glad you agree that it's your fault"—booted heels rang out hollowly just outside the door—"because you're about to receive your penance."

Videon strode back in, now wearing a knife on his belt.

He was followed by four of the ex-cons, one dusted with blood. The unfortunate Dr. Samuel Preston surely had a

Celtic quaternary knot carved into his forehead now.

A vast coldness crept over Nyko while something inside him came apart. Dr. Preston was dead because of him; it was his fault that he and Thomal hadn't joined Dev and Gábor in time to save the man. On top of that, Thomal had been shot, Nyko had been shot, both of them by Shọn, who'd joined the bad guys and was sinking deeper into a pit fast. Also all due to Nyko's failure. Nyko's jaw trembled again. His whole life he'd been everyone's hero, but now, as it turned out, his "heroics" had done more harm than good. To who else? For how long?

Videon dumped the gym bag at Nyko's feet again and checked his chains. The links were inch-thick, probably the type of chain used to moor large boats. Obviously these guys knew what it took to hold a Vârcolac.

"Fancy that," Videon drawled. "The big'un's still secure in his swaddlin'." He glanced over his shoulder at Nyko's face-puncher. "Told ye, Kevin. I can always recognize a bloke who's as off his tree as the rest o' us."

"All right." Kevin nodded at Shọn, apparently approving of him being "off his tree."

"Any road, back to business." Videon unzipped the gym bag and pulled out a pair of pliers. "I'll give ye one chance, half-Rău, to tell me where the secret entrances o' yer lair are. Fess up, and I'll leave ye be and get back to my evenin'. Keep yer gob shut, and"—he brandished the pliers at Nyko—"I'll have a go at yer happy sack."

Nyko gave the tool a dull look. The grade of the metal was cheap. He had much better tools at home.

"Naught? Brilliant. Get behind the tonk, Kevin," Videon ordered. "All o' ye are about to see what kind o' griff a bloke will spill when his ballocks are bein' torn from his body."

Kevin moved behind Nyko, two others planted themselves to either side of his chair, and the last of the four stayed by the door.

Shọn lounged at his radiator, his expression conveying

nothing of what he thought of his big brother about to be castrated.

Nyko met Videon's brutal black eyes with an empty gaze of his own. These next few minutes were going to go very poorly, and he was beyond caring.

Videon reached between the chains at Nyko's waist, fumbling for his belt.

Nyko hunched his shoulders and curled his hands into fists on the armrests of his chair. He was done with all of this. Done with threats of torture, done with pain, done with this night's confessions. Done with disillusionment. Done. A growl rolled like thunder out of his chest.

Shọn came to attention off the radiator.

Smiling sadistically, Videon snapped the pliers' jaws, *tick, tick,* as he yanked open Nyko's belt.

A red haze unfurled over Nyko's vision and through a *crackling* in his ears he heard his growl warp into a snarl, low and bestial, a sound borne from the depths of the earth.

Shọn shouted. "You guys need ..."—*crackle*—"... the fuck out. Now!"

Iron surged into Nyko's muscles, weighting them with power. Control slipped like smoke through his brain. *Want. Fight. Hurt.* He inflated his chest and the iron links exploded off his body, flinging in all directions.

A snaking coil of fast-moving chain headed for the ex-con on the right. The man ducked so low he fell down to one knee.

Nyko shot out of his chair, kicking out. His booted foot rammed Videon's stomach, propelling the half-Rău across the room. Videon's body slammed into the wall. A kerosene lamp rocked on its base.

Nyko spun left, grabbing that ex-con by the hair at his temples and yanking his head down to meet Nyko's upward pistoning knee. Ex-con's legs buckled. He sprawled on his back. Nose smashed. Out.

The ex-con at the door rushed him.

Nyko bunched his fist and felled the man with a single bone-breaking blow to the jaw. Feet went up as body thumped down. Teeth scattered onto floor.

Ex-con on the right pushed up from his kneel and charged.

Kick to the side of the knee went *crunch*. Lots of hollering. Screams faded as body tumbled through the charred hole.

Kevin attacked from behind, jumping on Nyko's back. Whirling, Nyko crashed back against the boarded window, broke through, and scraped body off. It fell to street below.

Videon roared off the wall, his gaze glinting Rău red.

Yes. More. Nyko's hand locked shut around the half-Rău's throat. He re-pinioned him to the wall, compressing windpipe.

Videon clamped his fingers around Nyko's wrist and pulled. Strong. Very, very strong.

Hissing through bared fangs, Nyko tugged the knife off Videon's belt and punched the blade into Videon's left eye. Eyeball popped like juicy grape. Knife punctured back of skull. White acid blood fountained, stinging Nyko's right cheek.

He stepped back, grunting and snorting, then glared around the room through the sweat in his reddened gaze. Three men visible. Videon sagged at the wall on his eye socket spike, two other bodies lay crumpled on the floor. Nobody else standing. Shọn gone.

Nyko turned and leapt through the now-open window. Three stories down. *Easy drop.* He landed next to Kevin. The guy stirred, even though there was a large stain of blood beneath his head.

Nyko took off at a run.

Chapter Twenty-Four

Țărână: same night

FAITH LIFTED HER FIST TO Amsterdam and knocked on the mural of pink and yellow tulips, flexing her toes against the inside of her shoes while she waited. Maybe she should just barge in. Nyko shouldn't be back in his room after being shot several hours ago, anyway. Her anxiety grew. He was probably unconscious on the bathroom floor!

The door opened and Nyko appeared.

"There you are," she gasped out. "Are you all right?"

He stared at her. His right cheek was speckled with about half a dozen small, spotted scars, like albino freckles, and a thick white bandage wrapped the upper portion of his right arm. His face was pale and blank as marble. The doctors were insane to have released him already. Thomal was still in the hospital, wasn't he? Although he'd been shot on the side of his abdomen, which was a more serious injury, but still...Nyko was clearly in pain.

She set her hands on her hips. "Hey, didn't I tell you to be careful?"

He just kept staring at her, his eyes as expressionless as his face.

Oh, this was bad. "I'm taking you back to the hospital."

"I'm fine."

"You don't look fine."

"Dr. Jess took the bullet out of my arm and sewed me up." He shrugged. "Why wouldn't I be fine after that?"

Because any normal person wouldn't be. But Nyko wasn't

normal, was he? He was a Vârcolac, and, honestly, she didn't fully understand that breed's healing capabilities yet. "At the very least this calls for one of my famous sundaes."

"Your what?"

She smiled brightly at him. "I make the best hot fudge sundae in the world." Since she only allowed herself one per month, it had to be great.

"I don't—"

"Listen," she plowed over him. "I know you're not feeling well, Nyko, despite your efforts to pretend you're fine. So I'll make you a sundae and bring it here and we can watch a movie together or something." She widened her smile. "We never had dessert after our lunch date, remember?"

Nyko muttered something under his breath, then stepped out into the hallway.

She frowned as he pulled his door almost-closed behind him. That certainly wasn't very…welcoming.

"I can't," he said.

She searched his face. "Nyko, if you're in pain, you should go back to the hospital."

"I'm not in pain."

"That's a lie. I can see it in your eyes." *Beneath a thick layer of distance.*

He turned his head aside, the bones of his jaw set rigidly. "I'd like you to go."

"I…" Then she sighed. Why did men hate for women to see them when they were hurt? "Okay. I'll come back tomorrow, and—"

"No," he cut her off. "I mean for good." His throat moved. "Go for good."

Her lips parted and all of the blood washed out of her head. "What's going on?"

If possible, his expression flattened out even more.

"Would you please tell me?" she pressed in a hoarse tone.

He muttered again, then said in a tight voice, "Do you

remember the story I told you about my mom stealing maps to get us three Brun boys out of Oţărât?"

"Yes."

"Well, I didn't tell you why she took such a risk to do that." His looked at her with those weird blank eyes of his. "It was because of me. I was twenty years old at the time, which meant the next year I'd be maturing into my blood-need. Mom knew I'd be in serious trouble if I was in Oţărât when I had to start feeding. There weren't any donors there, and unmarked females were obtained only through near-death fighting. She had to get me out to save me."

Nyko paced a few strides away from her and gazed down the hallway, his focus faraway. "We Vârcolac have only been living in these caves for about a hundred years, did you know that? Not long at all. But when we first came, the Om Răuhad already been here for several centuries, and they were less than thrilled by our intrusion, even though there was plenty of room for everyone. They tried to drive us out. A lot of battling went on over the years, and in the chaos of one of those fights, my mother got dragged into Oţărât."

Faith studied the lines of tension in Nyko's back, a sinking feeling growing inside her stomach.

"Lorke, my father, had no reason to keep her. Om Rău and Vârcolac generally can't interbreed. But he wanted to use Urzella as his toy, and, uh…" Nyko flinched. "To make the things Lorke wanted to do to my mom possible without her enduring excruciating pain, she had to bite and bond with him." Lines grew at the sides of his eyes. "By escaping into Ţărână, she consigned herself to death by removing herself from her blood source. Going back wasn't an option. She said she'd rather die than live under Lorke in Oţărât, a sentiment I could totally understand, but still…" A muscle in his face twitched. "Watching her waste away into a blood-coma was one of the hardest things I've ever had to do. Worse knowing it was for me she'd sacrificed her life."

Faith swallowed. A sick knot pushed into the center of her chest. She knew the visceral agony of losing a parent, how it felt like a soul could scream forever and it would still never be long enough to make the pain go away. But sitting bedside as a parent slowly died had to be debilitating on a level she couldn't fully understand.

"My mom died because of me." Nyko swung around, his gaze coming alive now, both haunted and fierce. "And now I've lost my little brother, Shon, and again it's. All."—he pounded his thick chest to emphasize each word—"My. Fault. I look around me, Faith, and I see my other brother, Jacken, half-crazed with worry over Toni. Will Raymond get hold of her and hurt her? Will everything be okay when it's time for the baby to come? Dev almost turned himself inside out when Raymond kidnapped Marissa, and a month ago, Arc lost his noodle when his wife went into labor while the whole community was shut down. I can't do it, Faith. I don't want a family anymore, not a wife or kids or *any* of it to worry over. I can't deal with knowing that, when it gets right down to it, there's not a single thing I could do to save them if they needed saving. Just the opposite, I seem to be the reason people get hurt. Bad things happen to good people, Faith, you said so yourself. It happens all the freaking time, but I'm sick and tired of being the one caught up in the middle of all that, feeling nothing but helpless."

Faith lost her breath as her heart reached out to this man. She'd never thought to see someone of his size and strength laid so low by pain and vulnerability and self-loathing. It nearly tore her in half. "I wanted to give up, too, when my parents died. I still want to curl into a ball because of my injured knee, but I don't. And you can't give up, either."

Shaking his head, Nyko walked back over to his bedroom. "I'm out of the hero business, Faith. Everyone's going to have to save themselves from here on out." He pushed his bedroom door open. "I'm sorry, but I can't see you anymore."

She grabbed his arm to stop him, tears stinging her nose. He was setting her aside, and…it shouldn't feel so awful and desperate—she barely knew this man—but it did. How in the world had she grown so attached to Nyko in only one date? *Since he loved watching you dance. Since he understood what it's like to lose a childhood to responsibility and hardship.* Was her heart already heading into this? She stared at his face. He looked handsome to her now: his messy hair, boyish, the solid block of his face, masculine, his off-center nose, charming, his black eyes, deep and mysterious. Even his lethal bulk no longer disconcerted her. A woman could depend on shoulders as broad as Nyko's, lean on them if she had to and know they'd hold up under just about any burden. Which all meant, *yes.* Her heart was heading into this.

"You're hurt right now," she said in a shaky voice. "And if anyone can understand that pain, I can. So when you're feeling better, I'll be waiting for you. We'll pick up where we left off today. Like you said we would."

Something moved across Nyko's expression. She could've sworn he'd momentarily wavered, but the emotion was gone too quickly for her to be sure. "There are tons of single men in this town: Jeddin, Breen, and Kasson from the Warrior Class are all great. Oh, wait, Kasson's dating Rachel. But there's Mekhel over in the lab, and Balc, who's an electrician and a cool guy." His tone was strangely blasé, too offhand for there not to be agony behind the names of all these future husband possibilities. "I'll talk to them, let them know I've no longer got a claim on you."

"No." She let go of his arm and stepped back, dragging her knuckles across her nose. "I don't want anyone else."

He didn't say more. Just bowed his head and closed the door.

CHAPTER TWENTY-FIVE

Topside: Nunu's Bar, downtown San Diego, two days later,
December 24th

FAITH INSTINCTIVELY CLUTCHED HER PURSE close to her
chest as their group approached the grubby beige door of
Nunu's. She couldn't believe Toni had chosen to meet Aunt
Idyll at a dive bar, although considering the topic of
conversation was going to be the Symbol Killer, it probably
did make sense to go someplace obscure and private. Plus,
there probably weren't many establishments open on
Christmas Eve night.

Three of the Special Ops Team members stayed outside
to surround the building: Thomal, Gábor, and a black-haired
Vârcolac named Vinz, whom she remembered from that life-
changing night in Țărână's garage. He had long sideburns and
was Nyko's substitute.

Why had Nyko been left behind? Faith had gnawed on
her fingernails for the entire twenty-minute elevator ride to
the surface as she'd considered options. Because his arm hurt?
His arm hadn't hurt two days ago when he'd been shot, so
that was doubtful. Plus Thomal was here, and he'd suffered a
worse injury. Was the team worried that Nyko would stick
out like a sore thumb at a topside bar? He would, but he
could've manned the perimeter like the others. Or had Nyko
purposely opted out of this mission because he knew the
Teague twins would attend a meeting with their aunt and he
was, once again, avoiding Faith. She clutched her purse
harder. That was the most likely and thus the most painful.

Warriors Dev and Jacken accompanied Toni, Kacie, and Faith inside. The dimly lit bar had cushioned burgundy-colored booths lining the walls and lamps of yellow-and-burgundy stained glass hanging from the ceiling over each. Faith relaxed a bit now that they were inside. With its offbeat color scheme and wood-burning stove, Nunu's wasn't without a certain quirky charm. Kind of a circa-1940s Sam Spade meeting place...although back then there wouldn't have been all the TVs playing sports.

As they passed the large polished wood, U-shaped bar to head to the back booth where Aunt Idyll already waited, the bartender tossed them a friendly smile.

"My girls!" Idyll jumped up, stepping over her small suitcase to open her arms to Faith and Kacie.

They rushed into their aunt's hug.

Open a Webster's Dictionary and look up the definition for a Pagan priestess or shaman—or shamanka, as a female priestess would be called—and there'd be a picture of Idyll O'Shaughnessy. She fit nearly every stereotype. This evening's outfit consisted of long ropes of beaded necklaces, bangles stacked at each wrist, hoop earrings, open-toed sandals, and a floor-length beatnik-style dress made out of the kind of rough-woven, patchwork fabric one might find on a carpet bag. The dress was sleeveless, exposing Idyll's slender arms; the forty-seven-year-old woman still had a svelte body concealed beneath the roomy folds of her clothing. One non-stereotypical part of Idyll was her hairstyle. It was cut short, layered, and colored a chestnut brown with blonde, streaking highlights—very modern and fashionable.

Tears pooled in Faith's eyes as the comforting fragrance of incense enveloped her, and she squeezed Idyll harder. She never thought she'd miss her crazy aunt so much, but when life went topsy-turvy, even a grown woman needed her mother, surrogate or not.

Idyll leaned back and beamed at them. "It's been so long

since I've seen you two. I was overjoyed when you said you were coming west for Christmas, although"—she glanced around Nunu's—"I figured we'd be eating cooked goose at home by now."

Another non-stereotypical thing about Idyll; she wasn't a vegetarian.

"Sorry, Auntie," Kacie said. "Our life has taken a bit of an unexpected detour."

"Well, it's served you beautifully, Kacie. Such roses in you cheeks!" Idyll gushed. "I've never seen you look better."

Kacie glanced at the group. "Aunt Idyll could always tell us apart."

"Yes, well, this one"—Idyll cupped Faith's cheeks between her soft palms—"always had the serious eyes." She gave Faith a tender smile. "Not much has changed, I see."

Faith ducked her head, gently extricating herself from her aunt's hold. There hadn't exactly been much to be happy about for a while. Over the past two days especially, faced with Nyko's unwavering rejection, her mood had plummeted to something more bleak and downcast than even when she'd first arrived at Țărână. Which was saying something.

Introductions were made.

Idyll shook hands with Toni and Dev, then hesitated when it came to Jacken. Pulling her hand back to finger one of her necklaces, Idyll observed him with open caution.

Jacken was wearing a navy blue, long-sleeved Henley shirt to hide his forearm tattoos, along with a dark brown leather jacket, under which Faith knew he also hid a varied selection of weapons. But there could be no disguising his hard-jawed face and black eyes.

"He looks like a bad guy," Toni said, a note of humor in her voice. "But he's really not."

"Yes, of course. Excuse me." Idyll didn't shake Jacken's hand, though.

They all slid into the half-moon-shaped banquette, Jacken

and Dev taking the outer seats, Toni sitting across from Idyll, and the twins in the middle.

The bartender arrived. "What can I get for you folks tonight?"

"A round of coffees for us," Toni said. "Make mine a decaf, please." Toni gestured at Idyll. "Ms. O'Shaughnessy?"

"Idyll," she corrected, her mouth edging downward. "It's nearly 9:30 at night. Won't coffee keep you awake?"

Toni smiled. "We work odd hours."

"I make a sick Tequila Sunrise," the bartender told Idyll.

"That'll be fine, then," Idyll said.

As the bartender left, Toni set a manila file on the table in front of her. "I appreciate your willingness to meet with us, Idyll."

"Of course. Faith said you're in need of my Celtic expertise."

Toni nodded. "It's about the Symbol Killer. Have you heard about that?"

"Yes. Ghastly stuff." Idyll leaned back in the booth. "Good gracious, are you trying to figure out who that serial killer is?"

"We already know who it is," Toni said, earning a lift of Idyll's brows. "We're trying to figure out his next move, so we can anticipate it and catch him." From her file, Toni extracted a drawing and set it before Idyll. "This is the symbol being carved into the victims' foreheads. We know it's Celtic and called a quaternary knot, and that the symbol is grounded in the concept of four, since it's divided into quadrants."

"Yes, very good," Idyll said.

Toni nodded at Faith. "Faith has explained that in Druidic philosophy the quaternary is a symbol of protection."

"Correct again." Idyll cast a pleased glance at Faith. "Nice to know someone was paying attention all these years."

"So what I'm wondering." Toni rested her hands on the file. "Is why a murderer would use a symbol of protection in his killings?"

"I can't imagine a single reason why he would." Idyll pointed to the drawing. "Are you sure the symbol is exactly this?"

"Fairly sure. I have pictures of the victims, if you would care to check for yourself." Toni pushed the file folder across the table to Idyll. "They're pretty gruesome," she warned.

"Don't worry about that," Idyll said. "I have an extremely strong stomach."

Faith looked sidelong at Kacie. *Isn't that the truth? Remember when Aunt Idyll killed a chicken with her own hands, just chopped the head off with a cleaver and proceeded to pluck it?*

Kacie's mouth quirked up at one corner. *We thought her spiritualism had finally graduated into the realm of making animal sacrifices.*

Aunt Idyll had merely laughed at their expressions. *The meat's freshest this way, silly girls.*

Idyll took out all five of the 8x10 crime scene photos and carefully inspected them. "Ah, see, it's not the same. The knot on the victims' heads has been cut through."

They all leaned forward to give the photo a closer inspection, except for Dev, who maintained his constant surveillance of the bar.

Aunt Idyll was right. There was a knife slice in the exact same spot on each corpse's forehead.

Toni glanced only briefly at the photos. "What does the cut mean?"

"Well, break a symbol of protection and what happens?" Idyll asked, her brows raised.

"You remove that person's protection," Jacken answered.

"Exactly."

"Protection from what?" Jacken asked.

Idyll drew a measured breath. "In ancient Celtic tradition, the soul reposes in the head. So when this killer un-protects the head, he exposes the soul of the victim."

"Exposes it to what?" Jacken probed again.

"To abuse, manipulation, theft…" Idyll suggested, shrugging.

The bartender approached with a tray of drinks, and Toni quickly shoved the crime scene photos back into the folder.

He set down five mugs and spoons, a small pitcher of milk, a pot of sugar, and Aunt Idyll's cocktail. "Just to let you know, we're closing in about an hour because of the holidays."

"Thank you," Toni said. "We'll be out of your way before then."

Idyll stirred her Tequila Sunrise, whirling the red grenadine at the bottom of the glass up into the orange juice. "However a person would have to possess immense power of a supernatural nature in order to perform a Celtic un-protection ritual successfully. Are you sure your serial killer has that sort of power?"

Jacken and Dev exchanged glances.

Faith knew what they were thinking. The instant her aunt had said the word "supernatural," the two warriors had gone on high alert. How much did Idyll actually know of such matters? How much could safely be told to her?

"You're not sure?" Idyll persisted.

Toni's face smoothed of expression. The situation had become tricky. If Toni either confirmed or denied the killer's possession of this kind of power, she'd be admitting to its existence. "Not exactly that."

Idyll eyed her curiously. "I can't help you unless you tell me the truth, Dr. Parthen. The entire, unvarnished truth."

"It's Toni," she offered the same correction. "And, I appreciate that, Idyll." Toni slowly added cream and sugar to her decaf. "But there are some things we don't discuss in public."

"You mean like this one"—Idyll gestured at Dev—"being a vampire." She smiled serenely. "Like that?"

CHAPTER TWENTY-SIX

FAITH BLUSHED TO THE ROOTS of her hair as Dev directed an accusing glare at her and Kacie.

Kacie shot Faith a panicked glance. *Did you say anything? Certainly not!*

"We didn't tell," Kacie squeaked.

"Of course they didn't." Aunt Idyll *pishawed*. "I read people's auras." She faced Toni again. "You're the first woman I've ever met who has the same aura as my girls, although yours is more powerful." Idyll pursed her lips. "You're different, aren't you?"

Toni's expression turned wry. "That's probably a discussion for another time."

"Most likely, yes." Idyll scrutinized Jacken skeptically. "I still can't figure out what you are, though."

"I'll tell you what I am," Jacken clipped back. "Freaked out by you, lady, that's what." He gestured to Toni. "Let's get out of here."

"Oh, come now, I didn't blow your cover." Idyll waved a hand around the bar. "We're the only people here. Listen, you won't shock me with whatever you have to say and you can trust me."

Toni checked gazes with Jacken.

Grimly, Jacken shrugged.

"Okay." Toni sipped her decaf. "The serial killer's name is Videon. He's part-demon and part-Fey, and he has power, yes, but not an enchantment ability...which is what I'm assuming he'd need in order to perform a supernatural ritual of the kind you've described."

Idyll considered that. "He's a Tenebris Mala," she murmured. "These are the dark evils of the Fey, called such because no matter what color their hair or skin, their eyes are always"—she glanced swiftly at Jacken—"black. They are descendants of Mórrígán, goddess of war, Queen of Demons."

Dev lifted his coffee mug. "I hate to bring this up," he said to Toni, taking a drink. "But your father controls Videon, and Raymond *does* own the level of power we're talking about."

Toni frowned.

"Actually," Jacken inserted, "during the debrief about the failed Preston mission, Nyko told me that Videon's starting a war with Raymond. So maybe Raymond doesn't control Videon anymore."

Toni cut a quick glance at her husband. "Videon without controls? Oh, that would be bad."

"Very," Jacken agreed.

"Excuse me," Idyll interrupted, looking at Toni. "Do you mean Raymond *Parthen*? The same last name as you?"

"Yes."

"Oh, my." Idyll's forehead puckered. "This is a bizarre alignment."

"Now why am I not surprised to hear you say that?" Jacken said in a dry tone.

Faith had the sense that the name Raymond Parthen brought up even more bad memories for Jacken than it did for her.

Idyll spun the bangles on her left wrist. "A shamanka friend of mine living in San Diego works for a man called Raymond Parthen on occasion."

"Works how?" Jacken asked.

Idyll's lashes fluttered. "Oh, I'm quite certain her patron never asked her to do anything untoward. But...I haven't been in touch with Moriah for several months, either."

"Would you mind getting back in contact with her to ask a few discreet questions?" Toni was still frowning. "We'd like to find out everything we can."

"Of course."

Jacken shoved his mug aside and leaned forward. "Whoever's involved in these killings, whether it's only Videon or both him and Raymond, I'd like to know why the hell souls are being un-protected as a part of it. Because I have a very bad feeling about the reason." He kept his dark gaze on Idyll. "You mentioned abuse, manipulation, or theft: how do we find out which?"

Idyll paused, the small creases on her forehead deepening. "I think we need to ask the cards." She rooted around in her purse, big as a small duffel bag and made out of faux brown leather with colorful beads and spangles on it.

Faith nearly moaned when Aunt Idyll pulled out a familiar pack of Tarot cards.

"Have you ever had a Tarot reading?" Idyll asked Toni.

Toni glanced at the cards. "Nope."

Idyll gestured at Faith and Kacie. "Neither have these two, if you can believe it." She mugged a face. "Too much mumbo-jumbo for them."

Faith blushed.

Kacie's face was the same shade of red. *We always used to scoff at times like these, but I think this evening is giving us a new perspective on our weird aunt.*

Faith sighed softly. *Yes, maybe Aunt Idyll isn't so much kooky as wise on a level we've never bothered to appreciate.*

"Black magic?" Idyll waggled her eyebrows, chuckling. "No. The Tarot is simply a tool for accessing the subconscious, a method to help us gain answers within our awareness that perhaps we don't realize exist there." Idyll picked up the cards and began to shuffle. "Some people call the subconscious the Higher Self or the Inner Guide. This guiding voice is always within us. We can't break our connection to it, but we can certainly ignore it. In fact, most everyday people do." Idyll set down the deck, forming the cards into a neat stack. "You have to be receptive to hearing your inner voice, Toni. Be at peace inside yourself, centered, and mindful. If you think this is mumbo-jumbo, our ability to seek out information will be limited."

A smile tilted Toni's lips. "The last year of my life has widened my perspective on many things, Idyll. You can trust I'm open-minded."

"Wonderful." Eyes bright, Idyll handed Toni the deck. "Shuffle the cards a few times, mention your father's name and the killer's as you do, then cut the cards three times to the left. After that, hand them back to me."

Toni did as instructed.

Idyll dealt the cards face up in front of her in a specific pattern: two overlapping cards in the center, four cards at each compass-point surrounding it, and four more on the left side to act as a "staff:" this pattern was considered to be the shape of a Celtic cross.

Even though Faith had never had a Tarot reading for herself, she'd certainly seen her aunt perform it enough times to understand the particulars.

Idyll studied the cards in silence. "My, but your power does come through, Toni. There are three Major Arcana cards in this reading. It's very rare that I see so many. Here." She pointed to the card at the western compass-point. "This is The Emperor, the commanding father figure, stern and authoritative." She glanced up. "Raymond Parthen, I would think."

"Sounds like a fit to me," Toni agreed dryly.

"He sits in the Past position, which indicates he's moving out of this situation." Idyll gave Toni a meaningful look. "This confirms he's not a part of the killings."

Some of the tension eased from Toni's expression. "That's something, I guess."

Idyll pointed to the southern compass-point. "Here's

Videon: The Knight of Pentacles. He sits in the position which designates the Root Cause of the problem."

Dev snorted. "Videon as a *knight*."

"This knight represents blunt, overbearing, and unfeeling qualities, especially since the card was dealt upside down. That position heightens the negativity."

"Ah," Dev said. "Makes sense now."

"Here." Idyll swept a hand toward the center, her bangles clink-clanking. "These are the cards that represent the Heart of the Matter and its Opposition."

Dev pointed to the Opposition card. "That one doesn't seem good." The card showed a heart being pierced by three swords.

Idyll's expression sobered. "It's heartbreak and loneliness. And in the Future position…" She pointed to the card at the eastern compass-point. "Is the Tower, chaos and upheaval."

Toni rubbed a hand over her forehead. "So we have chaos and upheaval in our near future," she summarized, "and heartbreak and loneliness in opposition to…what?" She pointed to the Heart of the Matter card. "What's this?"

"The Ten of Cups. Family." Idyll sat back, her fingertips resting on the edge of the table. "Not your family," she murmured. "But…" Her eyes swept over the spread several times. "Oh, Lord, I think I know what's going on. If I'm right, then I would have to agree with Jacken's assessment of this being extremely bad." Idyll indicated the manila file with a forward thrust of her chin. "Do you have the names of the victims in there?"

"Yes," Toni said.

"May I see them?" Idyll bent over and unzipped her suitcase, digging out a thin paperback from the side pocket. It was a guide to Celtic surnames.

Jacken extracted a paper from the file and handed it to Idyll.

Idyll flipped pages rapidly in her book as she looked up

each victim's last name. Finally, she closed the book. "It's as I feared," she said, her face white. "All five of the victims' names—O'Connolly, Fleming, Eagan, Dowdall, and Preston—are surnames from families from the County of Meath in Ireland: *ancient, original families.*"

"Original?" Toni repeated. "What does that mean?"

"County Meath is where the Hill of Tara is located, once the seat of power of the medieval High Kings of Ireland. It's a hallowed place. The first families who came from Meath are believed to be equally hallowed, so much so that they were used as sacred vessels, and their descendants, as well." She held up the list of victims' names. "Like these men."

Jacken furrowed his brow. "Vessels for what?"

"For power from the four Treasures of the Tuatha Dé Danann."

Toni glanced around the table, making a sweep of their group until her eyes landed on Idyll again. "You've totally lost us."

"All right, let's go back to the beginning," Idyll's voice took on the melodic cadence of a storyteller. "In ancient Celtic lore, the mother goddess of the Celts merged with the sacred oak and together they created the Children of Danu, or the Tuatha Dé Danann—these are the ancestors of today's Fey folk. These special beings migrated to Ireland from the four mythical cities of their origin, but before they left, they were given four magic Treasures, or talismans, one from each of their cities to protect them against the evil Fomoriians, who already resided in Ireland."

"The illustrious number four," Dev inserted.

"Very good. The number is quite meaningful here." Idyll took a sip of her Tequila Sunrise. "After the Tuatha Dé Danann conquered the Fomoriians, there was A Time Of One; a time when the Tuatha lived in Ireland in peace as a united group. That ended when the Milesians, the ancestors of modern day Gaels, came and conquered, forcing the Tuatha to flee into hiding. It was during this time of great upheaval that the Tenebris Mala decided to make their move into dominance. The only way the Tenebris could overthrow the Milesians, however, was to combine their dark powers with Tuatha enchantments. They needed the four Treasures—the Stone, the Spear, the Sword, and the Cauldron. All Fey power resided in these Treasures, you see. As you can imagine, it would've been disastrous if the talismans had ended up in the hands of such evil.

"So to protect these essential enchantments, the king of the Tuatha Dé Danann took half the power from the Treasures and concealed it in the souls of mighty Fey warriors, called Fianna, for safekeeping. Then he dispatched the actual physical Treasures to four hidden corners of the world to be guarded in secret. Modern-day Masters, those with The Knowledge, say the Treasures ended up in charmed places on earth: Romania in the Carpathian Mountains, Tibet, Argentina near the Iguazú Falls, and, funny enough"—Idyll made a wide gesture—"the forest lands of Balboa Park, not far from where we now sit."

Idyll pulled the straw out of her drink and laid it beside the glass. "The king was clearly taking care to make sure that Fey power wasn't concentrated in one place, which would've left it too susceptible to theft. Some power is contained in the Treasures—which are scattered—and some is kept in the Fianna warrior souls. These souls are passed from generation to generation of the people who came out of the County of Meath: original families, like I said."

Jacken's eyes narrowed. "So when Videon performs an un-protection ritual on a man with an original family last name, he's accessing the soul of one of these Fianna warriors?"

"Yes, but only if the bearer of the original last name is in fact a sacred vessel. Not all are."

Dev rasped a hand over his goatee. "How is Videon find-ing men with original family last names who actually carry these souls, then?"

Idyll shook her head, her face drawn. "I have no idea."

Jacken frowned. "And once Videon has access to the Fianna soul, what does he do? Manipulation, abuse, theft…?"

Idyll exhaled unevenly. "This is an intuition, a guess, mind you, but I feel strongly that he's stealing them. Take these souls, and a person gains immense Fey power." She waved her hand. "This Videon, however, would need somewhere to store them. As a Tenebris Mala, he couldn't take these souls into his own body."

Jacken paused, then cursed. "I think I know how he's doing it." He glanced at Toni. "Nyko told me that Videon's men were wearing amulets that gave off evil power. The men were regular humans, but had strength and healing powers that went beyond regular capabilities—and their scent was off." He turned to Idyll. "Is that a way to store these souls, with enchanted amulets?"

"Yes," Idyll said quietly. "The wearer would gain the soul's power."

"Christ," Jacken hissed. "Why the hell is Videon amassing an army of men with Fey power? For his war with Raymond or for something even worse? And how is he able to perform this un-protection ritual to do it? We never determined that, either."

Idyll fidgeted with one of her necklaces, the longest one with the carved wooden African beads. "It's worse than you realize. You see, a symbiotic relationship of sorts exists between the Treasures and the vessels. Because they've been divided, there can't be one without the other; the souls depend on the magic of the Treasures for their survival, and the Treasures cannot have complete power without that which is kept within the vessels. By stealing souls, Videon is upsetting the balance of all Fey power. If he takes too many, one of the Treasures will fall, and then all Fey power will cease to exist. That means those of us with Otherworldly gifts—

people like you, Toni, and me—will lose whatever makes us special. Videon, too, although he's obviously too stupid to know it. Their kind"—Idyll gestured at Jacken and Dev— "will likely die off completely."

Idyll touched the Tarot card at the northern compass-point of the reading. "See here? This is The Empress, the fertile, life-giving mother, our connection to the natural world. I believe she represents the mother goddess of the Tuatha Dé Danann. She sits in the position of an Alternative Future, which I sense means the continuation of the power stemming from her is uncertain." The thin lines on Idyll's face became more pronounced. "I'm telling you all, we're looking at a catastrophe of biblical proportions for those of us of the Otherworld, if Videon is allowed to continue unchecked."

Faith's lashes fluttered, then a clammy trickle of ice rolled down her spine. Who would've thought that these symbol killings could have such profound meaning hidden behind them. She glanced around at the circle of faces, finding nothing but grave expressions.

"Now it makes sense," Toni said, "why Raymond isn't involved with this. He's smart enough to know this kind of soul stealing wouldn't gain him power, like Videon thinks, but ultimately destroy it."

Jacken's gaze was still aimed at Idyll. "Is there anything in those cards that might tell me how I can stop Videon?"

"*You* can't," Idyll said. "If Videon can perform a Celtic un-protection ritual, then only the Tuatha Dé Danann have the power to stop him."

Toni's eyebrows popped up. "The Tuatha exist today?"

Idyll nodded. "As long as the Treasures exist, so will the Tuatha. They are the guardians, or *custos*, of the Treasures."

Jacken massaged the bridge of his nose. "Hell, if the Tuatha are in charge of protecting Fey power, then why aren't they stopping Videon?"

"They can't," Idyll said. "Not without a conduit from the

Middle World to the Shifted World. They're fairies, you see."

A tightness flickered across Faith's forehead. *Did Aunt Idyll just say…?*

Kacie had a perplexed expression.

Toni sighed broadly. "Just when I thought my life couldn't get any stranger. Okay. Explain about these worlds."

"There are worlds within worlds," Idyll said. "The Middle World is our here and now, our reality. The Upper World is in the stars where one goes to meet spirit guides. The Lower World also offers a place for guidance, but is accessed through use of a power animal. As a shamanka, I can travel to both the Upper and Lower Worlds. But fairies live in a Shifted World: a world that exists here and now, in today's Middle World reality, but is beyond normal perception." Idyll tucked the Celtic surname book into her purse. "The Tuatha can shapeshift to human form, but cannot use their power in that form. In their fairy shape, they can affect the Middle World somewhat with their dust. But to use the full strength of their power, they need to act through a person in possession of a fifth element enchantment skill. Fifth elements are the conduits."

"And let me guess," Jacken drawled. "You don't know any fifth elements. Because that would be too easy."

"No," Idyll confirmed. "I'm sorry, I don't."

Jacken's lips formed a hard line. "So here we are, sitting on the verge of an Otherworld apocalypse, and—"

"Oh, God." Toni breathed the words.

Everyone at the table turned to look at her.

The bartender was turning off the television sets. It was time to go.

"What?" Jacken prompted his wife.

"I was just remembering the enchantment designator I saw on Pandra. Dr. Jess thought it was the letter V, but…now I realize it's a Roman numeral five. *We* know a fifth element." Toni inhaled deeply. "It's Pandra."

Chapter Twenty-Seven

Ţărână: the next day, December 25th, Christmas

THOMAL EASED A BLUE-STRIPED BUTTON-DOWN shirt off a hanger in his closet, sending the wire triangle swinging. He vacantly watched it rock lazily on the rod. The hanger was bent in two places, but he couldn't find any appreciation for the interesting asymmetry of that. The color of the shirt also didn't splash against the backs of his retinas like it usually did, inspiring all kinds of creative painting ideas until he pushed those images aside. His view of the world was narrowing in on him every day, and it was beginning to scare the shit out of him.

He was fucked up all to hell, though; no need to ask Carnac the Magnificent to figure out that one. His marriage-that-wasn't-a-marriage didn't exactly make him want to cue the laugh track on his life, but it wasn't the primary thing messing him up. No, he and Pandra had settled into an uneasy routine over the last two and a half weeks. Every Sunday he came to feed on her to get strong for the training week ahead—although he'd needed a bolster three days ago when he'd been shot at the Park Place condominium complex.

He entered her bedroom without knocking. She stood at the bedpost. He feed on her, avoiding touching her as much as possible, then he spun an about-face and left. All this was accomplished without a single syllable spoken between them. During the week, they also never spoke or had contact. Although he did spy on her. A lot. Why that was the case, he didn't know and couldn't figure out right now because all of his conscious attention was focused on his brother's deterioration.

Arc was systematically cutting himself off from everyone who was important in his life, his wife, Beth, and his kids.

Me.

Thomal didn't think he and his brother had passed more than two words in the last couple of weeks. A whole lotta mondo bizarro still sat between them. Which sucked to high heaven. Thomal missed the solidity of their former relationship, missed the easy camaraderie that had always been between them. It was like being minus a limb.

Exhaling, Thomal drew his attention away from the swaying hanger, which he found weirdly disturbing, and shrugged on his shirt, the movement twinging the healed wound on his abdomen. He buttoned up, then jammed his feet into a pair of loafers, finishing dressing for Christmas dinner at his mom's house. Beth, Arc, and the kids would also be there. He had no idea what Pandra was—Distracted by his thoughts, Thomal jumped slightly when his phone rang.

He crossed to his nightstand and picked up his cell. "Hello."

It was his mother. "Arc's not coming tonight," she told him, her voice heavy with worry and disappointment.

Ah, shit. Thomal scrubbed a hand over his face.

"Beth will be here late," Vivy added. "The kids are with Claresta." She was the community's elementary school teacher, who also babysat her charges on occasion. "But Arc just called and said he wasn't coming at all."

This was getting fucking ridiculous. It was time for Thomal to quit waiting for his big brother to fix this, and do something about it himself. "I'll go talk to him. Sorry about dinner, Mom." He hung up and trudged out the door.

WHEN THOMAL STEPPED INTO HIS brother's living room, he found Arc sprawled haphazardly on the couch, knees wide, one arm looped halfway along the back of the sofa, the other hand wrapped around a bottle of Budweiser, which he had propped on his knee. Arc was watching a football game on TV, and looked exhausted, dark circles under his eyes and an unhealthy hollowness to his cheeks. A Christmas tree sat in the corner of the room, dark and droopy.

Thomal closed the door. "Hey."

Arc didn't acknowledge him. Just kept watching the game.

Annoyance and exasperation mixed in Thomal's gut and curdled. His brother wasn't even making the slightest effort to be reachable. Walking over to the television, Thomal snapped it off. "It's Christmas, Arc. You can't bail on your family today."

Arc shifted his gaze over, a dark aggression in his eyes revealing a rage so deep-seated it gave Thomal the willies. He was beginning to wonder if his brother would ever recover from what had happened.

Or if he would.

He did a lot of his own stewing and festering these days. Seemed stuck there, in fact, but the problem was, the man he usually turned to for help when he was screwed up was currently an equal mess. Dev should've been another option— he was Thomal's best friend—but the finer nuts and bolts of how Pandra had ended up in Thomal's life was, oh, a slightly embarrassing topic.

"Turn the TV back on," Arc ordered.

"We need to talk," Thomal said. "You're heading down the tube—we both are—and it's time we put a stop to it."

Arc's jaw jutted a bit as he tipped beer into his mouth. "No, we're not," he retorted.

That was such an obvious lie, it was insulting. "Man up," Thomal growled, "and face this."

A sheen of frost slipped over Arc's gaze.

Thomal's voice wrenched tighter. "We need to clear the

air between us about what happened."

Arc's response was a fulminating silence.

Thomal crossed his arms over his chest, a surge of his own anger sending acid through his stomach, which wasn't at all nice for the ulcer he felt he was already brewing. "Or," he snapped, "I suppose I could go talk to Dev about this, start off with, 'hey, man, if you had a brother and Marissa sucked his dick before hooking up with you, would that, like, make you want to kill lots of things all the time?'"

Arc roared off the couch.

Thomal had never glimpsed such fury on his brother's face. It probably should've clued him in that something bad was coming next, but he was shocked momentarily stupid by the sight, so nearly got his feet tangled under him when he was suddenly being hurtled backward, Arc's hands fisted in the front of his shirt.

"You think I need reminding about what went down that night?" Arc snarled, ramming him into the wall by the front door. "I was forced to *watch*." He emphasized that last word by pulling Thomal forward and slamming him into the wall again.

Air shot past Thomal's lips. The bleak, soul-shredding anguish on his brother's face kept him stalled out in a too-shocked-to-do-anything gear.

Arc showed Thomal a set of teeth clenched into a rigid line. "That vicious, black-eyed whore never should've had the chance to abuse you, Thomal. I failed!"

"Y-you…?"

"I should've saved you!" Arc's gaze lowered to the hand Thomal had clutched to his injured side.

Thomal didn't even remember doing that.

Arc shoved himself off Thomal and snarled again, though this time softly, like a wounded animal. He turned and paced a couple of feet away.

"Are you crazy, Arc?" Thomal said to his brother's back.

"We were both locked in chains. Murk was restraining you, too, and he's no lightweight, and Pandra is stronger than a dammed Cyclops. No way you could've—"

"No!" Arc rounded on Thomal. "I should've been strong enough to stop them from doing what they did to you." His face blanched a stark white. "To me." He rammed both hands through his hair. "I promised Dad," he added in a low tone.

Thomal breathed heavily for a couple of moments. "What does that mean?"

Arc dropped his hands. "Before Dad died, he made me promise to look after you. I…" His eyes glistened. "That night in the hotel room, I broke my word to him."

You promised Dad you'd…? Heat needled the back of Thomal's neck. Did that mean his father had been pretending when he'd acted happy about Thomal going into the Warrior Class? Well, fuck, if what Arc just said was true, then clearly Dake hadn't believed in Thomal's abilities. And, obviously, neither had his brother, seeing as Arc had bought off on Dake's plan. Tightening his jaw, Thomal yanked his button-down shirt back into place. "You can unload that guilt trip right the hell now, big brother. I don't need your babysitting."

"Yes, you do."

The flush ran from Thomal's nape up into his cheeks.

Arc's voice went toneless as he started reciting facts. "That night at the DoubleTree Hotel ten months ago when we went into Toni's room to help her and Jacken, Ren threw you out a four-story high window. The night we were at Scripps Hospital to kidnap Toni, Ren strangled you nearly to death. The night the Spec Ops team saved Marissa and the other women, you got shot. You got shot again on the recent mission to save Dr. Preston. Then when you were on the op to—"

"Jesus, Arc," Thomal cut in. "You act like I'm the only warrior who ever gets wounded. What about Dev taking an exploding Bătaie blade to the shoulder when Lorke was trying to capture Toni? Or—"

"Dev purposely threw himself into the line of fire to save her," Arc countered.

"Great." Thomal stepped back and flung his arms out. "So when another warrior gets hurt he's heroic, but when I do, it's because I'm being a doofus?"

Arc drew in a deep breath, then exhaled it in a long stream. "You've always had to work twice as hard as the other men for half the results, Thomal. Frankly, I've never agreed with your decision to go into the Warrior Class. Going from paints and brushes to fighting? I mean, come on."

Thomal's jerked his chin in, his stomach burning so hot now that a load of saliva dumped into his mouth.

"I've tried to keep an eye on you, but…" Arc sank down on the couch again and grabbed his half-empty beer, his knuckles white. "You'll excuse the hell out of me if what happened two weeks ago isn't sitting well. I hate losing. You may be used to it, but I sure the fuck am not."

Thomal's face actually hurt, he was blushing so furiously now. All these years, his brother *actually* thought of him as a doofus. The concept was beyond comment. He said nothing.

Arc glanced around the couch, then jammed his hand between two cushions and extracted the remote. He clicked on the TV, the gesture a pretty damned clear dismissal.

Thomal slammed out of his brother's house and stomped down the front steps, nearly bowling into Claresta returning with Lysha, Brynt, and the baby, Garez.

"Hi, Thomal," the teacher greeted him. "Merry Christmas."

"Hey," Thomal returned shortly, angling past her.

"I'm glad I ran into you," she said. "I've been wanting to ask you—"

"Do you think we could talk later? Now isn't the best time." *I'm kinda busy eating myself alive with self-doubt and guilt.* Dammit, if only he hadn't let a moment of weakness stop him from tearing out Pandra's throat, none of this would be happening.

Claresta inhaled a quiet breath. "I know your life is out of sorts right now, Thomal, but I could really use your help. I need you to teach Hannah and Willen Crişan's eldest boy, Ællen, how to draw."

"I don't do that anymore." *Going from paints and brushes to fighting? I mean, come on.* Hunching his shoulders, Thomal stalked on.

"Ællen is having the same problems you did in school," Claresta said softly.

Thomal jerked to a stop.

"Learning how to draw helped you, didn't it?"

Ah, shit. Thomal aimed a hard gaze across the street at nothing. What was he supposed to say to that?

CHAPTER TWENTY-EIGHT

Topside: La Mesa, San Diego, five days later, December 30th

THE FRONT DOOR OF APARTMENT 6D started to open…

John Waterson shoulder-rammed himself the rest of the way inside, sending Ria stumbling back with a sharp gasp.

He slammed the door shut behind him. "You really should check your peephole before you open the door," he grated between his teeth, the rage he'd been nurturing for a month adding a scratchy menace to his voice. "You never know who might be lurking outside."

"I did check. I just figured I needed to get this over with," Ria said forlornly. "I knew you'd come for me sometime."

"Yeah, well, where the hell have you been?" he demanded. He fucking hated stakeouts, and being forced to watch Ria's apartment building on personal time had only fueled his vile mood.

"Oklahoma," Ria answered. "I took my sister home to my parents, then stayed for the holidays."

That's right, *abracadabra*, the Mendoza case had been solved by Elsa's miraculous return. No ransom given over, no explanations offered from the kidnappers, just—*zam!*—Elsa stork-dropped back onto Ria's doorstep. *Sure.* Anyone who believed there wasn't more to the case than that, John had some beachfront property in Florida to sell them. Real cheap.

"I'm sorry about what I did to you, John," Ria said, giving him a pleading look. "But I didn't have a choice! The man who kidnapped my sister made me."

The man in question was the sociopath with the scar on

his lip who'd abducted Kendra Mawbry six months ago the night John had been shot. SDPD had acquired a description of the perp from Elsa upon her return, although clearly Ria had always known who the bad guy was. *Thanks for nothing, angel face.*

"Your blood was Elsa's ransom," Ria continued. "My sister's kidnapper said he'd r-rape and kill Elsa if I didn't get him a pint of your blood."

John froze. "What…? You mean specifically *my* blood?"

Ria nodded. "I overheard him talking to one of his men about it, and I guess there's something in your blood he wants. *Needs.* Some…element."

John took a quick step back as his heart ground to a shuddering halt. The night he'd been in the hospital after being shot, Dr. Edward Sevilli had approached John with the results of a blood test. *A strange element popped up in your blood work, John…nothing identifiable as strictly human.* John had been trying to convince himself this "element" was a mistake, but now here it was again.

A swallow worked its way down his throat. How in the world had Scar Lip known about John's so-called inhuman element? And what did he need it for? Shit, the maniac must know what it was! "What is it?" he growled at Ria. "What's in my blood?"

"I don't—"

She let out a squeak when he snatched her up by the arms. "What's the element?" he yelled, shaking her. Finally a chance to get some answers! "Tell me!"

"I don't know," she cried out, her face draining of color. "I really don't, John, I swear!"

He released her and jerked around, forcing several deep breaths that seemed to quake his lungs on the way in and out. "Dammit," he hissed. On top of his physical decay, now he was starting to lose it upstairs. He dragged an unsteady hand through his hair. Jesus H. Christ in a hot house, once again this case was back to blood. He had to get this figured out before he actually did go certifiable.

It was time to contact his mother.

BOOK TWO

CHAPTER TWENTY-NINE

Ţărână: eight and a half months later, August

LITTLE DEANDRA UNGUREANU APPEARED IN the doorway of the make-believe straw house, dressed to the nines in a piggy costume of Pandra's own making. "Not by the hair of my shimmy shim shim!" the young girl yelled at the top of her lungs.

Lysha Costache and Kristara Crişan, the two other five year old girls dressed in piggy costumes, exchanged a look across the small school stage—one girl from her "stick" house, the other from the "brick" one—then shifted over to check in with Pandra. Seven year old Ællen, the Big Bad Wolf, who was facing down Deandra, didn't say anything either.

"Oh." Deandra's face fell. "I mussed up my words again, didn't I?"

Pandra stepped forward from offstage, chuckling as she took Deandra's hand and urged her out of the pretend house. "Didn't I tell you not to give a toss if you fluff your lines?" Smiling, Pandra went down on one knee in front of the little girl. "No matter what you do, your parents will love it, I guarantee. So no worries, right?"

Deandra frowned a little. Her mother, Ellen the dentist, was a chipper sort, but Pedrr, the girl's father, was a bit of a brooding fellow, and Deandra tended toward his more serious personality.

Pandra waved over Lysha, Kristara, and Ællen, and the three scampered obediently to her side. "And you lot press forward with your lines regardless. After all…" Pandra threw her arms up in the air. "The show must go on!" Her over-exaggerated antics earned a round of giggles from the little girls, as it was intended to do.

Pandra laughed along with them, the moment of simple, innocent joy washing over her in a surreal warmth. Sometimes it was still difficult to believe she worked alongside Claresta at Ţărână's elementary school, even though she'd been doing so for several months now. Had anyone ever told Pandra that one day *she* would be helping to shape the next generation, she would've handed over her noggin for football practice.

Eight months ago, she'd done what was required and had a dab at a varied assortment of jobs in the community, chopping vegetables and stirring sauces at Marissa's Restaurant, putting up dry wall in the new bowling alley, handing dental instruments to Dr. Ellen, selling movie tickets at the Town Cinema, lifeguarding at the Water Cliffs, fixing cars with Llawell in the garage, slapping bandages onto boo-boos as nurse's aide with Shaston at the hospital, flipping burgers at the diner, and more. The only jobs she hadn't tried were at places where she was *persona non grata*. As in, she hadn't trained with the warriors, Thomal and Arc's domain—not to mention that Vârcolac whose fang she'd broken—and she hadn't worked at Beth Costache's TradeMark clothing store.

Both omissions had been just aces with her.

Although...she suspected Beth would've been willing to parley a truce with her, if given the opportunity. Which surprised the beans out of Pandra. She doubted she would've be so magnanimous had their roles been reversed. But Beth was the sweet and forgiving type. Arc, on the other hand, most definitely was not, and he stood as a massive, immovable blockade between Pandra ever becoming a member of the Costache clan.

Difficult to blame him too harshly for that, not after what Pandra had done to both the Costache brothers. If she could go back and change the night she'd gone spacky on the two, she would, for certain. Although that would first entail her going back and being reborn into a different family, one without a father who'd so seriously buggered her up, both with the power of his dark enchantment as well as his hot-then-cold method of parenting.

A lifetime spent with a father who would lull her into a false sense of security and wellbeing with his charm, care, and approval, only to clobber her, mentally or physically, in the next moment when she failed to please him or dared to defy him lay at the root of her actions against Thomal and Arc…and so many others. According to her therapist, Karrell, Pandra had resorted to subjugating and hurting people as a way to gain power in a world where she was essentially powerless. Not exactly the most attractive thing to learn about oneself. Even though, oddly enough, this was why she'd gravitated toward becoming a teacher. The role gave her a chance to love young, impressionable beings unconditionally, to accept them not *in spite of* their faults and mistakes but *because of* them. As had never been done for her.

Now the power in her world came from love, giving it and receiving it—from her sister and brother, Toni and Alex, the friends she'd made in the community, and these adorable young ones.

Too bad not from Thomal.

Over the last eight months her estranged husband hadn't shown any interest in becoming an actual bonded mate. His attitude toward her had moved from icy fury to cool indifference to brief moments of terse civility…and ended about there. She was doing her best to make amends to him. She'd already apologized—which he'd accepted, though brusquely—but beyond that she didn't know what to do. Except to keep her nose clean and work hard, which, hopefully, he'd interpret as a reason to give her a chance. They were biologically stuck with each other, after all. It would be nice if they could make a go of it outside of the nothing they currently had. No, not just *nice*, but in fact, necessary. Pandra had just come too far and grown too much over the last months to settle for less than true happiness. With Karrell's help, she was slowly coming to the conclusion that she deserved that.

"Hey."

Pandra turned on her knee. *Well, speak of the very devil himself.*

Thomal stood in the doorway of the classroom, a satchel of art supplies tucked under his arm. "I thought you weren't teaching today."

Pandra came to her feet, catching back a flare of disappointment. It should come as no surprise that her husband hadn't wanted to bump into her. "Just running a little late on rehearsals, is all. All right, lasses, off you go and change into your normal duds."

Lysha, Deandra, and Kristara rushed up to Pandra with their arms open.

Pandra bent over and hugged each girl in turn, the backs of her eyes prickling. She didn't think she'd ever get used to how grand that felt. As the girls dashed off, she glanced at Ællen. "You can go fetch your art kit now, lad. It's time for your drawing lesson."

The boy sprinted into the next room.

Thomal pinned his gaze onto the opposite wall, no doubt fascinated by the world map there, not just avoiding Pandra now they were alone.

'Course not.

"I'm glad I have a moment with you, Thomal," Pandra said, anyway. "I wanted to tell you what brilliant work you've done with Ællen. Confidence-wise he's an entirely different lad from eight months ago. Has he shown you his comic books yet?"

"What?" Thomal's eyes darted over to her. "No."

She smiled. "He will. He draws loads of them. At first he

didn't fill in the thought bubbles, so when we read them together, we'd invent the dialogue." She laughed. "But I think he got fed up with the barmy things I had his heroes saying, so now he writes his own words."

Thomal paused. "Does he still get the letters backward?"

"Sure." She shrugged. "Sometimes. But he doesn't care so much now." She nodded her head at him. "*You* did that for the lad."

Thomal set his art satchel on the communal table, turning away from her again.

She scooped up her sewing basket to take home with her tonight, along with Kristara's costume, which she'd noted had a tear along the sleeve. "Your dyslexia went away when you entered your blood-need, correct?"

"Yes."

"No problems at all with it anymore?"

"No." He hitched a shoulder. "Every now and then I misdial a phone number, but who doesn't?"

Pandra considered that. "I'm not sure if we should tell Ællen that, though. I don't want to raise his hopes, if it doesn't turn out to be the case for him."

Ællen raced back in the classroom, carrying a satchel similar to Thomal's. "Ready!" He plunked his satchel down, then gave Pandra a quick goodbye hug.

"Cheers," she said, smiling. "Have fun you two." She strode down the hall. Well, not quite *down* the hall. Actually, she stopped just outside the classroom doorway and clandestinely observed the two artists, unpacking their drawing supplies and chatting.

Today wasn't the first time Pandra had spied on Thomal while he worked with Ællen. She supposed it was poor form, like eavesdropping, but she was too fascinated by how much Thomal changed whenever he slipped into his creative side to resist watching. The moment he opened his artist's pad, the dark edges melted off him and the anger he wore like a shield dropped away. She'd stand in this hallway and watch, enthralled, as he put his very soul into everything he taught Ællen, becoming so engrossed in his art she couldn't figure why Thomal had ever gone into soldiering.

It touched her, deeply, to see him that way, and, ugh, she hated to be no better than a silly moo who got all squishy over a man because he had a secret sensitive side, not to mention being good with children and a nice, attentive bloke to his mum, but... Truth was, she loved those qualities about him. And the lost soul she sensed he was.

"Oh, I'm glad you're both here."

Pandra nearly jumped out of her skin as Donree, Toni's assistant, appeared at the other end of the hallway.

Thomal turned his head to look.

Ah, botheration. *Caught.*

Donree came the rest of the way down the hall and looked between Pandra and Thomal. "Dr. Parthen would like to see you both in her office right away."

When Pandra arrived at Toni's office with Thomal, Jacken, Dev, and Alex were already inside. Toni was seated behind her desk, and as they entered, she offered them a smile of greeting that didn't quite curl her mouth all the way. *Poor girl.* Toni had entered her last month of pregnancy—month *ten* in the Vârcolac gestational cycle—and she seemed to wear a worn expression all of the time. Her humanoid body wasn't especially well adapted to carry a baby for that long, so she was probably as uncomfortable as a woman could get, her belly stretched huge as a Goodyear blimp. Most days Jacken looked like he'd swallowed a prickly pear.

"There's been a symbol killing," Jacken told them without preamble.

Pandra came to a halt. "What? Again?" There hadn't been a murder since Dr. Preston's.

Soon after the plastic surgeon's unfortunate demise, the

community had engaged in a whirlwind of preparations to man an attack against Videon. The plan would've even included contacting Raymond, but mostly had entailed getting Pandra up to speed as a fifth element...so that she could perform the ritual to save all Fey life and power on earth.

Right. She'd felt no pressure a'tall when the dotty character Idyll O'Shaughnessy had come down to Ţărână to help Pandra. That'd been eight months ago in this very office, the Special Ops Topside Team of warriors also in attendance, watching Pandra make an utter hash out of it.

"First off," Idyll had said to her. "We want to practice out-of-body travel by having you journey into either the Lower or Upper World. Once you've mastered that, we can align the necessary four components for your journey into the Shifted World."

Pandra nodded mutely, still overcome from learning that she was an all-important fifth element.

Idyll held a small drum that she'd created out of a bowl and some canvas cloth. "I'll pound this at a steady rhythm of about four to seven beats per second. Your brain waves will soon follow that rhythm, then change to match it, putting you into the theta state necessary for a deep, meditative trance. Are you ready?"

Pandra grimaced. "Not particularly."

Idyll lowered her drum to the couch and gave her a motherly look. "Shall I help you relax a bit first?"

"Sure. Got any tequila?" Pandra had meant it as a silly quip, but as she was hit by a blast of hostile tension from Thomal, her chest heated. She and Murk had gone out for tequila after the "event."

She stiffened up tight after that. No fecking way could she relax now. But actually...the shamanka's voice was very soothing as she talked Pandra through some centering exercises. Soon, Pandra's body was melting into the chair, her brain switching to a soft *hum*.

She didn't think she'd be able to go any further than that. One part of her mind remained very aware of everyone staring at her, the hubby in particular. But as Idyll beat her drum, Pandra reached for the essence that was supposed to be inside her now and...*I'll be buggered.* She found it. Of all the things. It was like a different life-force, moving about inside her head, winding the *hum* into a vibration. Pressure built inside her ears, from the inside of her skull out. Her fifth element wanted to get out. Go places.

In her mind, a long, dark hallway appeared. At the end was a door, divine light spearing around the seams. She knew, without knowing how, that she would need to pass through that door to travel to the next sphere. All was fine. She felt absolute control within herself. Her fifth element would allow her to determine exactly where she went. Yet...as she approached the door, she felt a pull at something deep inside of her, something frighteningly deep. She didn't know what it was, but instinct told her to back away. Run, even.

She flipped her eyelids open.

Idyll stopped thumping her drum. "What happened?"

"I..." Pandra broke off. As imperative as this ritual was, an excuse like *I wimped out* seemed dreadfully insufficient.

Idyll set the drum aside again. "Out-of-body travel requires complete vulnerability, Pandra. You have to bare yourself to the Otherworld forces in order to be allowed passage. Otherwise there can be no trust between our world and theirs. Do you understand this?"

Complete vulnerability. Bare yourself. She understood. She just couldn't do it. She hadn't allowed herself to be completely vulnerable since she'd been out of nappies, so the idea wasn't the freshest.

Toni cast a sidelong glance at Thomal. "Maybe we should clear the room," she suggested softly.

"No." Pandra stood up, her throat constricting. "I'm

sorry. I can't do this." She'd left the office. Her guilt over letting everyone down had been somewhat relieved by the cessation of Symbol Killer slayings. She'd thought she was off the hook. No more.

"I'm sorry," Pandra repeated now to Toni. "I know I'm the one who's supposed to prevent these killings. I've tried to perform the ritual again on my own, but—"

"You don't need to apologize," Toni interrupted. "Rituals of a supernatural nature are tricky. I know you want to help. In fact, Alex has an idea that involves you. It's…a bit racy, though." Toni glanced at Thomal.

A scowl began to build on Thomal's brow. "What is it?"

Alex stepped forward. "I've been monitoring Pandra's topside email account," he said, then aimed at Pandra, "As you approved."

Pandra gave her half-brother an *it's okay* nod. A couple of months ago the Council had deemed Pandra sufficiently well-adjusted to community life to be allowed access to her old email account. She'd declined—unable to think of a single soul she'd like to have contact with—but, aye, had agreed to let her account be monitored.

"A man named Edgar got in touch with you," Alex said.

Pandra arched her brow. "Truly?" Before she'd been wrangled down to Ţărână, she'd heard Edgar had fallen off the grid.

"From the nature of the email, it was clear that he's…uh, attracted to you." Alex's cheeks stained pink.

Edgar must've been extra-descriptive this time.

"We thought maybe you could persuade him to take you to one of Videon's hideouts, then the warriors can storm in and deal with the rest." Alex dipped his chin and gave her a pointed look over the rims of his glasses. "I assume you realize that by persuade, we mean seduce."

Pandra quirked her lips. "You did say racy."

Thomal's scowl deepened. "We don't need her for that.

The warriors can follow this dude on our own."

Alex spread his hands. "Besides this email, I haven't been able to unearth traces of him anywhere. I can't tell you the first place to find this Edgar in order to follow him. If we want to get to Videon through Edgar, then Pandra is our best bet."

Toni cupped her belly with her palms, probably trying to relieve pressure on her lower parts. "Would you be willing to email Edgar, Pandra? Set up a meeting?"

"That would raise Edgar's suspicions," Pandra answered. "I stopped answering his emails ages ago. But I know of a sex club where he ponces about. Happens we could find him there."

"No," Thomal said shortly.

"Thomal," Dev interceded. "You heard Alex. This is our only way to Videon."

Thomal swung around. "So you'd be all kumbaya about Marissa doing something like this, Nichita?"

Dev regarded Thomal without expression. "Marissa lives with me in Țărână's family neighborhood and is pregnant with my child. I'd say our situations are vastly different."

Thomal's eyes flashed and the skin across his cheekbones reddened.

Pandra nearly sighed. *Jolly.* Such fun to discuss the sorry state of her marriage like this in front of everyone.

"It's still my call," Thomal gritted. "I'm also not thrilled with letting her go topside. If things get hairy up there, she can use the distraction to her advantage."

Jacken's black brows drew together. "Are you saying you think Pandra's a flight risk?"

There was a tick of a weird pause, like the room was thinking that such a thing wouldn't have been a consideration if Thomal and Pandra were a proper couple.

Toni shifted in her chair and grimaced. "This baby *lives* on my bladder. Pandra, don't you have *The Three Little Pigs* play to put on?"

Pandra paused over that comment, then realized what Toni was saying and chuckled. "Ah, indeed. Best I come back, then."

Thomal's eyes narrowed down to thin slits.

Jacken crossed his arms over his chest. "Look, Costache, you got something to say about this that outweighs the loss of all Fey power on earth, then by all means, let's hear it. Meanwhile I give your wife high marks for her willingness to step back to her old ways. Personally, I'm not happy about having to ask her to do that."

At least Jacken recognized how far Pandra had come in the last eight months.

Thomal's jaw flexed, muscles rippling up and down his cheeks. "I go with her. Every step of the way."

A snort slipped out of Pandra.

Thomal glowered at her. "You got a problem with that arrangement?"

"It's just that…you don't exactly fit in with the Iron Cock's usual clientele. They're a bit on the gritty side, and you're…" She shrugged. "Pretty."

"Then I guess you're going to have to hooker me up or slut me down or however you want to say it." Thomal's upper lip tightened at one corner. "You remember how to do that, right?"

She met his icy blue gaze for a long moment. "I remember."

CHAPTER THIRTY

FAITH CAREFULLY SMOOTHED OPEN THE vellum page on the top of her desk, lightly brushing her fingers over the raised gold lettering as she read the invitation. Idyll O'Shaughnessy and Garwald Istok, the distinguished part-owner of Garwald's Pub who'd stolen Aunt Idyll's heart within three days of her arrival in Țărână, were throwing a bonding celebration.

Faith smiled weakly. She was happy for her aunt, sincerely. Idyll was giddy as a schoolgirl, madly in love, and mated after spending her whole life unmarried because of being a Dragon. It was just…Faith shut her eyes, feeling an ugly coil of jealousy. Everyone who wanted a man around here seemed to have one.

Except for her.

She wouldn't have thought it possible to grow even more unhappy and lonely than she'd been before, but here she was, reaching new lows of miserable. And stuck. Leaving this backward town had gone from highly unlikely to extremely improbable now that both her twin sister and her adoptive mother lived down here. Not only that, but there was nothing left for her to do topside anymore. After eight more months of nurturing along her MCL with no improvement, she'd finally had to accept that her knee was permanently disabled. It was over. No more professional ballet.

"Acceptance" was one thing, though. "Moving on" was another. She just couldn't seem to find anything to fill the hole that'd been bored out of her soul by the loss of dance. What made matters worse was that all around her people were *living*, making lasting friendships, fashioning new careers, dating, falling in love. Getting mated.

Except for her.

She'd held out for Nyko for months, never dreaming the wait for him would be so interminable. In eight months that big lummox of a Vârcolac had never made even one move in her direction. She'd finally given up about a month ago and gone on a date with the owner of the community diner, Dănuţ Marga, who talked about himself the whole time and wasn't at all like an oversized teddy bear, and then Oszkar Vasilichi, Ţărână's head gemologist, who couldn't stop bragging about how much money he made for the community and had neglected to gaze at her as if she smelled like someone he'd get along with very well.

She'd given up after that. For good.

She'd tried to find meaning in other areas of her life by helping teach at Kacie's new dance school. But being at the barre reminded her of all her losses and failures, and she ended up just trudging through the motions. It was especially painful when Lysha, Deandra, and Kristara skipped in for the kindergarten class, dressed in adorable pink ballet gear. As the little ones rushed into the studio, Faith would rush out, choking back tears. Now that her name was forever off the ballet marquee, her maternal urges were on loudspeaker. She wanted babies, lots of them, and right away. But the only man she wanted as genetic contributor to her offspring—as mate, provider, and all-around hero—she couldn't have. Why was the cosmos also so determined to destroy her life on that score?

A tear spilled from her eyes and landed on Idyll's vellum invitation. Faith quickly sat back and—

She nearly fell off her chair when an ear-splitting siren started wailing.

CHAPTER THIRTY-ONE

Topside: downtown San Diego, three hours earlier

PANDRA GAVE HER BEST EFFORT to viewing Thomal with merely a clinical eye as he stepped out of the dressing room in her former leather clothing store haunt, *Rufskin,* located in Hillcrest, San Diego's gay district. But as her gaze traveled down to his crotch, her stomach went base over apex into some strange gymnastics because—

"Daaaamn, Costache," Gábor observed. "Those pants are way too tight, bro. You look like you have a vagina, but, like, a mutant one that's been injected with silicone or something."

Dev snorted.

Nyko didn't react. He was staring in horrified fascination at a mannequin wearing leather pants with the arse cheeks cut out of them. But then Nyko hardly talked anymore, anyroad.

"Screw this, I'm changing." Thomal took a backward step into the dressing room.

"No, it's perfect," Pandra interjected. "Your trousers need to be that tight for where we're going." And he didn't look like he had a vagina, rather the tight black leather formed a pronounced vee at his crotch, drawing focus to linger on the hefty bulge there. She exhaled tightly as her stomach did another backflip-double-tuck. Hells bells, she really needed to get some pull. After over eight months without sex, her nethers felt like they'd dried into an old husk. "Now let's put on your shirt." She pulled out a can of specialized spray paint and shook it with a *rattle, rattle, rattle.*

One of Thomal's golden brows hiked upward.

Gábor chortled. "Oh, this I gotta—"

"Say, mate," she said to Gábor. "Why don't you pop out and buy me my cigarettes. Camels. I'll need a lighter, too." She turned back to Thomal and gestured to their private dressing room. "Let's duck back in here. You'll need to take your real shirt off." And exposing a scaly dragon tattoo to public scrutiny was a topside no-no.

Thomal stepped inside and stripped off his shirt.

The door shut, enclosing them together. Alone. In intimate proximity. With one of them half-naked and wearing sexy leather pants. She heard herself breathe. She should get credit toward her debt of amends for this torture, shouldn't she?

She cleared her throat. "Turn around," she instructed him. "I need to spirit gum a layer of fake skin over your scaly dragon." Of course, she had to *touch* him to do that.

He gave her a dark look and didn't move.

She busied herself twisting open the bottle of spirit gum, just as casual as could be.

He turned around, and heat flushed through her. Cor blimey, her hubby had an outstanding rack of muscles cutting grooves into his v-shaped back. She licked her lips and went to work, begging her naughty bits not to juice up. A Vârcolac could scent that. After ignoring how firm and supple his skin was, she moved on to the rest of his getup, applying a temporary tattoo of a scorpion on the left side of his very kissable-looking throat, then preparing him for his spray-on shirt. She taped off his neck and halfway down his biceps, then tucked a towel around the waistband of his pants, her fingers brushing against the taut muscles of his lower abdomen. Her belly tightened. A few centimeters lower and…*best not to think about it, girl*. She chanced a glance at Thomal's face.

His eyes were focused across the dressing room, and they were dark and intense, his nostrils flared wide.

She swiftly moved on to the next task. Picking up the paint can, she proceeded to cover Thomal's torso in neon blue. That done, she added the finishing touches, dabbing purple hair dye onto the tips of his blond hair. Removing the tape and towel, she stepped back to view the finished product, and—

Love a duck.

"Well?" Thomal asked.

She couldn't answer, momentarily robbed of speech. She'd turned him into a one-thousand-horse-powered sex machine. Considering that his shirt was, quite literally, painted on, every chiseled, carved, cut, and sculpted muscle on his upper torso, along with the flat discs of his nipples and an old bullet wound on the left of his abdomen, were displayed for all and sundry to drool over. The getup accentuated the steely blue eyes and dizzying handsomeness that were already his claim to fame. He looked hotter than a sauna in Hell, and there wasn't a man, woman, or animal on earth who wouldn't want to jump his meat and two veg the second they took a gander at him.

She finally got her mouth to produce a sound. "That'll do," she murmured. "Now out you go, love. It's my turn to change."

He didn't say anything. Just left. As the door opened and he stepped out, she heard the warriors start in on him. The door shut, muffling the voices. *Right, then. Get yourself together.*

She tarted herself up in an ankle-to-neck leather bodysuit *a lá* Cat Woman. The garment might as well have been spray-painted on her body, too, it fit that tight. Like a second skin, it left nothing to the imagination, although it still did its job of covering the dragon tattoo on her back and her fecked-up belly. Metal zippers accented both sides of her calves, her left thigh, and her right breast. All the zippers were faux, except for the one over her boob. That one was unzipped, her breast swelling through the opening, appearing naked, when, in fact, it was concealed by skin-colored material. But it took a double- or triple-take to realize it, and the effect was eye-popping sexy.

"Wow," Dev said when she stepped out of the dressing room.

Thomal's jaw locked down.

"Hey, look," Gábor chirped. "It's the Camel Toe Twins."

Pandra called Duane to find out where the Iron Cock was tonight. Her former minion copped an attitude with her for being gone so many long months, but he also sounded creepily excited when he promised to meet her at the club tonight with Bo Bo. *Sorry, chums.* She planned to have all done and dusted well before those two showed. "Here's the address." She handed a piece of paper to Dev.

Ten minutes later they pulled up in front of a grubby four-story apartment building, the entire top floor of which was supposedly dedicated to the sex club tonight. They got out of the Dodge van, and Dev stepped up to Pandra and Thomal. "Here are your earpieces." He held out two on the palm of his hand.

Thomal took one.

She took the other and jammed it into her right ear.

"Gábor, Nyko, and I will man the perimeter." Dev glanced between the two of them. "We're here for you if you need us."

Thomal shoved his earpiece deeper. "I think I can say with reasonable accuracy that my old lady doesn't need help in the *seduction* department." He spun around and stalked inside the building.

She and Thomal had to walk up all four flights of warped stairs, the elevator being clapped out—hardly surprising in a place like this. They passed a long line of scantily-clad people assembled on the stairs. Hungry, devouring stares followed their progress, heads craning, although for the first time ever in an arrival at the Iron Cock, she wasn't necessarily the headliner.

At the top, she blazed up a Camel, puffing smoke sideways to avoid giving the bouncer a face full. "'Ow do, Curtis," she greeted the large black man. "Some good bagging off happening in there tonight?"

"There's a cover charge." Curtis didn't bother to look at her as he passed on this information. His attention was stuck on Thomal. "Economic downswing."

She *tut-tutted.* "Cor, what's the world coming to when good folk won't spend their brass on a proper felching or snowballing? Anyroad, get knotted. I brought a toy with me." She waved airily at Thomal. "He's my pass."

Thomal played his part, forming his lips into the kind of cocky smile that had Curtis rapidly reconsidering his straightness, his eyes nearly pin wheeling in their sockets.

She pushed past the bouncer and made her way inside, Thomal next to her.

The Iron Cock's typical dark, sordid atmosphere instantly engulfed them: loud music, streaks of white light slicing across the shadows, the suffocating heated *whoosh* of too many bodies packed into a too-small place. The smell of sweat and the distinctive musk of sex assaulted her senses. It had never bothered her before, but now she had to drag hard on her cigarette to keep the vom down.

Beside her, Thomal lifted his lip into a derisive sneer. "Look at them," he said, a glare aimed at the dance floor, where people were moving in an undulating mash of simulated sex acts. "They're making a travesty out of what sex is supposed to be. It's grotesque."

She held her Camel between the vee of her fingers and flicked her pinkie against her thumbnail as she surveyed the crowd. Edgar had to be here. The Iron Cock only operated one night a week, and he never missed. "Didn't know you were such the romantic type, hubby."

"With the right woman."

Pandra clamped her teeth into a tight grind. *Aye, that's right*. She was Dirty Pandra. Polish a pence to a high shine and underneath the gloss, it'll always be copper, never gold. She squeezed her eyes closed against a spike of temper. God's balls, why was she doing this? If she were back in Ţărână right now, she'd be making faces out of snack time pretzels and raisins for her students. Not being reminded of all the arsed-up things she used to do. And be.

She felt Thomal stiffen beside her, and turned to see what had snagged his attention. He'd spotted a couple in the act of oral sex, the man propped against a wall, neck arched and mouth open around moans the music was drowning out. The woman was on her knees in front of him, her hands wrapped around his naked buttocks, her cheeks hollowing and bulging as she worked the guy's stalk. Both the man and the woman were blonde, probably creating a decent facsimile of what Arc and Pandra had resembled the night of the "event."

Pandra's heart slumped into her stomach, and then both dropped away. *That's that, then. The end of the road, girlie-girl. Accept it.* Thomal would never forgive her. Time to give up the fantasy that he'd eventually see all she'd done to make amends and give her a chance. He'd never acknowledge the changes in her. *Never.* There was just too much wreckage on the road between them.

Oddly, such a thing would've been a doss for Old Pandra to deal with. But New Pandra had feelings, too many for her not to care about that loss. "Let's push off." Her voice grated through the narrow opening of her larynx. She'd come so far these last months, only to discover she'd moved the sum total of a gnat's whisker.

Thomal frowned. "You don't see the guy?"

She did, actually. Edgar was at the bar. He'd already spotted her, his gaze zeroing in on her as if through a gun sight. "He's here."

"What's the problem, then?"

She held her cigarette in front of her and stared at the glowing red tip as she worked to ice herself down, shoving emotions back into the trap of her ribcage like biting cobras. "Nothing," she said in a jaundiced tone. "Everything's brill." She mashed out her cigarette against the wall and tossed it aside. "To the dance floor, love. It's time to put on a show. We'll have to pretend to get into a fight." Her smile felt like it deformed her face into a unnatural mask. "Think you can pull that off, snookums?"

The hubby gave her a strange look.

CHAPTER THIRTY-TWO

THOMAL FOLLOWED PANDRA INTO THE sweaty, gyrating flotsam and jetsam of the worst society had to offer, the song *You Done Told Everybody* by Pearlene booming a dance-grind beat from several six-foot-tall speakers. Multiple pairs of hands caressed his upper body and grabbed his ass along the way, igniting a hot knot of aggression in his gut. *Fucking 'verts.* Everyone might think they had the right to take whatever liberties they damned well pleased because this was a sex club, but being treated like tonight's daddy-mack without even being asked didn't exactly put lead in his pencil.

One woman made a grab for his dick, another ran her tongue suggestively over her teeth at him, her huge tits joggling and bobbling; without benefit of upper body clothing, those things made quite a spectacle. Others might find those enormous jugs par excellence, but Thomal had the misfortune of being married to the hottest thing going on two legs. He'd turned impervious to every other female in existence the instant he'd sunk his fangs into a certain black-eyed half-Răŭ.

Pandra found a spot on the dance floor near the bar and started shakin' her thang. Taut, well-defined muscles flexed along her thighs and in her sweet ass, her body made to look even hotter by the tight covering of leather; like she was naked, but not really. It'd been a long time since he'd seen her wear something so sexy, and his balls were taking note of the outfit with a hard pull north. *Not* that he'd ever lost sight of how gorgeous she was for even a nanosecond.

Everywhere his wife had gone in the community over these past months, he'd gravitated to a place nearby. Partially out of a mate-thing, but also because of some strange… compulsion to watch her: observe the luscious curve of her calves when she scaled a ladder, ogle her perfectly formed rump as she bent over a playground sandbox, appreciate the way her bouncy breasts filled out a red lifeguard bathing suit. And watch her transform from black-eyed beast into some version of *woman*, vulnerable in some ways, wounded in lots of others.

Right before his eyes, Pandra had stopped being so ruthlessly contained. No longer did she listen to people with a blank, sphinxlike face, as if she was holding herself in constant readiness to react to the next bad thing coming down the pike—not a matter of *if* that bad thing was coming, just when and where. Which was a sad way to imagine her living, and the thought sometimes did weird things to his stomach.

These days she tilted her head when people talked to her, warmed her expression, *smiled*, which really weirded-out his insides, sending his guts slipping and sliding, like icing off the top of a double-layer cake left in the sun too long. And all the while Pandra had been making this miraculous transformation, Thomal had remained at a fucking standstill.

He just couldn't seem to figure out how to move forward. It didn't help that he wasn't sure what he wanted from Pandra. A part of him craved a wife in truth: somebody to come home to, a chance at a family, *regular sex*. But so much of those longings got ruined by the short-fused triggers littering the space between them: the word tequila, the cord that plugged his telephone into the wall, the shackles hanging in Ţărână's armory reserved for misbehaving Vârcolac. The sight of a blonde chick giving head to a blonde guy. Arc a ruined mess.

Hell, how could Thomal make a life for himself with the woman who'd so totally screwed up his brother? How could he allow himself to find happiness with the woman he should have killed?

He didn't know how. He didn't know what to do to save Arc or how to get his own head on straight. He didn't know how to quit being such a cold bastard to the woman who'd set all this crap in motion or even if he wanted to stop. And *if* he decided he wanted Pandra, he didn't have a clue how to take the first step toward her. No, the second step. Pandra had already taken the first with her apology. His dazzling response to that? A grunt. For shit's sake, he was such a total waste of skin about this whole thing, he was more impotent than even when his dick hadn't worked. A joyful thought.

Pandra spun around on the dance floor, her long hair whiplashing across his face, soft and filled with her sent. Tension landed square between his shoulder blades as his semi-aroused member launched upward another few inches. It'd been too long since he'd been inside his wife's warm kooch. *For-fucking-ever.* In eight months of sexual functioning, he'd only been laid one time. *Once.* Which was absolute bullshit.

Pandra wrapped her arms around his neck, her body moving sinuously against him with her dirty dancing. A quick slice of her eyes acknowledged the stiff length of wood she found in the vicinity of his zipper, but then she was peering over his shoulder, padlocking Edgar. She gave the ass gasket a smoldering look that oozed *if I get my hands on you, your clothes are coming off with my teeth.*

Hostile jealousy spread like peanut butter cement in Thomal's gut. He forced a swift breath. *Cool it, Costache. She's only on the mission.*

Yeah, but *was* she? His body was rubbing hers as closely as vice versa, yet he might as well have been a department store dummy for all the reaction he was getting out of her. He knew her sex-scent—every time he fed on her, his olfactory lobe got a knee-trembling blast of it—and right now it was nowhere to be found. Maybe she really did want to fuck Videon's scumbag friend. A girl like her had needs, after all, and she certainly wasn't getting any action out of Thomal's Fruit of the Looms.

"Edgar's watching us," she said into his ear. "Grab my arse or something, will you? He'll want to think he's nabbing me from you."

Well, gee… He complied, of course, grabbing and squeezing her moneymaker, ripe flesh over firm muscle in his palms, the solid curve of her lower buttocks rounding toward heaven's tightest gate. Lust shot through his balls and ransacked his brain. With his hands, he jacked her hips forward, anger and arousal surging through him until he was insane with the need to have her beneath him, legs spread wide, the vigor of his hips pounding his cock deep inside her body.

Pandra lurched out of his hold, ignoring him as she danced around, putting her back to his front. She rotated her caboose against his crotch, and he nearly groaned as he imagined taking her from behind and…*screw it.* He grabbed her by the waist and pumped his hips forward as if he was doing that very thing. The feel of her butt cheeks bumping into his member squeezed some pre-come to the head of his fully aroused staff. *Shit.* His pants were so tight, if he accidentally shot his wad, he'd probably blow his boots off.

With his mind still on a *screw it* path to trouble, he ran his hands up the side of her ribcage to—

She still wasn't paying any attention to him. He growled low, the noise scorching a path from his chest, up his throat, and through his nostrils. Hauling her around, he tangled a fist in her hair, forcing her to meet his eyes—*his* eyes. "Stop looking at that fuck pig."

She startled for a heartbeat, then she must've figured he was setting their fight in motion.

She gave him a hard shove.

He stumbled backward two paces, then caught his footing.

Pandra turned toward a tall, broad dude working his way through the dancers. Edgar. Her hips moved sinuously as she sauntered in the other man's direction, promising him all kinds of ecstasy.

Thomal lifted his lip in a possessive snarl. *She's playing the game. Chill-ax.* He watched a dark, venal desire come into his wife's gaze that guaranteed Edgar everything she wasn't giving to her own husband, and there was no *chilling* to be had.

Thomal stepped forward, manacled his fingers around Pandra's wrist, and jerked her back toward him.

Rolling with what she clearly thought was more of the show, her other hand shot out and cracked him across his face, rattling several back teeth. He staggered.

She spun away from him and launched herself at Edgar. Her legs wrapped his waist, her arms circled his neck, and then a nuclear bomb went off because…She planted her lips against the dude's in an open-mouthed, jaw-working kiss.

Vicious heat napalmed Thomal's entire body. Reasonable warrior went *see ya later, alligator* and bonded male Vârcolac came rampaging out.

His fangs ruptured out of his gums and he flew forward with a wall-rattling roar.

✧　✧　✧

PANTING FROM STREAKING DOWN FLOUR flights of stairs wearing five-inch heels, Pandra dove into the Dodge cargo van, making it inside just as the filth arrived. Three black and white cruisers squealed to a stop in front of the Iron Cock's apartment building, their bright lights strobing through the Dodge's windshield. The van door slammed shut, and Dev rammed his foot to the gas pedal, stonking it around a corner.

Pandra straightened in her seat, her outfit plastered uncomfortably to her body by sweat. The van was fitted with two long, removable bench seats facing each other. She was on the bench aimed forward, next to Nyko. Thomal and Gábor were seated across from her on the rear-facing one.

Several tense moments throbbed past.

Dev's hands were knuckle-white on the steering wheel. "Did anyone see your fangs during your shit fit?"

"I don't know," Thomal answered, tight-lipped, blood leaking from the corner of his mouth.

You should see the other guy, would've fit perfectly here. Edgar was now wearing his head backward and the Iron Cock was all but demolished. When a Vârcolac went berserk, he certainly didn't do the job half-arsed.

"Dammit to hell," Dev ground out. "You're on report, Costache, *and* I'm putting you on elevator cable duty next month."

"*What*?!" Thomal blasted.

"Oh, ho, ho," Gábor laughed.

That wouldn't be any fun. From what Pandra understood, a group of Ţărână's construction workers had to climb the half-mile elevator shafts once a year to grease the cables and check for fraying. She'd heard it was sweaty, exhausting, back-breaking work.

"That's assed up, Nichita."

"You knew what needed to go down on this mission," Dev countered sharply. "And you approved it."

Thomal's face darkened. "Maybe I didn't expect my mate to be quite so fucking thorough in her seduction." He rounded on her. "You *kissed* that cockbox, Pandra."

"No," she said quietly.

"I saw you," Thomal hissed.

"I mean, no, I'm not your mate. I'm a bottle of blood you booze up on whenever you need a fix." Her lungs hurt. Going back to smoking after so many months, probably. Or maybe it was the pain of being filled with too many cobras. "You don't have the right to call me a mate, or even to expect me to act like one, if you're not going to treat me like one."

Thomal's eyes flashed. "What the hell does that mean, Pandra? You *wanted* to bone Edgar?"

"Jesus wept." He was so stupid. And blind. "Why don't you admit why you're truly in a dither, Thomal?" She leaned forward in her seat. "Not because Edgar wanted to shag me. But because *you* did. Dirty, disgusting, hateful Pandra." Tears balled in her chest. Her stomach wrenched. "I fully realize that I've had a dear bill to pay for what I did. I understand that. So tell me what I need to do to pay it. *Tell me what I need to do* to earn your forgiveness and I'll do it, I swear. Because I can't keep living like this."

Thomal swiped the back of his hand across his bloody lip.

She sat back. "Living in Ţărână has...has done things to me, Thomal. It's changed me. It's not fair to show me all the possibilities in life and then not give me a chance to have them. Family and children, and..." A tear rose to the corner of her eye, but she blinked it back. "I've always known that I'd have nippers one day—it's what I'm bred for—but Raymond would've controlled them. Now there's this whole community, and...I want things. But if I can't have them, ever, then I *am* hanging on a meat hook as no more than your blood source, even if it's only fecking metaphorical."

Thomal stared down at the floor of the van, his face and neck rigid, his voice sadly absent.

So that's your answer. She swallowed once and shored herself up, puttying enough pieces back into place to say what needed to be said next. "You have to kill me, then."

Thomal's gaze bolted up.

She didn't waver. "Or if you can't, have someone else do the task. My death will free you." No actual tears fell, but on the inside, her heart wept huge, drowning droplets. "And me, as well," she added on a whisper.

Dev's grip tightened on the steering wheel again.

Nyko fiddled his hands together in his lap.

Silence engulfed them all like a malaise.

At last there was the *grumble* of the elevator moving, then twenty long minutes later, the bicycle chain *whisk* of the garage doors opening.

Then there was another noise.

As the five of them stepped from the van, they all heard it.

The community's emergency Om Răm breach alarm was blaring.

CHAPTER THIRTY-THREE

ŢĂRÂNĂ WAS UNDER ATTACK!

Faith raced out onto her bedroom balcony and looked down on Main Street, her heart thumping hard and fast. Women were screaming and running, some clutching children, most being rushed along by their husbands. Behind them, a swarm of dark-clothed men were bearing down on the fleeing townsfolk like an infestation of mutant black insects.

Faith gripped the railing as she watched people of the community being felled beneath brutal punches or bludgeoning clubs. *Kacie*! *Where are you*?! She frantically searched the chaos for her sister and her aunt. *Please, let them be—*

Faith gasped. *Marissa*! Dev's wife was falling behind in the confusion. Hugely pregnant, Marissa couldn't move at much more than an ungainly hobble, and as she lagged farther and farther back, two—*No*! Two red-haired Om Rău grabbed Marissa under her arms and scooped her off her feet.

Marissa's face went ashen with terror and her hands scrabbled protectively toward her swollen belly.

"No!" Faith screamed.

Dev Nichita appeared out of nowhere, seeming to rise up from the very cave rock. His eyes glowed pure murder, his fangs extended like twin white blades. He grabbed the two redheaded Om Rău by the backs of their skulls and rammed them at each other face on face. Their heads exploded like two plates of Spaghetti Bolognese thrown together.

Faith staggered back and gagged.

Dev snatched his wife into his arms and took off like

thunder for the mansion.

Faith pressed a hand over her mouth, her eyes watering from the bitterness in her throat. She thought she'd seen the worst of violence when Adonis had strangled Bald Guy, but that had been nothing compared to—

Her hand flopped down to her side as she gaped in awestruck horror at the man who'd just appeared on Main Street.

Nearly eight feet tall, he was *unreal*, dressed in a black leather loin cloth, short black boots, and that was all…besides the adornment of a T-shaped chain that swung from his pierced nipples down to his pierced navel. A glorious mane of bright red hair fell down his back and well past his butt, turning him into a creature both beautiful and savage.

Bulldozing through the crowd, the redheaded savage charged straight for The TradeMark clothing store. Without bothering with anything so insignificant as a door, he crashed through the plate glass window in a burst of jagged shards, stomping a mannequin in half as he stormed inside.

Beth Costache's petrified scream rang out.

Faith clutched a hand to her throat.

Faith, I'm here, I'm safe.

Faith swung her head around and peered at one of the balconies below, relief nearly taking her knees out when she saw her sister standing with a group of friends.

Oslo, London, Dublin, Berlin—all the second-floor balconies below were filling with people. Faith couldn't see Rome, directly beneath her feet, but could hear the frantic chatter.

Faith knitted her brow at Kacie as she shared a moment of worry and fear with her twin.

Bull-throated shouting called Faith's attention back to the town. She turned to look…and felt the blood drain from her cheeks. The redheaded savage was standing on a shelf of cave rock jutting over the town cinema. Faith could see him clearly. He was directly across from her balcony, about seventy-five feet away. He had Beth.

Another red-haired enemy was clutching Ellen the dentist, and still more Om Ră"u hovered behind the four.

Both women were white-faced and sobbing.

Beneath the shelf, several Vârcolac warriors were already scaling the cliff face: Dev, back on the scene now, plus Breen, Kasson, and Thomal, who was nearly unrecognizable with his purple-dyed hair and his sort-of clothes. Ellen's husband, Pedrr, was also trying to climb the rock wall, but kept falling off in his panic.

Jacken was standing in front of the movie theater, his legs planted wide, ruthless black eyes locked on the redheaded savage. Jacken had a knife in his hand, but no place to throw it. The savage was holding Beth directly in front of him.

Ellen's captor was similarly using her as a shield.

The redheaded savage gestured to Ellen. "Not one of the women I originally threatened to take, but she'll do." He laughed.

Faith cringed as the hair on her arms stood on end. Good God, that laugh was a chainsaw tearing through monkey bars—pure evil.

"You've captured two *mated* women," Jacken pointed out, his voice calm, but taut. "They're of no use to you, Josnic."

Josnic…Faith had heard this story. Over a year ago a faction of Topside Om Ră"u had been in the middle of handing over Marissa, Hadley, and Kendra to some of the Underground Om Ră"u when the Vârcolac warriors had come to the rescue and stolen the women. Enraged at losing these precious Dragons, Josnic, leader of the Underground Om Ră"u, had invaded Ţărână and threatened to take Beth and the librarian, Hannah, if his three women weren't returned. They *weren't* returned, of course, and the town had lived with Josnic's threat ever since. Today, it appeared, was the day of reckoning.

Josnic hugged Beth closer to his body, his forearm pushing up her breasts, and smiled meanly down at Jacken. "I can
still find something to do with mated women."

Beth whimpered, her lips quivering.

Josnic's voice lowered to impossible octaves. "You *owed*
me three women, Brun. You should've paid that debt with
ones that didn't mean shit to you when you had the chance.
Ejohn," Josnic addressed one of the Om Răū behind him.
"We have an unwelcome visitor."

Goodness, Faith hadn't even noticed Thomal, he'd moved
so stealthily. Now he was at the top of the outcropping of
rock, a knife clenched in his teeth like in the movies.

"Costache!" Dev yelled as the Om Răū named Ejohn
proceeded to step forward and drop a rock on top of Thomal.

But Thomal had already seen it and was rotating out of
the way—unfortunately, the sharp, twisting evasive movement
made him lose his grip. He fell.

Breen reached out to make a grab for him. For his efforts,
he was pulled off the cliff face, too.

Whoom! The boulder hit first, splatting apart against the
cave floor, then Breen and Thomal followed, both men
landing hard and rolling.

Shouts erupted behind Josnic and the air was suddenly
cacophonous with the sounds of combat. Faith's heart surged
forward with hope. The Vârcolac had launched an attack from
behind to save Beth and Ellen! She couldn't see the fight—it
was too far back on the outthrust of rock—but she could hear
the thuds of blow meeting flesh, ragged breathing, incoherent
oaths, and…and then the noises faded.

Josnic threw back his lion's head and laughed uproarious-
ly.

The back of Jacken's neck turned red.

"We go," Josnic said to his men, then his vicious black
eyes bored into Jacken. "Here's your woman's life now,
Vârcolac." Reaching up to the collar of Beth's blouse, Josnic

ripped it down the middle, tearing away her bra with it.

Beth let out a wail and fumbled to cover her bare breasts.

The women on the second-floor balconies upped the volume of their screaming.

Faith clasped both hands to her mouth, a wintry rush of panic washing down her spine. *Please, God, let somebody save her.*

But no other warrior was high enough on the cliff face to do something. Josnic turned around…so did Ellen's captor. They were leaving! Everything was going wrong too fast!

"Stop!" Faith called out, raising her arm. "Please! I'll go with you!"

Instant silence.

Josnic turned back around. His gaze swept the balconies, found her and pinioned her.

Faith dropped her hand back to her side and shuddered. She'd blurted those words out of fear for Beth and Ellen's welfare, but now that she'd spoken them, she felt their rightness.

Both Beth and Ellen had children, homes, husbands.

Faith had nothing.

She didn't even know how to live this new life she'd been handed, without the rigid discipline of ballet to guide her, without Kacie—not now that her twin had a mountain of friends—and without Nyko. She just didn't know how to exist in the shadow of so much rejection. And there it was: the deciding factor. It was time to go.

Her entire body iced with the thought of leaving, never again to see her twin or her aunt. Would they miss her? Yes, of course. At first. But they both had such full lives now. She stood on their periphery, anyway, and that was beginning to hurt just too much. Would she miss them? Immensely. Nyko, too. But it helped knowing that with this final act of saving two dear women, Faith could go out with courage. She'd been acting uncharacteristically cowardly for too long.

She didn't delude herself about this choice. Wherever that redheaded savage took her, it wasn't going to be a pleasant place. But she was a practical woman who'd spent the better part of her years dealing with life's harsh realities. She'd deal with this, too. And the odd truth was, she'd rather go someplace bad, where her unhappiness wouldn't be questioned and her hopelessness would make sense, rather than continue listening to her sister and aunt incessantly harp on her to *try* a little harder here in Țărână.

She was so sick of the struggle.

"You have to let both of those women go in exchange for me," she called across to Josnic. "You said that Jacken owes you three unmated women. Well, I'm an unmarked *Royal* Dragon, and that's worth three females, for sure."

Josnic's eyes blazed.

The community as a whole unfroze at that, voices from every direction shouting at her.

"Don't go!"

"Stop!"

"You have no idea what you're doing!"

"Faith, please listen…!"

Through it all, she heard Kacie's voice, the loudest, the most panicked and alarmed. But Faith forced herself to block her sister's protests from her ears. From her mind.

"Agreed." Josnic smiled, the expression somehow both attractive and menacing. "Krolan," he said, and a different black-haired Om Rău stepped forward, black teeth tattoos whirling up the entire length of both arms.

This Om Rău lifted a crossbow, sighted, and shot.

A bolt *zinged* past Faith's head and embedded in the wall of the mansion behind her. A long cord trailed from the end of it, and the black-haired shooter quickly hammered his end into the cave wall. Next he laid a pair of hand-holds over the cord and *whizzed* them over to her.

She caught them and climbed up onto her balcony railing.

Her pulse pounded into her throat. She gripped the hand-holds so tightly, her fingers throbbed.

The shouting of the people around her rose to a deafening high.

Below her, Jacken looked on the verge of blowing a vein.

Terror over what she was about to do shrank her stomach. She hesitated, trembling.

With a lascivious sneer, Josnic seized one of Beth's breasts in his massive fist and squeezed it.

"Let those two women go now," Faith ordered in a tremulous voice. "I won't come until you do." Sweat trickled from her armpits.

"One now," Josnic countered. "The other when you get here." He gestured to Ellen's captor.

The red-headed Om Rău took a step back from Ellen and kicked her in the rear end.

Screaming, Ellen flew over the side of the rock shelf, her arms flailing.

On the ground below, Pedrr shouted.

Dev sprang off the side of the cliff and snatched Ellen out of the air, tucking her close to his chest. They spun together, picking up speed. As they hit ground, Dev angled his body sideways, taking the brunt of the fall onto his shoulder.

Pedrr staggered over to Ellen and hugged his wife.

Faith's attention was pulled away from the scene by movement on one of the balconies adjacent to hers.

It was Pandra, dressed in...*my goodness*, some sort of outlandish leather jumpsuit. Leaping up onto her own railing, Pandra started hurdling balconies toward Faith.

A band of panic clutched Faith's lungs. *No!* If Pandra caught her and stopped her, who would save Beth? Not even one warrior was left on the rock face now.

Someone pounded on her locked bedroom door. The knob rattled.

No more time. Be brave, Faith! She leapt off her railing.

Wobbling on her hand-holds like a drunken acrobatics performer, she rode the cord for only a few feet before bumping into the large steel bars that surrounded the mansion. Wriggling her slender body sideways, she made it through the two-foot space that separated each bar, then crammed her eyes shut as she sped into open air.

Hundreds of voices rose in horror around her.

It felt like she zip-lined forever across the cave, until, finally, a large hand curled around one side of her waist, bringing her to an abrupt halt. Her feet happily found solid contact on the cave shelf. She started to exhale in relief…then caught an up-close view of Josnic, and the sight stopped the breath in her lungs. With his massive bone structure and body made out of Incredible Hulk parts, the Om Răn leader was even more terrifying than she'd realized. How had she ever thought of Nyko as big?

Josnic shoved her at Ellen's former captor, and then she was dealing with a different problem. Her throat pinched off and her eyes watered uncontrollably, blurring her vision. The red-headed Om Răn exuded a stink unlike anything she'd ever encountered, and she'd been around some very sweaty dancers in her days. But this was like…spoiled meat mixed with a hundred sweaty jockstraps and a swamp of rotten vegetation. Her head swam from the strength of it, almost making her think she was imagining it when she heard Josnic tell Jacken…

"Think I'll keep this one, after all." Laughing that horrible laugh of his, Josnic tossed Beth over his shoulder.

Faith shook her head violently, trying without success to voice a protest. Her tongue was glued to the roof of her parched mouth.

Zzzzzz…

All heads turned at the sound of someone else traveling down the zip-line.

It was Pandra. She'd looped a belt over the crossbow bolt

cord and was coming at their group, *fast*, her focus fixed on Josnic.

Josnic's gaze lit. He handed Beth off to one of his men and prepared to grab his new prize.

Pandra punched out her legs as she arrived at the platform, landing a two-footed blow dead-center to Josnic's chest.

Josnic hurtled backward, stumbling down onto one knee, his eyes flaring wide.

His Om Răeu brethren gaped, as well. It was probably extremely rare to see their enormous leader knocked down. Most likely never by a woman.

Josnic slowly lowered his head, peering down at his chest in abject shock. Blood was snaking from two holes there.

Pandra had stabbed him with her high heels.

Moving in a coordinated blur, Pandra leapt at Beth's keeper, dealing the Om Răeu an uppercut that knocked his feet out from under him. As the man took a trip down to the flat of his back, Pandra plucked Beth off his shoulder, then rushed to the rim of the rock shelf. She dropped Beth as gently as possible into Thomal's waiting arms below.

Thomal stared at Pandra, the look on his face as shocked as Josnic's.

Pandra paused, locking gazes with her husband for a long moment.

Josnic surged to his feet. His eyes flashed red and he bellowed a deafening roar.

Faith clapped her hands over her ears, swaying in her captor's arms.

Pandra straightened slowly, her focus never leaving Thomal. "Be free, love," she said so softly, Faith almost didn't hear. Pandra took a step backward.

An expression of utter panic spread across Thomal's face. "No!" he shouted. Setting Beth down, he started to claw up the rock face. "Pandra! Don't!" Rubble cascaded down.

Pandra turned toward Josnic, lids sealed, and lifted her chin to his blow.

CHAPTER THIRTY-FOUR

NYKO STRIPPED DOWN QUICKLY TO his underwear and boots, moving in a precise and unhurried way, even though panic was a hot knot of twisted metal in his stomach. He strapped on an utility belt, briskly filling it with one sheathed knife and two flash grenades. Cylindrically-shaped, flash grenades contained a pyrotechnic concoction that exploded into an intense white flare when detonated, effectively blinding everyone nearby for about five seconds. The accompanying loud blast also caused temporary loss of hearing and messed with the ear's inner fluid, throwing off balance.

Not that he had anything against fragmentation grenades. He would've used them on the Om Rău in a heartbeat if he could've been sure that Faith and Pandra wouldn't be within the blast radius. But the Om Rău had just grabbed themselves a Royal Dragon and a half-Rău, half-Fey female; they wouldn't be letting such catches out of their sights any time soon. Already bonded to Thomal, Pandra shouldn't have been considered one of their prizes, but there was some question as to whether the Topside Rău-Fey race was immune to the procreation block rendered by Vârcolac mating; which was why Raymond Parthen still hunted Toni.

"Stop what you're doing," Jacken ordered.

He was standing next to Nyko at the mouth of the Hell Tunnels in Stânga Town, his face reaching record levels of hardness, his eyes fierce. "In over a hundred years of living in these caves," his brother went on, "a Vârcolac has never made it through the Hell Tunnels. You won't, either."

"Maybe I will. Maybe I won't. Alex and I have already mapped over half the Tunnels. I only need to find my way through the other half." *Piece of cake in a million-degree heat, right?* He might've had a fighting chance if it was guaranteed he could get through the first half in a decent amount of time. But with all the sudden dips and sharp turns in those dark passageways, he'd only ever seemed to bump around on his practice runs.

"Listen to me." Jacken grabbed Nyko by the arm. "I know you're feeling like shit about losing Faith, same as every warrior in this town felt like shit about losing Gwyn. But do you remember why we didn't go after Gwyn, even though it was our fault and we owed her? Because *there was nothing we could do*. If you go in there, you'll end up dying for nothing."

"I have to at least try." Nyko shrugged off his brother's grip. "I couldn't live with myself if I didn't. This is all my fault." *Once again.* "Faith volunteered to go—she left the community—because of me." Because he hadn't done a danged thing to help her, just sat back with a bag of popcorn and watched her grow sadder and sadder. Congratulations to him. He'd succeeded in removing himself from hero status.

Yes, Faith's sister and her aunt had abandoned her, too, but those two had become too caught up in lives they'd never had before, or had ever hoped to have, to see what was happening. *He'd* seen, though. Which meant the sole responsibility for this sat squarely on his shoulders.

"Dammit, Nyko, stop being—"

"Faith's not Gwyn!" he shouted at his brother. "Take two seconds to imagine Toni in Oṭărât, Jacken, and then maybe you can understand what I'm going through. Faith is my woman, but I...I blew it. I let her down, and I'm not going to keep doing that. I'd rather die than do nothing, so if it comes to that, then it does."

A vein in Jacken's temple pulsed furiously. "Fuck it. All right. If you're so determined to do this, then I'm coming with you." He yanked off his shirt.

"No." He used his Big Brother voice for that one.

Thomal jogged up to them. "Hey, hold up."

Thomal had disappeared briefly to take Beth to Arc, who'd been in the rearguard battle with Nyko to squash Josnic. Their group of warriors had been waylaid by a new swarm of Om Răú, and both he and Arc had been injured, Nyko receiving a nasty knife wound to the left shoulder.

"I've been talking to Alex about the Hell Tunnels," Thomal said, "and I made this for you." He offered Nyko a large, flat rectangular-shaped something. "It's a map of the passageways. I drew it in three-dimensions, showing all of the hills and turns. It should help you get through the first part faster."

"You *made* this?" Nyko accepted the map, stunned.

"Yeah. I etched it into metal so it wouldn't melt in the heat, then edged the sides in high-grade rubber so you could hold onto it without burning your hands."

Nyko studied the map. Holy smokes, this was exactly what he needed. "This is fantastic." He gave Thomal another astounded look. "I can't believe you etched it."

Color rose in Thomal's cheeks. He shrugged. "I used to mess around with carving a while back. Anyway..." He pointed to the map. "See this fork here? Alex says that once you reach this point, you should be able to take either the left or right route and get into Oțărât."

"Okay." Nyko took a breath and said, "Thank you." Thomal might've just saved his life.

Thomal nodded shortly. "I'd go with you, if I could."

But without any Răú in him, he wouldn't last more than a minute in the extreme heat.

Thomal's jaw hardened. "Just get in there and get back, Nyko, all right? That's my woman in there, too."

Really? *Since when*? Nyko grimaced inwardly. Kind of an ungracious thought to have, considering Thomal's major contribution to the rescue operation, but…true nonetheless.

"I'm going with you," Jacken repeated, then gestured at the map. "There's a good chance we'll make it now."

"Good? I'd say *fair*, at best." Nyko tucked the map under his arm. "Even though I may have a possible way into Oṭărât now, my ability to grab the women then get back out, with an entire town of Om Rău to face down, is still a huge IF."

"All the more reason for me to come along and help fight."

"No." Nyko remained adamant. The mission was still too suicidal for him to bring along his brother. Not with Jacken becoming a father any day now. Nyko laid a hand on Jacken's shoulder and lowered his voice. "You have a wife and a soon-to-be-born kid who need you a lot more than I do for this mission. You can't go with me."

Jacken's lips compressed into a thin line. He stepped back, his hands on his hips.

"I *know* you know that," Nyko said.

Turning aside, Jacken stared off into Stânga Town.

"I'm sorry, I just can't allow it," Nyko maintained. "I'll knock you out if I have to."

Jacken scowled, then cursed. "At least feed before you go." He gestured at Nyko's knife wound. "You've lost a decent amount of blood."

"I don't have time. Every second that passes puts Faith and Pandra in more danger. Josnic and Lorke could be doling the women out to their men right now." Nyko aimed his steps toward the Hell Tunnels, but then paused. His chest jerked once. He turned back around, keeping his voice soft enough for Jacken's ears only. "You won't admit it, but you're worried about what kind of father you're going to make. We were raised by a complete ass, so we don't have the best model for that sort of thing. But…you're going to be a great dad." Nyko's heart folded inward. Dang, he'd really wanted to meet his niece or nephew. "I need for you to know that."

Jacken's nostrils flared and quivered almost imperceptibly. He recognized a final goodbye when he heard it.

Nyko grabbed Jacken by the back of the neck and squeezed hard, giving him a firm shake. A big brother silent message for *don't mess up your life when I'm not around to kick your butt.*

Nyko turned around for the last time and took off into the Hell Tunnels.

CHAPTER THIRTY-FIVE

Oţărât

THERE WAS A HORDE OF them.

Faith was awakened by their loud male voices, arguing, chortling, grunting, growling—they sounded like animals frenzied by the hunt, ready to move in for the feast.

And Faith was their kill.

Pain in her shoulder sockets told her she was hanging by her arms from bound wrists, her feet dangling God knew how many feet off the ground. And the worst: she was naked.

She flinched with the need to tuck her legs into her chest, every feminine instinct urging her to curl into a fetal position right there in midair, to cover and protect herself. She wasn't a prude or anything, certainly not. A woman couldn't be a dancer and be shy. How many times had she had to do a quick change backstage in front of men and women alike? Early in her career she'd even danced an avant-garde piece topless. But this was different. Without even looking, she knew she was vulnerable and helpless in the most absolute way imaginable.

She squeezed her eyelids tighter. Sensations beyond sight were making it painfully clear that she really, *really* didn't want to see whatever was out there: the stench of old sweat, human waste, rotting garbage, decay, and sour blood. A rush of bile plugged up her throat. More sweat slid over flesh that still felt sensitive and sunburned from her trip to get here through literal Hell.

God, that heat…

Two seconds into her journey through the Hell Tunnels atop her captor's shoulder and she'd started screaming. Five seconds, and not enough moisture had remained in her mouth to scream. By eleven seconds, the agony had driven her into unconsciousness. And such a horrendous journey could only have landed her someplace equally horrendous. Her chin quavered with the threat of tears, although her dehydrated body probably wouldn't be able to make any. *Faith, come on. See how bad this actually is.*

She pried open her eyelids. *Catastrophic.*

A small squeak of fright slipped passed her cracked lips before she could stop it. She was strung up next to Pandra—still unconscious, but fully clothed—at the far end of an arena of sorts: an area naturally created by a huge curvature in the cave wall. A violent-looking assortment of men, a couple hundred of them, were gathered in a seething mass fifty feet in front of them. Hair color was either black or red with no shade in between. Most of them were tall and muscular, all of them shabby, and every single man clearly needed to cut down on the caffeine. Or the testosterone. They were shoving at each other and snarling, already ripping clothes. Some were bleeding.

She saw Josnic among them. He was easy to spot standing head and shoulders above the rest and with that luscious red mane of his. Only one other man could match his towering height, and he was…was…

The personification of evil.

This man didn't have a single quality to soften his menace, like Josnic with his beautiful hair and teeth. Black-haired, this man's face was viciously constructed out of large, indestructible bones, his right temple marked with a tattoo of black teeth that sliced into the corner of his eye. His body—probably no more ruthlessly muscled than Josnic's—somehow gave the impression of being equipped exclusively to cause pain. He was shirtless, although his forearms were covered with strange spiked leather coverings. He wore black leather pants and combat boots with a ring of knives circling each of his calves.

A scream rang out behind her.

Faith whipped her head around to look over her right shoulder. She stiffened on her chain as dread dumped another load of adrenaline into her veins in a sickening flood. A man was dragging off a kicking and screaming woman by her hair…strange-colored hair, dark blonde several inches from her scalp, then brassy blonde for the rest of it. Like a bad dye job that had grown out partially, but not completely. The two disappeared behind an open-fronted building—just a roof and three walls—of what appeared to be a recreation area.

Inside, there were half a dozen television sets arrayed in front of three tattered couches, a couple of desks loaded down with computers, a beat-up pool table with the green felt worn in places.

Someone was moaning from the rickety building next door. This one had a medical red cross painted above the door and a steady billow of steam rising from a tin chimney.

She craned her head around to check out the left, finding the beginnings of a neighborhood…or an attempt at one. Ramshackle houses trailed far back into the cave, too far back for Faith to see them all, but the visible ones looked like they'd been put together on a song and a prayer. The wooden walls were warped and gaping, the ceilings lopsided or unfinished, the doors pitted and split. No drapes, fake plants, or decorations that could be considered quaint like there were in Țărână's family neighborhood.

In the middle of a cluster of these "homes," there was a squared-off space—what appeared to be a communal area— containing a couple of wooden picnic tables with benches, a large aluminum tub, a rusty stove, a refrigerator hiccupping along like it was on its last legs, a lineup of Sparkletts water containers, and half a dozen stacked barrels, some marked "supplies," others "sewage." Up near the ceiling, exposed electrical wires ran the length and breadth of the cave, snaking down in tangled vines to the houses and appliances. Naked light bulbs sagged from the uppermost wires at regular intervals. Again, crude and careless rather than quaint and homey.

The saying, *You don't know what you've got until it's gone,* never fit more appropriately than now. Țărână suddenly wasn't so "hick" and "backward" anymore, was it?

"Have you ever been raped?"

Faith startled, rattling her chain, and dropped her chin to look down.

A woman was standing on her left side, her neck angled up to meet Faith's gaze. She had honey blonde hair cut very short, nearly buzzed off, and was dressed for practicality in olive-colored cargo pants, a stained beige T-shirt, and dirty white tennis shoes. She had a clipboard tucked in the crook of her arm. Someone in charge? *Please, say yes.* This woman looked normal.

"No," Faith answered the question, her voice a mere croak. "I've never been raped."

"Good." The woman nodded firmly. "Because you'll get raped here, and the women who've been raped before handle it less well." She aimed her chin at where the shrieking woman had been. "As you saw with Kendra."

Faith repeated the name to herself. *Kendra...*She drew a quick breath. That poor woman who'd been dragged off was Kendra Mawbry, the Dragon woman the Vârcolac had saved, but then re-lost one night to the cruel Topside Om Rău Videon.

The clipboard woman exhaled roughly. "Unfortunately, Kendra doesn't listen to anything I say and gets herself into trouble all the time. Before her, came Ashling, a spoiled little rich girl who spends her time weeping about wanting to go home." She gave Faith a quick, clinical once-over. "I hope that's not you."

"I…I…don't…" Her words were hitching up inside her head. She'd made the biggest, dumbest mistake of her life agreeing to come to Oţărât. She'd way—way, *way*—overestimated how brave and practical she could be about this.

"I'm Gwyn Billaud, by the way."

She had to swallow twice. "Faith Teague," she managed to introduce herself. *Sorry I can't shake your hand, but I'm hanging from the ceiling naked.* Her lips quavered.

"Some pretty bad stuff is going to happen to you," Gwyn continued in a matter-of-fact tone. "I know what you're going through right now is *immense*. So it probably seems callous of me to stand here and talk to you about it while you're in your current position. But if I can prepare you as much as possible beforehand, it'll help you deal and settle in more quickly."

Faith glanced again briefly at the ramshackle neighborhood and nausea burned her nose. "Settle in?" she gasped out.

Gwyn made a sound that sounded almost like a laugh. "Oh, Oţărât looks bad now, but trust me, it used to be way worse. I've organized the place, and now we're cleaner, we have scavengers traveling topside regularly for supplies and water, we've formed groups for enjoyment—for playing cards and games and sewing and whatnot—and we have systems for safety, Faith. Important systems you need to follow in order to limit the abuse you suffer. You won't escape it entirely, but if you're smart, you can keep it to a minimum. Okay?"

Faith couldn't locate her voice to offer an answer. Not including the constant berating dancers typically tolerated from their choreographers, she'd hardly ever endured a harsh word: never from Idyll, rarely from Kacie. She'd certainly never had to put up with abuse of the magnitude this Gwyn was hinting at. Her dry tongue spasmed in her mouth against the urge to shout. *Why, why,* why *had she run away*?!

"In a few minutes there's going to be a fight for you and"—Gwyn gestured at Pandra—"this woman. Whoever wins you will become your mate. He'll be the first to have sex with you, marking you so you can have only his children."

Faith dropped down her eyelids in an extra-long blink. Children. By one of *them*. She couldn't think about that.

"None of the other Om Răµ will mess with you during that marking period, but afterward, it's open season. If you happen to be wandering by another man when the mood strikes him, he'll jump you. The only one who'll protect you in this instance is your mate. Partly out of a pride thing, but mostly because he's been properly motivated to do so. By you. Get on your mate's good side immediately, Faith, I mean it. I don't care if you abhor him. You need to please him. Find out what he likes and give it to him. And *never* refuse him sex. No matter what, *don't*. One time I had a raging urinary tract infection. That night my mate came to my bed. Do you think I wanted to have sex with him? No. What did I do? I shut my mouth and spread my legs."

Faith stared down on Gwyn, appalled.

"That was Kendra's mistake number one," Gwyn went on. "Her nonstop whining made her mate hate her. He won't do squat to protect her now, and the whole of Oţărât knows it. And you can see what happens." She gestured behind Faith.

Faith turned to see the man who'd dragged Kendra behind the recreational building just emerging, tugging his pants up. Barrel-chested with massive thighs and a puckered scar where his left eye used to be, he sauntered toward the main horde of Om Răµ.

A shiver wracked Faith's entire body, and—

She spotted another Om Răµ male intently watching Kendra's attacker.

This man was leaning against the cave wall on the other side of the red cross building, his crossed arms displaying an array of black teeth tattoos along his forearms—a requirement for this place, it seemed. He had spiky black hair, a down-turned mouth, and strange, bright-black eyes—eyes that shifted over to focus on her. After a moment, his lips tipped sideways, as if they shared a secret.

"W-who is that man?" she asked Gwyn hoarsely. His face was oddly familiar, even though she knew for certain she'd never seen him before.

Gwyn thought she meant Kendra's attacker, gesturing at him as she said, "That's Bollven. A real jackass. He'll get to you at some point. That's guaranteed."

Faith's brain fuzzed at the edges, her heart flatlining through a couple of missed beats. Weighing in at a hundred and two pounds, she wouldn't have a chance in a million against a man like that Bollven. If he wanted to rape her, she'd end up just like Kendra, kicking and shrieking. Panic filled her mouth with a flood of acid. "I can't do this," she said, her voice going high-pitched as she reached the end of her capacity to cope with sudden impact, like a crash dummy meeting a cement wall. Her next words stuttered out of her. "I-I'm sorry, but I can't."

Gwyn wrapped a hand around Faith's ankle and gave it a squeeze. "You can," she said firmly. "You *have* to. Listen, not all of the men here are bad. Relatively speaking, that is. You might get lucky." Gwyn gestured to the red-haired Om Rău who'd been Faith's transport into Oțărât. "That's Tollar, one of my best scavengers. He also looks out for his women really well. He mainly needs to bathe more. Krolan's not bad, either, and Ejohn…actually, he sucks. Cantorth's pretty good, and…wait, where's Cantorth?"

"Dead."

Faith turned her head at the same moment Gwyn did, and grimaced. Her shoulder sockets were really hurting now.

The woman who'd just spoken was an athletically built female with black hair hanging in dreadlocks down her back: an Om Rău by her black eyes.

Gwyn scowled at the woman. "Havel, I gave you a post to man. You're supposed to be watching the children."

"I know." Havel stepped closer. "But I need to warn you that this is going to be badder than usual, Gwyn. Some Vârcolac killed Cantorth and Frove, slammed their heads together from what I hear. So now the men are extra riled up, but Lorke and Josnic ain't gonna let anyone fight."

"Aren't," Gwyn corrected. "Why not?"

Havel pointed to Faith. "This one's a Royal Dragon, and that one"—she shifted her finger over to Pandra—"is one of them Rău-Fey females from topside. As special as they are, Lorke and Josnic want to pair them only with their pure bloodlines." Havel swept a gesture at the two tallest men.

Faith blinked rapidly, switching her gaze back and forth between Josnic and… Wait…*Lorke*. That black-haired horror who didn't possess a shred of mercy or decency was Nyko's *father*?!

"Which means," Havel sneered, "all of these pricks are going to take their stank mood out on the rest of us."

The words had just come out of Havel's mouth when an earth-shaking bellow rang out.

Faith cringed.

It was the one called Bollven. He stomped over to Josnic and began a snarled conversation with him.

Gwyn watched the argument. "Bollven disapproves of the decision," she murmured. "Understandably. He hasn't been given a shot at a woman in years."

Havel snorted. "Maybe because he gets up on everyone else's women alla time."

Josnic leaned toward Lorke and spoke to him. Lorke nodded his head. Bollven's lips snaked into an expression of malicious satisfaction.

"Bollven will be given the chance to fight," Gwyn translated. "For this one," she indicated Pandra, "since her ability to breed is in question."

A red-headed toddler scampered up and hugged Gwyn around the legs.

"Dange!" Gwyn exclaimed. "What are you doing out here?! You know you're supposed to stay in hiding when there's going to be a fight." She scooped the little boy up, kissed his pudgy cheek, and handed him off to Havel. "Go!" Gwyn watched the two leave, then glanced at Faith. "My son."

Proper manners probably dictated that Faith should coo about how cute the toddler was, but she was sort of hanging with her armpits stretched to the limit right now.

"He's Josnic's," Gwyn supplied. "I'm one of his women."

Faith blinked rapidly. *You're…?* Her thought cut off as an Om Ră0 approached her with a knife. She jerked on her chain, a breath hissing out of her. But he went over to Pandra and began slicing her leather jumpsuit off.

Meanwhile Bollven entered the center of the arena and bellowed again.

The Om Rău with the bright-black eyes stepped forward from the red cross building. "I challenge."

Bollven threw back his head and laughed.

Lorke laughed, too, but nodded his approval.

The two combatants circled each other.

Lorke headed toward Faith, his satanic gaze fixed hungrily on her.

"Wh-what's happening?" Faith choked.

"Lorke will take you," Gwyn said.

"No." Hysteria rose fast inside Faith. *He'll be the first to have sex with you, marking you so you can have only his children.* "Please, n-no." She clenched her bare thighs together against the sudden urge to pee, even though she doubted her body could make enough liquid for such an embarrassment. "I can't!" A scream clawed at her chest.

"Faith," Gwyn said. "Remember what I told you. Don't fight him. Faith? *Faith*, calm down and listen to me."

Faith cycled her legs in empty air. Somehow she managed to open her voice box, and screams burst from her, one after the other. Hot vomit piled into her raw throat, a terror unlike any she'd ever known blocking her breath. Strength ebbed from her, but she found voice for one last scream.

"Nyko!"

CHAPTER THIRTY-SIX

PANDRA SLITTED HER EYELIDS OPEN as the last of her jumpsuit was sliced off her body. She'd been conscious, but playing possum, for most of the confab between Faith and the woman calling herself Gwyn, so she'd heard the plan to pair that smidge of a ballet dancer with the arsemonger, Lorke.

Not too keen on that, was Faith? One could hardly blame the girl. The two leaders, Lorke and Josnic, were frightful creatures. Little wonder Raymond had never allowed Pandra to come down into Oţărât to deal directly with the Underground Om RăU. Even with her strength, she'd be hard pressed to defend herself against the two leaders should they decide to...well, do anything to her they fecking pleased.

"Nyko!" ripped out of the ballerina, and the one called Lorke stopped.

The gang of Om RăU went quiet, too, as that name bounced around the cave, then faded. Even the two combatants stilled.

That had been the bloody wrong thing to yell.

Lorke's gaze darkened to the shade of overturned earth, like ancient volcanic soil. "You Nyko's woman?"

Faith heaved on her chain, her lips bloodless and her eyes wide.

Lorke curled his mouth into what could only be termed a demon's version of smile. "Not anymore." Turning around, he stalked over to a bench, the lethal way he moved eerily reminding Pandra of Jacken, and grabbed a bucket and hammer.

"Oh, crap." Gwyn shot a worried glance at Faith, then backed away.

Faith's head swung around. "Pandra," she rasped out.

Lorke returned to Faith and set down the bucket below her feet. He shoved his hand into it, pulling out a small metal piece of something, his hand dripping with runny black fluid.

Teeth chattering, Faith stared buggy-eyed at him.

"Gonna have to mark you as mine," Lorke said. "Permanently erase *Nyko* from your mind." The name was limned with disdain.

"P-please," Faith chattered and choked. "D-d-don't…"

Lorke set the point of the metal item he'd fetched from the dark liquid on Faith's belly, several inches from her navel.

It was a tack…so the black liquid must be tattoo ink.

"No!" Faith flopped about on her chain like a carp caught on the end of a fishhook.

Drawing back his hammer, Lorke slammed the tack into Faith's belly.

A raw, throbbing scream poured out of Faith, her neck arching back, tendons standing on end. The dancer's entire body turned pasty in such a flash flood that for the briefest moment, Pandra thought that one tack had killed her. *But, no.* The dancer hadn't popped her clogs. White-eyed with terror, she strained a pleading look at Pandra again. "Pandra!"

"Faith…" Gwyn tried from several meters away.

Faith ignored her. "Help me, Pandra," she cried out. "Please."

Venting a sigh, Pandra lifted her head and opened her eyes all the way. Aye, she supposed she owned it to the girl to help her. She should've saved the dancer back on that jut of cave rock when she'd had the chance, but had let her grandiose gesture of sacrifice toward Thomal distract her from it. And here she was still alive, after all—an unhappy happenstance to have woken up to. Josnic was supposed to have killed her with that punch back in Ţărână. He wouldn't have wanted to snuff her, of course, preferring to save her for his use, but she'd seen Josnic's eyes flash Răul red, and she'd bloody well counted on him losing control and socking her too hard. Unfortunately not.

A second tattooing tack was slammed in. More high-pitched screaming.

All right, all right, keep your hair on.

Pandra peered up the length of her chain to the bolt securing it into the cave ceiling. The bolt was about half the size of her wrist. A real chuffer to dislodge by the look of it. *Right, then.* She gave her body a good swing, aiming to fling herself up high enough to grasp the chain with her feet. She didn't make it. Damnation, she'd lost all feeling in her arms. And a worse shower of shite was headed her way. Josnic had spotted her antics and was striding toward her, his chin dropped into a threatening angle.

No more fannying around, then. She concentrated on her power, shedding the debilitating deadness in her arms and the lingering ache in her jaw from Josnic's earlier knockout blow. She quickly searched for other wounds, but only found a strange iciness inside her, like her organs were coated in frost. *Ah.* Old Pandra was back, ready to hurt the first living creature who made her feel vulnerable. *Bully for her.* She needed her former self right now. 'Struth, she'd trade a year of her life for her immortality ring—which sounded kind of ironic, actually.

Grunting, she swung herself again, arching her legs far back, then forward, back, forth, until she hurled herself all the way up the length of chain this time. Latching the soles of her feet onto the metal links, she hung upside down like a chimpanzee, her long hair lashing about in a curtain of blonde streamers. Scrambling up the stretch of chain, she planted her feet on either side of the bolt.

Gawping faces turned up to the sight she must've made: stark bollock naked, squatting like a spider on the ceiling.

Below her, she saw the smaller Om Răµ take a pot shot at Bollven. Snarling, the two combatants threw themselves into a wild scrap.

Ignoring the punch-up, Lorke foraged in his bucket for another tack.

Shite. Pandra grabbed hold of the chain at the root and pulled on it, *hard.* Fissures snaked around the bolt. Cave dust, pebbles, and other rubble broke free and pissed down. Teeth gritted, she strained harder, muscles quivering. *Rum-rum-ka-shoom!* With the rumbling sound of a seven-point earthquake, the chain tore free.

She fell, bringing a sizable chunk of boulder attached to the end of her chain with her. Twisting a Triple Linde on the way down, she landed straight on her feet and already swinging, using her boulder like a medieval ball-and-chain mace. She whipped it at Lorke, but a group of three Om Răµ stood between her and her target and—*Thunk. Thunk. Thunk.* She swiped their heads off their necks with her boulder, red streaking the air in bloody ribbons.

The boulder continued its destructive path toward Lorke, but with so much warning of imminent danger, the Om Răµ leader easily ducked out of the way.

The boulder crashed to the cave floor, jerking Pandra into a stumble as it exploded apart into a herd of tiny pet rocks. *Buggeration.*

Lorke straightened with a deafening bawl of rage, his mighty yell sending more cave debris tumbling down from the gaping hole overhead.

It also triggered the other men to go into their Răµ states. Eyes blazing crimson, they began to lunge at nearby women.

"Code Berserk!" Gwyn shouted as she turned and ran.

The women who hadn't already been grabbed, scattered.

From the tail of her vision, Pandra saw Josnic closing the last bit of space between them. She lithely sidestepped him, moving to stomp on the length of her chain near her wrists to snap her bindings off. Hands freed, she rounded on the red-haired giant, her fists raised, manacles dangling from her wrists. She clenched her knuckles tight, her focus narrowed to a point. She was going to have to fight like she never had in her life to survive this. As strong as a Pure-bred male Om Rău was—and without her immortality ring to promptly heal her—it wouldn't take many blows to land her up the swanny.

Leaping to the offensive, she turned herself into a whirling dervish of violence, surprisingly making it through Josnic's defenses here and there. Not surprisingly, her hits and kicks had no blooming effect on him whatsoever.

"Pandra!" Faith wailed.

Pandra sidestepped again, putting Faith into her line of sight.

Lorke had his hammer poised over another tack at the dancer's stomach.

Taking two running steps, Pandra flew through the air, performing a textbook-perfect spinning back kick into the side of Lorke's head. *Down like a sack of spuds.* That was the corker. The not-so-grand part was that the maneuver had put her back to Josnic, and that cost her. Dearly.

A mallet-like fist came down on top of her head, like she was one of those wee critters in a Whac-a-Mole arcade game. And just like one of those sorry little moles, she went straight down into a dark place, a blinding nightmare of agony engulfing her. The cave floor rose up and slammed into her spine and the back of her skull. Manic stars pranced across the surface of her pupils. Her lungs socked in. She struggled to claw through the pain, to recover herself, but her limbs were suddenly made of resin, her brain, a rubbish bin clattering down a hill.

Come on, don't shag out. It was only one smacker, for crying out loud.

With a nasty growl, Josnic came down onto his knees beside her, his colossal arm cocked back to deliver another punch.

A bag of wank for you, girl. There was only one thing she could do.

She opened the cage door on her beast. A *crackle* darted through her ears. Her vision filmed over with red and her muscles inflated with strength. Pressing her teeth into a tight grate, she struck out with Răuˇ power.

Bones broke. *Crunch*—and again.

Josnic jolted backward, yowling.

She grabbed the chain strung across his chest and yanked. Nipples and navel popped apart, blood spraying in every direction like a hellish fireworks display.

More howling resounded in her ears. Josnic's mammoth fist missiled toward her face.

She lifted a forearm to block him, but…his power was phenomenal. Pain ruptured at the front of her head as the blow landed dead center on her nose. Her vision disintegrated. Blindly, she brought her head up with a sharp snap, nutting her attacker, their foreheads loudly *thumping* together.

A yell, then another punch from that gigantic fist.

Bone fragments burst off the bridge of her nose. Pain stripped down to agony. Her hearing changed programming to an out-of-tune radio station, Inga's voice singing. ♪*A little bird crssssh sat in the pear-tree…*

Then she was flying, Josnic scooping her off the ground and slinging her over his shoulder.

Will the rapist become the rapee in her final moments? Blood streamed from the shattered remains of her nose as her Răuˇ beastie slunk away. *Agony! Agony! Agony!* Her neurons fired the signal in her brain. Over and over and over. It dragged her into a deep, dark hole. That sorry mole again. She scrabbled about, trying to tear herself out of it. Her tongue turned gluey. Her brain spun in two different directions.

She jostled on Josnic's shoulder.

Daddy, help me.

Deeper she went. Bones inched toward her brain. Her frontal lobe throbbed. So much pain... The blurry specter of Death appeared, holding out a hand to her. Beckoning. She craned her head up to get a better glimpse of the ghostly form. A single tear leaked from her eye. *Thomal...be free, love.*

So much pain.

Death waited, hand extended. So patient.

She reached out to accept the specter's offer, her fingers oddly grey-colored, and—

A flash of lightening whited out her vision. A deafening *wa-boom*! followed, rocking her off Josnic's shoulder. She landed with a hoarse *oomph* and flopped over onto her side, her lids mere slits. Who knew death would be so dramatic.

But so it was.

Blackness overtook her, the last thing her conscious mind registering was the sound of her pulse dimming to nothing.

CHAPTER THIRTY-SEVEN

NYKO SKIDDED TO A STOP as the cave walls closed in around him, the tunnel narrowing ahead to an impassable gap. *Another wrong turn*! *Dang it*! Reeling around, he stumbled back the way he'd come, adjusting his grip on Pandra, propped on his right shoulder, and Faith on his left. Squinting through the deluge of sweat in his eyes, he tried to make out another route through the dim illumination provided by the heat-resistant light strapped to his head.

He found another tunnel and staggered down it. The steady boom of his heart and the whistling of his breath through the chambers of his lungs were the only sounds. He was so weak at this point he'd already dropped Pandra once, and Faith was starting to feel like she weighed one thousand pounds, not a measly one hundred. He should've listened to Jacken and fed before going off on this mission. The sky-high temperature inside these Hell Tunnels was rapidly finishing the job that blood loss from his knife wound had begun: utterly depleting him.

The smart thing probably would've been to leave Pandra behind and save himself the liability of her extra weight. After all, when he'd found her, she looked pretty close to dead, her nose nothing but a misshapen mass of pulp. But "pretty close" wasn't close enough for him when it came to dead…although if he kept scurrying about these tunnels like a mouse in a maze, searching for an exit but only finding more cave, then dead, as in *completely dead*, as in dead as a doorknob dead, would define them all. Soon.

And even though I may have a possible way into Oţărât, my ability to grab the women then get back out, with an entire town of Om Răuul to face down, is still a huge IF.

A little mission tidbit he was proving right about.

When it came to extracting his objectives, however, Nyko had defied the odds and accomplished that easy as pie. What do you know, but toss a couple flash grenades and every Om Răuul in town collapsed to the cave floor, rolling around with their arms clutched over their heads. He'd practically skipped into town, la-di-da…then had almost blown the whole easy deal by freezing up when he saw Faith suspended from a chain, *naked*, her belly awash with blood. And Pandra lumped on the ground looking very close to dead.

He'd somehow managed to get moving again—maybe inspired by the sight of a barely unconscious Lorke stirring— and grabbed both women. With chaos still reigning around him, he'd run through the dense smoke back into the tunnels, retracing his steps toward Ţărână.

Unfortunately, that's where the whole *easy* part of this mission had turned into mud pie.

It had happened about three hundred yards ago, to be exact. The Om Răuul, having recovered, had given chase, and in the process of whizzing and wagging through their own well-known tunnels, they'd cut him off from the sole route he knew would get him home.

Now he was staggering around inside a fire serpent's belly, completely off Thomal's map, blood loss and dehydration closing in on him at an exponential rate. Awhile back, he was fairly sure the soles of his boots had also seared off.

Footsteps! Ah, crud, someone was coming up fast behind him.

Nyko lurched into the next left, and—

His legs folded beneath him like a broken beach chair, dumping him onto his knees. Faith and Pandra slid off his sweaty shoulders and crumpled into a couple of sad heaps on either side of him. He moaned.

His pursuer slammed to a halt over him, breathing heavily.

Nyko sat back on his heels, keeping his head bowed as he mentally accepted the unavoidable. Suicide missions were supposed to end in death, after all. Too bad he was letting the girls down, though. He really would've liked to get them back to Țărână.

"Off your ass, Nyko," his pursuer ordered.

Huh? Nyko managed the impossibly difficult task of looking up. Through the hair caked into his eyes with sweat, he viewed his pursuer.

Shǫn, dressed all in black with darker black spots scattered across his shirt and pants. *Blood.* There was a smear of it on his chin, too.

"You wanna live?" Shǫn asked. "Come with me now. Quick." His younger brother grabbed him under the arm, trying to tug him to his feet.

Of all the things...

"Come on, man! Don't pussy out on me!"

Nyko didn't budge. His body felt overheavy, his big muscles no longer an asset, but a burden to his bones and flesh. "B-b-b..." he tried to explain. The words wobbled around on his tongue. His brain vacantly registered the wrongness of the situation. This was Shǫn, a bad guy now. "B-blood-need."

"Yeah, that's kinda obvious. But I know a place where we can take a break and figure this out, all right?" With a teeth-clamping growl of effort that spoke of how little help Nyko gave to his brother, Shǫn hefted Nyko to his feet.

Too tired. Just want to—

"Christ," Shǫn panted. "Try cutting down on the fucking cookies, Nyko, would you?" Shǫn scooped up Faith and Pandra. "You follow me," he warned. "Or I come back here and kick in your ornaments."

*Can't, can't, can't…*Nyko didn't know how he could, but somehow he did, one foot miraculously appearing in front of the other as he trailed Shọn. Thankfully his little brother traveled only about twenty feet down the tunnel before ducking into a cave opening. Here, Nyko was met with the unwelcome sight of a rocky ramp leading up at a steep grade. Up, up—Nyko huffed and puffed as he climbed, his muscles quivering so much it was like mini vibrator packs were jammed underneath his skin. The one thing that kept him going was the feel of the temperature cooling with each upward step he took. That felt very, very fantastic.

The ramp finally ended in a small, dome-shaped rock room. Nyko and Shọn collapsed together, cluttering the cramped space with their rough breathing. Nyko didn't know how long it took his lungs to return to normal functioning, but when they did, he heard the steady *plip-plip* of dripping water. He cranked his head to the side. *Holy Moly.* The cave walls were so slick here that the moist trickling had formed a small pool. Mortal thirst had his tongue automatically trying to dart out and lick his lips, but the desiccated slab merely succeeded in making a crackling sound. That couldn't be good.

Shọn crawled over to the water and cupped his hands in it. "Drink," he ordered through his own sips.

*Nice thought, but…*The pool could've been a mirage for how capable Nyko was of getting to it. The climb to this room had done him in. He was half-blind with fatigue, his whole body shaking to the point of near-seizures, his heart lollygagging in his chest, a dull *thump-bump* that threatened to give up completely any second. "What are you doing, Shọn?" His voice came out as a hoarse whisper, debility wringing it out.

Lifting off his hands and knees, Shọn sank back into a crouch, his forearms braced on his thighs.

"Last time I saw you." Nyko paused through a stomach spasm. "You shot me."

"Don't be a baby. I winged you. Thomal, too."

Nyko blinked slowly and painfully. It felt like his blood-need was moving into his brain, shriveling it up. "Am I missing a punch line here? Are you, or are you not, a Topside Om Rău now?"

Shọn's eyebrows shot straight up. "You're joking, right?"

"I don't hear myself laughing, Shọn."

"Aren't I here," Shọn countered, "saving your ass?"

Nyko set his jaw, his blood-need drilling out another borehole in his stomach.

"All right, yeah," Shọn conceded. "I was with them at first. But I've spent a lot of time with my therapist topside since you last saw me, and...she's helped me. I mean, I'll never forgive myself for what I did to Luvera, but Karrell has been getting me through the other stuff, a bunch of *Good Will Hunting* 'it's not your fault' kinda shit."

Nyko lay there, his throat cinched tight, strangling on *some possible way* to express the jumbled stew of anger and wretchedness within him. Finally, roughly, "Would've been nice to have been clued in on that a little sooner."

Shọn shrugged, highlighting the fact that his shirt was plastered to his body. "I wasn't ready to ask to come back to Țărână, yet. I figured what my therapy actually needed was for me to kill Bollven as payback for his near butt-reaming." Shọn flashed a mordant smile, long canines glistening. "Which I just did."

Nyko moved his teeth back and forth against each other, his bones hurting, like he'd been chewed up and spit out. "So glad you've got that all worked out, Shọn, that it was only a matter of you killing your tormentor rather than me being *the worst brother on earth*!" He tried to swallow, but his throat refused to do its job anymore. "Maybe if I'd known that a little earlier, I wouldn't have thrown in the towel on my own life. Maybe I could've had...I could've..." Druggedly, he turned his head to seek out Faith.

She was staring back at him with her amber tiger's eyes, her cheek pressed to the cave floor.

His heart rocked back and forth against his ribs.

"You came for me," she whispered.

Nyko wrenched his gaze away from Faith's and directed his attention to the domed ceiling, a tic in his cheek twitching. He supposed he deserved to hear the astonishment and disbelief in her voice, but it still rammed a ten-foot spike into his pride to know he'd done everything in his power to earn that doubt.

"Thank you." Faith's voice sounded small, calling to the Big Nyko side of him, the man who'd devoted his entire life to being everybody's most dependable good guy and had hated every living second he hadn't been.

"Don't thank me." He dragged his gaze from the ceiling to face her. "I know why you sacrificed yourself to Oṭărât, Faith. Because you lost everything in your life that mattered. I...I saw it happening to you, but never did anything to help you. I don't deserve your gratitude."

She only smiled. "You're here now, aren't you?" She cast a quick glance around the rock room. "Where is here, exactly? Are we safe?"

Safe. Ah, yes, all men who could leap tall buildings in a single bound strove to give that to their damsels. A knife turned inside him. "I'm sorry, but no. I..." *botched it again.* "I wasn't able to get us out. We're in some hidden room in the Hell Tunnels."

"Oh." Faith's teeth tugged at her bottom lip. "So what happens now?"

Nyko chugged his larynx until he managed to produce more sound. "You'll be all right. My brother knows the way out and—"

"Your brother?" Faith peered over Pandra's prone form to find Shǫn. "You!" she exclaimed. "I thought you seemed familiar. You must look like Nyko."

"Like *him*?" Shǫn's eyebrows flew up. "You really know how to hurt a guy, lady."

Nyko cut back in. "Shǫn is going to take you and Pandra out of—"

"Whoa, hold up," Shǫn interrupted. "What do you mean *me*? I don't have the juice for that. I just fought Bollven, I'm fried from these Hell Tunnels, too, and I haven't fed since yesterday." He narrowed his eyes. "Which reminds me…why did you keep sending my donor topside to me if you thought I was a bad guy?"

The wheels of Nyko's mind moved sluggishly toward his memory of the meeting to decide that. "That was Toni. She didn't want to give up on you."

Shǫn pushed his tongue into his cheek. "And you did?"

"You *said* that you wanted me out of your life forever, Shǫn! You sat there while Videon prepared to rip my balls off with a pair of pliers, which was my rightful *penance*, according to you." Nyko flattened his lips against his teeth, the force of that accusation hurting his chest.

"I'm not leaving without you, anyway, Nyko." Faith pushed up on an elbow and bent a worried look on him. "It's obvious that if you stay here, you'll die."

"That's kind of the point," Nyko said. "I'm too far gone to go any further."

"You could make it if you fed, though?" She turned to Shǫn. "Couldn't he?"

"Faith," Nyko gritted. "I can't ask my donor to risk her life coming into the Hell Tunnels." And even if Ruxandra insisted on coming to his rescue, she wouldn't make it in time. He was circling the drain here. *I'd rather die than do nothing, so if it comes to that, then it does.* Good thing he was okay with it.

"Don't be a hayseed, Nyko," Shǫn said. "She's offering you her own vein."

She's…? Nyko jolted his gaze over, saw the expression on

Faith's face, and… "Absolutely not."

Faith's brow crinkled, irritation and—*please, not this one*—hurt creeping in. "Why not?"

"Because…" The first saliva he'd felt in two hours wetted his mouth as his imagination conjured the taste of her—for only the billionth time—her blood loaded up with all her Royal strength and saturated with her unique, delicious Faithness: manna from heaven, surely. "Because…" *Because why, again*? "The decision to bond is a serious one. You can't make it to…to save my life. You'd be stuck with me forever afterward."

Faith gave him a potent glare. "I can make the decision for any reason I want to." Pushing to a full sitting position, she bunched little fists against her bare thighs. "The manual says I only have to be willing, and I am."

Willing. The word itself sent a stronger surge of bloodlust biting deep inside him. He stared at the light blue veins in Faith's throat with animal focus.

"Besides." She scooted closer. "You *owe* me a rescue."

He tensed all over, very aware that—even though her long, coppery hair was stuck to the front of her body, covering her nakedness—she was still very much *naked*.

"I'm afraid that means you're back in the hero business. So get over yourself, feed on me, and haul us out of this place."

His pulse beat in the corner of his left eyeball like a tic.

When he didn't move, Faith thinned her lids on him. "I'll make you, if I have to."

Shọn let out a snort.

Faith whipped her head around.

"You weigh, like, three pounds," Shọn pointed out.

Her look was pure challenge. "You might want to back up a bit." With a flourish, she swiped off the scent-reducing mud from behind her ears.

CHAPTER THIRTY-EIGHT

"AHHHH!" NYKO ARCHED HIS NECK, pressing his head into the rocky floor as a full-on blast of Faith's scent bombed the cave room, fumigating the entire small interior in the space of a second. It swirled, tickled, consumed...*yes, yes, yes, more, more*...The ventricles in his brain vacuumed it up and his lungs ballooned.

Shọn—never any good at managing himself around aromatic females—let loose a low, lusty growl, his fangs springing down into his mouth. And suddenly he was no longer a younger brother, but a rival male Vârcolac.

Nyko bolted upright and clamped a fist around Shọn's throat. He snarled, snapping his fangs inches from his brother's face, then let go.

Shọn reacted immediately to the not-so-subtle territorial communication and retreated back against the wall next to the entrance, his gaze black fire.

Nyko flopped back onto his spine, adrenaline spent.

Faith watched the two-second exchange with wide-open eyes.

A guttural noise spilled out of Nyko, his nostrils fluttering. With one hand, he gingerly cupped his crotch. His manparts were in serious jeopardy of being squeezed unto death by Faith's scent. It made him want to do the horizontal bop with her and stuff his aching balls down a garbage disposal all in one certifiable moment. With his other hand, he grabbed Faith's wrist and pulled her toward him.

She'd won. He'd feed on her. Of course she'd won. No

way did he have the strength to resist her now, not as battered down as he felt, not with his survival instincts steering him into a hard turn away from death, not with his possessive Vârcolac male roaring that he needed his strength right now to fight for his woman. And definitely not with Faith's scent making him yearn for her so badly—for blood, sex, love…throw in Parcheesi nights and shopping for antiques online, or whatever. He wanted the whole bonded kit and caboodle.

"Turn around," he barked at his brother.

Shon crab-walked in a circle until he was crouched with his back to the room.

He kept pulling Faith closer. She needed to get on his lap if he was going to take her at the throat. Wrist was another option, but her throat was where he wanted to be…maybe never leave. Her scent would be richer there, her skin softer, the act of feeding on her carotid, by some unspoken natural law, more intimate. He swallowed so loudly, he heard it echo up through his ears.

Faith got the hint and climbed aboard, her sleek dancer's legs straddling his hips, her bare derriere using his balls as a couple of couch cushions.

A moan escaped him on a long breath. "Go down the ramp a ways, Shon." He had no idea how loud he was going to get. Probably fairly loud.

His brother disappeared.

He reached up and grabbed a handful of Faith's sweat-soaked hair at the base of her head and gathered it into a ponytail. Coppery strands slithered off the front of her body, and then—

He smothered another moan. There were her breasts.

Perky, round, and white, like cream puffs topped with lush, red strawberries. They were on the small side, but to him, the perfect size. *More than a handful is a waste*, he'd heard the saying go, and Faith's offering would fit nicely into his palm. Not his whole hand—that wasn't even fair to ask—but definitely she'd fill his palm. She was packing a lot of curves, actually, more than he'd expected. In clothes, her frame was so slight, he'd worried she'd lean toward preadolescent, even underdeveloped. But, no, this naked body before him was all woman, hips gently flared, thighs shapely, the area between her legs like—

He felt the scorching heat of a blush. In all his years he'd never seen a woman's... femininity before, and the reality of how those curls looked, all silky and coppery, and how close she was to his own...area made his breath wedge deep in his chest.

Lust bit harder. With his hand on her nape, he pulled her to him. She scooted up his body and leaned over him, her nipples almost caressing his bare chest, but not quite. More of her scent atomized into his nostrils, and his loins filled with a heaviness his pelvic bones didn't feel equipped to contain. Need blinded him to all but the pulse at her neck, but somehow he pushed the warning out of his mouth. "The first bite hurts."

She paused. "Worse than an all-day ballet workshop with Vladimir Azarov, world famous Russian choreographer?"

Hunger thundered down his spine, and his hand quaked as he cupped the back of her skull. "That, I don't know."

"I'll be fine," she whispered.

Green light. He angled her head to the side, found her pulse, and broke her skin with his fangs.

She let out a squeak as he clamped onto her artery, his lips latching securely to her flesh. He sucked vigorously. A coarse sound broke from him as blood gushed over his tongue. *She's so...* Pleasure noises stampeded up his throat and—

And then he was gone. Time and place ceased to exist as he was pulled into a vortex of ecstasy.

I was empty, now I'm full.
I was hurt, now I'm healed.

I was missing, now I'm found.
I was dying, now I'm saved.

He drank and drank, like a man nearly starving his whole life getting his first true taste of unpolluted water. He drank until his fangs wouldn't let him take anymore, then with a huge gasp, he broke the seal.

I was half, now I'm whole.

Faith gazed down at him with hooded, Ființă-dazed eyes, her body loose-jointed on top of him.

Hot air streamed out of his nostrils. He'd never seen her look more beautiful. Setting her gently aside, he rolled onto his hands and knees, crawled forward, and stuck his face into the pool, drinking deeply. His cells twitched sharply in complaint. His staff was hard as petrified wood, ready to make love to Faith and complete their bond. His body howled for it. But on a dirty cave floor with hundreds of Om Rău still hunting them was no time for that.

When he had his fill of water, he leapt to his feet and stretched to his full height. *Wow.* In the time it'd taken him to stand upright, the world had acquired a whole new shape; colors were brighter, sensations sharper, scents richer, and his muscles were powering up with Faith's Royal Fey blood. It was like being in a state of Rău, but with none of the bad.

I was weak, now I'm strong.

He bent to pick up Faith. "I'm going to get you out of here, don't worry." He swung her up on his shoulder, Pandra onto the other, then trotted down the ramp to Shọn.

"All right, Magellan," he said to his brother. "Lead the way out of this hell pit."

Shọn turned his head to peer up at him. "Nice boner."

CHAPTER THIRTY-NINE

Ţărână

THOMAL REFUSED TO LEAVE THE Outer Edge—the area of town near the Hell Tunnels. He sat on the ground with his back propped up against The Shank Tooth, Stânga Town's dive bar, and waited. The muscles in his legs wouldn't stop twitching, pushing him to put his agitated energy to us and pace, but the fifty swords piercing his sternum, twisting that bone into spiky gristle, kept him on his ass.

So this was what it felt like to have his radar go off.

And from the grim look Jacken had exchanged with Toni, standing nearby with Dr. Jess, a bunch of medical supplies clustered around their feet, when Thomal had first toppled over from the excruciating pain, his level of agony was symptomatic of a mate not just being hurt, but *dead*.

A paroxysm of emotions rippled up his throat. He glanced sideways at his right bicep, still neon blue with shirt-paint, and wrestled with the monsters in his head, a myriad craptacular images of all the ways his wife could've possibly died. What had the Om Răm done to her? How had she spent her last hours on—? *C'mon, Costache, don't kill her off. Get in the zone, man, and keep hoping.* A bone-rattling shudder clonked his vertebra together. He tried to squeeze breath through his lungs, but didn't have much success. It felt like he was operating off deflated bota bags. His pain was severe enough that, even if by some miracle Pandra wasn't dead, she had to be hurting. Bad. That thought was about as welcome as the others.

He snapped his head up. The muted cadence of footsteps had just rolled down the Tunnels...hadn't it? He whipped his gaze over to Jacken. His boss had gone hyper-still. Yeah, dammit, Jacken had heard it, too.

Thomal struggled to his feet, his heart beating wildly, every hair on his head standing at attention.

Steel *hissed* as Jacken unsheathed his blade. There was no other sound quite like it, and it called the other warriors milling about to move forward, their own knives drawn, ready to fight in case it was a gang of Om Rău headed their way, instead of the three people who'd been *presumed dead* the moment they'd gone into the Hell Tunnels.

The sound of running grew louder, ringing out sharply in the stillness, beating a rhythm of urgency.

Thomal did the pins-and-needles thing, one hand braced against the wall of The Shank Tooth.

Nyko reeled out of the Hell Tunnels, dust flying from his heels, flecks of sweat and blood flinging off his back. He had Pandra and Faith supported on each of his enormous shoulders and a hand fisted in the scruff of Shọn's shirt, dragging him along beside—*Shọn?*

Nyko stumbled down onto his knees and deposited the women on the cave floor. Naked.

Oh, shit.

"Help h-her!" Nyko wheezed out. "I think she's dead."

All the blood drained from Thomal's head. It was obvious who Nyko meant. Thomal's pinging radar notwithstanding, Pandra's skin was an ominous grey color and her nose...*holy crap*. It wasn't even there anymore. Vomit scaled his throat and horror burned at the backs of his eyeballs. A sound rushed out of him. He didn't know what it was—a yelping growl?—alarm, worry, desperation, and grief mashed together. A whole lot of stuff he hadn't even known he was capable of feeling.

Toni held onto her pregnant belly as she hurried over to Pandra and knelt down at her sister's side. She felt for a pulse.

"Thready and weak," she told Dr. Jess. "She's barely alive."

The words washed over Thomal in a numb tide. He stood on the perimeter with his arms hanging loose. *Alive, but barely.* "Barely" wasn't good.

Toni fumbled in her lab coat pocket, pulled out a small box, and slipped Pandra's immortality ring onto her finger.

"Don't leave it on for too long," Dr. Jess warned. "Or her face will heal like that. Just stabilize her enough so we can get her to the operating room."

The numbness rolled up and peaked inside Thomal's head, bright animated Pac Men eating across the screen of his vision. "Operating room" wasn't good, either.

THOMAL SANK INTO A HOSPITAL waiting room chair and let his head wilt backward off his neck. The fluorescent lights glowed through the threads of his blond lashes as he relived the look on Pandra's face when she'd been on that shelf of cave rock. Her eyes had been such deep wells of pain, full of sorrow and regret, as if she wished things had worked out between them.

His lids fell closed. What the hell had he ever done to warrant her *regret*? Or her willingness to make the ultimate sacrifice of her life for him? The shutter clicked across the screen of his mind and he saw Josnic punching her. Pandra letting him. Because she'd wanted to die. For him. So *he* could be free. Him.

His own bitter regret climbed up into his throat like bile. He leaned forward, propping his elbows on his thighs, and clasped the back of his neck. He'd wasted a lot of time confused about what he wanted from Pandra, but he knew with absolute, no holds barred certainty that he didn't want her dead. *Might've been nice if you'd said something to her about that.* Because now his barely alive wife was going through hardcore surgery to have her face reconstructed, maybe on the verge of—

"What are *you* doing here?"

The question came at Thomal in a flat, hard tone. He didn't recognize the voice, and when he glanced up, he barely recognized the scowling face.

Nyko never scowled; the dude was generally all about playing down the child-butcher disguise he wore.

Only one explanation for the uncharacteristic frowny face. Everyone had seen the telltale bruise on the side of Faith's neck. Nyko had fed on her, but odds were he hadn't had time to close the deal with some doinking. Being inside the Hell Tunnels and chased by a crapload of Om Rău dipshits wasn't exactly conducive to the old in-out. So Nyko was half-bonded, which meant he was caught in a torturously painful, crazy-making state, the kind of condition that could turn a man even as mild-mannered and agreeable as Nyko into something rabid.

Thomal came to his feet, keeping a careful eye on the oversized Vârcolac. Where was a horse tranquilizer when a guy needed it? "My mate's in surgery, so I'm—"

"Pandra's not your mate," Nyko snapped. "You heard what she said in the van on the way back from the mission. She's a blood source to you. That's it. So don't you call Pandra a mate. Not till you've *earned* it." Nyko closed in on Thomal with several clipped strides and stopped nose to nose in front of him. Like in, literally, Nyko's nose touched his. "You hear me?"

The flow of Thomal's blood sped up, aggression sizzling in his veins, priming him for violence. *Stupid, stupid.* Nyko outweighed him by at least the body weight of two extra warriors and his fists were each as large as Thomal's head. He was likewise pumped up with Royal Fey blood and his every cell probably felt covered in cactus prickles. Best response would be to treat Nyko like a wounded bull on steroid overdose: with caution and probably a prudent spoonful of fear. Buuuut…

Worry had Thomal too hosed up right now to act wise

and careful about anyone trying to hand him more bullshit. He stepped back, not in retreat, but to better clash eyes with Nyko's. "I appreciate the heads-up, brother, but last I checked, my marriage wasn't any of your fucking concern."

Nyko snarled, the noise making it sound like his Răú was jonesing for some flesh to munch. "I almost died saving Pandra. So I'm not letting your critical, unfeeling face be the first thing she sees when she wakes up. I'm not letting *you*"— he rammed his index finger into Thomal's chest—"hurt her anymore."

Thomal snatched up Nyko's finger and bent it backward. Anybody else's finger would've had the decency to break. Nyko merely took his hand back and squared off for a punch, his gaze alive with fury.

Thomal angled his body sideways and flexed his shoulder muscles in readiness, his weight poised on the balls of his feet. *Bring it, you jumbo-sized bitch.* Coldness gathered inside him.

"Hey guys, what's up?" Dev was standing in the doorway that led from the waiting room into the hospital's main hallway, a hand still propping open one side of the swinging double doors. The man wasn't fooling anyone with his casual tone. He knew exactly what was going down.

Nyko sniffed. "Only helping Thomal find the door. Deadbeat husbands who never do anything for their wives aren't allowed to occupy this waiting area."

Heat rose from Thomal's neck to his hairline. Rage split his head. "You did *not* just say that. You *know* I couldn't go into the Hell Tunnels after my mate, but I gave you—"

Nyko threw a backhand blow, his bowling-ball-sized knuckles catching Thomal high on the face in a shock of ripping pain. The room went white as his chin snapped toward the ceiling, the skin along his cheekbone splitting open. Before he knew how he'd gotten there, he was sprawled on his hands and knees, Ferris wheels and tea cups spinning colorfully at the corners of his vision. He shook his head. *Ow!*

Nyko's huge feet bulged on the linoleum floor at the corner of Thomal's vision, carnival fun house feet. "What did I say about calling Pandra your mate?"

Dev stepped into the waiting room. The door *swished* once then vacuum-sealed shut. "Nyko," he said quietly. "C'mon, man. You're not yourself right now."

A steady rivulet of blood poured off the cut on Thomal's face and gathered on the linoleum. His fangs came down. Absurdly, he had the urge to squish his hands into the red pool and finger paint around with it. There was just so damned much of it.

Nyko's clown feet angled toward Dev. "Somebody's got to talk some sense into him, Dev, and you sure as heck aren't doing it." Nyko made a disgusted *huh* sound. "You've watched how Pandra has worked for Thomal's forgiveness. You know that she's earned a second chance from him. She almost died saving Beth, for God's sake—Faith, too! But you've let Thomal treat Pandra like dirt. Do you think keeping your mouth shut for the last eight months has done Thomal any favors, Dev? You think that's being a *friend*?" Before Dev could answer, Nyko pivoted toward Thomal again and grabbed him by the back of the neck, hauling him to his feet.

Thomal staggered a couple of paces before righting himself, then yanked out of Nyko's hold. "I've had just about enough of your shit, Nyko."

"Too bad. More's coming." Nyko fixed him with a baleful glare. "First and foremost, you're a coward."

What little remained of Thomal's good sense went the way of the dinosaur. "Excuse me?" His voice came from some dark, evil place. "What did you call me?"

"Ah, crap," Dev murmured.

Ferocity boiled up in Thomal, uncontrolled, his pride short-circuiting important safety mechanisms in his brain as he bore down on Nyko.

Another backhand lashed out.

Thomal blocked the punch, but, *hell*, that blow had been the decoy. The anvil that was Nyko's other fist slammed up under his chin in an excruciating uppercut.

Air roared through Thomal's ears as he toppled backward off his heels and met the floor with a near rib-cracking jolt. His mouth hung open. He stared mindlessly for a technical knockout count of eight, watching blue cartoon birdies do laps in front of his eyes. Tweety Bird's, *I tought I taw a putty cat*, wonged through his ears.

Nyko stepped up to his side, looming over his supine form like heavy metal's biggest and worst.

Dev maintained his position by the door.

Just gonna stand there, are you?

Here was a man who knew how to employ caution when it was warranted. Probably the reason Dev had been promoted into leadership while Thomal remained a lowly swabby. But then again, Thomal had never known his friend to back down from a fight, no matter how big or crazy the opponent, so maybe Dev's non-movement wasn't a sign of caution so much as an indication that Dev was taking Nyko's lecture to heart and getting on board with the gotta-smack-some-sense-into-Thomal plan.

Jagoff traitor.

Thomal probed the inside of his sore cheek was his tongue. *What to do, what to do?* Too bad backing down wasn't his style. No. Foolish feats of self-destruction apparently were. He laughed up from the floor. Maybe it was a cackle. Whatever it was, it sounded insane. "Thanks, Nyko. I think you cured my TMJ." He rolled onto his hands and knees, then took in a strengthening breath to keep himself from just sagging there. His eyeballs were doing some serious *Chutes and Ladders* inside his skull. He pushed to his feet. The room rolled sideways. Fun! "But, hey, I'm thinking before you get all righteous with your fists again, maybe you should consider this about the whole coward thing." He narrowed his eyes, even though it hurt his cheek to do that. "It takes one to know one, brother. You forgettin' there's another woman in this hospital who went into Oțărât to escape a man who's been a complete chump to her. Gee, I wonder who she is? Oh, yeah, it's *Faith*."

Nyko's face reddened. Not any sort of red, but ripe plum red, raw meat red. Say-your-prayers red.

Sighing expansively, Dev glanced over his shoulder, probably confirming that the emergency call button was still on the wall by the double doors.

Thomal dug his heels in. This time he wasn't worshiping the linoleum when Nyko struck out.

"You know what? You're right," Nyko said, his voice weirdly calm.

Confusion and surprise pressed in on Thomal's temples. *What's this? No hitting?* Couldn't be. He'd probably passed out, after all.

"I made all the wrong decisions about Faith," Nyko admitted. "But at least *I* made them, Thomal. Me, myself. You hate Pandra because Arc does. It's the only reason, I think, because I've watched you watch her, and I get the sense that deep-down you've wanted to forgive her. But you didn't, you *don't*, because you're too weak to defy your big brother. A coward, like I said, and it's pathetic."

Scorching anger struck Thomal's body like a lightning blast. He gave his nostrils a warning flare. "I'd rethink pissing in my Wheaties anymore, if I were you." *Or I'll smash my face into your knuckles some more.* "You didn't see what your half-Răv pal did to my brother. But I'm reasonably sure you *do* see how badly it's screwed up Arc."

"That stuff is between Arc and Pandra," Nyko said. "It's for them to work out. *Stop* letting it affect your relationship with her, Thomal. Get out from under Arc's shadow. You've been living there for way too many years."

The accusation slammed into Thomal. *Years*?! He glanced over at Dev. His friend's eyes dipped down. It was a stab in the heart.

Nyko shook his head, looking disgusted down to his very core. "Sack up and be your own man, will you? For once."

Thomal stood in place, mute and stiff as he tried to keep his anger churning so that the truth of Nyko's words couldn't get in and hurt him. Didn't work, entirely. He gritted his fangs against his bottom teeth. A humming sound invaded his head, and his body began to shake so hard, his vision bounced. Blood coated the side of his face and neck, slipping down to his shoulder and upper chest.

Turning shortly on his heel, he walked out of the hospital's main entrance on numb feet.

CHAPTER FORTY

FIRST THING THOMAL DID WHEN he returned to his Oslo bedroom in the mansion was throw up. Hanging over the rim of the toilet, he fed the contents of his stomach into the porcelain bowl, then dry-heaved a few more times as visions of the confrontation he'd just had with Nyko swam around in his mind. Not the violent part. *Fuck that*! It was the shit about Thomal and Arc.

You're too weak to defy your big brother.

Get out from under Arc's shadow. You've been living there for way too many years.

A lot of what Nyko had said felt unpleasantly right—*right*: what a screwed concept. But something wasn't fitting…or maybe missing, like a dirty, little secret he and Arc had both conspired to maintain. Thomal had no idea what, though.

Wiping a wrist across his mouth, Thomal hefted himself up from the toilet and got in the shower, weary beyond description. Sex club antics, followed by the Om Răuu breach, insane worry over his wife when she'd been carried off by Josnic, his destructive radar, more insane worry about Pandra when she'd shown up barely alive back in Țărână, Nyko beating some *sense* into him, and then being gutted by Nyko's accusations might've, oh, stressed him out a bit. Head bowed, hands braced on either side of the shower handle, he let hot water sluice over him.

Before Dad died, he made me promise to look after you.

You've always had to work twice as hard as the other men for

291

half the results, Thomal. Frankly, I've never agreed with your decision to go into the Warrior Class.

I hate losing. You may be used to it, but I sure the fuck am not.

Thomal's head sagged deeper between his shoulder blades, water flooding his eyelashes. What had he been doing all these years? Did he even know who he was...who he wanted to be...who he was supposed to be? Had he been living the wrong life this whole time and that's why he felt so pissed off? Cranking the shower hotter, Thomal squeezed his eyes until spots littered the backs of his lids. There were just too many possible boned-up answers to those questions for him to think about it right now.

He concentrated on returning his appearance to normal, using the special soap Pandra had given him to scrub all the ridiculous shit off himself: the scorpion tattoo on his neck, the dye from his hair, and his paint shirt. The soap smelled vaguely of acetone, and by the time he was done, he stank like a damned nail salon.

His wet feet slapped the tile floor as he stepped in front of the bathroom mirror. Normal? *Riiiight.* His golden boy appeal was gone for now, hidden beneath a leather mask of tension and confused hurt. His eyes looked like they'd been plucked out, rolled around in red glitter, then re-inserted into their sockets; like he'd been crying on the inside and it was bleeding out. A bizarre and uncomfortable thought. The cut on his cheekbone was still oozing blood. He opened his medicine cabinet, pulled out bandages, and butterflied the skin closed. He'd have a beaut of a bruise tomorrow. If he was lucky, the injury would turn into another scar: a daily reminder in the mirror about what a no-load he'd been these past eight months.

You've watched how Pandra has worked for Thomal's forgiveness. You know *that she's earned a second chance from him.*

Dammit, he *was* a coward. He grimaced. Fuck, but he

hated that word.

He toweled off, and dressed in blue jeans, a green T-shirt, and Adidas running shoes, then grabbed his art pad and pencils out of his satchel, taking a seat at his desk. No more escaping, no more avoidance. He was going to pour everything in him out onto the page. Be real…or be whoever ended up on the sheet of paper. Maybe figure some shit out.

An hour into the drawing, the realization hit him. *Hard*, like something between a bear trampling and an avalanche. He staggered to his feet, his stomach roiling with nausea again. Chucking his art pad on the desk, he took off at a run for his brother's house.

Barging inside without knocking, he stormed through the living room and found Arc and Beth in the kitchen.

"I'm a dunce," he panted, his lungs making tight grabs for air. "It took me nearly a year to figure this out, but I get it now, you know. It's finally in my head"—he jabbed two fingers at his temple—"who you're really angry with, Arc. Maybe I was too consumed by guilt before to see the truth, but now it's clear as a full moon. I mean you have every right to be pissed as hell at Pandra. I'm not saying you don't. I *saw* what she did to you, too."

Arc's expression blackened. "Go upstairs Beth," he said, his voice low and tight, sounding all kinds of full of suppressed violence.

"Why?" Thomal bit out. "So you can keep your wife locked in more of your cold silence. You've told her exactly Jack and shit about what happened, haven't you?"

Arc leveled a heavy stare at him.

White-faced, Beth left.

Thomal sucked in a breath and continued. "Let's not pussyfoot around this thing anymore. The person you're really enraged with is *me*." He paced away a couple of feet, running a hand over his hair. "Nyko told me I've been living in your shadow, and damn the hell out of me if that isn't true. I just realized that I've done a real number on myself all these years, letting my insecurities about you and Dad rule me." A weird grief clogged his throat. "You were always Dad's favorite, his pride and fucking joy. And on some unspoken level I think you and Dad both agreed you were better than me. *You* had to look out for *me*, right? *You* were stronger. *You* were the tougher fighter than your silly doofus of an artist little brother. I've lived with doubts about myself my whole life because of that."

He braced his hands on his hips. "But, here's something, Arc. When Jacken created the Special Ops Topside Team—an *elite* military unit—he chose *me* to man it, didn't he? Not you. And all that shit you said about me getting hurt all the time? I don't lack talent, Arc. I go balls to the wall with everything I do." He shook his head. "That night in the hotel with Murk and Pandra, I saved your life. For the first time ever, *I* saved *your* life, big brother, and I think deep-down in a place you're ashamed of, you hate me for it."

A muscle jumped in Arc's face.

"All this time," Thomal forged on. "I thought I was feeling guilty because I didn't kill Pandra when I had the chance. It made all my doubts about my choice to become a warrior rise up and bite my ass. But now I realize that *this* is what I've been feeling guilty about." And if he was a poet, maybe he could appreciate the wretched irony of sacrificing himself to a loveless marriage so that Arc could go home to his wife and kids and have a long and happy life…only to have that very sacrifice be the thing that destroyed his brother. But Thomal wasn't feeling particularly poetic at the moment. "And here's another thing. Pandra didn't deserve to die. There's a lot of goodness in her—even that night I picked up on it. Look how far she's come over the last months. While you and I remain the Last Angry Men. Well, I'm done. I want my marriage. And until you can get your negativity under control and stop giving my mate the stink-eye, I want you out of my life."

The skin over Arc's cheekbones flared red while the rest of his face went pale. "Don't," he said through tight lips.

Thomal inhaled a shallow breath as pain drilled into his chest, coagulated, then dropped like a lead blob into his stomach, kept going and sagged into his legs. His knees went oddly nerveless. The relationship he'd always thought he'd had with his brother was *gone*. The support, camaraderie, the solid foundation they'd always shared as the almighty Costache brothers, two against the world, had only ever been a wax statue. Put under the extreme heat of intense scrutiny, it'd melted. What had they ever really been?

Thomal braced a hand on the kitchen island before he fell down. "You're not a bad man," he said in a raspy voice. "The things you've said to me…I know you didn't mean to hurt me on purpose. You just couldn't stand to have the image of yourself as the better man destroyed, and…and that's not your fault, either. Dad planted the idea in you." Thomal licked his lips. "You also didn't fail me the night with Pandra by not saving me, okay? Now that I'm seeing things more clearly, I'm grateful Pandra came into my life. Because if she hadn't, I never would've figured out that I've been living a lie." Thomal's voice dropped lower, became more scratchy. "I love you, Arc, but I need to figure out who I am." *Be your own man, will you? For once.* Could he be the warrior who also painted? Well, why the fuck not? "And I'm sorry, but that means I need to get some space from you for a while."

He couldn't bear to see any more of his brother's reactions to what he was saying. There was a good chance he'd waver. So he just turned around and walked out the door, gripping the handrail as he picked his way down the front steps, moving like a one-hundred-fifty-year-old man. He paused at the bottom, pulling a hand down his face. It'd been one helluva last twelve hours. If he had anything left in his stomach, he probably would've fertilized the fake plants at the bottom of Arc's porch steps.

His cell phone beeped. It was a message from Nurse Shaston. Pandra was back in her bedroom. Not even a Vârcolac could've recovered from major surgery that quickly, but such was the miracle healing power of Pandra's ring. She still no doubt needed rest. He shouldn't bother her. But as he started walking, a visceral, nearly violent, need to see her set his unsteady feet on a path directly for her door.

He knocked softly on Budapest. A second later the door swung open, and he was met by the sight of his wife wearing a pair of deconstructed jean shorts and a blue tank top with thin pink stripes on it, her blonde hair caught back in a low pony tail.

He nearly startled. Her face looked shockingly beautiful, without a hint that the middle of it had been concave a few short hours ago. But such was the healing power of Dr. Jess, who had mad skills in just about every discipline, including plastic surgery. 'Course the man had been studying medicine for over a hundred and twenty years.

Pandra gave him a blank stare.

Before he could get something earthshattering out of his mouth like, "Hi," she turned around and walked over to her bed, bracing her spine against the post and clasping her arms behind her back. A wave of heat flushed through him, most of it landing squarely in his cheeks. That was the position she took every time he came to feed—the position he'd demanded she take. Jesus, she was going to let him *feed* after everything she'd been through?

"Please…" He stepped into her room. "Uh…I just came to…I wanted to check on you, that's all, see how you're doing."

"Why?"

"Why?" *Always answer a question with a question when stalling for time.* He didn't know what to say. *Because I care*, would sound unbelievable. He said it, anyway, and, yeah, Pandra's eyebrows slanted.

"Truly?" she asked. "All of a sudden, I'm your twinkle, am I?" She took a step away from the bedpost and tilted her head to one side, studying him as if he was a laboratory curiosity. "Nyko told you about Josnic raping me, didn't he?"

What…? Thomal's stomach jacked up into his chest to play bumper cars with his heart. Holy shit! *What*?!

"His nibs can finally forgive me now that I've received a proper comeuppance for my sins, is that it?"

The room spun away, disappearing into the eye of a twister. He groped behind him for some place to sit. Nausea exploded in the pit of his stomach. His legs stopped holding him up and he sat down abruptly on the carpet.

Pandra gave him an astonished look.

Her words made another round inside his head, resounding like a hard clapper against his ears. Black rage at what had been done to his woman surged through him with such force he was powering to his feet in the next blink and moving in a blur of speed for the door. "I'm going to kill him!" he gnashed through the points of his fangs, welcoming his anger, if not the reason for it. Fury was so much better than—

"Thomal—stop."

Something in Pandra's voice brought him up short. He turned back around, his breath hot inside his lungs.

"You truly didn't know about what Josnic did?" she asked quietly.

"No," he fairly growled. An animal rose inside him. If he wasn't on his way to inflicting some *extremely painful* revenge on someone in about two seconds, this room was going to get annihilated. "And for the record, I would *never* wish rape on you as payback. I never wanted you dead, either, so that I could be free of you. I would've come after you in the Hell Tunnels, too, but I'm not a half-Răscu, so I couldn't."

She watched him for a long moment, more of that laboratory curiosity look, then sat on the edge of her mattress, hooking her insteps on the bedrail. Her bare feet somehow made her seem kind of vulnerable. Hard to believe her body had been crowded into a black leather slut suit earlier this evening. "I wasn't raped," she said. "Josnic was carting me off to do the deed when Nyko arrived."

The admission jarred Thomal. Then her words sank in all the way. *I wasn't raped.* He pressed the heels of his palms to his closed lids. He could barely think straight, but...but... Dropping his hands, he spoke around the thickness in his throat. "So you're okay?"

He heard her soft inhalation. "Oţărât wasn't exactly tea with the fecking queen, but"—she shrugged—"more or less."

"I'm sorry." That just fell out of his mouth, lamely and without the necessary elaboration; there was so much he was sorry for. But because this mole hill actually was a mountain, he wasn't sure how to even begin to scale it.

"Why the change in attitude toward me?" she asked.

He ran a hand across his nape. Guess he was going to have to find a way. "I suppose this," he said, pointing to his butterfly bandage. "Nyko beat the pride out of me. Or maybe it was more like he was beating *truth* into me, making me acknowledge things I've known all along. About you."

She smoothed her palms down her thighs to her knees. "Like what?"

"Like how hard you've worked to change. I should've given you props for it, Pandra, but I've been tangled up and not seeing things straight for a long time. I...I just couldn't get past Arc's hatred of you, and my own guilt. But I want you to know that I've put Arc out of my life for now so—"

"No." Her eyes flew to his face. "No, Thomal, I don't want that. He's your brother, and you love him dearly. The last thing I'd ever want is to come between you two."

"This isn't entirely about you, Pandra—not at the core. It's about me figuring out who I am outside of being Arc's little brother. Until I get that squared away, I can't redefine my relationship with him on the level it needs to be. If that makes sense."

She nodded, but her eyes were sad. "I still feel right gutted for being the one to upset that apple cart, though."

"Don't." He stepped further into her bedroom. "I'm coming to realize what a good thing it is…this stuff with Arc. It's a son of a bitch to deal with, yeah, but…it's necessary." He exhaled. "Can we…? I'd like to move forward, Pandra. Put the past in the past. You're my bonded mate, and I'd like to give our relationship a chance, if you'll…" He shuffled his feet. "I don't deserve a chance. I never gave you one. I've spent eight months blowing it, so I wouldn't blame you if you refused to change things between us—kept it with me just coming to you for feedings and that's it—but…" He swallowed, the tendons in his throat going taut. "I'm hoping you won't."

She gazed into his eyes, so deeply that for a moment he saw the thin border of her pupils against the black of her irises. "I suppose that depends on if you can forgive me."

He twisted his mouth, probably his whole face, the idea was so stupid. "There's nothing to forgive, Pandra."

She shook her head and began to speak.

He cut in. "You didn't rape me, okay? I volunteered for that mission."

"Thomal," she chided softly.

He rubbed a hand over his non-injured cheek. "All right, look, you were troubled at the time you did that stuff to me and Arc. I know that. But you're not the same woman you were back then." He shoved his hands into his jeans pockets. "Truth is, I didn't come here to forgive you, but to ask you to forgive me."

She sat there in silence, her lips moving together and her hands rubbing her knees.

He scraped his fingers inside his pockets, collecting lint under his nails.

"Say, do you want to go out?" she asked him suddenly.

"Neck a few pints at Garwald's or something?"

He paused, frowning internally, then his pulse bounced out of rhythm. She was asking him out on a date? He barely stopped himself from yelling, *Hell, yes*! "Are you sure you feel up to it?"

Chapter Forty-One

GARWALD'S PUB WAS A BLEEDING wasteland.

True, six hours ago the town of Ṭărână had been under Om Răo siege, but shouldn't the bar have been packed out because of that, all and sundry itching to get pie-eyed and forget the whole sordid hash? Just as well the place was deserted. Pandra didn't fancy a crowd of folk gawking at the unprecedented of sight of her and Thomal out together, on a date, of all the blooming things.

The whole situation seemed surreal.

He seemed surreal, like a prince out of a fairy book or some such, the soft overhead lighting turning his hair to corn silk, the green in his shirt bringing out aquamarine highlights in his eyes, and the smile he kept aiming at her rather intimate. Even the wound on his face, now swollen angrily and heading from red to marbled black, worked for him, making him look more masculine.

Thomal led her to an inconspicuous booth in the back, despite the lack of populace, and guided her into a seat. "Everyone's gone to ground," he told her as he slid into the side opposite. "The thing about Vârcolac, when threatened we fight like hell, but afterward we hole up with our loved ones. Males especially need to keep wives and kids in our line of sight, assure ourselves they're all right."

"You're a protective lot." She smiled wryly. "I've noticed."

"Take your average, run-of-the-mill Vârcolac, and you've got a very protective guy. Remove all women from his life and his chance to procreate, then return the possibility of a family

TRACY TAPPAN

back to him in the form of extremely hard to find women, and his protectiveness shoots into the stratosphere."

Luvera arrived at their table with a friendly expression, nothing at all unusual about her, as if it was bog-standard to see Pandra and Thomal sitting together. No gawking from the bar mistress, at least. "I can't believe someone actually showed up tonight," she chuckled. "I was getting ready to close."

"Oh, hey, we don't want to hold you up," Thomal said in a conciliatory tone. "I know you're probably tired."

Luvera was four months pregnant, an amazing turn of events, considering Alex—a non-Vârcolac who couldn't scent his mate's fertile time—had managed to get his wife—a Vârcolac female who only ovulated about twice a year—with child in under five months. Proud papa was certainly strutting his stuff around town over that accomplishment.

"No, I'm fine," Luvera said. "I've got some inventory to do, anyway." She glanced between them. "Can we keep it simple, though? A couple of beers and pretzels, maybe?"

"Brilliant for me," Pandra said, even though a better decision probably would've been to abstain from alcohol altogether. Her Rău beastie was jiffling about inside her tonight, eager to come back out after being released earlier in Oţărât, then afterward, pumped up with enchanted surgery drugs and her nasty immortality ring. But, feck it, the day had been a ruddy pisser. She could let herself get half-cut, at least.

"I'm cool with that, too," Thomal said.

"Great. I'll be right back." Luvera reached over and gave Pandra's shoulder a soft squeeze. "Glad to see you're fine, by the way." She bustled off.

"Okay, so are you ready?" Thomal asked, a mischievous glint entering his eyes.

"Come again?" The playful expression on her husband's face was nearly curling her toes. "Ready for what?"

"We're going to ask questions to get to know each other better."

"Are we now?" She cocked a single brow. "You mean like favorite food, favorite song, that sort of thing?"

"No, that'd be boring. Things like, best childhood memory, worst date. Personal stuff."

"Personal? Gads, sounds like a mare."

"A what?"

"That's short for *nightmare*."

Thomal chuckled. "Come on. It'll be good for us."

Soft music began to pour out of the bar's speakers, a mellow song by some woman—Norah Jones, possibly.

"You go first." His chuckle settled into a smile that could've made angels weep. "Tell me a memory from your childhood, a good one."

"Well, lawks, there are so many to choose from." She sighed, thinking back, then latched onto the first thing that popped into her mind. "I had a pony when we lived in England." She perked up. That was a grand memory, right? Every kid wanted a pony.

"Whoa, you lived in England?"

She tossed him a sardonic look as she gestured to her mouth. "The accent."

"I just thought…" He shook his head. "Never mind. Where in England did you live?"

"In a smashing mansion on the Sussex coast." Sitting back in her booth, she traveled back in time and wandered the hallways of her childhood home, seeing the gleaming hardwood floors, exquisitely crafted furniture, flowered wallpaper, soaring mullioned windows with views of magnificent gardens and gentle green hills, long hallways with rows upon rows of doors…one door in particular. She halted before it. "Ah, here's a memory." In her imagination, the door loomed larger than life, like a portal Finn McCool might use to come and go. "In that mansion, like in any other place we've ever lived, my father had a den, a room he kept all to himself, extremely private, entrance strictly forbidden. I was about eleven, pre-pubescent and full of my own invincibility, and I took a dare from my older brothers to sneak inside."

The sides of Thomal's eyes crinkled with amusement. "Uh, oh."

"Mind, I didn't get caught. I beetled it in and out, I was so scared."

Luvera swept by, dropping off two foaming beer steins and a basket of soft pretzel nuggets, then whisked off.

"While I was inside," Pandra went on, "I saw on the shelf behind my father's desk a framed photograph of a toddler girl, sitting on a lawn and holding a red ball: Toni—I knew it instantly. *Only* her. None of Raymond's other children had the honor of making it into his precious man-lair." Pandra took a sip of her beer, licking the foam from her upper lip. "It was then that I knew I wasn't my father's favorite, after all."

Thomal's chin went down. "*That's* your good memory? Seriously?"

She picked up a pretzel nugget and nibbled on it. "Aye, it took all the pressure off, see. Right-o. My turn to ask. Best kiss?" The name Hadley appeared before Pandra's eyes in fat balloon letters. *Hadley was sweet and nice and affectionate. She would've been a great wife, a fantastic mother to my children.* Pandra wanted to pop the letters. With a knife.

"No way." Thomal laughed again. "I'm not answering that. A gentleman doesn't talk about other women with his wife."

"You're a gentleman now, are you?"

His lips slanted. "I have my moments."

She snorted. "I'll let that one go for now. Here's another. Most embarrassing memory?"

"Ah, hell." Thomal sat back, rolling his eyes. "Okay. When I was ten, my dad caught me in the bathroom trying to jack off, sweating bullets, my face all torqued up in pain."

"Jesus wept—*ten*?"

"I know, I know." He made a face. "Dad obviously

thought he had a few more years before he needed to explain the Vârcolac dick blockage sitch-o to me. I got the lecture right then and there, of course."

"Cor blimey, did you even have pubes, yet?" She tossed the pretzel nugget into her mouth and licked the tips of her fingers.

Thomal watched her closely. "Um…you know, I'm not saying. Back to me. How'd you get the scar on your belly?"

Her hand froze in the act of reaching for another pretzel, her fingers twitching over the basket. Raymond sauntered toward her, the tap of his Gucci loafers pounding through her teeth. *What a perishing disappointment you turned out to be, Pandra.* She felt the slimy ribbons of her intestines snaking through her hands, and—Flushing, she set her palm back down on the table. "Pass."

"No passing."

"You passed on the kiss question."

"That was different."

"Bollocks."

"I didn't want to offend you."

"Awww, I didn't know I was so sensitive."

His eyes danced. "You are. Definitely. Now, c'mon. I'm trying to get to know you, right?"

"By rooting about for a bad memory?"

"Looking for both sides of your story is all."

"Aren't you flaming generous."

"I am. Feel free to unload on me. Ease your burden."

She sniffed. "I'm not burdened, mate."

"Ah, ha. Then the story about your scar should be no big deal to tell."

She glanced down, the lure of Thomal's teasing, handsome face filling her chest with an unexpected pressure: eight months' worth of cobras squirming around to get out, no doubt. "Very well, you want a bad memory?" She raked her focus back up to him. "Here's one: I was eleven, snuck into my father's den on a dare, and found out that I wasn't his favorite anymore." A fluttering tightness rolled up her throat.

Thomal's eyes darkened to cobalt, the gold around his pupils like rings of fire. "Sounds like a helluva day," he said softly.

She trembled with the sudden urge to wipe the tenderness off Thomal's face with her fists. An expression like that could cultivate too much hope inside her chest, tempting her to let her cobras escape, to be free of them at long last. She'd be a prize idiot to do that. There wasn't anything about this night, *him*, that she could trust. How many times had he barged into her bedroom, feed on her without a single word, then turned around and walked right back out? For crying out loud, a handful of hours ago, she'd been Dirty Pandra to him.

She trembled again. Everything that writhed inside her, every emotion that hurt and injured and plunged her soul into defeat, ate through the spaces between her ribs and tore out of her. "You want more of the nasties?" she asked sharply, a snarl reverberating inside her head. "Here's a stand-out memory: remember the time you told me you hated me for ruining your happily ever after with Hadley? How about that one?" she spat.

He startled, a muscle in his cheek twitching.

"I know I deserved your anger and hatred at the time, Thomal. But now here you are, asking me to dive headlong into intimacy with you, spill my guts, when I know I'll always be your second choice. How can you even—?"

"You're *not*." Deep grooves set into the sides of his mouth. "I said that about Hadley being so great to hurt you. I...Pandra, I..." He turned his head aside, his Adam's apple bobbing as he clearly struggled for the right words. "You wanted to know about my best kiss?" He brought his turbulent gaze back to her. "I don't have any good ones. And do you know why? Because I always pick the wrong women, *always*, even going back to my first kiss. It was with Trinnía.

You know her?"

"Ţărână's hairdresser," Pandra said. And probably the most dishy Dragon Vârcolac in existence, besides Jennilîth. Figured.

"So you've seen her. She's a damned piece of fluff. A great girl, yeah—no offense to her—but that kiss was like, Jesus, so ridiculously *careful*. Lips all nicey-nice, when what I wanted to do was crush her against me and get my tongue going hard and wet with hers. And with Hadley…? Even worse. I had to walk on tiptoes around her all of the time. I hated it, but couldn't admit that she was wrong for me because I was so in love with the *concept* of her, or what she meant: wife, sex, family, blood that didn't taste like a drunk's upchuck. Then Fate came along and picked you *for* me: the absolute best mate. A woman who's tough enough to call me on my shit and kick my ass back into line when I need it, but who's also soft enough to crawl around on the floor playing with a bunch of school children. Someone who's strong enough to come out the other end of a sucky upbringing with the fight still left in her. But who did, definitely, get battered down by a doucher of a father, and so could stand a husband who *really* wants to make her happy."

She stared at him as needles of emotion pricked at her tear ducts. If he was expecting a comment, he wasn't getting one. Her throat had started to shrink roundabout his admission that Hadley was the wrong woman for him, and had battened down completely when he'd said he wanted to make her happy.

"Don't let all these months of my hard-headedness cloud the truth of what I'm saying to you now. Okay? Please."

A single tear slipped from the corner of her eye and forged a path down her cheek. She pressed both palms over her face. *Arr*, what was this? She couldn't remember the last time she'd cried.

"Oh, shit. Please, don't cry, Pandra."

Another sob wrenched out of her, and another. She tried to choke back her tears. This was ludicrous. What would Raymond say if he saw her like—? She immediately cut off the thought. Sod him! She'd gotten herself into a sorry state because of too many years spent keeping her feelings locked away. Sod him! Sod him! Sod him! Pressing her palms more firmly to her face, she wept harder.

"That's it." She heard Thomal shift along the stretch of his seat. "I'm coming over to your side and hugging you, because, seriously, you're killing me with this."

She felt the vinyl of her booth give, and then Thomal's warm body was next to hers, his arms enfolding her in an embrace. The gentleness of his touch was both foreign and welcome in one amazing instant.

She hiccupped. "If you ever hurt me again…"

"No way," he came back. "Not happening."

"I realize that you might sometimes, by accident." Tears gushed uncontrollably, soaking her palms. "But if you ever do it on purpose, I'll quit you, Thomal. I swear it. No second chances."

"You have an absolute deal on that." He drew her closer.

She sank against him. Her lips wobbled and her spine shook. *Bugger me.* "Why did you have to snub me for so bleeding long, you god-awful toe-rag?"

"I'm so sorry," he whispered against her brow.

A spasm of pain clutched her sternum. *Cobras, cobras, so bloody many.* They *twanged* out of her, fast and straight, like cartoon snakes miraculously transmuted into arrows. Her heart expanded and filled her chest, taking up the space left beyond. She nestled her face into one of Thomal's sturdy pectorals, his scent filling her nose. She loved how he smelled…although tonight there was an unwelcome hint of strangely scented soap about him. But underneath that he was pure Thomal, a scent of darkness, almost like a foreign spice, and danger, like polished steel, but also earthy, natural smells, like what color and light and texture might smell like if those things had scents.

Warmth flooded her veins, spreading calm through her. Her stomach did a punch-front forward flip and round off cartwheel—gymnastics again, like when she'd seen him in his shaggable glad rags in *Rufskin*. She sniffed back the last of her tears. "I have a term," she said, taking some of his shirt in her hand and rubbing it between her thumb and forefinger.

He ran a palm lightly down the curve of her back. "Whatever it is, I'll do it."

"I want us to have sex."

CHAPTER FORTY-TWO

PANDRA CUT A SHARP RIGHT out of Garwald's, Thomal hurrying at her side, both of them legging it down Main Street. Several meters from the mansion, they broke into an outright run, and by the time they were halfway up the grand staircase, she'd already wrapped herself around him—legs clamping his waist, arms enfolding his neck…lips kissing a path up his throat. Thomal uttered a growl.

Pounding up to the second floor, he kicked open his bedroom door, sending the wood panel banging against the wall, and in five long strides, he was at his bed, tumbling her onto the mattress and coming down hard on top of her. Her insides clenched with quickening desire…and the instinct to roll him beneath her and take control. She never let a man be on top during a tupping.

But then he levered his own body up, bracing himself on straight arms as he gazed down on her with a wolfish expression, his lungs working. "You know what I'm thinking?"

An unsteady laugh broke from her. "I'd say the possibilities are too endless at this particular moment, love."

"I was thinking that we've never even kissed." He lifted a hand and brushed the pad of his thumb across her lower lip.

She gave him a heavy-lidded look. "An oversight you plan to rectify, dare I hope?"

The dark centers of his eyes lit. He took her lower lip between his thumb and forefinger and tugged gently on it as he lowered his head at the same time. His lips met hers, his

310

fingers sliding to rest at her chin. The sweet taste of his breath washed over her tongue, his mouth warm and soft and greedy. She drank him in…and grew more thirsty. Intoxicated. Sparks of fire skittered up and down her spine as he molded his lips to hers with soft caresses, his attentions caring and reverent.

An unfamiliar uneasiness spiraled through her. Palming the back of his neck, she pulled him closer and slanted her head to the side, roughening the kiss into something hard and hungry. Familiar. Comfortable.

Thomal groaned into her mouth, then lifted his head and offered her a crooked grin. "I definitely have a best kiss now."

She smiled back. "Go shut the door."

"Hell if I'm moving." His voice was a hoarse snarl.

"Thomal." She gave his shoulder a shove. "You want every Tom, Dick, and Harry to see us at our business?"

"Right now? Don't care." He angled his hips forward, prodding her vadge with the hard length of his stalk.

A low moan came out of her. Another move like that and she'd be throwing prudence to the dogs, as well. "If you go close the door," she coaxed, "I'll be in the buff by the time you get back."

He was off her at Dragon speeds, blasting over to the door and slamming it shut before she even had a chance to blink. He turned to face her, chin down, peering at her through the fan of his lashes as he kicked his shoes into the corner. Then his pants came off, revealing that magnificent dobber of his, driving out from a golden thatch of hair.

She ran her tongue across her lips. Her nipples tightened.

He prowled toward her, pulling his shirt off over his head, a task that rippled and delineated an astounding array of muscles, tendons, and ligaments. And then he was standing in front of her, arrogant and strong and proud, a sexy smirk aimed at her. "You said something about naked?"

"Oh." She laughed. "Didn't mean to muck about, hubby, but you're a right distracting article." She hauled off her tank top and cast it aside along with her bra.

His gaze dropped to her naked breasts and lingered there…for so long that a blush actually rose. He was looking at her as if he'd never seen anything more beautiful.

"Gonna have to attend to those." With a hand on her shoulder, he urged her down flat on the mattress, and leaned over her, his lips lowering to within a scant inch of her nipple. He hovered there, his hot breath slipping over the crest of her breast and rolling in a lightening tide of warmth down the sides.

She squirmed. If she grabbed him by the temples and muscled him down the rest of the way, would that be bad form? His tongue darted out and flicked over just the tip. Her eyes fell closed as her nipples crinkled and her vadge warmed.

He placed a kiss just below the cleavage of her breasts, leaving her aching nipple behind as he forged a path downwards.

Frustration twitched and pulled at her.

He must've heard her teeth come together. He chuckled low in his throat. "I'll be back, horndog." He kissed lower. Then stopped.

She angled a glance down at him.

Eyes the color of steel ice were pinned on her belly. His fingertips traced the ugly scar there. "You've been hurt so much in your life," he whispered, bending forward to brush his lips over her scar.

Every muscle in her body tightened. Bristling with irritation, she shifted rigidly under his touch.

"Tell me what happened to you."

"No."

Thomal straightened. His gaze was cloudy and filled with a poignant ache. He took a step back.

The absence of his body heat chilled her. *My, what a recognizable feeling.* Her fingers curled inward.

"Maybe it's too soon for this," he said. "Too soon after

Oțărât. Too soon for *us*."

"Why?" she snapped, sitting up. "Because I'm unwilling to subject myself to your pity?"

"My—?" He looked at her as if she was a complete nutter. "Because *I'm* one of the people who've hurt you so badly, and you understandably don't trust me, yet."

"You've been nice to me all of a few hours, Thomal. What the bleeding hell did you expect?"

"Exactly my point." Turning around, Thomal grabbed his blue jeans off the floor.

She narrowed her eyes as she watched him tug on his trousers. Anger slithered a hot coil through her body. She vaulted off the bed, stalked across the room, and wrenched the door open. "All right, then. Get out."

He stopped dressing, his shirt draped over the palm of his hand.

"That's what you do best, isn't it?" She squeezed the doorknob, forcing it from a circle to an oval. "Leave."

A sinew bunched in his cheek. "This isn't me rejecting you, Pandra. The total opposite. I don't want to get into that bed with you until it can be more than fucking. I want it to…I don't know, to mean something beyond the obvious: that we're both horny as shit for each other."

"*Mean something*?" She scoffed at the concept even as little muscles in her belly jumped and a queer bolt of panic closed off her throat. Old memories rose up: a poor mark in algebra class, second prize at the boxing club tournament, her inability to master Russian. Any less-than-perfect performance had been cause for disappointment to flicker through Raymond's gaze, his encouraging smile to turn so utterly false. And now here she was again, standing on the edge of a precipice where she was certain to disappoint. Because she had no idea how to make sex mean anything.

She stalked back over to Thomal and snatched his T-shirt out of his hand. "And here I thought you liked it rough, old boy. What was all that piffle about no tiptoeing?" She tugged the shirt on over her head, glad when the hem fell to the tops of her thighs. She didn't want to be naked anymore. "Was that just a load of tut?"

"Look," he said in a measured tone. "You told me no second chances. So I'm not going to mess this up. I've done every wrong thing I could possibly do with you, Pandra, and I don't want to keep doing that." He dragged in a deep breath, the muscles across his chest tensing. "I don't mean to ask too much of you. I know you don't love me. I…this is the first time we'll be together since the night of…" He trailed off.

Her eyes drifted sideways, away from him. "And what if it *can't* mean anything?" She fingered the soft cotton of Thomal's T-shirt. Her heart suddenly felt watery.

She heard a frown enter his tone. "You mean ever?"

She shrugged stiffly. "Sex has always been about blowing off a proper head of steam for me, Thomal, usually involving violence to some degree." She turned to look at him. "Something I'm sure you can attest to. There's a good chance I'll kick ten balls out of you when we're done." Especially should it *mean something*. How heinous.

"You can certainly try." A thread of amusement ran through his voice.

Her skin flushed hot. "Flaming hell, now isn't the time to get mangled up in your male ego. I'm dead serious here."

"So am I." He scratched the side of his face. "I'm not afraid of you, Pandra."

She planted her hands on her hips. Everyone was afraid of her, the fool. "You ought to be. Stuff your Dragon speed and your Vârcolac strength. You can't beat me."

He shrugged, his expression remaining neutral. "That's something we'll never find out for sure, because I'm never fighting you again. If you come at me with violence, I'll combat you with love—kisses, hugs, and a bunch of dorky jokes, poor you."

She gaped at him. She had no words for that, not a one. Nor did she have any idea what the devil she'd do if he actually followed through and played smoochie face with her nasty half.

He walked over to her and reached behind her, gently closing the door, grinning as he said, "This is my bedroom, by the way."

She flushed.

"Now you and I are going to do that thing couples do when they don't have sex." More humor rippled through his tone. "I think it's called cuddling."

CHAPTER FORTY-THREE

PANDRA PULLED HER HAND FROM Thomal's when he tried to lead her to the bed, and instead strayed to the other side of the room. Her husband's eyes followed her as she went over to his desk and slumped down at it. Cuddling? Playing *little spoon* to a man's *big spoon* was another precipice she didn't care to approach.

"What's wrong?" Thomal asked quietly.

She peered up at the ceiling. "Why do you have to make everything so bloody complicated?" She spun around and started to prop her elbows on the desk. Then froze. *What the dickens?* She picked up the art pad off the top of the desk and stared down at the drawing with her lips parted, utterly stupefied.

She heard Thomal move up behind her.

A landslide of emotion and heat tumbled through her. She turned on her chair to gape up at him. "Is this how you actually see me?"

Tenderness filled his gaze. "That *is* you."

She looked back down at the portrait he'd drawn of her, her throat closing off around an emotion too unfamiliar to name. Embarrassment? Pride? A sort of giddy *that's me* wonderment? Her likeness stared back at her, the mouth turned in a smile both ironic and gentle, the depth of the eyes so… No…no…it was…

Pandra outlined the edge of the art pad with her finger-tips. For as long as she could remember, she'd felt like her soul resided on the outside of her body; that she had one, yes, but it was separate from her, walking hand-in-hand, perhaps, without a great deal of influence. Somehow Thomal, with no more than charcoal, dark pencils, and his own gifted hand, had merged the two, body and soul in one. That was the only way she could think to describe the indescribable *something* that he'd put on the page. In essence, he'd portrayed the woman she'd always wanted to be, and it was the furthest thing from Dirty Pandra in existence. "How did you do this?"

His eyes warmed on her. "I was feeling inspired." He stepped nearer, his fingertips drifting beneath her jaw. His body heat floated around her.

The hint of a shiver touched the base of her spine.

"I have a way of seeing the truth in people," he told her. "Even that night in the seedy hotel room, I sensed you were more than just some half-Ră

u bully." His fingers floated partway down her throat, then wandered away. "It's why I didn't kill you."

She lifted her brows slightly.

He smiled. "When I was feeding on you, I couldn't drain you dry, but I definitely could've ripped your throat to shreds."

She exhaled a short laugh. "I wondered about that. I thought perhaps there was some natural Vârcolac law against hurting a host."

"Nope." His mouth angled a bit. "Why would you let me bite you, if you weren't sure about it?"

She smiled thinly. "Self-destructive risk-taking was sort of my go-to back then."

Thomal's mouth canted more to the side.

She glanced down at her portrait again, marveling once more at the image staring back at her. "You *are* a dab hand at capturing a person, Thomal. Whyever did you give it up?"

He shrugged. "I suppose I figured it wasn't manly. I had my dad and Arc to compete with in the household, and being an artist felt like a disadvantage."

She didn't know about his father, but he was overestimating Arc's level above him on that score. "There are many different ways to define masculinity."

He laughed. "No, there aren't."

She made a moue of her lips.

"But, yeah, if you mean that it's time to figure out who I am based on who I want to be, I agree."

She snorted. "Welcome to the club on that." She carefully set the picture back on the desk. "Maybe," she murmured, "we're closer to each other than either of us realize." She looked up at him, holding his gaze for a long moment. "Remember earlier how you said you wanted to give our relationship a chance?"

He nodded.

"Do you truly think more waiting is going to help us build a marriage? We've already been circling each other for eight long months."

"Probably not."

"I know you're trying to be good to me, and I appreciate that, but can it be enough that I *want* to trust you? And that I'd like to try and have relations with you which are…uh, special."

A smile concentrated in his eyes.

"I need you to *show* me how to be, hubby. Cuddling isn't going to do that."

His lips curled silkily. "Well, hell, now you've made it a challenge." He took both of her hands in his, kissed the tops of each, then helped her stand and led her over to the bed.

She sat down on the mattress and scooted to the middle, leaning back on her elbows.

His eyes changed color, darkening and deepening. He prowled onto the bed, climbing up her body and nudged her knees apart, his pelvis coming to rest between her thighs.

The weight of his body stirred her aggression awake, like the mythological Echidna roused from her cave. That was her, half-woman, half-snake monster… *No.* She forced the portrait Thomal had drawn of her to her mind's eye, and checked herself. *This isn't an act of domination. He isn't trying to make you vulnerable. He's trying to make love to you.* She drew in a full breath and looped her arms around his neck. *This is Thomal, not an enemy, but an artist down to his very soul.* She lifted her mouth to his, and he took the invitation, his lips exploring hers with lazy heat, his tongue making a silky journey along the line of her mouth, coaxing her lips apart. His tongue crept inside, and she met it with an easy swirl.

Groaning, he shifted on top of her. He had a lob on again…if he'd ever lost it entirely. His fingers crept beneath her shirt—*his* shirt—grazing up the side of her ribcage on a route toward her breast. His hand found her flesh and encircled it. He slowly broke their kiss, his lips peeling centimeter by centimeter away from hers, as if he couldn't bear to leave, but had been called away to other, compulsory endeavors. Pushing the shirt up to her collar bone, he ducked down to her nipple and sucked it into the moist well of his mouth, his lips fastening onto the erect berry with exquisite care.

Her blood slowed to a sluggish crawl through her veins, her heart wavering. It'd been so long since she'd been touched by a man, and never like this. He was being so damnably gentle—something she hadn't expected after all that talk of being horny as shit and crushing a woman against him with tongues going hard and wet. Could a man be gentle while bonking? Thrusting dobber, pounding hips…doubtful. That offered a measure of comfort. She gripped his perfectly formed buttocks and pulled him tightly against her, encouraging him to enter her.

Air rushed out of his nose and mouth, but he resisted her impatience. Tugging the shirt all the way off, he flung it aside and found her other nipple, his tongue swirling and lapping around the erect point.

She moaned. The man had the softest tongue ever.

"Okay," he whispered. "This was actually a very good idea." He left her breast to move down her body, placing kisses along her flesh to her waist, as he'd done before. And again, he hesitated.

She snapped her teeth shut. For crying out loud, not more of his—

"No questions," he said in a gravelly voice, unbuttoning her jean shorts. He pushed them down her legs, along with her knickers. "Whoa," he breathed out, peering at her nethers. "You have hair now."

"Part of my new persona." She twisted her ankles to slip her clothes the rest of the way off, then edged her thighs open a little wider. "You approve?"

His gaze lit. "Baby, I'm about to show you how much." He bent his head and placed a kiss on her small patch of curls.

Damnation! She slammed her legs together, one of her knees clonking his chin.

"Ouch!" He lurched back. "What the hell, Pandra?!"

"Bugger off from down there, Thomal."

His eyebrows scrunched together. "Did I do something wrong?"

"No. I just don't go in for that."

His brows changed positions, ascending high on his forehead. "Do you mean no guy has ever gone down on you before?"

What did he truly think? That using sex to violently blow off steam entailed her lying like a sacrifice before a man, her legs flopped wide while his mouth fiddled with parts best left to her own self?

He laughed throatily. "My badass, half-Răn wife, the cunnilingus virgin." He swept a hand across his chest. "I feel honored to be the one to change that."

She held her thighs firmly shut. "Not on your Nellie, mucker."

He shook his head at her, the look on his face intractable. "Pandra, you're my bonded mate. I have to scent and taste you, or I'll go crazy. And I mean that literally." He set his chin on her closed knees and gazed down on her, his eyes glinting blue flames. "I'm Vârcolac, honey, so, you know, I'm very orally inclined."

"Oh, piss." She scowled at him.

His lips spread into the kind of broad, fangy grin that highlighted his handsomeness to a near heart-stopping degree.

Her belly went all squidgey. Hells bells, the bugger knew he was irresistible when he did that.

"Nothing bad, I promise." He coaxed her legs apart. "All good." His attention fastened keenly on her nethers as he mattress-jogged out of his blue jeans, his knees pumping to fling his trousers off. Sprawling between her thighs again, he pressed his face into her nascent pubic hair, nuzzling the curly nest.

She cursed, her legs instinctively jerking.

Thomal shot back into a crouch. "Okay, listen up." He pointed a finger at her. "No more shutting your legs on me, you hear? No matter what. As strong as you are, you'll pop my skull like a rotten grapefruit. We solid on that?"

She made a face at him. "Away and shite."

"If you don't like something I'm doing, tell me, and I'll stop. Give me your word."

"I can't believe what a chuffing arse you're being."

A bold smile curved his lips. "You smell extremely good, by the way."

She reddened. "All *right*, for crying out loud. Do your stupid thing."

He dropped down onto his belly and pushed his hands against her inner thighs, spreading her legs wider.

Her stomach balled. She latched her eyes onto the ceiling, as if the spot of chipped paint up there could keep her from killing her husband between the vise-grip of her thighs.

The tips of his fingers found the inside of one of her knees. He sketched a figure eight there, then trailed his touch along the flesh of her inner thigh to brush near her feminine core.

She held her breath.

A single finger glided up the side of her opening, over the hood covering her clitoris, then back down the other side. Back up he went to the area just above her clitoris, where— she expelled her held breath—he stayed. His finger made little circles around her clitoris, around and around, skimming over her tight bundle of nerve endings, over and over.

Broken gasps escaped from between the barrier of her teeth as her nethers filled with a carnal heat. She tingled and shivered; her belly quaked; her pelvis grew heavy.

Thomal inhaled deeply, as if testing the air for a scent. Grunting once, he dipped his head down, and her womb quickened as his tongue probed into her sex. He shoved his tongue deeper into her hole and groaned in what sounded like sheer rapture. She clenched her toes into the bedsheets as he lapped at her opening, murmuring, "You taste so good," between strokes, the exquisite feeling sending her heart into a wild staccato beat against her ribs. His tongue smoothed in an extra-slow path all the way up to her clitoris, and the game changed again.

A large breath escaped her as a flush of ecstasy coursed through her body. Thomal pressed his tongue against that button and held it there for several long seconds, the soft, focused pressure chasing away any lingering tension. Her thighs fell wide and the clench melted from her toes. Her mouth slacked open around erratic pants as he made small, sliding movements against her, all energy, feeling, friction concentrated on this most sensitive part of her. Frissons of electricity plunged down her legs.

He added a finger to her torment, tucking it inside her, easily sliding on her wetness. He moved it in and out, all the while his tongue softly rubbing. A sound of pleasure slipped out of her, raspy and awestruck. Her hips surged to meet his strokes. Tension returned, but in a good way, a bound-up, anticipatory pull in her womb. Her inner muscles tightened as her husband's tongue and finger worked in concert, and between one second and the next, she was coming, her spine lifting, her sheath squeezing and throbbing. She hissed, gasped, moaned.

As the shocks left her body, Thomal sat back on his heels, his eyes black with lust, his dobber standing erect as a Beefeater guard from the middle of his crotch.

Was it even bigger now?

"Want more of that," he growled. Taking his dobber in his fist, he moved between her thighs, positioned himself at her entrance, and pushed inside her.

A groan rolled up from the pit of her chest as she felt her flesh close around him.

Thomal let out some kind of animalistic snarl. No more niceties now. He pummeled her with his thrusts, deep, hard, fast, nothing eloquent or expert, but with a passion so raw and real that inside her she felt places open that'd been closed her whole life. She'd expected comforting familiarity to come with his aggressive passion, but instead her breathing took on a frantic tenor. What if he was lulling her into a false sense of security? *That's what you do best, isn't it? Leave.* She couldn't lose this...

A guttural rasp broke past Thomal's lips, the noise sounding like it'd been wrenched from deep within his soul. "Jesus, yeah," he ground out. "Yeah." Rising above her, he entwined his fingers with hers and pressed her hands to either side of her head, locking eyes with her in an intimate hold. His velvet shaft was an unrelenting force inside her. His gaze never wavered. *This isn't me rejecting you, Pandra. The total opposite.*

Her vision fuzzed as another orgasm slammed through her, these shockwaves stronger than the last. "Thomal," she whispered.

His muscle-ridged chest and taut belly crushed her into the mattress as he came down on top of her for his final strokes. "So fucking good," he panted softly into her ear, then sank his fingers into her hair, grabbing up fistfuls of it as he captured her lips in a rough, devouring kiss. He rooted himself firmly against her, his butt muscles clenching tight, his length pulsing rhythmically as he filled her with his seed…filled up all the empty, lonely places she owned. His ragged moan of completion poured into her mouth, then he collapsed on top of her, her name tumbling from his lips.

Panting, she hugged him close, all hot, steamy skin.

He sprawled boneless on top of her, gasping and sweating, his heart hammering as if it meant to scarper off from the cage of his ribs.

She caressed her hands down the cool scales of Thomal's dragon tattoo, petting his creature as she waited for him to regain himself.

Thomal muffled a chuckle against her sweat-dampened throat, then, "Wow." He straight-armed himself above her, a strange smile spreading across his face as he singsonged, "Little Jack Horner sat in a corner, fucking this cutie pie. Stuck in his thumb, made the bitch cum, and said, 'Hell of a lad am I!'"

She laughed, openmouthed and with a full lung of air. "What the *devil?*"

A larger smile bloomed in his eyes. "I told you I'd combat your need to kick my ass with dorky jokes."

"That was a limerick, you gonk."

"How about this, then?" He settled down on his elbows, his chest caressing her breasts. "Tomorrow morning we head into Țărână's family neighborhood and pick out our house. Oh, and those kids you want to have. I'm totally on board with making it happen. Whenever you want. Soon."

She opened her mouth, closed it, opened it again. "For crying out loud, stop. I'm not feeling the need to lace into you. Truth is…" She made a show of snuggling beneath him. "I'm feeling rather contented and satiated."

"Hmm." He pulled out of her, then rolled to her side, propping his head on his hand. "It was my sexual prowess, wasn't it?"

She chuckled. "Dare I shovel more fodder onto your ego?" She dashed a hand over his soft hair. "But, aye, I never knew sex could be so smashing."

His expression was one of pure pleasure. "Me either." He traced a finger along the flesh of her arm.

She smiled. "What you just said, about the house and the nippers? Let's do that."

Making a sound in his chest, Thomal rolled on top of her. "What's this? Ready to go again?"

"Just need a tiny bite," he said, lowering his face to her throat. The pointed tip of a fang traced the path of her carotid artery. "Then, yeah."

They made love and slept, made love and slept, all through the night. The early hours of stupid o'clock had just arrived by the time they were finishing with their fifth go-'round…and were interrupted by a fist pounding at the bedroom door.

Panting on top of her, Thomal's head bolted up from her neck, his fangs still elongated. "Somebody's about to get killed. Go away!" he shouted at the door.

"Thomal." It was Breen. "This is important, man. I wouldn't be here disturbing you if it wasn't."

He grumbled. "All right. One second." He kissed Pandra on the nose as he slid out of her. "Sorry, baby." Rolling off, he hopped out of bed and grabbed his blue jeans, tugging them on.

Wrapping herself in the bed sheet, she climbed off the mattress, too. "It's okay, love. My vadge could use the rest, anyway."

He glanced askance at her as he pulled on his T-shirt.

"Nuh, uh." He crossed the room, and she followed. "What's going on?" he asked as he opened the door.

Breen, who already leaned right heavily toward Pure-bred pale, was white as a corpse. "It's Toni."

At the mention of her sister's name in that dire tone, Pandra lost all feeling in her limbs. She must've made some kind of horrified sound, too, because Thomal's arm instantly came around her shoulders.

Breen looked at the two of them through the long sweep of his black bangs. "She went into labor soon after Pandra got out of surgery. We didn't want to bother you with the news, because Luvera said you guys were, um... But there were complications with the delivery, so now you need to know." Breen's throat appeared to be struggling with a swallow. "Toni almost died and she's in critical condition."

CHAPTER FORTY-FOUR

NYKO SET THE GLASS PITCHER in the Bruns' kitchen sink and poured iced tea into it, sloshing most of the liquid over the high rim. *Darn it.* His hand was shaking as badly as if he was a one-hundred-thirty-year-old, palsied man whose main claim to fame was not messing his Depends after his morning pureed prunes. Him in the kitchen was proving to be the proverbial bull in a china shop—the very reason he was using the sink for this iced tea chore, instead of the counter. It was also why he'd left brewing hot coffee to Beth Costache, who'd gone home to her kids a while back.

He'd broken two glasses early in the morning when they'd all first holed up here: one, two, right in a row—*crrrr-ash.*

The startling noise hadn't earned much more than a dull stare from the two other men, Dev and Shǫn, who were here with Nyko to sit vigil with Jacken. Everyone was too shell-shocked and grief-stricken to do anything but act spacey. Dev still had blood on his jeans: Toni's or the baby's? Who could tell, so much had just...come out of her.

Nyko pinched his eyes closed, his stomach lurching sick-eningly. Bracing his palms on the edge of the sink, he leaned heavily on his hands as memories of the scene in Țărână's hospital dropped on top of him like jagged rocks: Jacken, wild with panic, rushing into the waiting room for help; Dr. Jess, frantic over Jacken's stillborn baby; the sight of Toni on the delivery table, white as paste and nearly unconscious, looking like she'd been through the wringer. Which she had.

No woman brought a child into this world easily, but

giving birth to a Vârcolac baby was a unique chore. Instead of contractions, the laboring woman went through what could only be described as sonic blasts. These were earthquake-like, the pulsations rolling off the womb strong enough to break windows, knock nearby people off their feet, and fell bookshelves. So as soon as a momma-to-be went into labor, she was locked into a belly container on the delivery table to protect the surroundings and the doctor. The container restricted movement, so the uncomfortable momma was made even more uncomfortable, and worse, no pain meds could be given for such a thing as sonic blasts. She had to suffer through it. The single upside was that delivery time for Vârcolac babies clocked in at much less than what it would be for a regular human kid. Vârcolac were birthed in anywhere from four to six hours. The rare woman went eight.

Toni had gone *ten hours* by the time Jacken came rushing into the waiting room.

For some unknown reason, Toni never switched from the sonic phase into pushing mode. Her womb just kept blasting away, propelling Toni toward a state of exhausted death. Dr. Jess finally decided to break protocol and have Toni push even while she was blasting.

That's when Nyko, Dev, and Shon had been called in from the waiting room and tasked with holding mattresses around Toni in order to protect the hospital machinery and Dr. Jess. Nyko had been the one to brace the mattress behind the doctor, stumbling and grunting as Jess got slammed back into the mattress again and again... Until finally, Jess had managed to extract the baby, limp, blue, and silent. Following that was more bad. Toni's final sonic blast catapulted the afterbirth out of her body along with a bucket's worth of blood, which hit the floor and splatted all over Dev. Then she coded.

Paddles! Doc Jess had yelled, then sharply commanded the rest of them to *Go!* the last thing any of them hearing was

Clear!

Jacken lost it.

Stumbling out to the waiting room, a long, moaning growl rumbled out of him as he started to make the ugly shift into Rău.

Goosebumps raised along Nyko's flesh. If Jacken changed to his beast side now, with such stark emotions ruling him, there was no telling if he'd ever make it back out. "Jacken!" Nyko leapt forward and grabbed his brother. "Stop! I need you to stay focused—for Toni!"

Expelling another gravelly animal sound, Jacken sagged forward at the waist.

Nyko quickly hooked his arms under his brother's armpits, his forearms wrapping over Jacken's shoulders, to keep his brother from nose-drilling into the floor. "I need you to stay in touch with your radar," Nyko said.

The two of them scuffled around the waiting room, head to head, like two Sumo wrestlers going at it. A chair got booted across the floor.

The occupants of the waiting room pressed back, the males body-shielding the women. Some of the wives were weeping, loudly, while others were stone-cold silent. Difficult to tell which was worse.

"Feel your radar and tell me if Toni's all right," Nyko told his brother. "*Is* she?!"

An eternal pause, then, "I don't know," Jacken moaned out.

Nyko squeezed his brother harder, motivation for Jacken, a hug of relief for himself. That had been a relatively normal-sounding response. "You do know."

Jacken breathed audibly for several seconds. "Yes…she's not…she's not dead."

The surrounding women muffled relieved cries against their men.

"She's bad, though. Christ, Nyko, she's really bad off."

Which turned out to be very true.

A few minutes later, a harried Dr. Jess had rushed out to give them an update. Toni's blood pressure was dangerously low, making the next twenty-four hours crucial for her survival. The baby, who'd been resuscitated, was doing only marginally better than Toni, and so was also facing an uphill climb to remain alive. After that, Dr. Jess had shooed them all off, not wanting anyone under foot for the stressful work ahead of him, but he'd promised to keep them informed of any changes, good or bad.

So now here they all were, huddled in the Brun household, one heckuva sorry group.

Dev, who had a pregnant wife due in two weeks, looked to be permanently choking on a handful of red hot chili peppers. When Marissa had come by a few hours ago to drop off an egg and cheese breakfast casserole, Dev had ordered her to "Go home and lie down!"

Shọn looked way out of his element for what to do in the situation, having never been particularly close to either Jacken or Nyko, but there was a lot to be said that he was here and trying.

Jacken's state of messed-up-ness went without saying.

Nyko himself was trying to manage all of these grim happenings while stuck in an excruciating half-bond. No. *Excruciating* couldn't even begin to describe this extra-special form of torture and insanity. Maybe this: it felt like every inch of his skin had been ripped off his body, dunked in boiling oil, then reapplied with serrated needles. And whoever had tacked his flesh back into place had done a slipshod job. His skin kept coming off his muscles, scraping, chafing, abrading. There wasn't any part of him that didn't feel completely wrong. He would've been willing to hack off his knife-throwing hand to be done with it.

But the only relief for him lay with Faith and what was between her thighs. Crass, but true. If it wasn't for his absolute refusal to leave Jacken even for one minute, he would've long since succumbed to his fierce primal drive, run to Faith, and without finesse or prelude, mounted her. So, he supposed on one hand it was good that he was being held here. Because in the light of clearer thinking, he had to face facts: Faith had offered up her vein to him to save his life. He, in turn, had partaken of her generosity because he'd grown too weak to resist. Those two things combined put their pre-bonding solidly into the *desperate times call for desperate measures* category. And after all of the other hurts he'd already inflicted on her, he didn't want to add to those by losing control of himself and humping her escape option into oblivion. That would amount to them being blood-bonded by force, which wasn't the best beginning for a strong, long-lasting marriage.

Unfortunately for him, he had no idea how long a half-bond worked at forcibly pulling a man toward completion before it finally let its talons out of the guy. The data was sketchy on that, seeing as so few Vârcolac had ever made it through this horror to the other side. But if he was stuck here long enough in the Brun household, maybe he'd return to an *un*bounded state, and then Faith would be off the hook. And all the screaming inside his head would finally shut off.

He gripped the edge of the sink in tight fists. The mere thought of giving up Faith sent ropes of flesh unfurling off his body, his atoms sprouting lethal spikes. His knuckles throbbed, his tight jaw ached, but those feelings were absolute joy compared to the merciless vise of lust that had a grip on less-mentionable parts of his body. *Thinking about it so much is really helping, too.* Forcing himself to straighten off the sink, Nyko picked up the pitcher of iced tea—his hand trying to play the bongos instead of following his commands—and carefully set it on the kitchen island near some glasses. He squeezed his quaking hand into a fist. He didn't know how much more of this he could take.

Time leaked by like sand through a partially corked hour-glass.

Pandra, uncharacteristically teary-eyed, showed up with Thomal at one point. Then Alex Parthen, who was finally tracked down at a computer seminar topside, arrived, not just teary, but full-on sobbing. Jacken bear hugged Alex for a very long moment.

Time, that cow, wouldn't move fast enough…yet somehow steadily trudged forward, moving from day hours to evening to night. During it all, somber neighbors came and went from the house, quietly checking in and dropping off food. ESPN played constantly on the television, though Nyko doubted anyone actually watched it. The weary vigil-keepers stared at the screen until they began to drift off; Dev and Shọn flopped out on the couch, Alex with his head down on the dining room table, Luvera slumped asleep in a chair next to him, Pandra cuddled up in an armchair with Thomal.

Huh. Nyko supposed now wasn't the time to ask about *that.*

Nyko stayed in the kitchen, pretending to putter, when he was really just fidgeting, certainly not sleeping, what with being stuck in this wanna-stick-my-willy-inside-Faith-and-come-like-a-fire-hose mood. *Jeez.* He really wished he'd stop having such crass thoughts.

Jacken, not surprisingly, didn't sleep, either. He continued to do what he'd been doing as soon as he'd come home from the hospital: sit in an armchair, his palms planted on his knees, and stare at the floor. Twice he'd changed the program and gone to the bathroom. He never ate or drank or even—

There was a soft knock at the door.

Nyko cast a quick, hopeful glance at Jacken, then strode swiftly and silently to open it.

It was Marissa. She was biting her lower lip and her brow was knotted.

Nyko hated the F-bomb, but he dropped it now when he

shifted his focus down to her swollen belly. In the last months of pregnancy, a momma-to-be got strapped up with a labor alarm that warned of oncoming sonic blasts.

Marissa's belly lights were presently winking like a Star Wars X-wing fighter during a Death Star attack, and, whoa, maybe he'd been spending too much time with Alex, lately.

"Oh, no." Nyko clunked his head onto the doorjamb. "Dev's going to crap himself."

"I know," Marissa groaned.

At the sound of his name, Dev sat up from the couch, blinking sleepily. His vision cleared on Marissa, and—he was on his feet, over the back of the couch, and at the door in a single leap. His eyes rounded on his wife's flashing belly lights. "Dammit to hell, Marissa, I told you to lie down, didn't I?"

"It's not my fault." Marissa's voice cracked. "I didn't overdo it, I swear."

Dev jammed his fingers into his hair. "Shit! All right—*dammit!*—let's go." Dropping a steady battery of F-bombs, he pounded out onto the porch and took his wife's arm, leading her down the steps. "Fuck, fuck, fuck…"

"Nichita, hold up." It was Jacken, angling passed Nyko and heading out onto the porch. "I have to tell you something, all right? You need to know that Marissa is going to be fine. She's not going to have complications like Toni did because… Listen, what I'm going to tell you is private, just between us." Jacken went down the porch steps and lowered his voice. "When Toni was sixteen years old, she had a baby."

Marissa gasped softly.

Oh, wow. Nyko pulled the front door into a thin seam.

Jacken dragged a hand through his hair. "She never talks about it, because she feels so guilty about giving the kid up for adoption. Unfortunately, she represses it so deeply she didn't even tell Dr. Jess about it as a part of her medical history. The poor guy had no idea what was going on in that delivery room until I brought it up. At that point he figured out that Toni's body was confused from birthing a human baby before. Her womb didn't know how to shift into Vârcolac labor. So, you see, there was a clear reason for Toni's problems." Jacken turned to speak directly to Marissa. "Have you ever given birth to a human baby?"

The motion of Marissa's lashes released a tear down her cheek. "No. This is the first time I've ever been pregnant."

"Then you won't have any problems, Marissa, just like all the other women in this town who've had plenty of healthy Vârcolac babies without a hitch: Hannah, Ellen, Beth, Maggie. Right?"

"Yes." Marissa looked at Dev.

Dev pulled in a deep breath, still tense, but now more focused. "Yeah. Okay. Jacken's right. You're going to be fine, Riss. I'm going to make sure of it." He hauled Jacken into a single-back-slap hug, then gave Marissa a quick kiss. "Sorry that I fell apart on you for a second." Scooping his wife into his arms, he took off for the hospital.

Jacken watched the two of them go. When they disappeared around a corner, he turned and, without a word, went back to his armchair.

CHAPTER FORTY-FIVE

NYKO STOOD JUST BEHIND JACKEN'S left shoulder, his eyes fixated on the Plexiglas bassinet inside the hospital baby room. He didn't know how he stopped himself from rushing over and peering into it, his hands clasped beneath his chin like he was *oohing* over a basket of puppies. Probably because Jacken hadn't moved past the doorjamb, yet, so he couldn't. Or Alex.

It was six o'clock in the morning, twenty-four hours after Toni had coded and six hours after Marissa had gone into labor. A short time ago, Dr. Jess had come to the Brun household to make the welcome and long-awaited announcement that Toni had stabilized *and* a healthy Baby Brun was hungry. Would Jacken like to come to the hospital and give his child a bottle?

In joy, profound relief, leftover debilitating shock, or whatever, for now Jacken remained frozen in the doorway, staring at Dev, who *was* hovering over the Plexiglas basinet and peering at its occupant, a smile on his face. Dev was also holding a blanket-wrapped bundle in his arms.

"Everything…go all right?" Jacken asked Dev.

Dev met Jacken's eyes and smiled. "Delivery was textbook."

"I enjoyed that part, too," Dr. Jess said wearily from where he stood by the bassinet.

"Marissa's sacked out," Dev added. "Tired as hammered shit, but *really* great."

"Okay, good." Jacken exhaled a careful-sounding breath. "Good." He aimed an inquisitive look at the bundle. "And?"

TRACY TAPPAN

Dev's smile returned, lighting his entire face. "A healthy baby boy. We're naming him Randon."

Jacken nodded slowly.

Nyko sensed a muscular tension in his brother, like Jacken was holding up a wall of unstable bricks, so freaking exhausted and ready to let them go, but unable to relax his hold quite yet.

Jacken transferred his gaze to the bassinet, then over to Dr. Jess. "I don't even know what Toni and I had. In all the turmoil, it just…"

Jess's gaze warmed kindly. "You have a daughter, Jacken."

"No, you've got an *angel*." Dev peered into the bassinet again.

Nyko laughed, utterly delighted. *A little girl-angel niece. How cool.*

Jacken started in on nodding again, the monotonous gesture speaking of how many hours this man had spent dazed and terrified, his life teetering on the edge of utter annihilation. If Jacken had lost both Toni and his child today, even *one* of them, no way he would've ever… *No.* Nyko didn't want to think about it anymore. Too many hours of sitting with that possibility had already twisted his gut into a lot of knots.

"And…she's okay?" Jacken asked Jess. "I mean, she came out looking really…"

The baby came out looking really *dead*, so Jacken was right to be concerned about her wellbeing. Nyko shifted his feet, the knots in his stomach tightening. Heck, maybe he was the one who couldn't let go of the stress bricks.

"Yes," Dr. Jess answered. "I've done some preliminary tests on her—visual acuity, hearing, brain wave function, and she passed splendidly. I believe she was extremely tuckered out by the extensive labor before. But she's proving as strong as her mother in recovering." Jess placed a hand on the bassinet. "Would you like to come meet her?"

336

"Yeah, uh…" Jacken rubbed a hand over the middle of his chest, probably a double-check: *radar's still chill? Yes.* Like a sleepwalker, Jacken strode up to the bassinet, Nyko and Alex on either side of him.

All three men peered down at the wriggly occupant.

"Oh, man!" Nyko exclaimed. "She's adorable!"

Dev had been right. Jacken's daughter *was* an angel with a head full of strawberry-blonde hair, just like her momma's, a tiny rosebud of a mouth, and long lashes resting demurely against her cheeks like dollhouse fans. Dressed only in a diaper, she was also modeling a lot of pink, vibrant skin. She appeared to be a healthy baby, for sure.

Alex moved to the head of the bassinet and smiled down at his niece. "No way that's your kid, Jacken. She's too cute."

Jacken snorted. The noise sounded kind of soggy.

The baby's lids lifted, and the group of them laughed.

"Hello, *there's* Jacken," Nyko said, gazing into his niece's lustrous pure black eyes.

Jacken made another sound in his throat, then he tucked his face into the crook of his arm.

Nyko grabbed ahold of his brother and dragged him close. The man was *spent*.

"Ah, crap," Jacken said into his arm. "After everything I've gone through tonight—in my whole life—*now* I break down."

Dev moved over to Jacken's other side. "All bets are off when it comes to a guy's kid, man. I've been blubbering for hours. Hell, I might sympathy cry again now, you don't quit soon."

Jacken laughed, a jerky sound, still damp around the edges. "That's it, then. From here on out, we're banned from the gym. *Shit.*" He wiped his eyes a little on his sleeve before he brought his head up. "I need a drink of water; I need to feed; I need a nap; I need my wife to wake up." He gripped the edge of the bassinet. "I was never supposed to have this kid, then I lost her, and now here she is, looking like Toni, and…Christ."

The baby pursed her sweet little lips and let out an indignant squeak.

They all chuckled again. It seemed like none of them could get enough of her.

"She's hungry," Dr. Jess observed brightly. "Are you ready to feed your daughter, Jacken? I've already prepared a bottle."

Jacken let out a long, long breath, the load of bricks finally rolling off his shoulders. "That would be amazing." Reaching into the bassinet, Jacken wrapped his daughter in a blanket and, careful to support her neck—as he'd learned reading baby books—gently picked her up. "Hi there, little one," he said in a soft voice Nyko never would've guessed his stiff-jawed brother could've produced. "Your name is Sharanna."

The baby instantly stopped her fussing, peering at Jacken in wonderment.

"Look at that." Alex moved nearer for a better view. "She knows her daddy. Guess all that time talking to Toni's belly paid off."

Jacken tucked Sharanna's blanket under her chin. "Nyko, you getting it, yet?"

Nyko peered more closely at the baby. "Getting what?"

"The last twenty-four hours have been the worst in my life, and you know that means something when I say it, considering where we come from." Jacken accepted a bottle from Dr. Jess. "Yet, I can safely say everything I went through these last hours was so fucking worth it." Jacken slipped the nipple into his daughter's mouth and smiled. "You think maybe you can learn something from that, big brother?"

Nyko watched Sharanna suckle happily, her gaze fastened on her father. To be looked at like that would be…the most amazing… An object the size of a baseball wedged into his throat. He swallowed, but the sucker stayed.

Jacken glanced up, the sudden intensity in his eyes wrenching cords in Nyko's stomach. "Go to Faith. Stop being afraid, you big chowderhead."

Nyko blinked, but stood like stone, the knots in his stomach rooting him to the spot.

Jacken shifted the baby in his arms. "Am I going to have to hit you?"

"It worked for Thomal," Dev drawled.

Nyko startled back to himself. What the heck *was* he doing. "No, that's all right. I'm going now. In fact"—he pointed at the doorway behind him—"you don't mind if I run, do you?"

FAITH CLICKED ON HER NIGHTSTAND lamp and leapt out of bed, whirling her bathrobe around her body as she raced for her bedroom door. The only reason anyone would be knocking at six-thirty in the morning would be for news about Toni. *Finally*! Faith had been lying awake in bed all night. She must've choreographed an entire ballet in her head by now. Whipping open her door, she—

Her heart fell. *No*! Nyko looked terrible. Dark bruises of exhaustion lay under his eyes, his face was drawn into a mask of pain, and if she didn't know better, she'd say it was raining in Ţărână—he was drenched. So the news was bad. She clutched her bathrobe. "Oh, no."

"Toni's okay," he quickly assured her. "The baby, too. Sorry to wake you, but I thought you'd want to know."

"Yes." She felt her shoulders sag. "Oh, thank goodness." She took a few moments to breathe, then gave him another once-over. "You don't look so well."

"Don't feel so well, either." He pushed an unsteady hand through his unruly hair. "And then some."

Touching her hand to the doorjamb, she gazed at him tenderly. "It's been a long night." She wanted to get her hands in that hair of his, tame it, caress it. "Do you want to come in? I mean, if you have to get back to your brother, I understand…"

"No. Jacken was the one who made me get my butt over here."

She inched a brow up. "He did?"

He smiled halfway. "I guess he was getting sick of watching me melt."

"Well, what does he expect, considering all that's been going on?" She reached for Nyko's hand. "Come inside, Nyko. I don't bite." The pun was lost on him. Or…something was more off with him than she realized because—

He pulled away. "I-I can't, not until…" He paused to swallow. "Our bond isn't complete, Faith, which means I'm feeling *extremely* driven right now. Once I step into your room, I—"

"What?" she interrupted sharply.

He frowned at her. "What, what?"

"What are you talking about? That's what." *Not complete?* She put her hands on her hips. "You fed on me. We're bonded."

"But… No. We didn't have sex after I fed, so…no."

She stared at him, her jaw coming loose.

"I have to, uh, ejaculate inside you in order to…" He reddened. "Didn't you read the community manual?"

"Eight months ago! I can't remember everything I read *eight months ago.*" Also, she'd skimmed it, figuring Vârcolac culture wouldn't ever have anything to do with her. She'd lived all but the last few days in Ţărână with one foot out the door. Groaning softly, she dropped her head into her hand. All this time she'd thought she'd had him, and she hadn't. And now… "Oh, God. You've changed your mind about bonding with me, haven't you?" Tears rolled down her cheeks before she even knew she was going to cry. *Why* couldn't she get her life together in this town?

He jolted to attention. "No. Nonononono."

She turned and strode back into her room, plopping down onto her iron-framed couch.

Nyko gave her bedroom a panicked glance. "Ah, heck." He took a careful step inside, planting his boot cautiously, as if the carpet was quicksand. "I'm not afraid of being with you anymore," he said, closing the door behind him. "I got scared about not being able to protect the people I love, and I gave up when I should've listened to you and kept fighting. But…I just saw in Ţărână's hospital how stupid I've been. I know I may not be able to save everyone, but I've had a lot of practice with saving, so I'd say I'm pretty good at it by now. The odds are strong for me being able to keep you and our children safe. Strong enough for me not to live in a hole."

She blinked. "Our children?"

Another blush rose to his cheeks. "Yes, I'd love it if we, uh…but I need you to be sure about us before we press ahead, because…well, a couple of things. First, you let me feed on you to save my life, and I need to know it wasn't only for that reason. That may sound stupid, but please try to understand that no woman has ever liked me before: in a romantic way. Women are terrified of me, then once they get used to me, they think of me as…I don't know, a nice protective ogre. So I can't seem to wrap my brain around the idea that you could possibly want Big Scary Nyko as a mate. I'm sorry, it doesn't compute, so I need to be dead sure." He ducked his head. "Do you think of me that way? Um…romantically?"

She wiped her tears on the sleeve of her bathrobe. "Of course."

Grimacing, he scuffed the toe of his boot against the carpet.

"You think I copped to that too easily? Like I haven't been paying attention?" She crossed her arms. "I love that you adore children. I love that you take on the job of watching out for the other warriors, because they're tough, strong guys, so who else is there? I love how dedicated you are to your brothers and how much you clearly respected and admired your mother. I love your nimble fingers and nice laugh. I love that you took an interest in ballet, purely for me, and even amateur that you are, you noticed I dance with passion. I love that you think I smell like cookies—you can thank Kacie for that secret. I love that for the first time in a long time, I feel like there's someone in my life who's strong enough to carry the load when I can't. I love *you*."

His throat moved visibly.

"And, you know, love has a funny way of carving out attraction from something that wasn't there before. I saw you as handsome right after our first and only date. But things really heated up for me yesterday in that cave room. It was the first time I'd seen you without a shirt. Your muscles are spectacular, and I thought all of your tattoos were kind of wicked artistic—although I probably shouldn't think that, considering the horrible way they were put on. But here's the blunt truth: when I sat on your lap, your penis and testicles felt big, and that made me want to hump your lights out. How's that for feeling romantically inclined toward you? Enough? Are you going to pass out?" He looked on the verge of it, and as much as he weighed, if he toppled over, he'd probably crash right through the floor. "Listen, Nyko, if you want to date some more, to be completely sure, then—"

"Please, no," he groaned. "This half-bond is killing me, Faith. I don't think I can bear it much longer."

She pulled her chin in. "Wait. Are you saying you look like this"—she waved her hand up and down his body—"because of *me*?"

His lids sank down as if pulled there by lead weights.

Answer enough. "God, Nyko, I don't know how to convince you. I spent *eight months* waiting for you. What else do you want me to do? I'm not sure I have the energy for another

Greek tragedy demonstration after Oțărât, but if you—"

"No." He pressed his large palms over his face. "Nothing. No more." He groaned again. "I believe you."

"Well, good." She saw that his hands were shaking. "Okay… So…? Do you want to see my ballerina tattoo now?"

He dropped his hands and, despite the saucy way she'd said that, his expression was very serious. "I really do." He started toward her, tearing his shirt off over his head—as in, actually tearing. His pants came off in the next moment, his boots, socks, *everything*.

Faith opened her mouth, but no sound came out. Right in front of her was a panorama of muscle-packed male, Nyko's naked state once again putting on display his savage body art. The black, interlocking teeth covered his entire torso, sweeping up his abdomen, over his broad chest, up and over his shoulders, where, on the right, they disappeared beneath a square of gauze bandage. He didn't have a single tattoo below his waist, but…That penis and testicles she'd just mentioned? *Oh, my*.

Nyko followed her line of sight to his crotch. "That'll pop up once I feed on you again, and don't worry, my bite won't hurt this time." He plucked her off the couch by her armpits and carried her, feet dangling, to the bed. Setting her on the edge of the mattress, he pushed her bathrobe off her shoulders, then hiked her nightgown over her head.

Suddenly bared, her nipples puckered. She didn't think she'd ever been stripped so fast. His eagerness was… She hid a smile. Lying back, she rolled slightly onto her left side and lifted her right hip to him. "There she is."

Nyko pressed two fingers to her ballerina tattoo as his gaze traveled the length of her body. "How the heck did I end up with such a porcelain doll for a mate? I was supposed to bond with a woman who was part-hippopotamus or something."

"Come here." She settled flat on her back. "You won't

crush me. Just prop yourself up on your elbows."

But he didn't move. Something was happening to his face…

It took a moment for her to figure out the expression— she'd never thought to see anger on her sweet Nyko—but he was livid, eyes fiery, the sides of his jaws bulging, his heavy fists clenched so tight that she could see the tendons stretched out from his knuckles. It took another moment for her to determine what had set him off. He was staring at the red and swollen patch of skin on her belly.

"What. Is. That?" The question was squeezed out between his teeth.

She covered the area with her palm, catching back a flinch. *Ouch.* The skin was still very sensitive.

He pushed her hand aside. "Are those two black *dots*?"

"Um…" She wasn't scared, per se, but seeing Nyko like this wasn't fun.

"Lorke tacked you, didn't he?"

There wasn't any point in lying. "Yes. After I called out your name, he said he had to mark me as his."

Nyko's upper lip peeled off one of his fangs. "That ass hates me." He tapped the tattoos on his neck. "Because he couldn't break me."

"Look, honey, what's done is done," she said, sitting up. "It's two measly dots, and they don't even hurt that much, but if we keep thinking about it, then it will ruin our night together and that will be a victory for your father." She studied Nyko's face. "Right?"

He seemed to be taking in what she'd said. The lines of anger were easing from his expression.

She reached for Nyko, setting her hand on his hip. "Let's not allow him to do that." She tugged him forward, lifting her face for a kiss.

His lips came down, but had barely touched hers before he fell on top of her.

"Ooof."

"Sorry," he panted. "And fair warning. I'm not going to be very good at this."

His body heat flash-charged to a dizzying temperature, a raw, animal scent coming off him. She placed her hands on the heavy slabs of his shoulders. "You don't need to rush." But he clearly wasn't capable of anything else. His heart pounded violently against her breasts as his mouth dropped to search frantically at her throat. Exhaling a feverish breath against her skin, Nyko angled his head deeper into the bend of her neck. Pressure increased.

She tensed for the space of a second, instinctively clutching his shoulders harder at the sensation of her skin being punctured. Then she relaxed. Oh, he was right. His bite didn't hurt this time. There was only that incredible warmth, as if her body contained a small sun, heat blooming from the inside and moving out, pushing pleasure everywhere she had nerve endings. Sighing softly, she lolled her head back into the mattress and reveled in the feel of Nyko sucking vigorously, his steady moans vibrating against her chest. Something about this was so…intimate.

Pulling his fangs out with a final groan, he started in on a mad poke-about with his erection, the head of his sex jabbing her pelvis bone, her mons, her clitoris. She nearly yelped as he bumped into her anus. *Goodness.* It was time to get her hand down there and guide him to—

The rounded head of his sex seated in her opening, and with a jerk of his hips, he plunged inside her.

She cried out softly, stunned by the fulsome weight of him. The walls of her sheath rippled, adjusting to his size and dimension, her deepest muscles grabbing at his length. *Oh, yes.*

Shuddering, Nyko barked out a shout, then went still, his breathing ragged and his expression utterly flabbergasted.

She bit back a smile. *Oops.*

He stared at her in panic.

She gazed back at him through a sparkly vista of Fiinţă-generated stars. "It's okay."

"I knew I was going to be bad, but not *that* bad."

"It was the half-bond, honey. It was making you crazy." She might not be a Vârcolac expert, but she could tell that much. "Don't worry about it."

His tongue dragged along his lips. "I'm not going to be like this always?"

She grinned. "We'll try again in ten minutes and you'll see."

He studied her smile. "What's that? It can't be the look of a satisfied woman."

She giggled. "I *am* happy. We're married now, aren't we?"

He paused, then exhaled a low chuckle. "My one, awesome pump did do that."

She laughed, the joy of the moment soaring through her. At long last, she had her man.

He opened his mouth, as if to say something more, but a low growl rolled past his lips instead.

The smile was startled off her face. She'd never heard him make a sound like that before.

He looked as surprised by the noise as she was. Hefting himself off her, he knelt on the mattress at her feet, blinking, then he rubbed his eyes. "I'm seeing red," he said.

She levered herself up on her elbows. "What does that mean?"

"I'm starting to go Rău. But it feels like it's moving out of my control, like I'm drunk or something." He pressed a palm to his ear. "Why in the heck—?"

She sat up. "Has this ever happened to you before?"

"No. Never."

"Oh." She gazed down at her wrists, still chafed raw from being strung up in Oţărât, her heart wringing through a sieve. "It's me, isn't it? You're having a negative reaction to bonding with me."

"Oh, crud." The edges of his nostrils fluttered. "It *is* you."

Of course it was, because her life had *just* got on the right track.

"You're ovulating."

She glanced up. "What?"

"And as I'm bonding to you and becoming your mate, I'm scenting it. Dang it, I'm going to glaze out and go into procreation mode on you, Faith, as soon as the bond is complete."

Procreation mode...oh, *that* she remembered from the manual, it had struck her as so unfortunate that a male Vârcolac couldn't be emotionally involved in the creation of his own baby. As soon as he scented his mate's fertility, he checked out into a state of quasi-unconsciousness, a state in which he robotically had intercourse with his wife until she was impregnated. From what Faith had heard, the act could sometimes last quite a few uncomfortable hours.

Suddenly leaping off the bed, Nyko charged over to the curtains that were closed across her balcony window and wrapped the cords around each of his wrists. "Go," he ordered. "While you still can. When a half-Răuu shifts into procreation mode our beast comes out."

"But won't that put you into bonding withdrawal?" She understood that well enough; the whole town had watched poor Thomal Costache go through it. Which meant that if she left, depriving Nyko of the ability to scent her, he would have to endure more misery after all that he'd just gone through with a half-bond.

"I'll deal with it. Now, go! I don't want you to face down my Răuu our first time together."

She didn't move, held immobile by a riot of emotions churning inside her. There was, of course, relief that Nyko wasn't having some kind of weird allergic reaction to their bond. Also frustration at herself for not following the manual's stern warning about bonded females testing their fertility hormones daily—although it was a little late to discover that directive also applied to *prospective* bonded females. And angst over the thought of her man possibly suffering. But those feelings were almost immediately smothered by biological need. She was ovulating right now. It didn't take a straight-A student to figure out that if she and Nyko continued to make love, she'd get pregnant. And, yes, it was probably stupid and irresponsible of her to think of starting a family with a man she hardly knew. There was always plenty of time for babies and all that blah, blah, blah. But she ached to have a little being growing inside her. *This* man's baby: this man who loved children so much. And who loved her.

"I think I'll stay," she said simply.

He pressed back against the balcony window and widened his eyes on her.

She positioned herself in the middle of the bed and lay flat on her back, wracking her brain for the manual's guidelines on how a woman should conduct herself during Vârcolac mating. Sweat beaded her upper lip. How she wished she hadn't skimmed that part.

A barbaric howl roared through the room and the curtain rods ripped out of the wall.

Chapter Forty-Six

The <u>SHIFTED</u> World: Balboa Park, San Diego, four months later, December

STANDING WITH HIS FEET PLANTED like he owned the Meeting Tree, his powerful arms crossed, Erigeron steadily lifted his upper lip into a sneer. Drawing his blade to deal with this assembly was taking on more and more appeal. He'd just cast a quick glance up through a tangled mesh of naked branches at the position of the new moon and discovered they'd been at this quibbling for an hour.

It was never a quiet affair when the head *custos*, or custodians, of the four clans met, but this was worse than usual. The topic currently under debate—the ongoing theft of Fianna warrior souls, which could equal death to them all—was understandably charged with emotion. Everyone had an opinion about the next step to take, and the racket of so many dissenting voices was coming close to splitting Erig's head.

The lead *custos* of Clan Salix, the largest clan, and once the only—until *bellum libertatem*, or the War of Freedom, had divided them into four—was shaking his fist at the representative from Clan Tsuga. *Stupidus*. Tsuga might be the smallest band of Tuatha Dé Danann, but they were brutes, all.

Even the captain from Clan Kigelia, the most peace-loving and earth-nurturing, had his diamond-white eyebrows clamped in a frown.

Erig needed to end this. They were getting nowhere. He shot a quick, sideways glance at each of his two lieutenants.

Zigadenus was zipping around in short spurts, his red hair

hanging forward in a sharp point down his nose. The churning prospect of violence had Zig in a state of hyper glee, but if the man didn't stop his annoying, spastic flying, he was going to get swatted. If not by Erig, then someone.

Erig switched his gaze to his other side, finding Daucus hovering in the air about a foot away. Erig's sneer grew. *Are we boring you?* Daucus was focused on something outside of the Meeting Tree, giving Erig a view of the back of his blue hair.

Erig shifted his focus to see what was so important.

Across the field, Clarkia had her face stuffed in a honey-suckle, her wings aglow, her bottom wiggling as she went deep for the nectar.

Getting drunk again, the *maldulsa*. Which meant Daucus would be dipping his stamen in her carpel later tonight…*if* the man could still function after the lesson Erig would be teaching him about the downfalls of distraction.

Beyond Clarkia, countless Fey lanterns twinkled, swaying from branches above and about the tree houses the Tuatha made for themselves. Clan lands sprawled out from this Meeting Tree like spokes from the center hub of a wheel, sometimes covering more than a mile in certain directions before Balboa Park ended and civilization began. Save for due west. About five hundred yards in that direction, the territory of Erig's people, the Dryads, or Tree Fairies, ended abruptly at a powerful ward demarcating them from the Earth Fair-ies…despicable fungi, every last one.

Between the Earth and the Tree, there were thousands of Tuatha Dé Danann living here. Yet should Middle World humans tromp through these lands—and in the daytime, they sometimes did—they would see only tree upon endless tree with their humanoid eyes. Such was not the case with animals. Predatory birds and canines posed the only true danger to the Tuatha. Besides dark magic.

Erig turned back to the assembly and opened his

mouth—

"Enough!" Conium bellowed, the leader of Clan Salix's *custos* beating Erig to putting a stop to this mayhem. "It has been over a year since Fey power was first threatened. Too long. We've had meeting after meeting, and solved nothing. Eight warrior souls have now been stolen. Too many." Conium's fist came up. "Clan Salix will take over direct guardianship of the Stone, and *we* will resolve this."

Erig's wings went rigid, blasting a spray of golden dust into the air and lifting him several inches off his bough of the tree.

Daucus' head snapped around, Clarkia's rump forgotten.

Zig burst into a series of streaking zings, leaving angry contrails of glittering dust in his wake.

At least now there was silence. Anxious, breath-holding silence.

Guardianship of the Tuatha Dé Danann Treasure changed from clan to clan every one hundred years, and Erig's clan, Cercis, had nearly seventy-five years left guarding the precious Stone. To have that responsibility taken away would be the highest insult. Just the suggestion was.

Eyes hot, Erig caressed the hilt of his dagger, his fingers lethally tracing the intricate hawk design: the heraldic emblem of his clan. "When the fifth element opens the portal in the Middle World," he inquired mildly, "will Alnus be able to open a door on this side?"

Eyes shifted.

Conium's face went red as a hibiscus all the way to the tips of his pointed ears.

Alnus was Clan Salix's mage, and while Salix might be the most powerful clan in many respects, Erig's boasted the most powerful of all the mages. The wise Picea. Everyone knew she was the only one with magic strong enough to manage a portal opening.

Even so, Salix's leader clearly didn't appreciate Erig calling attention to this lack. Conium's wings stretched to their fullest extent and gave a huge *whomp* of a flap, the resulting swoosh of air sending a hapless Kigelian tumbling off into the next tree.

"It is now wintertime," Erig said in a profound tone.

Everyone knew what this meant; it was the only season in which contact could be made with those of them in charge of the Stone. For a fifth element ritual to be successful, all four elements had to be in place: the season of winter, the direction of north, the element of earth, the Treasure of Stone.

"Clan Cercis," Erig continued, "will soon have this resolved in battle. Picea has foreseen an interconnection in the near—"

"Look!" A Tsugian pointed a dirty finger skyward. "She comes!"

The assembly turned as one to look up.

Picea.

The queen mage was seated majestically on a carpet woven of sticks, leaves, moss, and flowers, carried along—for show alone—by four stout Cercisian attendants. The half dozen or so ladies of her court flitted gracefully around her, leaving sprinkles of fairy dust here and there. Picea was dressed in a flowing gown of indigo blue which rippled, wave-like, around her. Her blue-black hair, touched with grey in a pattern of neat checkerboard, was caught in an elaborate design of twists and curls.

Erig caught his breath. *Please say it is time.* He glided straight upward, revealing himself to his mistress out of the masses.

Picea met his gaze. "It is time."

Erig exhaled a huge breath. He chopped a hard gesture at his ranks of Cercisian *custos*, waiting in wing-humming anticipation just outside of the Meeting Tree. "We go north!"

Erig and his men took flight, speeding their way through the moon-dappled darkness along aerial pathways the Tuatha had traveled for hundreds of years. Wind streamed through Erig's short hair and occasionally whistled musically off his wings.

They arrived at the site of the portal well ahead of Picea and her attendants. Erig flew in an impatient, repetitive Z pattern while he waited. He gripped the hilt of his blade. His blood was stoked.

Picea finally arrived on her carpet and came to a floating halt. She held out her palm, and it filled as if from nowhere with a small pile of sparkling white dust—the only of its kind.

The mood went solemn.

Moving forward, the *custos* bowed their heads before her, bobbing lightly in the air, wings whispering.

"Tonight," Picea said, "you fight for the *Sidhe* race. You fight for the humans who are our allies in magic. And you fight for the pride of your clan."

Erig drew in a deep breath.

"*Boni vobiscum*," Picea blessed them.

Erig slowly released his breath.

The grounding principle of the Stone of Destiny, the Treasure they guarded, was *The Stone knows the heart of man.* Only a Tuatha Dé Danann with an unblemished heart would succeed in this, and thus Picea had said, *Goodness be with you.*

Emotion expanded Erig's chest. Although he might be tarnished in many ways—ways he wished he could forever forget—he never doubted the purity of his heart as a *custos*.

Picea tossed the white dust over their ranks.

Erig shut his eyes as a luxurious heat traveled through the tiny ribbed veins of his wings and flowed into his body, the strength of Picea's magic coursing through him.

"You may pass," Picea announced.

Erig lifted his head.

A long, cylindrical tunnel made of what looked like clear gel was now visible at the portal site. Where it terminated, Erig couldn't see, but it had to end with the fifth element on the Other Side. The portal couldn't have been opened otherwise.

"Erigeron," Picea summoned.

He coasted over to her.

More white dust appeared in her hand. She titled her palm, pouring the dust into a pouch of indigo velvet, then handed it to him. "You will need this to access the villain's True form."

To fight his evil magic. Erig hooked the pouch onto his belt. He met his mistress's gaze for what might be the last time, then darted into the tunnel, Zig and Daucus flanking him, the thirty of his other men following.

Five minutes into their journey, the fifth element appeared, her image blurred through the gel of the tunnel, but...wait. *Her?*

"A woman," Daucus remarked, incredulous.

Erig slowed.

Blonde-haired, the fifth element sat cross-legged on the forest floor with her fingers dug deep into the soil. Her head was sagged back on her neck, evincing her deep, meditative state, and oddly, a man, also blond but *not* a fifth element, was seated at her side, an arm wrapped around her. Nearby, an older woman thumped a drum, and about six others observed.

Erig continued onward, slower now. He *thrummed* his wings in a hailing signal.

The fifth element's head came up and she opened glassy eyes to him.

Erig wrenched to a halt, cocking one knee back and angling his wings to catch the most wind resistance. A Tenebris Mala!

"*Infernus*," Daucus cursed.

Zig narrowed his eyes and hissed a string of even nastier curses, any one of which would've sent his mother fluttering out of her tree.

Erig's hand automatically lowered to the velvet pouch at his waist, but he checked himself before he could extract any of Picea's dust. He shouldn't let impatience lead him down a wrong path. It was the fifth element's responsibility to expose her True form to them.

Erig waited, his tension sending erratic spurts of dust off his wing-tips.

His men buzzed softly behind him, all but motionless except for the small wing movements needed to remain aloft.

Finally, a ghostly impression of the fifth element's human body materialized out of the top of her blonde head and rose into the gel tunnel, completely naked. Taking on her True form, her hair lightened to the color of Erig's hair then lengthened, twisting in teasing curls around her thighs, and her eyes changed to a sparkly blue. Her skin was smooth and unmarked…at least in front.

"Hold," Erig ordered his men. He flew forward to inspect her.

On the ground, the fifth element's human body jerked.

Her True form in the gel tunnel faded.

Erig slowed again.

Back on the ground, the fifth element's male partner moved to sit behind her. He put both arms around her and squeezed tighter, whispering something into her ear.

Her True form flared back to full visibility.

Erig continued forward, circling her. No blemishes on the back side of her, either. He completed his circuit and nodded at Zig and Daucus. She could be trusted.

He winged his way to the front of her and stopped in a hover. "Fifth element," he said formally. "The Tuatha Dé Danann beg your leave to travel a conduit to the dark evil threatening Fey power."

There was a long pause while she just stared at him. Her eyes shone in wonderment and an awestruck smile spread across her face.

First time seeing a fairy, is it? Erig cleared his throat.

She blinked once, then lifted an arm straight out from her body. Another gel tunnel opened along her arm's trajectory.

Erig glanced at his lieutenants. *This is it. Battle.* He zoomed down the new pathway.

It wasn't a long flight. Maybe only two minutes passed before Erig found himself in a dingy living room, a black-haired man the sole occupant. No, there was another…a woman slumped, beaten and unconscious, in a corner.

Erig snarled.

The black-haired man bolted to his feet. He couldn't see Erig and the other *custos*, but obviously could feel the intensity of their presence. *And this*—Erig shoved his hand into the velvet pouch and threw a fistful of white dust at the man.

A dark blob began to rise out of him.

The man threw back his head. He had a scar on his lip and one milky eye. The other eye was the solid black of a Tenebris Mala. "No!" he yelled, clearly feeling the pull of his True form leaving him.

Erig back-stroked out of the way as the dark blob took on a sinister shape, its form pockmarked and stitched from end to end with scars. Erig knew, without knowing how, that the blob would grow into the most fearsome creature he and his men had ever battled. Kill it, and the black-haired Tenebris Mala would lose his power to perform an un-protection ritual. The magic of the Stone would be saved.

Erig yanked his blade out of its sheathe, and with a savage roar, surged forward.

✧   ✧   ✧

Țărână

NYKO STOOD IN THE MIDDLE of the stage—a stage that had been built all of about one week ago at Garwald's Pub for regular jam sessions by Alex's band and other entertainment, like tonight's talent show. He was acting the role of male sort-of-ballet-dancer, which he didn't mind because it merely consisted of him standing in one place and throwing Faith and Kacie into amazing displays of acrobatic ballet. Faith had tried to talk him into wearing tights for their performance, but he'd *no way'd* it. That would've gotten him eaten alive by ribbing from the warriors, and he wasn't very good at returning their banter. So he was dressed in black pants and a white dress shirt.

The spectators *ooh'd* and *aah'd* as he tossed the sisters to either side of him into turns—called pirouettes. They rotated with admirable precision, looking so alike...except Faith turned with a bit more fluidity than Kacie, was wearing a brace on her knee, and had a blue-and-red dragon on her back. Nyko dropped his gaze to his wife's belly, flat as could be, even though she was four months along. He flushed, pleasure and pride both. Inside that beautiful woman grew his kid. Yeah, speaking of ribbing...Nyko had taken a lot over losing his virginity and impregnating his mate all on the same night.

Nyko peered through the bright lights to the audience, spotting Shọn in the front row. His little brother was almost watching Nyko more than the girls, no doubt making sure Nyko didn't drop anyone precious. *As if.* Nyko was handling a pregnant wife.

But Kacie was Shọn's squeeze.

The day Nyko and Shọn, along with Pandra and Faith, had emerged from the Hell Tunnels, Kacie had flung her arms around Shọn's neck and thanked him for saving her sister with a peck on the cheek, then dashed off to accompany Faith to the hospital, leaving Shọn with his jaw down on his chest. From there the rest was, as they said, history. It was the general agreement that those two would bond any day.

Nyko shifted his gaze over two seats, finding Luvera, eight months pregnant and looking it, and next to her, Toni was holding Sharanna on her lap. Toni had spent a full month in the hospital after her near-fatal birth, which hadn't been a breeze for either Toni or Jacken. Once Jacken got his wife and daughter home and settled, though, things had gotten serious.

Over the past couple of months the warriors had been making ready to save the human women trapped in Oţărât, memorizing the routes of the Hell Tunnels given to them by Shọn, sharpening their knives, and buying heat-resistant suits.

It was time to go to war.

At least topside one less worry awaited them now that Pandra had successfully performed her fifth element ritual and stopped Videon. Some questions still remained unanswered. No one knew how Videon had acquired an enchantment power enabling him to perform a Celtic un-protection ritual or why he'd kidnapped Elsa Mendoza in the first place, and, most disturbingly, they didn't know why Videon was creating an army of amulet-wearing super beings. Ignorance was never fun, but Nyko figured Videon would play his cards soon enough, then they'd all know what was up…and probably need to build an Ark or some other Chicken Little *The sky is falling* stuff.

One thing they had discovered was how Videon managed to identify the vessels. Videon had kidnapped Moriah, Idyll's shamanka friend, who was an aura-reader, too, and had forced her to check out men with original family surnames and "see" which ones were carrying these important souls. He'd kept the poor woman in custody up until the time when he'd been stopped by Pandra and no longer had a use for the shamanka.

Idyll said that Moriah was taking an extended vacation in the Bahamas.

Nyko shifted his gaze over a few more seats and found Pandra cuddled next to Thomal. Those two were a solid couple now, and Thomal was really changing because of it. He'd recently painted a portrait of Toni and Sharanna that had every momma in town lining up outside his door.

After Nyko had cleared his head from his half-bond, then his procreation glaze-out, then his post-reproduction hibernation, he'd felt pretty bad about beating up Thomal. But, well… maybe it'd done some good. Unfortunately, Thomal and Arc still weren't back to normal, but they seemed to be slowly improving.

The music ended, and Nyko took a bow with Faith and Kacie, then the three of them left the stage, passing Alex along the way—his band was the final act.

Backstage, Nyko hugged his wife. "You were so amazing out there," he told her.

Faith beamed up at him, but before she had a chance to answer, someone tugged on his sleeve. Jacken.

"Everything set, Nyko?" he asked.

Dev was standing beside Jacken, his silver eyes bright with excitement.

"Yep." Nyko pulled the remote out of his back pocket. "Which one of you wants to do the honors?"

Jacken snatched the remote out of his hands.

"The fuck?" Dev protested.

Jacken lifted his lip at his friend. "I've been dealing with him a lot longer than you have, Nichita."

"You bonded with Toni in January," Dev countered. "I got together with Marissa in October. That's only nine months difference, so you can shove—"

"You know what, Devid? My cow died last night, so I don't need your bull." Jacken smirked.

"You're a dildo." Dev made a grab for Jacken's shirt collar.

"Guys," Nyko intervened. "Alex is starting."

Both men's heads swiveled toward the stage.

Alex was standing in front of a tall microphone, strumming his guitar and singing. Nilan, Barbu, and Iosif, his bandmates, were jamming behind him.

"*Now*," Dev hissed.

"No," Jacken said from the edge of his lips. "I've been watching him rehearse, and a high note is coming up where Alex opens his mouth really wide and—ah!" Jacken jammed his thumb down on the remote activator.

A long stream of purple ink sprayed out of the microphone and hit Alex directly in the back of his throat.

Alex choked and stumbled back, his fingers tangling discordantly in his guitar strings.

The audience gasped into silence.

Oh, man, jeez. Nyko buried a smile. How cruddy was it that he'd contributed to Alex's embarrassment—the man was a friend—but...dang, he couldn't help but feel proud of his handiwork. That had worked perfectly.

"Alex...bro..." Gábor said, ending the silence with a chortle from the third row. "You look like you just blew Barney the Dinosaur."

As if on cue, a mouthful of purple "spunk" spilled past Alex's lips and dribbled onto his shirt.

The silence broke completely, then, a gale of rollicking laughter sweeping through the bar.

Flushing a mottled red, Alex whipped his head over and located Dev and Jacken backstage.

The two men were *beyond* laughter, sagging into each other's arms.

Staggering over to Nyko, Jacken and Dev tugged him into their huddle of hilarity, and despite still feeling sort of bad for Alex, Nyko couldn't hold back his guffaws anymore.

That *had* been one heckuva great practical joke.

✧   ✧   ✧

Hey, I hope you enjoyed reading this enemies-to-lovers romance. Intense in spots, wasn't it? But all ended happily between Pandra and Thomal—of course!

If you're like me, you pick up a romance novel to enjoy a little escapism, so if BLOOD-BONDED BY FORCE did its job for you and effectively transported you to a different reality, please consider writing a review. Other readers may be looking for the same type of journey.

No time for a review? You can also *anonymously* rate a book with stars alone.

Thank you!

✧   ✧   ✧

Book Four in The Community Series
MOON-RIDERS
Breen Dalakis's Story
Available now!

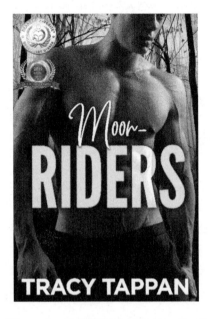

★ **Readers' Favorite Gold Medal winner for Paranormal Romance** ★
★ **Kindle Book Awards TOP FIVE Finalist for Romance** ★

In a moment of unbridled lust, a vampire warrior accidentally life-bonds to the carefree woman who doesn't want him, his slip-up stripping them of their chance at happiness…unless they find a way to stand together against their haunting pasts.

Learn more at tracytappan.com.

✧　✧　✧

Sneak peek of MOON-RIDERS, Book Four in The Community Series...

Charlize slammed the community manual closed. *Bam!*

Breen peeled his eyes open wider. If he'd had any energy, he might've startled.

She thundered over to his armchair and came to a rigid stop in front of him, her hands planted on her hips.

The position bowed open the neckline of her robe, but he tried not to notice the view. He might not be a sitcom guy, but basic male instinct for doing whatever it took to calm down his woman so he could get laid again told him that ogling Charlize's tits while she was jammed up would only make her more jammed.

He met her gaze, which was glaring hot.

"You were a *virgin*!?" she hissed at him.

He blinked slowly. Now why would that piss her off? Was this another hidden meaning thing? He tried to reason it out, but his brain was a gigantic yawn.

"You screwed me like a wild man. How the hell does a virgin do that?"

He carefully studied her enraged expression. She was very, very angry. She was shouting every word at him, which he didn't mind so much. He didn't mind the fury in her gestures, either. No. It was when things got quiet—same as right before his father struck with one of his barbed remarks—that Breen didn't like. Those barbs stabbed a man like a cold blade. For all the brutal hits Breen had taken in his life, and seen others endure, he'd never encountered anything able to do a man more damage than one of Ungar Dalakis's perfectly aimed criticisms.

"Why the hell aren't you answering me?" If Charlize's voice turned any more sour, it would be sauerkraut.

He scooted up in his chair. "You told me not to talk to you."

"Oh, for God's sake. Don't be a dick."

Yeah, so…the name-calling wasn't a favorite.

Charlize's mouth tautened until her lips were a stiff, red knot. "I asked you a direct question."

He shrugged. "I don't know. I guess I've been thinking about sex for a long time."

She *piffed*. "Every man does that."

"Not like our breed. A Vârcolac reaches sexual maturity at the age of twenty-one, but because there's been no one for us to mate with for years—only you Dragons, who showed up on the scene recently—we've had to wait forever to have sex. I'm thirty-nine. That means I've been thinking about sex for eighteen years."

She gaped at him, her mouth just hanging open for a long moment, then she turned around and stomped a couple of paces away. "I don't know which number is more appalling to me. The thirty-nine or the eighteen." Beneath her bathrobe, her spinal cord was a tight stretch of bones.

Thirty-nine was actually young in Vârcolac years. He wasn't sure what to say about the eighteen. "Why does the virgin thing bother you?"

She spun back around, her glare reigniting. "Because the hell if I want to be anyone's memory." The edge of her jaw quivered. "Now I'll forever be your *first*."

First and *only*. Vârcolac mated for life. But probably he should keep quiet about it. She was already upset enough. He scratched his temple. "I'm not sure what you want me to do about it. I mean, I can't undo it." Virginity was one of those things.

Charlize crossed her arms beneath her breasts. The new posture was better than when she had her hands on her hips, and… No, actually, it wasn't. "No, you can't undo it, can you?" she snapped. "*Any* of it."

Breen wasn't able to stop himself. He was acting on instinct.

When Toni had said that, she'd cast him a sideways glance, and even though her expression wasn't accusatory, it wasn't exactly forgiving either. Like maybe at some point in this disastrous chain of events, she believed he should've known what the hell he was doing.

Learn more at tracytappan.com.

ABOUT THE AUTHOR

Tracy Tappan is a bestselling and award-winning author of gritty romance and the creator of the Choose A Hero Romance™ reading experience, a brand-new concept in storytelling where the reader controls the ending. You can find out more about this exciting new trend at www.choosea hero.com.

Tracy's books in paranormal and military romance have earned both bronze and gold medals in the Readers' Favorite contests, have finaled for the USA Book News and Kindle Book Awards, and won both the HOLT Medallion and the Independent Publishers Book Award (IPPY) bronze medal for romance.

Tracy holds a master's degree in Marriage, Family, Child Counseling (MFCC), loves to play tennis, enjoys a great glass of wine, and talks to her Labrador like he's a human (admittedly, the wine drinking and the dog talking probably go together).

A native of San Diego, Tracy is married to a former Navy helicopter pilot, who retired after thirty years of service and joined the diplomatic corps. He and Tracy currently live in Rome, Italy.

Visit her website and join the gang on her monthly newsletter for giveaways, publication updates, and other fun and sexy news. www.tracytappan.com.

.

Printed in Great Britain
by Amazon

46230787R00215